THE
WELL-MANNERED
ASSASSIN

A LSO BY ALINE, COUNTESS OF ROMANONES

The Earth Rests Lightly
The Spy Wore Red
The Spy Went Dancing
The Spy Wore Silk

The
WELL-MANNERED
Assassin

Aline,
Countess of
Romanones

G. P. PUTNAM'S SONS
NEW YORK

FOR BUD

G. P. Putnam's Sons
Publishers Since 1838
200 Madison Avenue
New York, NY 10016

Library of Congress Cataloging-in-Publication Data

Aline, Countess of Romanones, date.
   The well-mannered assassin / Aline, Countess of Romanones.
      p.   cm.
   ISBN 0-399-13863-3 (acid-free paper)
   1. Carlos, the Jackal—Fiction.   2. Terrorists—Fiction.
3. Assassins—Fiction.   I. Title.
PS3551.L364W4   1994   93-47588 CIP
813'.54—dc20

Fic.

Printed in the United States of America
1   2   3   4   5   6   7   8   9   10

This book is printed on acid-free paper.

"Murderers, in general, are people who are consistent, people who are obsessed with one idea and nothing else."
—Ugo Betti, *Struggle Til Dawn* (1949)

"As a rule what is out of sight disturbs men's minds more seriously than what they see."
—Julius Caesar, *Gallic War* (58–51 B.C.)

ACKNOWLEDGMENTS

I would like to thank some of those who over the last three years have helped me in one way or another. First and foremost, John S. Palmer, who has collaborated with me throughout the book. Friends in the intelligence services of five different countries have provided me with pertinent information on Carlos, and I would like to thank them, especially Teniente General Emilio Alonso Manglano, Director General of Spain's CESID. For access to the archives of *ABC*, Madrid's daily paper, I want to thank the editor, Luis María Anson and also Joaquín Amado. For valuable technical advice I would like to thank Donald Jamieson, Ben Perry, Commander Peter W. Harris, USNR. Thanks as always to John Taylor of the National Archives, Washington, D.C., and to Edouard Sablier, terrorist specialist, author of *Le fil rouge*, and to Brian Crozier, foreign affairs specialist and author of *Free Agent*.

I certainly want to thank my editor, Neil Nyren, my literary agent, Lynn Nesbit, and Eric Simonoff of her staff for reading my manuscript and being enthusiastic. My wonderful secretary, Mary Beth Hughes, and my exceptional publicist, Paul Olsewski.

But let me mention also my gratitude to the privilege of living, at least part-time, in this great city of New York, whose stimulating atmosphere, created by all those exceptional and unusual human beings who inhabit it, constantly inspires me and not only helped me finish this book, but encourages me to want to do many more.

AUTHOR'S NOTE

This book began as a nonfiction account of the illegal sale of nuclear weapons material. To a minor degree, it was also about Carlos the Jackal—perhaps the most feared terrorist and assassin in the world, and a man whom I knew personally—but as the story proceeded, Carlos's vivid personality took over. Gradually, the account changed to concentrate on his activities, and I developed a fictionalized story that was nevertheless based on actual facts.

My relationship with Carlos began in 1977, when, as I relate, he delivered documents to my home in Madrid, though my later contact with him was not as extensive as I describe it. Many of the other characters are actual persons, with their real names, though in some cases I have changed names of people and places for security reasons. Before I started the book, I was under the impression that Carlos was dead. But Carlos is nothing if not resourceful and a survivor, and so when I later learned that Carlos was still very likely alive and living in a Middle Eastern country, it became especially important for me to fictionalize the story, in order to protect certain people in the book.

Because I live in a country where, unfortunately, terrorism is endemic, and because over the past twelve years I have given many lectures in the United States on that subject, I have had the opportunity to meet and consult with a wide variety of world specialists on international terrorism. It is my hope that this story will give the reader a heightened awareness of the great threat these international terrorist organizations represent for people living in every part of today's world.

PROLOGUE

*I*n December of 1990, as the entire world awaited the outcome of the standoff between President Bush and Saddam Hussein, I was in the beautiful Al Bustann Palace in Muscat, capital of the sultanate of Oman in the Arabian Peninsula, participating in a confidential conference of high-level experts who had gathered to study the threat to world peace posed by Iraq's invasion of Kuwait. Among the forty-five people present from sixteen different countries were intelligence agents, high government officials, cabinet members, and General Norman Schwarzkopf, who left his post with the Sixth Army in Saudi Arabia to join us for one day. Though our host, the Sultan of Oman, had guaranteed the safety of his prestigious visitors, in view of the escalating violence in the Middle East on the verge of war, such a guarantee of course had only the force of courtesy.

The horrors of chemical weapons, secret production of nuclear arms, and uncontrollable, indiscriminate terrorism were the focus of scrutiny during the meeting—dangers which had not existed when I first began my career as an intelligence agent during the Second World War. The group itself convened twice a year in various parts of the world; and as a consequence of my work in intelligence, I had been a regular member for twelve years. Like other participants, I took advantage of the information we shared to advise key officials in those countries where I had connections.

Meanwhile, the news from the international press concerning the mounting tensions between nearby nations charged the meeting's atmosphere. Each of us was highly aware of the gravity of the moment.

On the second day of the conference, Edouard Sablier, a world-famous French expert on terrorism, spoke about his specialty. Terrorism, he said, was no longer a merely localized phenomenon, it had become a truly international threat. Terrorist networks had rapidly expanded throughout the world.

I knew too well what my colleague was talking about. And when he went on to mention the name "Carlos the Jackal," my back stiffened with a fear I hadn't experienced in years. With rapt attention, I listened to the Frenchman's report.

That evening in the luxurious royal palace, surrounded by exquisite mosaics, multitudinous fountains, graceful arches, and intricately carved ceilings, the Sultan gave a banquet in our honor. As we were waiting to be seated, I spotted the Frenchman sitting on a silk cushion on the floor across the salon. During the course of his talk, he had mentioned that Carlos had been reported killed in Beirut. Curious, I decided to ask him if he knew any more about the manner of Carlos's death.

When I approached, he stood up graciously, and when I went on to mention my interest in Carlos the Jackal, he looked at me with mild curiosity. But when I said that I had in fact been personally acquainted with Carlos, he eyed me with new interest, took my arm and led me to a corner where we could talk in confidence.

"Comtesse, if you have met Carlos, you probably agree that his most advantageous asset is his charm," the Frenchman began, "his pleasant appearance, and refined manners. He is a genius at employing flattery, gifts, and kindness to obtain access to people he intends to kill. In fact he attempted to assassinate a dear friend of mine in London in just that manner." He shook his head sadly. "A ruthless demon, but a resourceful and brilliant man."

My new friend's troubled voice surprised me. "But Carlos is dead!" I said. "And now you're talking about him as if he were alive. You said today that he was reported to have been killed in Beirut. In fact that was the reason I approached you, to learn more about his death."

"Madame la Comtesse," he said, looking into my eyes, "never believe anything you hear about Carlos the Jackal, no matter how credible the source. He is the master magician. All we can do is to examine the smoke he leaves behind as best we can. Now would you kindly tell me everything you know about him?"

A shiver went up my spine as I realized that Carlos might still be alive. Glancing around the room, as though the mere mention of the name could conjure the presence of the famous terrorist, I returned my attention to my companion, who then offered me his arm and smiled. "I can see you were well acquainted with Carlos."

I managed a wan smile.

"Let me guess, you're remembering his eyes," he said.

I shook my head grimly. He was absolutely correct—yet I had seldom seen Carlos's eyes. For the terrorist usually wore dark sunglasses. But on those occasions when his eyes were visible to me, they were as cold, glittering, and black as *azabaches*—pieces of jet, like the eyes of a wild animal about to strike.

MY FRENCH FRIEND'S hunch was correct. Before writing this book, I learned that Carlos was reported to be alive in Syria. I deliberated at length over just how much of my story I could safely tell. And so here is the result of my decision, as close to the truth as I dare recount it.

Chapter 1

June 1977

*T*he first time I saw Carlos, nothing about his appearance or attitude prepared me for the havoc he was going to create in my life later on. I was perched on a ladder in my living room in Madrid, placing pieces of our collection of blue-and-white china on shelves on either side of the fireplace. The doorbell rang, and a minute later the butler came in.

"Señora Condesa," Andrés announced, "a young man is here from the Señor Conde's office. I told him the Señor Conde had left, but he insists that he must see you."

I told Andres to show the man in. When I heard him enter, I must have turned too quickly, and lost my balance; a precious piece of porcelain started to slip from my hand. With a gymnast's agility, the young fellow lunged to my side and made a grab for it. But it was too late, and the valuable Ming dish crashed to the marble floor in a mass of spiky shards. For a moment we were both silent, staring helplessly at the priceless broken plate. Then he darted to pick up the pieces; as he did so, a sharp bladelike edge sliced his hand, and a gush of red blood spurted out, dripping on the white marble. The sight of so much blood gave both of us a shock, and stunned we stared at his right hand.

Coming to my senses, I screamed for someone to bring towels. Andrés came running in, and behind him Felisa, the cook. They gazed horror-stricken at the dripping blood as I led the fellow into the kitchen and grabbed some cloths to stop the flow. Felisa was useless, she stared, trembling at the bleeding hand, but Andrés was more helpful, producing several white linen napkins. The gush continued while I struggled to wrap the wound and pack it with ice. My wounded patient began to speak softly to Felisa. "Good woman, do not worry. This small cut is nothing. It's more painful for me to see you suffering for my fault. Smile and I will feel better."

My knowledge of first aid was primitive but the outpouring finally stopped, and I was able to tear a strip from a linen towel, make a sling around his neck, and place his arm in it.

The young man then directed his attention to Andrés, who was struggling to remove a spot of blood from the lapel of the fellow's well-cut business suit. "That is kind of you. I only bought this suit last week in the Corte Inglés. Next time I try this trick of cutting my finger to get attention, I'll be more careful about the stains," he joked. However, the sweat trickling down the fellow's brow and the damp black curls forming on his forehead indicated that the wound was still hurting him. He was attractive—a bit taller than Andrés, olive skin, a round face, a regular nose and a large mouth with full lips. But what startled me were his thick, dark sunglasses. Even though he was indoors, he had not removed them, not even during the turmoil of his accident.

After that, everybody calmed down; and with his kind attention, even Felisa's crying ceased. Andrés now smiled, obviously enchanted with our visitor.

"Sorry I didn't have time to pick up all the pieces," the young stranger said to me. "Should have. That broken plate was my fault." I took his arm and led him back toward the salon. "If I hadn't burst into the room . . ." he continued.

"Not at all," I interrupted although I was desolate at my loss. "The broken plate is my fault alone."

As we walked back into the salon, the young man went on, "I'm still so very sorry about this, and so grateful for your bandaging my wound. No one has ever taken such care of me. Frankly, I'm not accustomed to such attention." His low, very masculine voice was agreeable and engaging, the accent softly South American. He asked permission to smoke, and carefully pulled a cigarette out of his pocket and lit it; a waft of pungent Turkish tobacco encircled us. As he went on speaking, his manner conveyed comfortable self-assurance. "With all the confusion, I have not yet introduced myself," he said. "Forgive me," he made a slight bow, "Carlos Evertz Fournier, *para servirle*—at your service. I work in the Centro Asegurador Insurance, your husband is president of the company, as you know. I was asked to deliver an important envelope to him personally, or to you." From the inside pocket of his jacket with his left hand, he managed to remove a long, blue envelope, which he handed me.

We chatted for a few moments, and when he learned that I intended to continue hanging the collection, he begged me to allow him to help.

"What a lovely room!" he commented as he handed me the first piece. The walls had been lacquered yellow as a background for the valuable china. "And this collection of Chinese porcelain is extraordinary."

Not everyone realized the quality of our blue-and-white collection, and I was surprised. Yet Carlos continued to surprise me during his subsequent visits; for he became the person designated to messenger papers from my husband's office to our home.

During one of these times, he pointed to the carnations on a table in our library. "My mother had a lovely garden in our house in Venezuela. Carnations like these," he said as his hand brushed one of the large red blossoms, "were her favorite."

"And they are mine also," I answered.

From then on, whenever he was delivering documents, he invariably appeared with a bunch of red carnations. Later, the sight of red carnations came to remind me of Carlos. Before long, my husband was teasing that Carlos had fallen for me. And when I made Carlos a gift of a Paco Rabanne tie I had bought in Paris, Luis complained, "You haven't given me such a tie for years. What does that fellow do to make such an impression?"

The truth was that Carlos was not only polite to me, but to others as well. For Felisa, he often brought some little thing—an inexpensive silk scarf or a bottle of eau de cologne. His visits were welcomed by my children, too; for them he was an encyclopedia of information about soccer teams and players. One day I found him in the garden with my youngest son, imitating the way the Italian goalie had dived and missed the soccer ball the day before, enabling Real Madrid to win by a goal. His slow motion re-creation was so funny that we both just stood there, laughing.

Perhaps the incident that most endeared him to me occurred the day my secretary's mother was being buried. In Spain the dead are not embalmed, so there is a law that they must be interred within twenty-four hours after death. I had learned about the sad event at the last minute and was struggling to start my car, which had a low battery, when Carlos pulled up in the office van. He insisted on taking me to the convent where the body was resting, and when we arrived, he politely accompanied me inside.

Stepping from the busy sunny street into the silence and dimness of the convent and then into the dark, barren funeral room was a shock. Four candles in gigantic bronze candelabras at the center of the large, nearly vacant room marked the corners of a simple pine coffin, before which two black-robed nuns were bent in prayer. From their hands dangled long rosaries, and their fingers slowly caressed each bead. The flickering light cast a spooky glimmer on their gloomy black habits and the half visible body in the box. The monotonous murmur of their voices repeating a litany made a melancholy background. No other sound was audible from the deep shadows around them, and for a moment I thought no one else was in the room.

Then a small figure rose from the darkness, and Cristina, my secretary, approached to embrace me. At first I did not notice that Carlos had quietly gone to a bench where her three small children were huddled; but I saw him lift one sobbing child on his knee and pull the other two close to him in a warm embrace.

Cristina and I knelt down next to the coffin. My breath caught in my chest as I looked on the tiny figure wrapped in a stiffly starched white sheet, the rigid folds of the chalky cotton enshrouding the head in the classic Carmelite nuns' headdress. The stark simplicity of the dead body engulfed me.

After a few minutes, Carlos must have realized that this spectacle was too depressing for little children; silently, I saw him leave the room with them. When I emerged a half hour later, three joyous children were lapping up the remains of ice-cream cones, and happily hanging on to Carlos, who was regaling them with stories.

The next day Cristina met me on the steps of my house. "Oh, Señora Condesa," she said as she arrived. "Carlos Evertz is the kindest man I have ever known. After you left yesterday, he drove me and the children to the cemetery, and on the way told them a lovely story about angels. It made the burial so much easier for all of us." She sighed deeply. "And," she went on, "he must have guessed that I had difficulty paying for my poor mother's funeral. I know he is not rich himself, and yet, when he dropped us off at our building, he obliged me to accept some money for the children's school." She looked at me closely, her eyes shining and moist. "It wasn't a small sum," she added quietly.

Over the next months, Carlos was sent to our house frequently to make deliveries; and if I was home, we would talk for a few minutes, sometimes about a recent soccer match or the last bullfight. I learned that his favorite matador was Antonio Ordoñez, who was also one of mine. Ordoñez had retired recently, but we both hoped that the great bullfighter would return to the ring. Carlos also adored another of my passions, flamenco.

Gradually an easy, companionable relationship grew between us, though we were by no means close. I might not see him for weeks at a time, during which he would never enter my mind.

Such was the case one day in October, which saw me on an Iberia plane on my way to a wedding in Bad Tölz in Bavaria with Luis. We were soaring upward through sumptous folds of white clouds on a flight from Madrid to Munich. Life was pleasant and beautiful that warm fall morning, and I was anticipating with joy the four days of balls in ancient castles, shooting parties in the Bavarian mountains, and rides in horse-drawn carriages through the open country. It would be a fascinating holiday in a place I'd never visited.

The plane leveled off, the steward served drinks, I settled deep in a book, and Luis dedicated himself to his newspaper.

Luis and I—so close and attached to one another in so many ways—were in fact also opposites: For instance, he was close-mouthed and secretive, where I am outgoing and enthusiastic. In appearance my Spanish husband has a northern European look—medium height, pale-green eyes, light-brown hair—while I am a brunette, in fact more of a "Spanish" type.

After my long acquaintance with Luis's introspective manner, I should not have been as astonished as I was when I realized why he was shoving the daily newspaper before my eyes.

"Look at the headlines, my dear," he said. "They have something to do with one of your favorites."

I glanced at the large black print, which described a terrorist attack on innocent civilians at an airport someplace in Europe. Eleven persons were dead and another nine gravely wounded. I looked up and asked him why such a story had anything to do with me.

"Not everyone is as friendly with a terrorist as you are, darling." His statement was absurd, and my look told him as much. He went on. "I didn't mention this to you when it happened, because I was afraid you would be too upset, but last week the police surrounded the Centro Asegurador building and burst in with automatic weapons. They were after the world's most dangerous terrorist, a bloodthirsty killer." Luis paused and smiled a half smile. "Your friend."

"That's ridiculous," I answered quickly. "How would I know a terrorist?"

"I'm referring to Carlos Evertz, my dear, the fellow you are always telling me is so charming and well-mannered. That's who the police were after. But he escaped. He fled from the building only seconds before the police had it fully surrounded. Something or someone tipped him off. It happened when you were in Pascualete." Pascualete is the name of our ranch in southwestern Spain.

I was absolutely stunned. "Nothing appeared in the press," I managed to say.

"No. The police kept this very quiet; and I also thought it was best for the company to keep the story under wraps. But the police did tell me that the man has a reputation for miraculously eluding capture. They call him Carlos the Jackal."

"Do you mean to tell me Carlos Evertz is Carlos the Jackal?" I asked.

Luis nodded.

"But, Luis, how is it you never told me this? How could you keep me ignorant of such an incredible event? Something you knew would especially affect me?"

"Darling, I'm sorry." He took my hand in his. "I didn't want to frighten you unnecessarily. Perhaps I was wrong. At any rate, today, when I read the paper, I decided I'd better tell you. If I don't, somebody else from the office eventually will." Luis looked at me thoughtfully. "There's another reason, too. Frankly, although John Derby's opinion on this matter might be useful, I was afraid you might rush to him with the story and he would drag you into a search for this international criminal. I didn't want to put you in that danger."

John Derby, code name Jupiter, had recruited me into the OSS during the Second World War. He was now one of the most experienced undercover agents in the CIA and had been my spymaster for years. Derby's cover as an international businessman with offices in forty-eight countries enabled him to operate espionage networks in every part of the world.

Jupiter had recruited me in 1943, when I was twenty. After training in the first U.S. espionage school, I'd been sent to work with a group of twelve fellow agents in "neutral" Spain, in reality a hotbed of murder and intrigue. Six hundred Gestapo agents worked closely with the Italians and the Japanese there; many of them trying to uncover where the Allied forces planned to launch their invasion of Southern Europe. Three years later when I married Luis, I had no thought of continuing my espionage work. But several years after that my old spymaster realized that my grandee title and influential Spanish family provided a perfect cover for obtaining information, and he repeatedly asked me to rejoin the Agency. The intoxicating excitement of undercover work made it much harder to give up than I had expected, and in 1954 I finally agreed to work again with Jupiter. Since then I had been involved in several exciting operations and had been regularly submitting reports.

Luis's reluctance to let me become involved with Jupiter did not surprise me. He'd always disapproved of my espionage work; and I suspected this was the main reason he hadn't told me about Carlos's escape. He and I rarely discussed that side of my life, though now and again in the past, when I was certain that a mission Jupiter had assigned me wasn't hazardous, I had informed Luis about it. However, my small attempts at candor hadn't changed his mind; he never approved of my continued association with a foreign country's intelligence service, and he himself did not want to be drawn into undercover activities either.

Overwhelmed by my husband's news, I stared out the window. Against the blue sky, fluffy clouds like stiffly beaten egg whites drifted past. The more I recalled his charming manner and kindness, the harder it was to accept the idea that he was a vicious terrorist.

"The funny thing is," Luis was saying, "Carlos was an excellent employee. During the eight months he was with us, the director told me he was one of the best salesmen we had." Luis caught my eye. "Hard to reconcile with what one of the police detectives told me, that Carlos has murdered dozens of innocent people. Just before coming to Spain, in fact, he killed two French policemen and one of his own colleagues."

I returned his stare in disbelief. Luis wasn't finished. "And the police captain who led the raid on our office also told me Carlos has been connected with all the major terrorist groups—the PLO, the Baader-Meinhoff of Germany, the Red Brigades of Japan and Italy. You name it. He tried to blow up an Israeli airliner at Orly Airport with a Russian rocket launcher. In Paris he drove by a Jewish bookstore and threw a grenade through the front window, killing one woman and wounding six others." Luis shook his head.

"How did he ever get a job in your company?" I asked, as the Iberia steward appeared with delicious-smelling trays of roast partridge in a sauce of grapes and mushrooms. I looked at the food and regretfully declined. Luis's news had killed my appetite.

"He had well-forged papers," Luis went on. "In appearance they were authentic—his identity card, his working permit, too. We are always cautious about whom we hire, you know."

"He must have taken the job to hide out, as some terrorists do," I said.

"No," Luis replied. "That seems doubtful. More likely to get information on key people. His job gave him access to many prominent people and the possibility of entering their homes. Maybe he's plotting the kidnapping of some of them—maybe of you and me—in order to get a good ransom. Just shows, you can't trust anyone these days." Luis sighed as he took up his fork and knife, then added: "Maybe, after all, one of your old CIA friends might know more about him than the Spanish police."

My husband picked up his newspaper again, and I looked back out the window, turning over and over in my mind the incredible news. As I was absorbing the shock, someone handed me the program and guest list for the wedding, which was being passed around the plane. The groom was the son of a friend from Sevilla and the bride was a German princess. Over five hundred people were expected, mostly from Germany and Spain, but there were Americans as well as guests from other countries. I scanned the program of shoots and balls, but I was too distressed to be interested and finally let it drop on my lap.

Luis picked it up and skimmed over it. "Ah," he said without further comment. "It looks like John Derby will be there."

"Yes, I knew that," I answered, struggling to register the names on the paper he put again in front of me. "Jupiter called last week to check if we were going. He told me he had already refused the invitation, but that if we were going, he would go, too."

"Good. This time, for once I might soften my attitude towards your friend Derby," Luis said. "Maybe it would be useful to ask him about Carlos Evertz. But," he met my eyes, "this doesn't mean that I'm willing to have you mixed up in the pursuit of a terrorist . . . or any other business he might have in mind."

"Don't worry, darling," I said. "During the next several days, I intend to enjoy the wedding festivities, not work at espionage."

He flashed me an "I-don't-really-believe-you" look, accepted a glass of the excellent Marques de Griñon red wine from the attentive Iberia steward, then settled back in his seat to continue reading. But I was still thinking about Luis's news, and the possible reasons why Jupiter had abruptly changed his mind about attending the wedding. Now it did not seem to me a mere coincidence that this decision so closely followed Carlos's recent escape in Madrid, especially since John might have been informed that Carlos was working in one of Luis's companies. My spymaster's actions were always calculated and purposeful. I knew I would hear from him.

Chapter 2

When we landed at the Munich airport, the customs' officials kept me busy, but all the time I had my eyes open for John Derby. I was explaining to the officer why I needed so many ball gowns, and why Luis needed so many hunting rifles, when I saw Jupiter's familiar figure in the passport line. Leaving Luis to struggle with the luggage, I made a beeline for him. It had been a number of months since I had last seen John Derby. His scrubbed, reddish face appeared fuller than in years gone by; but aside from that, he had hardly aged. Boxing, tennis, and martial arts kept him fit, and I was sure that he also maintained his skill with firearms and other weapons. John spotted me as I approached him, and greeted me with his usual calm warmth. "Aline," he called out, "it's so good to see you! It's been far too long!" Then, while he placed a kiss on each cheek, I whispered into his ear that I wanted to talk to him privately about a serious matter. Lowering his voice, he responded that it was just as vital for him to talk with me. "Aline, I'm working on one of the most hazardous operations of my career," he murmured. "We're trying to put a stop to a very shrewd gang of murderers." As I was about to ask him to tell me more, he put a hand on my arm. "Careful, friends are closing in on us. We'll talk later."

Glancing around, I saw Domínguin, the bullfighter, approaching; other friends were now milling nearby as well. Further confidences were impossible. So—curious and troubled—I retraced my steps to where Luis stood with the customs' official. I'd been right, Jupiter's appearance here was more than just a pleasure trip. The operation he'd hinted at was a matter of considerable consequence—and, I surmised, I was going to be involved in it, whether Luis liked it or not.

Quite soon our group was led to a pair of buses, which would deliver guests to the Bavarian town of Starnberg and the hotel nearby—once a private castle—where we would be staying for the next four days. Unfortunately, John Derby was assigned to the other bus; so my curiosity had to wait.

The narrow roads wound through thickly wooded hills and wondrous emerald mountains—some round and fat like puffy cakes jutting up above lush green valleys, and others as sharply pointed as church steeples. Lakes—great silver mirrors aimed at the sky—shimmered like jewels. Yet, even as I enjoyed the lovely scenery, I couldn't force from my mind Luis's news about Carlos, and John's brief declaration had me tingling with curiosity and excitement.

As we approached, the spires and slate roofs of the ancient castle were silhouetted against a cloud-struck sky. The lovely building looked like a gigantic bird nestled on the large lake's edge. When we descended from the bus, musicians in hats with feathers, dark leather shorts, and green loden jackets regaled us with a jaunty tune. Then abruptly the air resounded with the boom of a cannon. One slow rhythmic burst after the other exploded in a welcoming salute, a custom of the bride's princely family. All the merrymaking in such delightful surroundings made me look around and wonder: Did John expect to meet evil men in this idyllic place?

Our cozy suite was overflowing with vases of orange and purple wildflowers; through the open window I could see the lake and surrounding mountains. Most of the wedding guests were staying here, in the castle; but a few were lodged in an adjoining building—also ancient—which was now part of the hotel complex.

Before I could unpack, a knock came at the door. When I opened it, an attractive German girl stood there, looking radiant. Her name was Inge Schmidt; we'd met her the previous summer in Marbella, where she had been squired around by handsome Francisco Cabanellas, whose nickname was Paco.

Paco Cabanellas was very successful, and very wealthy, for a young man who had arrived in Marbella penniless about eight years before, and who for some time had worked as a mechanic. Later he became involved in the shipping business. Luis and I had met him at various times during the August social whirl, but we never became friendly with him, for my husband considered him a cheat. Once they'd been playing together in a foursome on the Monteros Golf Course, and according to Luis, Cabanellas's scorecard in no way reflected the number of shots he took. Luis was also skeptical about Paco's reputation as a hardworking young business executive, for he rarely seemed to spend enough time in his company's offices in Málaga to earn the kind of money he needed to maintain the jet-set existence he enjoyed in Marbella.

I recalled an afternoon during the past summer when Luis and I had watched Paco from the terrace of our house in Marbella, as he skimmed over the water in a fancy racing boat. "That's the most expensive racing boat out nowadays," Luis told me. "It's called a Magnum, or Cigarette. It can reach speeds up to eighty miles per hour . . . a marvel of design, way ahead of its time. Paco probably bought that one from his friend Nicky Maniatis. He's that rich Greek shipowner I saw at the Cocas last week, remember? Maniatis owns a company that distributes them."

Capturing the heart of Inge Schmidt had been a prime factor in the growth of Paco Cabanellas's social prestige. Inge was an only child, and a prominent figure every summer in Marbella—at the bullfights, in the nightclubs. Her father Hans was the chief executive of a major German industrial conglomerate, and one of Germany's wealthiest men. Hans doted on his pretty daughter.

"Oh, Aline!" Inge cried excitedly, entering the room and giving me an affectionate hug. "I read in the papers that you were coming to the wedding; and I decided to drop in to welcome you to my country."

We stood in the doorway, half embracing each other. "The papers claim the bride is the most beautiful princess in Germany and that the wedding is going to be filled with important people from all over the world," she gushed.

"How's Paco?" I asked as she released me.

"Sweeter than ever," Inge's deep-blue eyes sparkled happily. "He'll be staying in the building next door," she added. "I've never met anyone like him. Even my father is impressed. Not his usual reaction to my beaux."

She brushed aside a curly strand of straw-colored hair. Then, glancing at her watch, she continued. "In fact, Paco should be arriv-

ing any moment, so I can't stay long. He's coming in from Düsseldorf on a private plane."

"My heavens. I'm impressed. No one I know in Spain has a private plane."

Inge laughed. "Oh, the plane isn't his. He chartered it. He does
that often. He's doing extremely well. He now has several businesses with offices in Barcelona and Málaga, and in a few foreign
countries, too."

"In fact," Inge went on, "Paco took me recently to a shoot in
Italy, and all he did was buy me presents," she continued. "When
we stopped over in Rome, he bought me this bracelet in Bulgari."
She lifted a milky arm, gracing a shiny gold and diamond chain
bracelet. "Isn't it beautiful?"

Though I shared Luis's misgivings about Inge's boyfriend, I had to
admit that the bracelet was lovely. He may have been a cheat at
golf, and he may have liked to galavant around Marbella nightclubs
until dawn, but clearly Paco was doing something right in his business dealings. His dark good looks doubtless had a lot to do with
Inge's attraction to him, but it would take more than a handsome
face to impress a man like Inge's father.

Inge chatted with me a while longer; but she was worried about
being on time for Paco, so she dashed away a few moments later.

THE BALL THAT night was to begin at nine with dinner and cocktails. I was still unpacking when my old friend Ava Gardner came
sauntering into my room, carrying in her arms a pale-pink ballgown
embroidered in sparkling stones. Ava was still a ravishing beauty
despite her fiftyish years, her tempestuous marriages (to Mickey
Rooney, Artie Shaw, and Frank Sinatra) and affairs, and her burn-
the-candle-at-both-ends way of living. She threw the shimmering
dress over the back of the chaise lounge and plopped down. "Do
you think this dress will be all right tonight, Aline? I've dragged it all
the way from the other guest building where they've lodged me,
just so you could give me your opinion." Grabbing a cigarette from
the table, she bent to light it. "Adolfo assured me it would be perfect with a tiara, but my tiara is in the bank in London. I had hoped
to pick the damn thing up on the way here, but the f——ing film I
was doing kept me busy until the last minute. If I'd taken a plane to
London, I would have had to wait for another to get here, and I
wouldn't have arrived on time." She puffed heavily on the cigarette,
"I'm so f——ing mad. All those Wagnerian broads will be wearing

their tiaras. Mine is supposed to be one of the best in the world and I don't have it with me."

"At least you're here," I said, "and that's what's important. Someone said that Audrey Hepburn telephoned from Rome, there's a strike at the Rome airport and she has no idea when she'll arrive. Spanish friends traveling by way of Venice are also held up. And the Duchess of Windsor was coming, too; but she's had another ulcer attack and her doctor won't let her travel. So you're lucky to be here." I picked up the pink gown. "This dress is perfect, and you'll look better than any other woman, even without your tiara. So don't give it another thought."

After Ava left, Luis arrived—he'd been taking care of his shooting gear. A damp breeze had begun to chill the room; and when I went to close the window, Luis joined me to take a look at the view. Evening seemed to have come abruptly, and a damp mist was easing down into the valley from the nearby mountains. As I looked out in silence at the dim outline of the lake, I told him about my conversation with Jupiter. I mentioned that Jupiter was tracking some very dangerous people who could be in the wedding group. There'd not been time to tell John about Carlos, I added.

For a moment Luis said nothing. Both of us stood absorbed in our own private thoughts.

"Guapa,"—beautiful—Luis said quietly, breaking my reverie, "in order to calm yourself, ask John Derby what he knows about Carlos Evertz . . . and if he knows where that damn terrorist might be now. But I don't want you to let him involve you in tracking the fellow down. In fact, on second thought, maybe Jupiter is after other game than Carlos." A wry smile creased his face. "If that's the case, then I wouldn't be surprised—with your accustomed eagerness to do an operation with him—if you forgot about Carlos."

"You're absolutely wrong," I said, peeved. "I intend to ask John about Carlos, nothing more. And I will avoid doing anything that might upset you."

"Ha!" Luis blurted out. "Not bloody likely!" His eyes met mine. "I'm so certain you'll rush to work with him that I'm willing to bet that by the end of this wedding Jupiter will have you involved in some kind of undercover work. Well, what would you like to bet?"

"Anything you want," I responded with fervor. "Since I haven't the slightest doubt that I'll win."

"Anything?" Luis said, grinning at me. I could see he was enjoying this. "How about a present of the winner's choice? There's a pair of emerald cuff links I've been admiring for weeks in Luis Gil's shop in Madrid. He also has a beautiful gold cigarette case that I like almost as much."

"Marvelous," I said, warming to the idea. "I've been admiring Imelda Marcos's black pearl necklace for years. I'd love one like it."

We shook on it. Then he took my face in his hands and gave me a gentle kiss. "We'll see," he said, as he turned and walked toward the bathroom to bathe before dinner. He paused at the doorway, "By the way, the bet is good only if he asks you. John must ask and you must refuse. Otherwise you haven't proved anything."

"Ah, but how will you know whether he asks me or not?" I said, thinking myself very clever.

Luis raised an eyebrow. "My dear," he said, smiling ironically, "of course I trust you."

He disappeared, and I stood there a moment, wondering why I wasted energy raising my voice and getting excited, while Luis always managed to have the last word. His quiet authority, mixed with irresistible charm and humor, had stolen my heart over twenty years ago. And he continued to enthrall me.

Chapter 3

That night, John Derby arrived while I was standing near the entrance to the grand hallway of the castle. We then made an effort to separate ourselves from the stream of guests. In the soft light of crystal chandeliers, we wandered among elegantly dressed men and glittering women in lavish ballgowns and jeweled tiaras, but it was difficult to find a quiet nook in the crowded rooms. German castles, although sumptous, have smaller rooms than their Spanish counterparts. Finally we managed to find a place where there were relatively few people. But we had to go outside the castle to do it, out onto a terrace overlooking the lake. Fortunately, it was heated by overhead lamps.

A dance band was playing fox-trots, while around us small lanterns spread a soft yellow glow. Jupiter leaned against the railing, staring through the French doors, observing the people milling about inside. I told him about my encounters with Carlos, and about the excitement at the insurance office when the Jackal escaped. As I talked, John gave every appearance of just taking in the scene in the ballroom inside. But I could see he was scanning the other room as well, looking for someone. Aware that we might not have much time to speak alone, I briefly detailed the story of Carlos's appearances at the house. I told John about Carlos's delivery of documents, and about the various incidents where he displayed his generosity, and—of course—about the carnations Carlos liked to bring me. "Quite frankly," I told John when I'd finished, "I considered him a friend."

To my chagrin, John knew little about Carlos other than what was public knowledge. But he nonetheless had strong opinions about him. "My God, Tiger," he said ("Tiger" was my old code name in the OSS, and his accustomed nickname for me), "that bastard is about the most evil, dangerous character you could have come in contact with. I'm truly sorry to hear that he got to know you so well." He paused thoughtfully. "I do not believe it is generally known that he went underground in Madrid," he continued. "Vaguely, I remember hearing that he was still in Algeria." He meditated a moment longer, then exclaimed. "I've an idea. Remember your old friend Serge?"

I nodded. Indeed I did. Serge Lebedev was an ex-KGB agent who had defected through me about five years before. He'd been chief of station of the KGB in Tunisia and later in Morocco, where I'd met him. Apart from several sessions with him during his debriefing in Washington, I'd neither seen nor heard from Serge again, although I'd asked Jupiter about him several times, for I considered Serge to be a close friend.

"Today Serge is one of our specialists on European and Middle Eastern terrorists. He handled many of them when he was head of the KGB in North Africa. Not only is he familiar with the intricacies of all the various organizations, but he is personally familiar with many individual terrorists. For years, he supplied them with weapons and other assistance from the Soviet Union. If I could get you two together, Serge might be able to answer most of your questions. And your information about Carlos's personality and behavior should be useful to him as well." Jupiter extracted a small pad from his pocket and scribbled something. "You'll either hear from me or from him." He looked up. "And, by the way, Serge has a different name nowadays—same initials, but he's now called Steve Lederer."

The possibility of seeing Serge again pleased me, but that didn't diminish my anxiety to learn about the "hazardous" operation John had mentioned that afternoon. I had never heard him use such a drastic term when referring to his work; and I said as much when I asked him to tell me about it.

"Well, it's not going to be easy to brief you in a few words," he answered, "since the investigation I'm working on is complex and far-reaching. And, though I can't tell you all you might want to learn now, perhaps the most urgent thing for you to know is what I've just learned in Bonn from our COS there"—the Chief of Station. John's voice stopped then, and he continued to scan the people moving back and forth in front of us. He took so long to speak that my patience was almost at an end. Finally he resumed, "Someone is using a Spanish shipping company to transport high-tech weaponry and explosives to some of our Arab enemies and other dangerous people around the Mediterranean. There is a possibility that the man who runs the show is here tonight . . . or the *men*, for there are doubtless more than one of them. We don't know yet whom they are, but we do know that they move in the social circles like people that are invited to an affair such as this one."

Wafting out to us came muffled words in several languages, mingled with the sound of ice clinking against crystal. A full moon reflected the jagged mountains and lofty pines across the lake's surface.

"John," I said, "please tell me more details. Anything you can . . ." I was annoyed that after all these years he was still so secretive with me. But I held my tongue.

"Sorry. True enough. I should tell you more." He began to speak slowly, his breathing short and nervous. Although this manner of speaking was customary with him, tonight I sensed he was especially anxious about how much he should reveal to me. Whatever he told me would not be the full story, I knew that. Above all, my spymaster was cautious. In the faint light, the terrace shimmered, as the lake had earlier that day. The romantic setting was a strange background for an espionage tête à tête.

"Briefly," he began, "a terrorist group is involved in obtaining materials and designs for the manufacture of nuclear weapons and selling them abroad. This activity obviously represents a critical danger for the whole Western world, for it's much more likely that a nuclear war will be started by an arrogant, unstable dictator of a small nation in possession of a nuclear weapon than by the Soviets.

"The group I'm after is made up of cutthroats, pure and simple. It's terribly dangerous." He gave me a stern look. "I know how much you'd like to take part in the operation, Tiger, but I really hate to get you mixed up in this one. So I should probably leave the matter at this point and send you back to the wedding festivities."

His last words, he knew, did not discourage my interest in the operation. On the contrary, they fanned my curiosity. But I also knew that tight-mouthed Jupiter, having told me this much, actually wanted me to collaborate with him. "Don't worry, John," I said, as sweetly as possible. I was accustomed to wheedling information from him. "Your knowledge about these things can benefit me, and perhaps I can help . . . from the sidelines," I added.

"Good," he smiled. There were times when Jupiter could produce a raffishly winning, charming grin, and he had that look now. "So listen carefully," he went on. "A few years ago the United States and its allies developed a Coordinating Committee for Multilateral Export Controls—COCOM. The purpose of COCOM is to police American technology for the manufacture of nuclear weapons so it will not be sold to enemy countries. Certain European manufacturers, however, have been breaking COCOM regulations by exporting this material to various unaligned countries."

So that was why John had interrupted his busy schedule and accepted the invitation for the wedding! I listened attentively. "Some of the shipments of calutrons are being transported on Spanish ships."

"What the dickens are calutrons?"

"Calutrons are used to refine uranium, to enrich it to weapons-grade quality. We abandoned using calutrons some time ago for more efficient methods, but the process still works. We believe that a few wealthy, powerful individuals are buying them, and other critical components, in Germany. The materials are then trucked through Spain to freighters in Barcelona and Málaga." He paused for a moment, then added, "This material usually goes to Algiers, then to Libya; and in that way is passed on to other hostile countries in the Middle East." His tone now became so low I could barely distinguish the words. "We suspect one of the buyers is a Spaniard. He could even be someone you already know."

Investigating and exposing traitors had always fascinated me. Already my mind was scanning the people I knew who were involved in transportation or shipping. But Jupiter had not finished. "Tiger," his voice went on, "I have to repeat: The people involved are real killers. But there's a lot more. You should know . . . I have some clues."

This was the moment I had promised Luis to tell Jupiter that I could not work with him. But I said nothing, easing my conscience with the thought that if Luis knew the guilty party might be a Spaniard, he might be willing to help also.

Other people were closing in on us. A man who introduced himself as Karl von Ridder interrupted John when he graciously stretched out his hand to light John's cigarette. As Jupiter bent over the flame and then straightened up to thank the other man, I was struck by the similarity between the two of them. Ridder, like John Derby, was of medium height and had a solid build, like a middleweight boxer. His face, like John's, was square, the nose narrow and chiseled, the eyes were oddly disarming and deep set.

As soon as Ridder moved on, Derby hastened to add, "Our informant tells us that the person connected with the Spanish company has recently been in Germany, negotiating a major transaction. A lot of Spaniards have come to this wedding, and several German industrialists whose companies produce calutrons or small arms are also here." He moved his head from side to side. "The possibilities are tempting, don't you think?"

A Spanish shipowner and a German industrialist! The words immediately made me think of Inge Schmidt—and of her father and her boyfriend Paco Cabanellas. Paco had just flown in from business in Germany, I recalled. . . .

No, I said to myself a moment later, that's too easy. And I quickly discarded the notion. Paco may cheat at golf, I thought, but he's certainly not involved with terrorists and weapons' smugglers! And Inge's father is well thought of by everyone. I'd have to look further.

At that moment Karl von Ridder approached us again, this time with Ava Gardner, and our conversation was cut short. Ava's beauty and vivaciousness had been creating a sensation all evening, as usual. But when I noticed the easy manner between Ava and the German (he was a banker, I learned), I couldn't help concluding that more than an evening's brief friendship united the two. . . . In fact, a subtle electricity embraced them. Were they lovers? I asked myself. Had they once been?

Earlier that day, Ava had promised me that she would stay on the wagon, but I could see that she had not kept her word. Ever since I had known her, alcohol had always been a problem and heavy drinking had taken a toll on her looks. But you couldn't see that tonight. Tonight she was ravishing.

Grabbing each of us by an arm, with von Ridder trailing behind, Ava pulled us across the terrace into the dining room. Ornate white damasked tables loaded with heavy antique silver were set for dinner. The room echoed with the clatter of footsteps and the rustle of satin and chiffon. Silver covers had been lifted from the sumptuous buffet. Though I hoped to continue my conversation with Jupiter, the seating arrangements, I presumed, would not place us near each other, although German protocol was less strict than Spanish. At least that's what the Duke of Windsor had once told me, lamenting his bad luck in his youth: While visiting Spain, he had been placed beside the same elderly dowager Duchess night after night.

In other words, it was going to be difficult tonight to ask John to tell me something about his clues.

Meanwhile, elaborately uniformed menservants stood behind each buffet table. The array of exquisite foods was spectacular: roast lamb resting in a bed of mint and chestnuts and surrounded by tiny crisp potatoes; what appeared to be an entire flock of fowl—ducks and pheasants cooked so their rich savory skins were crisp; golden brown quail reclined on beds of stuffing filled with nuts and raisins.

IT WAS MUCH later, about two in the morning, when people were beginning to leave, that I noticed that Ava was now very drunk. She was running her fingers through her dark, reddish-brown hair, making it tumble around her face—always a sure sign that she had had too much to drink. "That old guy with lots of medals really knows how to dance a waltz," she was commenting to a German count at her side. Then the band played "One for the Road."

"This song always makes me sad," Ava mused, as if to herself. She was thinking of Frank Sinatra, I knew. The tune had been their favorite. Ava hardly ever talked about Frank . . . only when she had consumed too much alcohol. She had never stopped loving her ex-husband. But when they were married, neither of them could break free of their jealousies. And in the end they destroyed their marriage.

She stood up. "I think it's time I went off to bed," she declared in a slurred voice. The remains of a glass of red wine was in her hand; there was a flush across her cheekbones; and her eyes were feverish. The others at her table hardly noticed, but I knew Ava was apt to do rash things when she was in this state. "If I stay any longer I'll fall into someone's coffee," she went on with a giggle. I realized then that she was in no condition to find her room, which was in the hotel's small second building, a slight distance from the castle.

"I'll go with you, Ava, so you won't get lost," I said.

As we walked out through the front hall, arm in arm, Ava laughed raucously, for no reason, and then dropped my arm and began to run toward the door. I grabbed her key, which she had forgotten, and raced after her down the steps leading outdoors. She walked a short distance over the thick green grass that surrounded the castle, and then stopped. "F—— these shoes!" she cried, as she stooped to take off her gilt slippers. Then barefoot, shoes in hand and laughing wildly, she began to race over the grass, wet with evening dew. Her pale dress streamed out behind her. "Ava!" I called "You've forgotten your key." But she didn't hear me.

The night was too chilly for bare feet, but the grass was too wet for thin, fine leather. So I reluctantly followed Ava's lead and removed my own shoes.

The air slid off the lake in cool currents, breathing hints of winter, only weeks away. The lake itself was festive with long, undulating ribbons of light from the castle. All was quiet except for strains of music and laughter. The windows of the castle spilled light onto the lawn; but beyond their inviting perimeter, all was darkness. Ava plunged on past the light, and I hurried to keep up with her. As she advanced in front of me, all I could see was her dress shimmering in a ghostly cloud.

She reached the driveway. "Hey, be careful, Ava!" I cried. A large black Mercedes was pulling up to the building. "There's a car with no headlights just in front of you."

When I reached the driveway, the tiny sharp stones of the gravel hurt my feet, and I slowed down. As I neared the small building where Ava was staying, the car stopped. Two men emerged and started to walk toward the main entrance.

"You scared me, you jerks!" I heard Ava call out to them indignantly. "You almost ran into me. Why didn't you have your lights on?"

In the dimness, I saw the two figures nearing Ava. When I drew closer, a man's voice murmured something inarticulate as he continued to walk past her. Before he melted into the shadows behind the other man, a light on the corner of the building gave me a clear view of his face. For a split moment I thought he was General Oufkir, a man I had known in Morocco. Then I realized that this was preposterous. Oufkir had been dead five years. The reason for the similarity between the two men was the deep scar that ran across the man's cheek, and his Arab looks. But when he turned to glance in my direction, I saw that he was not at all like the famous Moroccan general who had masterminded two plots to assassinate King Hassan. This man's face, although handsome in a way, was not as strong and compelling as Oufkir's had been. This man may have earned his scar fighting, but his degenerate face indicated that he was more familiar with pleasure than battle.

When I reached Ava's side, the men were already entering a side door into a private suite. A path of light streaked out of one of the suite's rooms. Then they disappeared inside, the door shut behind them, and the light evaporated.

Ava turned to me, whispering, "I didn't like that guy's looks. What would someone who looks like a crook be doing in this place?" Her words still came out in a slur. "Evidently, not only wedding guests are staying here," she drawled in the Southern accent she only fell into when drinking. "Aline, we'd better check. Come on." She pulled me into the darkness near the room where the men had disappeared. The energy behind her gesture made it clear that drinking had not diminished her forcefulness. "That slug's up to no good," she mumbled. "I hope he's not lodged near me."

With one hand tugging on mine, she crept silently along the wall. I was surprised by her move, but also delighted. Nothing was more enticing for me than an investigation—no matter what kind. And anyhow, Ava couldn't be left alone. She stopped at the window and crouched low, pulling me down with her. Muffled voices, too low for us to understand, reached our ears. Moving further into the shadows, we reached another window where the voices seemed more audible. Ava was thrilled at the excitement. I laid a hand on her shoulder to steady her. I didn't want her to make a sound that would give us away. The men's voices were now clearly angry, but little of what they said was comprehensible. Expressions like *cobarde*—coward—and *cabrón*—foul goat—reached us; terms Ava understood well; and with each curse, she pounded my arm in glee. But after a while the voices calmed down; and she grew bored, indicating she wanted to leave. Just as we were about to sneak away, someone inside opened the window, probably to get fresh air. And we both sensed that if we stirred, they would hear us. Their conversation now reached us clearly. The speaker appeared to be only inches away. A nervous, insecure Spanish voice was saying, "I'll try to deliver as soon as I can." I've heard that voice before, I said to myself. But I couldn't remember where.

"What about the money?" replied someone else, also in Spanish. "I risked my life. The Germans are no fools, you know." This voice was firm, with a southern Andalusian—or maybe South American—intonation. And I knew this voice as well. But in the strange context, I couldn't place it.

Then we heard yet another voice. He also spoke Spanish, but his accent had a strong foreign sound. "You've got to get rid of them. Both of them. Use any means you want, and if you need help, you know where to go. Either finish with them once and for all . . . or we'll get somebody else to do it." The tone was as threatening as the words.

We both froze. Ava tapped my arm lightly, and we remained like statues, not daring to breathe.

"You've already been paid—in American dollars. If you don't deliver within ten days . . ." the voice menaced. With the warning hanging in the air, there was a moment of silence before the first speaker answered. "You trusted me enough to let me take risks for you before." This man's tone was full of resentment and at the same time carried a tinge of fear. "Now that I have a few financial problems, you're threatening me," he went on. "I don't want to get mixed up in your kind of business. That wasn't our agreement."

Ava was as quiet as a mouse, but not for long. The men—I couldn't make out how many there were—began to speak faster and moved away from the window. Since Ava's understanding of Spanish was limited, she soon became restless again, and yanked on my arm.

Gradually the voices became indistinguishable. The men must have moved to another part of the room. Signaling each other, Ava and I began to creep through the darkness toward the stairway that led to the building's main entrance.

As we were doing that, the door of the suite reopened and the lawn was once again flooded with light. We raced across the narrow beam and reached the stairway before anyone emerged. When I put my foot on the first step, Ava was ahead of me. For a split second, I glanced back. Two men were standing inside the open doorway, talking to someone invisible to me inside the door frame. In outline they seemed very like the two men we'd seen before.

When they turned to leave, Ava was already climbing the staircase. But I remained on the steps in semidarkness, watching the two men file by in front me. The first, the Arab with the scar, passed without noticing me and I was able to take a good look at him. I'd never seen him before tonight, and his evil expression made me hope I'd never see him again. He jumped into the car, which was standing in the shadows. Suddenly the headlights of the Mercedes splashed their cool white glare on the other man, who was now walking past me. He paused like a wild animal frozen in a beam of light. He was somewhat over medium height, almost stocky, with a massive beard and a thick moustache, and long hair half-covered his face. Even if I knew this man, I thought, he would be difficult to recognize. Yet something in his stance, in silhouette, struck me. As he passed by, he looked up without changing pace, and I blinked in astonishment. Although I had moved up onto the shadowed staircase when the headlights came on, he must have seen me, too. I knew those eyes, though I was used to sunglasses concealing them. I felt certain that I was looking into the cold penetrating stare of the man who for months had delivered Luis's business papers. I almost called out, "Carlos?"

But he strode on with no sign of recognition. His failure to recognize me made me doubt myself. And yet, although he had been only ten feet away, maybe he'd been blinded by the glare of the headlights and had not recognized me in the shadows. But the man, whether Carlos or not, must have realized that a woman was standing on the steps. Could he suspect that I'd overheard the comments inside the room? Whatever was the case, he reached the car without glancing back. As he opened the Mercedes's door, he looked briefly in my direction before jumping in. Then the engine roared, and the car sped away.

I was left staring out into the blackness, my heart thumping. Meanwhile, Ava was on the porch above me, and I turned to join her. When I reached her side, she was searching in her silver evening bag. I handed her the key and led her through the building to her door.

There was no doubt in my mind that these men were terrorists—they could even be the men Jupiter had told me about. Had I actually seen Carlos, I wondered, or was I imagining it? My only thought was to tell Jupiter what I had seen as soon as possible.

Ava was now not only drunk but frightened. "They're beasts," she mumbled. "That's what most men are. I want to forget them."

"Ava," I said, trying to sound unperturbed, "now that you're safely in your room, I must rush back to the castle. We'll pick you up for lunch tomorrow. I want to look for Luis, I haven't seen him for over an hour." The last thing I wanted was for Ava to notice that I, too, was frightened.

As I ran back over the lawn, the dew on the thick grass was wetting the ostrich feathers on my white chiffon gown. Lifting my skirt, I stumbled along, hardly aware of where I was. If the man I had seen was Carlos, I could be in danger. The horrifying litany of recent terrorist atrocities all over Europe started to run through my mind—car bombs in Spain, the massacre of Israeli athletes in Munich, murders in Italy, airliners shot out of the sky. . . .

As I neared the castle, the lights which before had been streaming through the windows illuminating the trees and greenery outside had dwindled. But despite the dimness, I recognized Jupiter's familiar figure descending the wide entrance stairs to the driveway. I almost cried out in relief. He was alone, and happened to look my way. He gave a bemused smile when he spotted me traipsing across the lawn barefoot, with my skirts pulled up around my knees. I waved and he stepped out onto the gravel to meet me halfway. I couldn't wait to tell him what I had just experienced. It was sheer luck to have found him so soon.

When I reached the stone gravel of the drive, I bent down to replace my slippers. As I did so a car came wheeling out of the shadows, it seemed from nowhere, and nearly knocked me over. Instinctively, I stepped back, just in time to see a black Mercedes come to a screeching halt. The back doors flew open. Two men leapt out and moved so quickly that I could not distinguish even their contours in the murky light. To my horror, they pounced on Jupiter and dragged him without a sound into the car. The doors slammed and the car tore off.

Everything happened so quickly and in such deep shadow that it was impossible to make out the plates on the car or to determine if it was indeed the same Mercedes I'd seen only moments before, although I sensed it had to be. I stood paralyzed, and then without thinking, I let out a scream. As if the speeding car was controlled by my voice, about two hundred meters away, it stopped abruptly. Again the rear doors flew open. This time a body was hurled out, bouncing on the ground in a way that told me the person was either unconscious or dead.

My breath stuck in my chest as I stared at what had to be my friend, lying inert on the gravel. Instinctively, I ran toward him, regardless of the idling Mercedes. As I did so, I had the vague impression that something else had triggered their departure. Whatever the cause, the big black car sped off, and this time it did not return.

As I ran, my legs felt incredibly heavy and dreamlike, each step dragging in a kind of slow motion. I just couldn't seem to get there fast enough. The closer I came to him, the higher my pitch of terror grew. Finally I reached the quiet body which was facedown on the gravel. Kneeling beside John, I slipped my hand around his throat to feel for a pulse. To my relief the whisper of a rhythmic beat was palpable beneath his damp, cold skin. He was alive but unconscious; there'd been some kind of a blow to his head, and judging from his body temperature, he was in some kind of shock. I was aware that he should be moved only by a doctor; the blow, or smashing into the hard driveway, could have broken his back. Turning my head from side to side, I searched for help, but no one was in sight. The night was black, most guests had already retired.

I raced back to the castle and up the stairs. Once inside, the happy laughter indicated that a few people were still partying. And directed by their sounds, I found the Baron von Schlegel and his wife sitting alone at a table in the now almost empty ballroom. Fortunately I'd met them hours before, and when I told the baron what had happened, without a moment's pause he came to my aid. In no time he had a doctor and an ambulance for John Derby.

The rest occurred swiftly, as if all other events of that night were compressed into one brief moment: Luis at my side as I again kneeled next to Jupiter; the mad dash to the hospital miles away; and finally, sometime just past dawn, Jupiter opening his eyes in a barren hospital room, the signal that his injury was not fatal.

At that point the chief doctor stated that Mr. Derby had a concussion and that he did not know yet how serious it was, but that for the time being, sleep would be the best cure for him and for us as well. In the backseat of the rickety old taxi on our way back to the castle, Luis cradled me against his shoulder. Through sleepy eyes I looked at the mountains awash in the blue morning light, and felt only gratitude and relief that Jupiter was going to live.

Chapter 4

The next morning I awoke close to eleven, feeling as though I had fallen from a high cliff. Every muscle in my body ached, and I groaned out loud as I rolled over and opened my eyes.

"I know how you feel, darling," said Luis, who was dressed and sipping coffee by the window. He stood and came over to the bed. I reached out my hand and he sat down beside me.

"That was quite an ordeal last night," he said. "I have spoken to the hospital. John is resting and the skull fracture seems to be what they call 'hairline.' So the recovery will be swift. He is miraculously lucky."

I already knew this about Jupiter: Cats and some spies have nine lives. But I always worried about my friend. In his business, death could be around the next corner. It seemed to me that he took too many chances . . . although this event was certainly not due to his risking his life.

"Can he see anyone?" I asked.

"No, not yet," said Luis, "though possibly this evening."

I lay back against the mass of pillows and tried to gather in my mind all the details that I could remember about the car and the men at the hotel. I wanted to be especially accurate when I told Luis that I thought I'd seen Carlos getting into a Mercedes only minutes before Jupiter's accident. I knew Luis would be hard to convince; it wasn't his way to take such things seriously.

Luis was watching me. Then he reached over and poured me a cup of coffee from the tray. "I've spoken to the police," he said quietly.

"What?"

"Yes, they were here quite early, the hospital must have notified them about the accident."

"Luis," I said excitedly, now thoroughly alert, sitting straight up, "that wasn't an accident!"

"Well, for the purposes of your spymaster's cover, not to mention your own, my darling, that's the best light to cast it in, wouldn't you agree? Apparently they managed to get a few words out of John Derby, and that's how he accounted for it. You made the same decision last night when you spoke to the baron, didn't you?"

"Of course. I have to consider John's cover," I said. Then I told Luis all I could remember about my experiences after I left the party with Ava.

He listened thoughtfully before speaking. "The men you saw when you were with Ava last night sound to me like hotel guests who are not members of this wedding party; and they will probably not appear here again. Please darling," he went on, "don't be worried. Most likely, since my news about Carlos yesterday was a shock, you had him on your mind. In the dark it's easy to confuse people.

At any rate, those thugs, whoever they are, are far away by now. Their business has nothing to do with us. And if John Derby is mixed up in an operation that puts his life in such danger, I insist again that I do not want you to have anything to do with it. What happened to John last night is an example of what could happen to you.

"Stay away from John's current operation," he said with great intensity. "Please, darling."

"Don't worry," I said. "I don't want a crushed head. But I do want to find out more about Carlos." Then I told him that Jupiter was going to put me in touch with Serge Lebedev, since he thought Serge and I should share our information about the Jackal. Luis agreed this was a good idea. He knew Serge, and said that an ex-KGB agent should also have some practical knowledge about terrorists that would be interesting to know.

Luis glanced at his watch. "If you think you can manage it, we're scheduled to meet Ava in her hotel lobby in about forty-five minutes. I think the best thing we can do is proceed as though this were an ordinary day. Since there are five hundred guests here for the wedding, John Derby's absence is not likely to cause a stir. The baron has agreed that the less said the better. We both decided it was better not to talk to the other guests about the incident. It could spoil the wedding celebrations." Then he grabbed his cigarette case from the table, put it in the inside pocket of his jacket, and lightly kissed my cheek. "I'll see you downstairs."

Chapter 5

While waiting for Ava, I spoke to the desk clerk in hope of learning the name of the man who was staying in the corner room. The clerk was young and officious, with a sparse brown mustache and thick eyeglasses. Despite my best efforts, I could see he was determined not to be cooperative. He refused to look in the registry for me, saying with great pomp that he was not at liberty to reveal the identity of guests of the hotel.

At that moment Ava arrived in the lobby amidst a flurry of attention. She always turned heads, but today when she bustled into view wearing tight black stretch ski-pants and a short black mink parka, not a single person failed to note her arrival. Small diamond earrings sparkled, offset by her dark, reddish-brown hair, swept back from her face. She was also wearing an enormous pair of black sunglasses.

"Is this squirt giving you any trouble, Aline?" she asked.

I could see she'd already had a run-in with the desk clerk. She'd probably asked the same question I had. Although Ava was usually warm and kind to almost everybody, this concierge was precisely the kind of obnoxious fool that drew her ire.

"Good morning, Miss Gardner," he said stiffly.

"Ava, he's been very helpful. Let's go," I said, grabbing her arm and tossing a thank-you over my shoulder to the relieved clerk.

Outside in the glaring sunshine, Ava removed her glasses. "Will you look at this, Aline?" she said, pointing to her face.

Her lovely violet eyes were puffy and bloodshot. Even the most expert makeup couldn't disguise their condition. There was no point in suggesting that half a dozen fewer drinks in the evening would have made a world of difference. So I patted her cheek, said she looked fine, and suggested we hurry.

However, she wanted to talk, and we paused as she pointed to the corner room where we'd been eavesdropping. "Actually," she said with a conspiratorial gleam in her eyes, "I've been playing detective. And I found out who is staying in that suite." She looked at me. "It's that young Spanish guy, Paco Cabanellas." She touched my arm. "So what do you know about him, Aline?"

I gave her a brief rundown of Paco's background, thinking all the while about Jupiter's information: Someone was using a Spanish shipper to transport high-tech weaponry. Is that how Paco got his wealth? I asked myself. It also occurred to me just then that it may have been Paco's voice that I thought I had heard last night.

And the other one, again I surmised, was Carlos.

"There's a strange woman in that suite, Aline," Ava was saying. "She almost ran into me this morning when I first came upon her. She was disheveled, only wrapped in a dressing gown as she came out of that room. Well," said Ava, "I didn't look much better myself.

"Anyhow, those horrible men were running around in my head all night. And as soon as I awoke, I looked out my window to find out how close that room was to mine. My god! If you can believe it, I saw the same car that nearly hit me last night! At least I'm almost sure it was. It was pulled up almost under my window. Two men were standing next to it talking. I couldn't tell if they were the same creeps as last night, because I only saw the top of their heads, and I never really saw them well, anyhow. But as I watched, out came this gorgeous young broad who ought to be in the movies. She's that beautiful, even in a dressing gown. From her gestures I could tell she was really giving it to them. My curiosity got the better of me; and since I wanted to do some jogging, I went down to see what I could find out." Ava was loosening her parka and plumping up her hair as she spoke. "And what do you think? On the steps I almost bumped right into that dame. She looked fantastic, like a gypsy—jet black hair, great slim body. She was still steamed up when I passed her."

Luis was waving to us from the car, so we jumped in, but Ava went right on with her story. "And do you know what she did?" Ava said, "Maybe she recognized me. At any rate she pulled me down beside her on the steps, as if we were old friends, and began to tell me that she knew somebody was going to be killed today. Can you imagine?"

"Who is this woman?" Luis asked her.

"I don't know. That pimp at the desk wouldn't tell me. But she's okay . . . nice. . . . Maybe she drinks a bit, or uses drugs. I don't know, but she has that look. Still, she's a beauty, even without makeup. Very young, speaks bad English, and . . . she tells fortunes."

"What?" I was wondering if Ava had completely sobered up.

"Yes. She told me she's good at reading hands. I wanted her to read mine right there, but she was too excited about this killing that she swears is going to happen today. She said that she can forecast these things."

"Did you see her at the party last night?"

"No, she wasn't there. She said her brother wouldn't let her go, and that she wasn't invited anyway. She told me that wouldn't stop her though, and that she would have gone if she had wanted to. And I believed her. She's willful like that, I can tell. But I ended up liking her, all the same. She's a live one.

"Before I left her, I asked her about the men in the Mercedes. And she told me that one is a bastard, but one is nice. She refused to give me their names, though. I couldn't even figure out if she actually knew them well . . . or if she was simply giving me a witchy, 'fortune teller's' version of them."

Ava's strange account only served to unnerve me more than I

already was. Meanwhile, according to our decision not to get a rumor started, I dared not tell her about the attack on John. When we pushed through the door of the mountain lodge, which was the scene of this morning's wedding event, the happy sounds of joyous voices and several accordions were more than welcome. Three entertainers decked in traditional lederhosen and green Bavarian jackets were harmonizing, and people were already dancing to the peppy song. Most guests had already arrived, and some were warming themselves in front of a huge stone hearth. The setting was charming. Rustic wood tables encircled a small dance floor; large windows gave a view of the beautiful mountain peaks surrounding us. The food was hearty and delicious; the gaiety of the music contagious. Luis and I joined the couples on the floor.

As soon as lunch was over, those who were going shooting were advised that the gamekeepers were ready and waiting. My husband, Dominguín, and Karl von Ridder, the German banker we'd met the night before, donned their shooting boots and clothes, and picked up their rifles. Standing at the window, I watched as they followed the gamekeepers along a steep narrow path on the edge of the mountain. The cliff had a sheer drop which, from my perspective, looked nearly vertical. They walked in single file, their heavy rifles balanced on their shoulders, their knapsacks strapped to their backs. Ava was at my side, her hands wrapped around a shiny new camera she had been using to take pictures of everyone.

"It would sure be easy to kill someone going down that path. Just a little nudge and they'd be tumbling down that cliff," she said. "I'm glad nobody tried to get me to go shooting."

I laughed. "You know, I was thinking the same thing. We're both still under the spell of the men we saw last night." At that moment I would have especially liked to tell her about John Derby . . . and to startle her with the news that I suspected one of those men we saw was a famous terrorist called Carlos; but naturally I held my tongue. To change the subject, I asked her if she knew Karl von Ridder.

"Umm," she said with a chuckle. "I knew him well."

"Really?" I didn't mention that I already suspected as much.

"Well, I met him between marriages."

"He really doesn't seem your type," I said, laughing. "I thought he was a reserved German banker."

"Oh, he is!" cried Ava. "But nevertheless, he's absolutely my type." She let out a melodramatic sigh as the men circled down the path and out of sight.

"Where did you meet him?"

"In Munich. I was making a movie. He was a friend of the producer. Took us all out for fabulous dinners and drank everyone under the table. The best drunk I ever met." Ava had a sincere admiration for people who could outdrink her. "Now he's married. C'est la vie!"

Ava looked pensively for a moment at her camera, then turned around and took a few pictures. The thought of the banker cast a momentary shadow over her high spirits. But then an Austrian archduke beckoned her to the dance floor; and with a wink she handed me the camera and went to join him.

Many wedding guests were leaving, but the place was obviously a popular one for its spectacular setting; and more people were arriving all the time. Inge Schmidt came in with Paco Cabanellas and another couple, and invited me to join them for coffee. Paco then introduced me to R. K. and Nancy Rhodentus.

I recognized the couple immediately, though I'd never met them. R. K. Rhodentus was the Texas billionaire whose wedding in Paris to an American fashion model half his age had made headlines in tabloids about two years ago. R.K. was on the boards of several major European insurance companies; and he had some kind of important connection with Exxon. He'd also made dubious headlines years earlier, due to a messy, long drawn-out divorce with an American heiress. His current wife couldn't have been more than thirty, and was even more beautiful than the photographs I'd seen of her in fashion magazines—small, delicate, fragile-looking, perfect. But when Nancy Rhodentus offered me her exquisitely manicured hand as we were introduced, I was slightly taken aback to notice a tiny, but visible, scar running in a vertical line from the right side of her nose to the top of her lip. Rather than detracting from her appearance, strangely enough, it had the effect of making her otherwise flawless features more entrancing. A flicker in her expression told me she was aware of my observation, and that she was sensitive about the scar.

Nancy's husband, R.K., was not in the least a fragile flower like his wife. He sat back in his chair and extracted a large cigar from a gold case inside his jacket. He was an enormous man, well over six feet tall, with an expansive belly, round ruddy cheeks, and a shock of thick white hair.

"I hope I won't disturb you with this, Countess," he said, waving the cigar jauntily in my direction. "Please tell me if I do." He held the cigar unlit, waiting for my permission, watching me with hazel-brown eyes that told me he was smart, assured, and tough.

I gave him a smile and a nod.

Then he proceeded to put himself through an elaborate ritual of sniffing, snipping, and puffing, which eventually culminated in stretching out his legs and sighing in blissful contentment as a turban of thick blue smoke unraveled around his head.

"Cigars are my only vice," said R.K., with an engaging smile. "But my dear wife is a chocaholic."

I looked at Nancy—and especially at her perfect figure and flawless complexion—and estimated that the last time she'd done more than allow herself a taste of chocolate had probably been about age three.

Meanwhile, something in this woman attracted my curiosity. Under the surface of her porcelain skin, I could almost see tension pulsing. She was like a thoroughbred just before a race. I'd known several young models who had married wealthy older men for their money, but something about this woman made me believe her case was different.

Inge Schmidt was smiling at Nancy—R.K.'s remark about the chocolate must have amused her, too. And then she turned to me. "You wouldn't believe what a wonder woman this friend of mine is. She's the perfect wife!"

"Isn't that the truth," beamed R.K., placing a fond hand on Nancy's delicate wrist. Nancy smiled at him and shook her head at me, as if to say, don't listen to any of this.

"I'm prepared to believe you," I said lightly to Inge and R.K., wondering why Inge had such a special opinion about this mysterious girl.

"She's everything from R.K.'s social secretary to his chief business consultant," said Inge, answering my unspoken question. "She staffs their houses, hires his pilots, and selects his bodyguards. And she still has time to dress better than anyone I know. In comparison I feel stupid."

Nancy was indeed chic today in a smart Valentino suit, and her fabulous cheekbones were subtly enhanced by a delicate makeup. But Inge's remarks had not satisfied my curiosity.

"Sometimes I actually feel that I am R.K.," said Nancy, with quiet humor, taking up where Inge left off. "I almost think I can read his mind and predict what he'll do better than he can. He's a sharp negotiator when it comes to business, but believe it or not, he's like a big cuddly bear. And when it comes to all his other affairs, he's helpless."

"To you I'm a cuddly bear, darling, but I'm afraid most of the world sees me as a grizzly looking for a good meal."

Nancy clasped her husband's large hand in hers in a warm, loving gesture. R.K. was still creating a small storm cloud of smoke above his head. "I confess, I married Nancy for her beauty," he said. "And I had no idea then how smart she was. Now I don't make an important decision without her."

Nancy shook off the compliments with a pretty toss of her taffy-colored curls. "I don't know what would have happened to me if I hadn't married R.K.," she said quietly. "I often feel that my life began when we married."

R.K. chuckled and squeezed her hand. But as I looked at this woman, I thought she was probably telling the truth. Some radical change in her life was probably what I had detected earlier and had not understood. She had the restless air of a fugitive, albeit a charming and beautiful one. In her eyes was the nervous desperation of someone who has narrowly escaped a hard fate and who still doesn't quite believe her good fortune. And at the same time there was something touching and genuine about her unassuming manner. I decided immediately that I liked her.

R.K. took a deep puff on his cigar. "My wife's only imperfection is that she admires other men," he said chuckling.

"I do?" she said, seemingly sincerely surprised.

"What about that Greek shipbuilder you were going on about the other day?"

"I only said he seemed intelligent and attractive," protested Nancy in mock alarm.

"Well you can't blame her, R.K.," said Inge. "We all feel that way about Nicky Maniatis."

"Who's that?" I asked. "Already I'm dying to meet him."

"Oh, he's really interesting, Aline," said Inge. "Dark Mediterranean type, with very white teeth and a marvelous smile. He builds absolutely smashing yachts and speedboats."

"Don't you know him?" asked Paco. "He's a good friend of mine and was in Marbella this past summer off and on. I'm surprised you didn't meet him." I remembered vaguely then that Luis had.

R.K. explained that one of his sons who was currently in the Caribbean was using a yacht designed and built in one of Maniatis's shipyards for an elaborate underwater project. The boat's shallow draft was perfect for maneuvering in small harbors, he explained; and he was so pleased with it, he'd commissioned another, much larger one—in fact, practically an ocean liner—that would be finished in the early spring.

"What kind of underwater project is your son doing in the Caribbean?" I asked.

"I'm very proud of Bob," R.K. responded, puffing with satisfaction on his cigar. "He's a veteran of the U.S. Navy SEAL program, which means he survived the toughest military training in the world, involving scuba work, explosives, small arms, knives, and hand-to-hand combat." He carefully tapped the ash from his cigar into an ashtray. "To graduate from that program, you have to be a real man. Anyway I'm delighted he's pursuing my oldest hobby— looking for gold, Countess." He chuckled. "Spanish gold from sunken galleons." Turning to his wife with a smile, he said, "Who knows, darling? Maybe the sexy Nicky will deliver the new yacht personally."

Nancy rolled her eyes.

"I'm kidding," said R.K. "He's a perfectly nice man, Countess."

"And rich, too!" cried Inge.

"Enough!" said Paco, with a laugh.

As if on cue, a group of stags came racing down the slope outside the window and distracted everyone's attention. Inge and Nancy both jumped up to go outside to watch. Even R.K. lumbered out of his chair and went out to the balcony veranda that surrounded the lodge. Paco and I were left to finish our coffee. He was a good-looking young man, tall, with dark hair. But he had a nervous manner that put me off a bit—like a man who has just passed a bad check and knows it.

"I didn't see you at the ball last night," I said.

"No, I wasn't invited. I went to bed early. I've been traveling too much lately, and I was exhausted," he said. "I wanted to be rested when the Rhodentuses arrived. They're tireless sightseers."

He stretched like a contented cat in the sun, then stood up and suggested we join those on the balcony. As we walked out, I said, "Inge mentioned you'd taken her to Italy for a shoot. I didn't know you liked to shoot, Paco."

His long-lashed dark eyes brightened. Evidently I'd hit on a topic that delighted him. "Yes, it's a new diversion of mine. We were shooting doves," he said, holding open the rustic log door that led to the balcony.

Below us, the cliff plummeted sharply down into rocky gorges and deep green depths. Far below, the spire of a church in a distant village nestled in the arm of the valley. Nancy, Inge, and R.K. had circled around to the other side of the balcony. As Paco and I leaned over the railing to get a better look at the retreating stags, I wondered how this young man had made such a remarkable success in business so quickly. And now had time to take up shooting as well? I asked him, "When did you take up shooting, Paco?"

Paco laughed. "Perhaps it seems strange to you, since we've usually met in nightclubs. But ever since my business began to improve and I could afford it, shooting became a passion for me. Recently I bought the Fernández de León *finca* near Toledo, where I'm planning partridge shoots this fall."

"I've been there once," I told him. "It's a lovely old place, isn't it?"

"Oh, yes. But it was very rundown when I bought it. It's taking quite a lot of fixing up. But the shooting is marvelous."

"I also like to shoot, Paco," I told him, hoping that he wouldn't notice that I was obviously fishing for an invitation. "And Luis is, of course, a top shot," I added.

"Yes," he said. "I've heard that. So why don't you and Luis come to shoot with me next month?" He pulled a small red datebook from an inner pocket. After turning over several pages he said, "How about the last weekend in November?"

Actually, my acquaintance with the estate he'd just bought was more than passing; I knew it well. It was one of the most beautiful in Spain, and had the reputation of offering a phenomenal amount of game. It was said that twelve top guns could bag almost a thousand birds a day. The purchase price on the property must have been staggering.

"I'd love to," I said. "But let me check with Luis. He may be already busy that weekend." I suspected my husband would refuse, considering his reservations about Paco. But I wanted to accept. Young Paco Cabanellas intrigued me—especially after I'd learned that his had been the suite where Ava and I had been eavesdropping last night.

A chill breeze had started to blow; and with it came a cluster of clouds that blocked out the sun, as if a winter storm was brewing. I hoped my husband would finish his shooting soon, for it seemed like a good time to return to the castle. Just as Paco and I were about to go inside, Nancy Rhodentus came around the far end of the veranda with a devastatingly beautiful girl. She was tall and slim with brilliant black hair, and she was wonderfully dressed in black high-heeled boots, an expensive sable jacket, and a small hat of the same fur. The pair were still quite a distance from us when Paco placed his hand on my arm and turned me around. But I had not moved far before I saw the girl walk straight to the railing and lean like a gymnast far out over the ravine in a motion that took her feet off the floor and my breath away watching her. She let out a shout of almost feral pleasure, and thrust her body out even farther. For a brief moment I had the impression she was going to jump. Just a few minutes ago, I'd felt vertigo only looking over the railing. In the next instant, Nancy pulled her back, and the girl was standing flat on the deck again, pulling her coat collar tight to protect against the cold blast of the wind.

Paco hurriedly deposited me inside, where I joined my old and very close friend Carmen Franco, who was just putting on her coat. Lovely, brown-eyed Carmen was the only child of General Francisco Franco, Spain's leader for almost forty years. He had been Spain's most famous and popular general during Spain's long, tragic Civil War. And at the war's end in 1939, he had been named chief of state by the victorious army. Carmen never took advantage of her father's powerful position and was generally admired for her unassuming manner. She had married a handsome doctor, Cristóbal, the Marquis of Vellaverde; the couple were a popular twosome in Spanish society.

A few minutes later, Carmen and I now joined the many guests descending the mountain path which was so narrow we proceeded in single file. Meanwhile, billowy clouds were massing overhead, skimming the peaks and ridges. The wind was beginning to howl; and in another ten minutes, the sky had turned ominous. My boots crunched on the path, and despite enjoying the clean, sharp air, I was anxious and fearful. For the first time since meeting Ava that morning, I was alone with my own personal worries pressing on me like the nagging gusts.

Although Luis had assured me that Jupiter would recover completely, Ava's story of the young girl's prediction that someone would be killed was weighing on me—the same young girl who moments earlier was threatening to fly off into the gorge? I wondered. At this very moment Jupiter lay unprotected in a hospital room. If the men in the Mercedes had intended to kill him last night, and knew they had failed, nothing would stand in their way now. I decided to speak to Jupiter about a guard.

The glowering sky pressed down against the treetops. I hoped a winter storm wouldn't delay my husband's return from the shoot.

Chapter 6

My anxiety grew, as hours passed and Luis did not arrive. No storm developed, fortunately, so his absence was even more perplexing. Often he'd return from a shoot later than I expected—tracking a wounded stag or helping a friend find his trophy in the thick brush—but surely on this night he would have hastened back to meet me. We were planning to see Jupiter at the hospital before going on to the evening's party.

I heard steps echoing through the hotel corridor as many of the others returned from the shoot. I went so far as to grab my bag, ready to depart the instant Luis appeared. But after the footsteps died away and my husband remained absent, I dropped my things and went to telephone the hospital once again.

"Stable," reported the evening nurse. Not "excellent" or even "good," but at least out of immediate danger. I stood in the window watching the shadows of early evening settle over the lake. Finally I couldn't bear it any longer—I called the concierge and asked for a car. I would go ahead to the hospital without Luis.

The drive through the dark mountains seemed far more treacherous than in the early-morning light. I was forced to steady myself in the backseat as the driver negotiated the sharp hairpin turns; the almost perpendicular drops by the roadside appeared like cavernous black holes deep as Hades. When we reached the hospital I nearly leapt out of the car.

Inside—to my intense relief—the nurse at the desk told me that John Derby had been moved from intensive care to a private room in a quiet section of the hospital. She gave me the directions, then returned to her duties. As I rounded the corner, to my surprise, I saw the hulking figure of Manolo, Jupiter's houseman in Marbella, sitting hunched with worry on a small chair before a door at the end of the corridor.

"Señora Condesa!" he cried, and stood to greet me.

"I'm glad to see you here, Manolo. How is Señor Derby?"

"He's resting, Señora Condesa, but his head has been paining him quite badly," Manolo said, making a dramatic gesture with both hands clutched to his forehead.

I looked at him with some alarm. "But he's better now?"

"Yes, I think so." Then he told me he'd just arrived, that he'd called the hotel early that morning merely to speak to Jupiter, and had been horrified to learn that his employer was in the hospital. So, he'd taken a plane immediately.

He was pleased to know that I thought he'd done the right thing; I patted his arm, and proceeded into Jupiter's room. Gently, I opened the door. Only a small bedside lamp burned. My spymaster sat propped against pillows at a sixty-five-degree angle, his eyes closed. I stood by the bed, my throat constricted with worry. Even in the dim light the pallor of his complexion was alarming. After a moment, however, his eyes opened, and he looked at me. I tried to smile, but in truth I was frightened.

"You look like you've seen a ghost, Tiger," he said in nearly a whisper.

I smiled. "Last night, I was afraid that was exactly what I was seeing. You scared me to death."

He was silent and closed his eyes again. After a while he said, "I can't describe this headache. I've never felt anything like it."

"What did the doctor say?"

"That the headache will probably continue into the night. That the blow is no more serious than what happens when I'm knocked out boxing." Boxing was one of John's hobbies, but I doubted he'd ever been knocked out. He was probably trying to raise my spirits. "But I wouldn't want you to experience this kind of pain," he went on.

"And tomorrow you'll be rid of it?"

"Yes. Or most of it, at any rate," he added. "And I'm free to go, as soon as I feel comfortable."

I was astonished. It seemed Jupiter's luck was holding. His eyes remained closed. And it was clear that conversing was difficult. I realized he was in no condition to listen to my account of last night's events.

"May I come again tomorrow?" I asked.

He opened his eyes and smiled, "Yes, in fact I would appreciate it if you would come in the morning and pick me up. I intend to go to the wedding. I'll have Manolo bring my things here from the hotel, so I can go directly to the church."

"Are you serious?"

"Perfectly. I had a glimpse at the faces of the two men in the car last night . . . just before they smashed my head. I want to look for them. I have a hunch those fellows are still hanging around."

"You're going to take that kind of risk?" I could barely control my voice. It seemed crazy for Jupiter to make himself a target.

"It would be more of a risk not to. After all, I'm the only one who would have any clue of their identity," he said.

"I have a lot to tell you," I said quietly. It was now more urgent than ever to tell him that Carlos himself and an Arab with a scar may have been the men who attacked him; but his frown of pain stopped me.

"Well, in that case, I expect you to come a little earlier tomorrow," he said with a slight smile. I could see our conversation was exhausting him, so we quickly concluded our plans, and then I left him to mend in peace. I said a brief goodbye to Manolo, who assured me he would stay by "el señor" throughout the night.

WHEN I BURST into our suite a few minutes later, it was Luis who was now anxious about me, and not the other way around.

"My god, Aline! I've been out of my mind with worry," he said. He stood up, but agitation and relief conspired to stop him in his tracks.

I explained that I'd been so worried about John Derby that I'd gone to the hospital to see for myself how he was, and that in my rush I'd forgotten to leave a message. Luis then came over and put his arms around me. "Darling," he said, "calm down. I can't say how relieved I am to see you. I've been imagining all kinds of disasters."

Then he shook his head. "Sit down," he continued. "I'm afraid I have bad news."

Chapter 7

"*You remember Karl* von Ridder, don't you, the German banker?" he began. "He was one of the many people we met last night?"

"Of course. I was talking to Ava about him this afternoon. What happened?" I cried.

Luis, who was still dressed in his hunting clothes, started to remove them. He took off his boots. Picking them up, he nodded to me to follow him into the dressing room. "He was nearly shot this afternoon, and he suspects it was a deliberate attempt to kill him," Luis said.

"My heavens, how awful!"

"No one knows about it yet. But he's certain that he has become a target for terrorists."

"Why, for goodness' sake?"

"Because sympathizers of the Baader-Meinhof gang have been committing assassinations in an effort to force the government to release terrorists who did not die in the group's suicide. Those remaining are blackmailing and kidnapping wealthy Germans in retaliation. Ridder is the perfect target for what's left of the Baader-Meinhof gang." Luis continued to undress and hang his hunting gear on the clothes horse.

"Was he hurt?"

"No. But he was certainly frightened. I was the nearest to him and heard the shot. I'd been tramping through the woods with him for hours. And after the shot, we tracked back to where we presumed the gun had been fired, and combed the area, looking for footprints. But we found nothing." Luis went into the bathroom to open the tap on the tub.

"After what happened to John Derby last night, perhaps the police should be advised about this, whether it disrupts the wedding celebrations or not," he said. "The situation for anyone here, it seems, has become unsafe. Frankly, a madman may be wandering around." Luis paused thoughtfully. "Von Ridder's experience this afternoon is extremely strange," he continued. "The gamekeepers in this part of the world are especially cautious; so it's not likely that the shot was a stray bullet. They place each gun personally, and indicate the precise area where each hunter can stalk game. No, this accident is very strange. That is, if it was an accident."

"Darling, you could have been shot as well."

Luis smiled at me. "I wasn't near enough. And anyhow, Karl is convinced that the shot was meant for him. He told me, in confidence, that this was not the first time he's had a close shave. Since I can count on his discretion, I told him what happened to John Derby last night. He didn't see any connection, however, unless someone is deliberately trying to jinx the wedding of this nice young couple." He shook his head wryly. "Maybe a spurned jealous suitor?"

Luis wrapped himself in a white terry-cloth robe while waiting for the tub to fill. Already the steamy air was fogging the mirrors.

"Do you suppose the shot may have come from a poacher?" I suggested.

"No. It's difficult for a poacher to get on the property. The game-keepers are vigilant, especially when there are several guns out there at the same time, like today. And besides, a man of Ridder's caliber doesn't exaggerate."

"But what do you know about von Ridder? Ava seems to like him very much," I said.

"Not much. At the bar downstairs just now, I ran into Rhoden-tus, who knows him very well. They went to school together. Harvard, I think he said. And Rhodentus filled me in on the other attempt on Karl's life," Luis added. "A rifle shot through the window of Karl's car on his way to the bank. His chauffeur was driving. Fortunately, at the moment the shot went off, Karl leaned down to pick up a paper that had slipped from his lap. Imagine, a simple gesture probably saved his life!"

"Luis," I almost shrieked as I again thought of the young girl's warning. "Do you recall Ava's story about the pretty girl's prophecy that someone was going to be killed? She didn't just say someone was going to die; she said someone was going to be killed."

"Yes, I do. Although the whole idea is ridiculous. Prophecy? Not likely. More likely: some silly woman's mutterings." His eyes met mine. "But to be truthful, I also remembered Ava's story, ever since I heard the shot this afternoon. But still, one shouldn't pay attention to such things . . . although I must admit that the girl's words sound less rash to me now in view of what has happened."

"The only reason I take the girl's words with any seriousness is that Ava also saw her talking to the men in the Mercedes that we saw last night," I said.

"Now, you're not sure of that. There you go magnifying things. However, perhaps we should advise the police after all," Luis said.

"No. We can't do that. I mustn't draw attention to Jupiter. As soon as he is better, he will know the best way to deal with these frightening incidents. Did you tell anyone about what happened to Karl this afternoon?"

"No. Only Rhodentus. Karl didn't want anyone else to know; and after all, it's his affair."

I looked at my watch, and jumped. "Luis, we're going to be late. I'll have to dress quickly, but you can be ready before me. Go on ahead and I'll get there as soon as I can."

WE WERE EXPECTED at a formal ceremony in another castle nearby to view the *tableau de chasse* of the day's game. As is customary in Europe after a shoot, the bag would be displayed, and guests who had shot a stag or chamois would be given one of the property's coveted silver emblems.

Almost the first person I saw when I arrived at the neighboring castle was Karl von Ridder. After all I had heard, I was curious to make up my own mind about this man who charmed movie stars and courted the bullets of terrorists. Looking into his deep-set, intelligent blue eyes, I could fully understand Luis's instinct to trust him.

He bent gracefully over my hand. "Countess," he began, "your husband did me a great kindness this afternoon."

He stood smiling at me with an easy manner. The similarity with Jupiter—his build, the shape of his head, his height—was marked. All of a sudden an incredible idea struck me. So far I had only one explanation for the assault on Jupiter: that the men did it to threaten him. For that was the only explanation I could come up with as to why they beat him and then threw him out of the car. But what if they had not been after Jupiter last night at all, but Karl? In that case, when they saw their mistake, they struck John in the head and threw him out of the car. The thought left me suspended for a moment.

Although there was nothing classic or regular about von Ridder's features which would mark him as handsome, I understood the reason why Ava was so impressed by him. She had a weakness for men with his kind of "charisma."

"Please come join us," von Ridder went on. "I'm with old friends. I think you'll enjoy our conversation. We're discussing sunken treasure. In fact, Spanish sunken treasure." He then led me to the sofa where the Rhodentuses were seated. They were talking animatedly when I sat down, and I overheard their last phrases.

"Sunken treasure? Is that what you were talking about?" I said. "Please tell me more."

Karl quickly and briefly filled me in. It appeared that he and R.K. had done a special study of ancient nautical maps with one of their professors at Harvard back in their college days. As the years passed, they had both kept up their interest in treasure maps. And now that their children were old enough to participate in treasure-hunting expeditions, Karl and R.K. were underwriting a full-scale search in the Caribbean, with both their sons as project leaders.

The idea had been Karl's, whose son, Alex, was a close friend of R.K.'s two sons, Robert and Rick. Alex and Robert were both outstanding athletes, while Rick, R.K.'s younger son, was more the intellectual, recently graduating magna cum laude from Harvard. Rick was about to join the older boys in the Caribbean.

"They're after a Spanish galleon that sank in 1668, loaded down with gold from Mexico and Peru!" cried Nancy. Clearly Karl's and her husband's enthusiasm was contagious.

"You should see the 'official' telegrams we're getting from the boys," said R.K.; both he and Karl smiled broadly at the thought of their sons' adventures.

"Well, I don't know what you're all doing here," I said with a laugh. "It sounds like the most exciting place to be, at the moment, is the Caribbean!"

My comment seemed to cast an unexpected somberness over the three of them. After such high spirits, that baffled me.

Karl was quick to perceive my confusion.

"Yes, Countess," he said quietly, "we would all like very much to be there, but I have serious problems to face here at home. And my friend," he pointed to R.K., "does not want to go without me. We hope things will be cleared up shortly; and then we will both go."

Since I still looked perplexed, von Ridder went on, "I might as well tell you about it, since we are with the only friends right now who are aware of my predicament. Perhaps your husband told you of the incident this afternoon?"

I nodded.

"Well, I worry that such attempts could be made against someone in my family as well," von Ridder said. "I'm relieved to have my only son happily occupied where no harm can come to him. But my wife remains in this country, and could be in danger."

R.K. looked at his friend with an expression of deep concern. Just then Luis approached our group and both men rose to make room for him. When they began to talk about shooting, I transferred my attention to Nancy.

She was thrilled about the search in the Caribbean, and she went on to confide that the enterprise would not only provide her and R.K. with a hobby they could both enjoy together, but it would also give R.K. a nice break from business pressures. The project would give him an opportunity to see his sons as well, she went on to tell me. For R.K. hardly knew them: Their mother had brought them up and had kept them away from their father. "There's a lot of bad blood between R.K. and his ex-wife," Nancy added. "But we will be going to the Caribbean in January," she went on gaily. "And this spring we expect delivery of our new yacht. We've called it *La Sirena*. R.K. and I are planning a second honeymoon on it."

I laughed. They appeared to have barely finished their first.

"But in the summer we will make Marbella our home port," she said, "which is another reason we are delighted to have met you and Luis. I understand you have a lovely house there. Tell me about it."

I insisted that Nancy and R.K. come and see for themselves, and told her that we would be there all of August. Nancy listened attentively. Again I noticed the tiny white line that traced from nostril to lip. And without wanting to, my glance lingered there.

As if I had spoken aloud, Nancy ran her forefinger lightly across the scar. Her lovely brow creased; and a flitting expression of fear for a moment transformed her countenance and told me that her scar might be the reminder of a not so far-off, mysterious tragedy.

Meanwhile, R.K. and von Ridder were chatting with my husband.

"This fellow Francisco Cabanellas bumped into me as I was leaving the hotel tonight," von Ridder was saying. "I've met him several times in Frankfurt. He's been kind enough to invite me to a partridge shoot in Spain next month. You may have heard of the place. It's called La Romana, near Toledo."

"Yes, that used to be a great shoot," responded Luis. My husband, I knew, was surprised to learn that Paco Cabanellas had bought such an expensive property. But Luis's expression rarely betrayed what he was thinking.

Von Ridder went on to say that he'd met Cabanellas at his bank when Paco had come in to transact some business. He had found him pleasant and intelligent, and he'd accepted the invitation, and hoped that Luis and I would be going, too. Luis looked mildly surprised; but I hastened to explain that Paco had invited us to the shoot earlier in the day, but there'd been no time to tell him about it.

"We've been invited, too, and are looking forward to it," R.K. added. "Karl tells me you are reputed to be a great shot, Luis."

"Not at all," replied Luis. "Most of my friends shoot better than I do."

Maybe it was the compliments, maybe it was just Luis's fondness for the sport—whatever—but to my astonishment, he said, "I don't know my plans for that weekend, but if I'm free, I'll go."

After that, Nancy and I began to talk about the latest Paris collections, when suddenly she became distracted. I followed her concerned glance. Standing alone in the doorway stood the beautiful young woman I'd seen that afternoon on the veranda. "Uh-oh," Nancy murmured, as if to herself. "Here she comes. What does she want now?"

"Who's that?" I asked Nancy. "She's certainly the most striking woman in the room."

Nancy shook her head in dismay, "Oh she's beautiful all right, but crazy. Completely crazy." Then she leaned over to Inge Schmidt, who had a few moments earlier sat down next to her. "Look who's in the doorway. See what you can do, Inge. Somebody should get her out of here before there's a scene."

Several admiring glances were already being directed toward the ravishing newcomer. And as we watched, two men joined her. Inge jumped up, "Too bad Paco's not here," she announced. "He can handle these moments better than I can, but I'll see what I can do."

My curiosity about the girl was not to be satisfied just then. For a butler appeared, informing us that the *tableau de chasse* was ready. Luis eagerly pulled me to my feet. "Let's go," he said. "I want to see how the Germans do this."

Assembling the day's game in an attractive design was an ancient custom that was still practiced in Europe. The gamekeepers often created patterns and layouts with the birds or the big game that were surprisingly artistic.

Descending the broad staircase to the park surrounding the castle, we found ourselves among tall trees and spacious green lawns, melting into shadowy hills. Four gamekeepers were holding tall poles supporting blazing torches. These cast flaming streaks of golden light over the chamois and stag stretched out in the motif of a star. The head gamekeeper blew a strident note on his horn, and all was silent. The men clasped their hats to their chests, while our host pronounced a prayer. This ceremony was followed by a few words of praise for the animals that lay at our feet.

Across the sober circle, Karl von Ridder was standing solemnly, bathed in the pale flickering light. As I looked at him, I was struck again by how closely he resembled John Derby. In the darkness, among trees and bushes, they could easily be mistaken for each other.

Next to Karl von Ridder, wrapped in a long, pale mink coat, was the beautiful and mysterious young girl. Karl was observing her intently. She noticed, and looking up bestowed upon him an especially pleasant smile. Another blast of the horn tore her attention away, as she watched our host bestow the shiny silver medals. As soon as the ceremony was over, I sneaked out of the circle and grabbed my husband's arm. As we walked together back toward the castle, I said, "How physically similar Karl and Jupiter are."

He stopped in his tracks. "You've got something there," he said. "One could easily be taken for the other." And then he gave his head a doubting shake. "Still," he said, "I don't know. I wonder if an assassin would be apt to make such a serious mistake."

The buzz of voices behind us became louder, and friends caught up with us. Together we went inside to enjoy the buffet dinner and dancing. A Viennese waltz was playing in the adjoining room. Karl von Ridder appeared and pulled me to my feet. Together we joined the whirling dancers in the high-ceilinged ballroom, and were soon flying around the floor. The sensation was glorious. One, two, three . . . one, two, three . . . one, two, three . . . The lilt of the music acted like a drug, and the rhythm beat through my head, as we went swinging around and around. When the music stopped, I told Karl I'd never danced such an exhilarating waltz. He thanked me for the compliment. "It's a dance that's in my blood," he smiled. "I wouldn't know how to dance a *pasadoble* as well as a Spaniard," he said. "And only an Argentine really understands the tango. Americans are the kings of the foxtrot. So we Germans have to have a speciality, too."

As he was talking, my eyes were drawn to a scene across the ballroom. Inge Schmidt was standing at one of the doors, firmly barring entrance to a woman in a long, red evening dress. A second later I realized that this was again Ava's mysterious young girl. She had removed her coat, and her strapless gown revealed lovely bare shoulders. She was clearly the most eye-catching woman in the room. But Inge obviously did not want her to join the party. The young girl appeared to be pleading with her. Then in one rough, brusque movement, Inge pushed the girl backward with such force that she almost lost her balance. The girl's expression turned fearful. And as Inge continued to shove her, she turned around and ran off. Inge was now looking in my direction and I was shocked to see her normally pleasant face twisted into a hard cold mask. Obviously there was some mysterious reason why some people wanted to keep this young beauty out of circulation. Jealousy? Possibly, I thought, but hardly likely. Whatever the reason, Inge suddenly appeared a different person from the woman I had known until now.

Chapter 8

The wedding day dawned sunny and warm. Looking out the window at the group gathering for the trip to the church, I wondered if Jupiter would be able to make it after all. Manolo had called and said that if the doctor agreed, he would drive the Señor. So I should not come to pick him up. Below, in the broad expanse in front of the castle steps, beautifully dressed men and women were climbing into two buses for the trip to the church. The smiling groom was speaking with a priest whose long black cassock and round-brimmed *teja*—hat—made it clear that he was Spanish.

A few minutes later, as my husband and I climbed into the already crowded bus, Luis remained standing in the front, while I went toward the back to take the only seat left. I was pleased to find that my place was next to the mysterious young beauty. This was going to provide me with the opportunity to find out who she was.

As soon as I sat down, the girl complimented my lace mantilla and went on to say that she regretted that she hadn't brought hers. Then she startled me: "I saw you sitting with that liar, Nancy Rhodentus," she told me, her dark eyes flashing with anger. "Humph!

She probably told you I was crazy. That's her usual line when she wants to make sure no one talks to me.''

The strange, dark girl looked at me. Her eyelashes were the longest I'd ever seen. Her lovely smooth olive complexion had practically no makeup. The innocence and sweetness of her small heart-shaped face, led me to judge that she was no more than twenty years old. "She's a real bitch, that Nancy," she continued bitterly. "As false as they come. And Inge Schmidt's worse! They hate me and I hate them. They're terrified I'll tell all I know about them. And I know a *lot*, I can tell you!" Without encouragement, she continued to talk so quickly and forcefully that I had no chance to ask her name. Most of her words were full of venom; and most of her venom was directed toward Inge and Nancy. Both of them seemed to be the bane of her existence. "They're both jealous of me," she declared.

"Poor R.K.," she went on. "He has no idea what a witch he's married. And Inge, what a horror she is! Wait till she sees me at the wedding today. She ordered me not to go." Then with a toss of her beautiful head, the young girl added, "As if I was still a minor and could be bossed around by that German cow! But to hell with her!" Her fury left me speechless. There was no need for me to express an opinion. And indeed, she didn't give me the opportunity. For just as she finished her tirade, she grabbed my hand. "I like to read hands," she said, in a voice that was once more—shockingly—sweet. "I'm good at it, probably because I have gypsy blood." She fingered my palm. Unfortunately, time was running short, the bus was already entering the small town where the wedding ceremony was to be held, and was about to park. It came to a stop in the quaint town square, and people stood up to leave. There was no time to build up to the question that was just then most on my mind, so I just blurted it. "You seem to be Spanish. What's your name?"

The girl's large dark eyes opened wide. "Why, I'm Sofia Cabanel-las—didn't you know? Paco is my brother." The bus was already half empty, and she thrust my hand back in my lap with a force that belied her delicate build. "I don't like what I see there," she said, nodding toward my hand. "But I can tell you you'd better be careful." And as we were stepping down from the bus, her last words were, "Stay away from those two witches, and don't tell them I warned you!"

When I met Luis, he asked me why I looked so startled. The strange girl was just behind me, so I could not tell him until we were further away.

Finally I said, "I've just learned the most amazing thing. That gorgeous creature is Paco Cabanellas's younger sister." He was about to answer, but I hushed him with a raised hand. "That's not all," I went on. "Did I tell you that I found out from Ava whose suite we were standing outside of two nights ago? It was Paco's. And I'm beginning to strongly suspect that Paco Cabanellas was the Spaniard I heard talking that night. That means he's working with Carlos . . . because I still believe Carlos was also there."

"Darling, all of that is *extremely* unlikely," Luis answered. "First I do not believe you saw Carlos. And secondly, it was not Cabanellas Ava saw coming out of that room, it was the girl. The girl could be staying there, and her brother could be in an entirely different part of the hotel. Again, you must be careful about your speculations."

As he was speaking, friends joined us and we walked across the village's picturesque plaza. Green and gold flags in the bride's family colors were suspended from all the balconies. Musicians in colorful costumes tooted loud, merry songs on a collection of antique horns. The German guests—the women dressed in wide-brimmed hats and elegant outfits—were already entering the ancient church, while masses of villagers thronged around to watch. So far I had not seen John Derby, but even if he had been there, it would have been difficult to locate him in the crowd.

Leading our Spanish contingent, the priest strode ahead and we promenaded toward the church, struggling against a strong breeze which whipped at the voluminous folds of our mantillas. I clutched the heavy black lace of my own, so the wind would not knock over my high comb. Ava Gardner, who was near me, looked ravishing with the only white mantilla in the group. This lovely antique had been a gift from Dominguín, the bullfighter, during their romance years before.

"The Spanish Inquisition," someone cried humorously when they saw us, then others took up the chant. "The Inquisition . . . The Inquisition." I couldn't help but be amused. Indeed, I realized, we must look very foreign in this ancient German square.

Then I saw an unusual man in the crowd. I felt him staring at me through his sunglasses. He had short curly hair, a thick, dirty-looking beard, and he wore a filthy, dark beret. Today the moustache and the long hair he'd worn the other night was missing, but still I was certain it was the same person. An icicle climbed my spine. Carlos! As I gaped at him, he turned and disappeared into the mass. The incident could not have taken three seconds. My heart was throbbing, not only out of fear for myself, but also for

John Derby. Where was Jupiter? Was Carlos searching for him right now? Or for Karl von Ridder?

Luis was tugging on my arm, urging me to hurry. And I let him lead me. My thoughts were in a turmoil as I climbed the church steps. Why would a world-famous terrorist be taking chances hanging around where an informant could tip the police? At the top of the steps, I turned and searched the crowd, but there was not a sign of the man. I entered the church still shaken. Had I really seen Carlos? Or, after so many unusual happenings, was my imagination running away with me?

Soft organ music sounded through the large ancient Gothic church. The altar was covered with white lillies; and it flickered in the glow of hundreds of candles. And yet, despite all the beauty of the moment, I was still stunned. Even though two full days had passed since the night I saw Carlos with the Arab, and when Jupiter was attacked—my nerves were still frayed. And now Carlos is again nearby, I said to myself. What does that mean? The ceremony seemed endless, with three priests officiating in three languages. And it was not until each pew emptied in a prearranged order and formed a cortege to parade through the town square that I finally— and with great relief—caught sight of Jupiter. He looked pale, but amazingly alert. However, our protocol places in the stroll to the wedding luncheon in a nearby palace made it impossible for me to rush to him.

Later, when we were drinking champagne in the palace, Jupiter and I separated ourselves from the others, and I unloaded all my information and preoccupations. When I told him that Carlos and the Arab had been in a black Mercedes, very similar to the car the thugs had used when they grabbed him, he put a hand on my arm. "I never saw that car clearly. I've been wondering about it."

"The problem is that because of the darkness," I told him, "I couldn't tell if it was the same one. Even in daylight, I can barely tell a Mercedes from a Ford."

"What bothers me most about the whole episode," John said, "is that this incident seems to indicate that my cover has been blown. This will be disastrous for my work, and for those who work with me as well . . . as you do. I can't understand how that could have happened."

I told him then about the attempt against Karl von Ridder, and explained my theory that the assassin could have mistaken him for Karl, which meant that his cover was not blown. After I finished, he looked at me skeptically. "Actually, John," I went on, "think about it. You've seen Karl. He does look a bit like you. The same height and build. The graying hair."

John rubbed his hand over his thinning scalp. "But he has more of this stuff," he said ruefully. "Unfortunately, as much as I appreciate your analysis, your theory does not convince me."

"Well, all the same, my theory is still plausible. In the dimness of the night, they may have been waiting in that car for Karl to come out of the castle party, and they made a mistake. When they took a closer look, they realized they had the wrong man."

"Perhaps. Anyhow, you've given me something to think about, Tiger. I see you are finally becoming an experienced agent. Maybe in another few years . . ." His teasing told me that he was well on the road to recovery.

"You mean your expert advice and example have finally borne fruit?" I added.

"If you are right that Carlos is in the neighborhood, he may be connected to the latest news I received from Bonn. Two modern land-to-air missiles were stolen yesterday from an American military depot not far from here, along with a large quantity of sophisticated explosives. That's right up Carlos's line. Our people fear an important operation is underway. When terrorists accumulate a large amount of explosives like plastique, that's the usual purpose. Whoever they are, they already have enough for a very powerful bomb."

Now that Jupiter was feeling better, his mind was totally focused on business. "If Carlos was one of the thugs who attacked me," he continued, "Serge's opinion is more necessary than ever. For both of us. I'm anxious for you to talk to him; but he can't come to Europe for several weeks yet. When he arrives, I'll arrange a meeting someplace convenient for you both. And by the way, he was delighted to learn that you two will be getting together again."

Then with a nod of his head Jupiter directed my gaze across the room. To my surprise, Karl von Ridder was chatting with Sofia Cabanellas. "That reminds me," Jupiter's voice had become livelier as he observed them, "our COS also told me this morning that a female terrorist—a former member of the Baader-Meinhof group—could have worked her way among these people." He raised his arm in a wide swing which encompassed the wedding group. "Conversations have been intercepted. One player is a female."

"What language was she speaking?" I asked.

"German. But with a decided foreign accent. Of course, the accent could be put on to disguise her identity."

"If you're thinking of that little girl, Sofia," I said laughing, "you're wrong. Few Spanish women are likely to be mixed up with terrorists."

"Don't underestimate your sex . . . or your husband's homeland. The nationality of a terrorist doesn't make any difference," he said. "Quite a few highly educated women from wealthy backgrounds have taken up some terrorist cause or other. And many are quite ruthless."

"Before our conversation ends, John," I asked, changing the subject, "could you tell me more about those calutrons you mentioned the other day? Isn't that what you said was being shipped through Spain? How big are they? What do they look like?"

"A disassembled calutron can be shipped in a crate about eight-by-eight-by-twenty feet," he explained. "And weighs about four tons." He was going to say more, but friends began to close in on us, and hastily Jupiter and I set up a means of contact for the future weeks.

Hours later, when Luis and I were alone, I told him that Jupiter believed a woman terrorist was nearby. My husband laughed. "Well, you might not have to look far. I met a woman tonight who is so devastating and wild that I believe she could do anything. Paco Cabanellas's sister." Then he went on to say, "In fact, your friend John Derby was having a pretty good time with her himself, especially for a man in his condition. He was with her for a long time."

For an innocent young girl, I mused, this one is arousing the attention of several very sophisticated men. Could this be part of a deliberate plan?

Chapter 9

During the following two weeks, Luis and I made a pleasure trip to Budapest and Prague, which gave me a respite from my other preoccupations. Then, before returning to Spain, we went to Paris to visit the Duchess of Windsor. She was lonely, for she had never recovered from the Duke's death four years before. Luis and I had met the Windsors during our honeymoon in New York. And after finding ourselves in many of the same places over the next years, we became close friends. Eventually Luis and I ended up as the Windsors' house guests during our many visits to Paris, where they had made their home.

As usual, Martin, her Spanish chauffeur, met us at the airport, and at first our arrival at the lovely house in the Bois de Boulogne was much the same as other visits over the years. Germaine, the wife of the caretaker, emerged in her navy-blue cape from their small house at the entrance to the property and smiled as always when she opened the gilt-spiked iron gate to the curving drive bordered by the bushes the Duke had planted years ago. Then Georges, the butler, at the foot of the palace steps waited for us in his usual welcoming stance. A footman in gray trousers and blue-black tails opened the car doors. All gave the impression that life was unchanged.

In the entrance hall, the Duke's royal dispatch box, one of the few items he had taken with him when he abdicated, sat in its accustomed spot on a large table, a sign that guests were expected. The Duchess was planning a small dinner that evening in honor of General Wilhelm Schuster, the German representative to NATO.

The Duchess appeared at the top of the wide, curved staircase, and leaned over the wrought-iron railing. She looked thinner than ever, but nevertheless lovely and serene in a sapphire-blue suit, a color that the Duke preferred, for it brought out the unusual violet hue of her eyes. The three pugs were yelping and snapping around her feet—as always—but for once she seemed oblivious to the cacophony. This was the first noticeable difference from the usual routine of greeting at the Duchess's home. Part of the charm of arriving at the house in the Bois had always been the repartee between the Duke and the Duchess as they strained to greet us above the racket of the pugs' barking. For a moment, the Duchess seemed at a loss. Then she rallied, calling down to us, "Aline, Luis, how wonderful to see you! Come upstairs. You're just in time for tea."

When we reached the landing on the second floor, where they had always maintained their private apartment, she embraced us both. "My dears, I'm so glad you're here," she said as she led us into the "boudoir," her small, intimate salon that overlooked the garden. In this room, the four of us had spent many happy hours together. And it was here where the Duke's absence seemed most palpable. Both the Duchess and I noticed Luis glancing toward

H.R.H.'s chair and shaking his head. Immediately he checked himself and started to compliment our hostess on the orchids on her desk. He knew they had come from her greenhouse.

When she spoke, her tone was hasty and nervous. "I'm afraid you may find the dinner tonight a bit boring, although I did my best. I have a new pianist. Someone told me he's good. These NATO people can be dreary sometimes. I hardly know the general who's coming." Then she changed the subject entirely. "Aline, Edouard will be here at five to do my hair. Should I send him up to your room?"

I would be wearing a black lace sheath over chiffon. The dress had simple lines, which looked best, I thought, with a low chignon. So I told her I would be happy to have Edouard's help.

Georges arrived with the tea, and we caught up with news about friends, while Luis and I gobbled tiny cheese puffs and miniature round pieces of toast with a sliced olive on top. Nothing substantial ever accompanied the tea in the Windsors' house. The Duchess never took tea at all, and watched as we served ourselves.

Before we knew it, Georges was announcing the arrival of Edouard. The Duchess jumped from her chair. "Oh, I must fly! I haven't even looked at the table plan yet! And the maquillage man will be here, too. See you both downstairs at eight." Luis and I hastened out to climb the stairs to our guest suite on the third floor.

Upstairs, our two bedrooms and bath were cozy and inviting. My dress had already been pressed by Marie, the second-floor maid, and hung with delicate blue tissue paper holding the perfectly pressed sleeves in place. A bath had been drawn. The fragrant aroma of Guerlain bath oil filled the air. From the desk in my room, I picked up the blue sheets of paper with the Windsor crest that contained the week's invitations and showed Luis the seating chart for the evening's dinner.

At eight-thirty we had all been gathered in the grand salon on the first floor for nearly a half hour. I knew the habits of the household. Dinners were always served promptly. So the entire staff would be in suspended animation over the delay. Georges stood in the doorway discreetly signaling the Duchess that the guest of honor still had not arrived. She lifted an eyebrow without interrupting her animated conversation with glamorous bejeweled Marie-Hélène de Rothschild. Georges departed, having understood that dinner would be kept, but not indefinitely.

Just then a flurry of activity in the foyer gathered momentum, and a minute later a very flustered General Schuster made his entrance. With hurried steps, he approached the Duchess, apologizing profusely for being late. Just as he was leaving his home, he said, he had received terrible news. At this he drew a breath as if to gather himself and remember his surroundings. "Terrible news," he repeated more softly. "A dear friend of mine was killed this evening as he left his office. His car had been rigged with explosives."

"How awful," the duchess said. "Would he be anyone we know?"

"Perhaps. He is . . . was . . . a famous banker in my country. Karl von Ridder."

"No, I don't know him, but how horrible to lose a friend that way. Do you have any idea who could have done such a thing?"

"Terrorists," said the General. "The authorities have identified the explosives. And a terrorist group has already taken credit for the attack."

Luis and I both had overheard. "I was just shooting with Karl a few weeks ago," my husband, visibly shocked, told the General.

I remained speechless. Memories of whirling around that ancient ballroom, propelled by the rhythm and force of Karl von Ridder's strong arms flashed back to me. That charming, dynamic man . . . dead! I couldn't believe it.

The General stared at us blankly. He was clearly moved by the death of his friend, and far from eager to talk more about the loss. Immediately, I thought of Jupiter. Perhaps von Ridder's assassination meant that he was now safe and had never been the target.

At dinner I was seated next to the General. As the meal progressed, the excellent wine and delicious food relaxed him, and we began to converse. As each new wine was served, the footman leaned over and whispered softly in each guest's ear the vineyard and year. Eventually the General asked if I had met Karl von Ridder, too, which opened the way for me to tell him that Karl believed someone had tried to assassinate him during the shoot.

General Schuster shook his head. "That's not probable. Terrorists don't make spontaneous attacks. They study the victim's movements for weeks, sometimes months, before deciding how and when. Everything is carefully planned. No, no impromptu bullet would come from a terrorist. Perhaps a hunter strayed from his assigned area; that could be an explanation." He was thoughtful for a moment. "The government," he went on, "advised Karl that he was on a hit list. That, perhaps, would have encouraged him to interpret any accident as the work of terrorists." He stopped and sighed softly. "But still, clearly Karl had premonitions that something like this might happen." So did Sofia Cabanellas, I thought. Had she actually been passing on information she was witness to and using her gypsy prophecy as a way to let others know? I asked myself.

"Do you think the government will find the assassins?" I asked the General then.

Evidently that question was also on his mind, because he launched into a long discourse about terrorism. He explained that terrorist groups usually hire foreign agents to plot the attack. And they, in turn, employ other trained specialists to execute it. The group's leaders—the actual planners—most often leave the country before the violence takes place. "For that reason," he said, "it is difficult to apprehend them. But there is every possibility that those who manufactured and placed the bomb will be captured."

For some time we talked about terrorist atrocities in various European countries, and then he said something that made me swallow in one lump the piece of chicken I had just put in my mouth. "Some professional killers are especially hard to track. Often they come from privileged families, and have had the advantages of the best schools. They dress well and appear to be law-abiding citizens. For example," he went on, warming to his topic, "take the most feared terrorist of all—the one they call 'Carlos the Jackal.' His father was a wealthy lawyer in Caracas."

I did not tell the General that I was acquainted with Carlos, much less that I very likely ran across him again in Bavaria recently. Jupiter had already passed my information to the proper officials. And I didn't want the General to be aware of my special interest in the terrorist. However, the General's mention of Carlos inclined me to suppose that his government had already considered the possibility that Carlos was the one who managed the operation that murdered Karl von Ridder.

Later, sitting on a sofa next to the Duchess, with the General facing us, another name that interested me came up in the conversation. The ivory candles in the wall sconces were flickering, and the pianist was playing Cole Porter's "Just One of Those Things" extremely well. Apparently, both the Duchess and the General had met Nicky Maniatis, the Greek shipbuilder so admired by Inge Schmidt and Nancy Rhodentus, at an American Embassy dinner a few weeks before. The General was saying that Maniatis had entertained him after dinner with his amusing stories. He'd made a good impression.

"Oh, I don't agree with you about that man, General," the Duchess declared. "In my opinion, he shouldn't be allowed near the American Embassy. I was shocked to see him there. He's so anti-American, it's appalling. I made a point that night of not talking to that Arab."

"But, he's Greek," I interrupted. "I haven't met him, but I know some of his friends, and they all say he's Greek."

"He's about as Greek as I am," the Duchess replied in her decisive manner. "Actually he's Palestinian . . . at least his mother is Palestinian. I know all about him. My chef Antoine used to work in his mother's kitchen. He has told me all about that fellow Nicky. And I can tell you, what I most hold against him is the anxiety and trouble he has caused his mother, always getting into scrapes, and mixing with the most terrible friends."

"He seemed such a pleasant, intelligent young man," said General Schuster.

"Well, I'm sorry to contradict you, General, but I most certainly know all about him," said the Duchess emphatically. "Nicky made his mother's life miserable. She was constantly having to get him out of jail. He even robbed her . . . and he robbed her friends, too. In fact, Antoine left because of the havoc Nicky caused in that household. But that means, of course, that I have one thing to thank Nicky Maniatis for. If it weren't for him I wouldn't have my marvelous chef."

The General shook his head, looking as though he had absorbed all the shocks he could sustain in one night. Standing up, he thanked the Duchess for her hospitality, and then left as quickly as courtesy allowed.

"Poor man," said the Duchess, after he had gone. "Well, he wasn't the least bit boring. But heaven knows I would prefer boredom to his accounts of the terrorism that is going on nowadays. You know, he told me that the bomb used to kill that German banker was similar to one that killed your friend the President of Spain a few years ago. Apparently the same kind of device was used; and they were both detonated at a distance in similar ways. Surprising, isn't it?"

Somehow, I wasn't surprised in the least.

Chapter 10

Jupiter, of course, learned of von Ridder's death as soon as I did. And when Luis and I returned to Madrid from Paris on Sunday afternoon, Maria Luisa told me that Mr. Derby had called several times, and would keep trying. Luis had a men's dinner that evening and my intention was to stay home and unwind. After my husband departed, looking dashing in black-tie, I settled in for a quiet supper upstairs with the anticipation that I would be hearing from Jupiter. I had placed several calls to him in New York and Washington when we'd first arrived home. So he knew where I was; and I knew that I should now sit tight and wait for him.

The evening passed, however, without a word from him. But just before dawn the phone on my bedside table blared. I picked up the receiver groggily, and was assaulted by a sound very like crackling popcorn. Jupiter's voice came over the line, thin and reedy, interrupted by intermittent "dead spots."

I sat bolt upright, pushing my hair back and grabbing for a pen and paper, just in case.

"Ridder . . . dead," I made out. Well, I knew that, but obviously Jupiter was giving the event a special significance, as he had every reason to do. His terse voice told me that this call was not going to be an exchange of ideas. Wherever he was, he was calling to tell me something specific; I didn't waste his time by asking questions.

"Two attempts failed . . . may have brought in Carlos to guarantee success . . ." he said; and my breath stopped. "Find out all you can about his time in Madrid working in the insurance company. . . . Will send dossier. . . . Be careful. Remember he's a killer. Since you've been seen with me often, you have to be extra watchful," he added. And then the voice was gone.

I sat in my bed and watched the dawn fill my garden with its moody light.

That morning, a few hours later, I called Alvaro Satrustegui, the director of the insurance company, Centro Asegurador. And he suggested that the man to speak to was Alfonso Domínguez, who had been Carlos's immediate supervisor and was the person who knew him best.

The man who was shown into my salon that afternoon was not someone who would ordinarily have much truck with terrorists. Alfonso Domínguez was tall for a Spaniard, slender, with light-brown hair, neatly trimmed, and soft, gentle-looking brown eyes. He had the warm manner of a person who perhaps grows beautiful flowers or is a particularly good father. There was a considerable irony in hearing about Carlos the Jackal from a solid man like him.

It turned out they had shared a desk together. Alfonso had been assigned to train him as a salesman. And even now, he was quietly enthusiastic about Carlos. I could see that the favorable impression Carlos had made in the beginning had not been completely destroyed by what came to light later on.

On the day of the police raid, he and Carlos had been seated together at their shared desk talking about one of the female employees at Centro (the girls in the office found Carlos devastating), when the phone interrupted them. Alfonso picked up the line, and a harried voice asked for Carlos. He handed the telephone over to him. And then, a moment later, Carlos dropped the receiver and ran out the door. Seconds after, doors crashed open, and the police entered armed and ready. But Carlos had vanished.

When Alfonso finished the story, his face wore a bewildered expression, as if he still couldn't quite believe the truth about his one-time friend.

"Were you close to him?" I asked, pressing the obvious.

"Oh yes," said Alfonso, "I would say so. He was very kind to me and my family. When my wife delivered our daughter, for instance, Carlos would drop in to see her, and would often bring her some special treat—candy or an amusing book. To this day, she refuses to believe that he's a terrorist."

"Did he get along with other men as well as he did with women?" I asked.

"Well, perhaps not." Alfonso smiled the bashful smile that I'd come to realize was characteristic of him. "What annoyed some of them was his phenomenal success. He sold more insurance in the short time he was with us than many of them had sold in their careers."

"Really?"

"Well, many of his sales later turned out to be phony. But none of us knew that at the time." Alfonso was thoughtful for a moment;

then he continued. "Sometimes I used to see Carlos on a street corner near the office," he said, his brow wrinkling as though still perplexed. "He was often standing there talking with rough-looking types."

"Carlos always carries a gun. Did you know about that?" I asked.

Alfonso nodded yes. "He usually wore a pale trenchcoat . . . sometimes even inside the office. That didn't surprise me, though, because he was constantly running in and out to see clients. Now I imagine that he was wearing it so he could hide his revolver."

"Didn't that bother you?"

"No, he told me openly that he carried one. He was—well—a bit 'eccentric' . . . 'different.' You know? I took it for that and nothing more."

Alfonso's last words were, "If you ever see him, Condesa, please tell him I said hello. He was a good friend to me."

A quick call to Alvaro Satrustegui, thanking him for setting up the appointment, yielded additional details. According to Alvaro, as the police were entering the building, they noticed a man who fit Carlos's description leaving it. But because the entrance hall was crowded and the man was surrounded by other people, they let him go to avoid a massacre.

"What do you mean, to avoid a massacre?"

"When he's in a tight spot, Aline, he's been known to produce an automatic weapon from thin air and slaughter everyone in the vicinity. The police were aware they were risking a bloody shootout."

IT TOOK TWO days for Jupiter's dossier on Carlos to arrive. "Jerry"—the chief of station in Madrid—called from a telephone booth outside the embassy to tell me he had documents for me, then gave me the address of a small shop that dealt in ancient manuscripts and old books on the Calle Lagasca. He suggested that I drop in there at five o'clock that afternoon and ask for Ovidio Díaz, the proprietor.

I never visited Jerry's offices in the embassy, of course, since the local employees knew he was the COS, and a meeting there with him would have blown my cover. When I first started working with the CIA in the fifties, I met regularly with my CIA contact in some obscure street or other. But one day a friend happened to see me with a "strange man" and commented on it to my husband. In consequence, Luis insisted that this could not happen again.

But a visit to an old book store was perfectly safe and respectable, since our friends knew I was interested in old books and ancient manuscripts.

The shop's entrance was three steps down from the street. Descending into a little stone vestibule, I pushed open a heavy, old door and pulled on a small iron bell which announced my arrival. As I walked inside, I relished the familiar smell of old paper and parchment. Meanwhile, no customers were there . . . and no shopkeeper, either. But in the silence that greeted me, the sound of a whistling kettle told me someone was in the back.

As I waited, I looked around. The tiny shop was cluttered with yellowed manuscripts—on shelves, on the floor, piled high in a half-open closet. Tattered, worn, leather-bound books were stored in an antique bookcase against the far wall. Marvelous hand-colored maps, dating back to the twelfth century, hung in thin black frames on the whitewashed walls. But a map lying on the counter was especially intriguing. It showed the province of Guadalajara, where my husband's family had many properties. The town of "Romanones"—our title originated there—was clearly marked. Evidently, the little town had been much more prosperous way back in the twelfth century than it was today. I hoped I could buy this little treasure for Luis.

"Yes, I thought that map might interest you, Señora Condesa," said a scratchy voice behind me. I was startled, not having heard footsteps. When I turned, I found myself looking into the long face of a tall, exceedingly thin man. It was of course the proprietor, Señor Díaz. He wore thick glasses over watery pale eyes; and although he scarcely appeared to be forty, he was almost entirely bald. The hand he stretched out to me had long bony fingers, his face was pale and gray, and his overall mien was disconcerting, even eerie. And yet he wasn't at all scary or funereal. In fact, there was much that was sensitive and artistic about him. I wondered if he played the piano, or maybe the guitar. Then I decided he looked more like a mystic than a musician.

It surprised me that such a strange man would be a confidant of the Agency. Yet when he smiled, the slightly distant expression, the furrowed brow of a shortsighted person disappeared; they were replaced by a warmly intelligent look. He pointed to the border on the map I'd been examining. It had been etched and painted in gold leaf by Benedictine monks, he explained. Then he picked it up carefully and placed it under the counter.

"I've made tea, Señora Condesa," he said. "Perhaps we can talk inside."

He indicated the passageway directly behind the counter. But before following me, he went to the front door and drew the bolt. Turning, he smiled again, almost coyly, saying it was bad weather for customers.

In the small, attractive sitting room, a lovely antique table had been set with Limoges porcelain and hand-embroidered linen, bespeaking good taste and refinement. He poured the tea from an ancient pewter pot, chatting as he did so about the map and the place where he had found it. Then he rattled on about other neutral topics. But finally, as though perceiving my growing impatience, he changed his tone. "I've been told, Countess, that you are interested in obtaining information about Carlos, the terrorist. Unfortunately, I had a firsthand encounter with him. I was in Paris when Carlos was making a name for himself."

He glanced at me, seemingly to register my interest. I asked him to tell me as much as he could.

"I was at the Louvre doing a fellowship in restoration," he began. "I have a special interest in old maps, as you can see. But I still had time to pursue other goals. And Carlos, alas, became one of them. I had a personal encounter with his handiwork before I was asked to be involved with him professionally."

He paused to offer me more tea and to refresh his cup. I was struck by the graciousness of his manner, now that he seemed to be at ease with me. He was as Old-World as his maps and books.

"I was with a dear friend," he continued. "We had been walking in the Tuileries, and then down the Champs Elysées. We stopped outside the popular drugstore there . . . you must know the one, Countess. My friend wanted to pick up something. She was flirting with me; and I was delighted, of course. She was quite lovely. Van Eyck would have adored her." I tried to picture the type of woman who would flirt with this gaunt, strange-looking man. Señor Díaz went on. "She told me to wait outside, because she was going to buy a surprise for me."

He stopped for a moment, as though he'd lost the thread in his story.

"My friend had been studying painting in Paris; she was a gifted artist." He paused again. "She was inside less than a minute when the explosion went off. I thought I heard her screaming; but it must have been my imagination: When I found her, she was unconscious.

She was taken to the hospital with the many others who were caught inside. Two people had been killed and twenty-three others injured. Apart from bodily contusions, only my friend's hand was badly injured . . . burned. And the surgery to save it severed many of the major nerves. She can barely hold a paintbrush now and has given up her profession entirely. She's like a ballerina trying to dance in heavy, steel-toed, rubber boots. It has made her a bitter woman, which is probably the worst injury of all. And she was one of the 'lucky' ones. Others lost limbs and eyes.

"While waiting in the hospital for her to regain consciousness, I wanted to kill the man who placed that bomb. It was Carlos, of course, although at the time I didn't know that, nor had I ever heard of him, in fact." As he spoke these words, an enormous crash made me bound from my chair. But Ovidio Díaz for a moment remained paralyzed in his. Then slowly he got to his feet. A large mirror on the wall behind where I was sitting had fallen. Miraculously, it had not fallen on me. It now lay scattered in sparkling pieces all over the floor. Again, I remembered the day Carlos had first appeared in my house.

My companion was obviously stunned. Then his expression became despondent. "Oh," he gasped. "I hope this is not a bad omen for you." I decided not to tell him about the Ming dish that had smashed the first time I met Carlos. . . .

We both knelt down and together picked up the largest pieces. "Don't worry, please," I said. "I'm not superstitious." This was not true, but I wanted to console him, since he looked so upset. "The pity is your mirror is destroyed."

"No. No. The mirror has no importance for me. But its fall could be a warning. I must admit I am unnerved." He then handed me a single small shard of splintered glass. "This may sound ridiculous, but dropping that in water will dispell any bad luck that's coming soon. You might want to stop by the Retiro Park on your way home and throw the piece in the lake there. It's not much out of your way; I'll do the same as soon as I have time."

I tried to hide my smile as I opened my purse and placed the broken glass inside. It then occurred to me that Señor Díaz was now feeling his girlfriend's tragedy more than I had realized at first. I felt sorry for him.

Fortunately, in short order, my host went back to briefing me about Carlos. He was so well informed about the terrorist that I told him I suspected he had written much of Carlos's dossier. He nodded. "That is true. Part of it I did write, but the greater part, you will find, was written by Carlos himself."

He went on to tell me about a diary the French Secret Service had shown him. It was written by a double agent called Michael Moukharbal, who was a close associate of Carlos's. After Moukharbal was killed, his notebook proved to be a revelation to the police.

"That's when I became involved," said Díaz. "I followed the leads in Moukharbal's notes."

"You mean like tracking down an ancient map?"

"Exactly," he said with a smile. "Moukharbal was picked up by the police on one of his trips to Paris. Among his effects they found a photograph of him with two men: One was a known German terrorist. The other was Carlos. At the time, Carlos was still unknown; and the police did not yet associate him with the bomb in the drugstore. Nevertheless, the police felt obliged to interrogate anyone connected to Moukharbal, a known terrorist. Somehow when the police went to talk to Carlos, Moukharbal managed to telephone him to warn him.

"At the time, Carlos was living with a girlfriend at 9 Rue Toullier. When the commissioner knocked, Carlos was ready. Music was blaring as he opened the door, guitar in hand. He invited the policeman in, even offered him a glass of wine. Behind Carlos, two Venezuelan friends strummed on their guitars, something loud and Latin. Meanwhile, the commissioner showed Carlos the photograph and asked if he knew Moukharbal. As Carlos placed a lazy arm around his pretty girlfriend's shoulder (his girlfriends are always pretty), he told the commissioner he'd never seen the man before. The commissioner then opened the door and asked his two men outside to bring in Moukharbal, whom they had brought along to identify Carlos. At that moment, Carlos pulled a .38 caliber submachine gun from behind his girlfriend's back and opened fire, shooting Moukharbal, killing the two policemen, and seriously wounding the commissioner. After the volley, Carlos went to Moukharbal, who lay slumped and bleeding, kicked him savagely in the head, and fired two more bullets directly into his face. Then stepping over the bodies, he ran down the stairs, yelling, 'I am Carlos! I am Carlos!'

"From that day on, Countess," Ovidio Díaz went on, "Carlos has been the most hunted terrorist in the world. His photograph was published in newspapers and circulated in airports throughout Europe. Meanwhile, Carlos sought refuge with Venezuelan and Cuban colleagues, who smuggled him out of France to Algiers."

Although I was spellbound by Señor Díaz's story, when I looked at my watch I realized that it was late and I had to leave. As we walked back into the shop, my host drew some brown paper from under the counter and proceeded to wrap a neat package. Then he tied the bundle with twine and handed it to me. A long skinny finger pointed to the parcel I now clutched under my arm. "That report will enable you to understand the terrorist's character better than anything I could tell you. It's a detailed description of Carlos's first operation. He wrote it himself, and sent it to his boss and several colleagues he wanted to impress. The French police found photocopies of it when they raided a weapons depot Carlos had established in a house in Villiers-sur-Marne in France (weapons depots are among Carlos's trademarks). As you will realize when you read it, Carlos is supremely vain. And, I have no doubt, he would have liked his story to have been published in the newspapers. The man's ego is astounding. Be that as it may, the report is well written. There's no doubt he's a gifted man. Too bad he uses his talents as he does. Meanwhile, I hope you will never have to face him yourself."

Walking to the door, he unbolted it and stood aside. "Call me, Countess, if you have any questions. It has been a pleasure to receive you. And don't forget to throw that shard of the mirror into the lake."

Luis and I were giving a dinner party that evening; so it wasn't until I was undressing for bed that I was able to untie the twine and unwrap the dossier. To my astonishment, the beautiful map of Guadalajara was tucked inside, along with the typed pages of Carlos's dossier. A small white card was attached to the map. "Hoping you and the Count will enjoy this. Ovidio Díaz" I was touched, and felt a tinge of guilt that I had not thrown his piece of mirror into the Retiro Lake as I had promised. The map rested on the table by the window overlooking the garden. Luis was already in bed and almost asleep. So when I suggested he look at Señor Díaz's thoughtful gift, he mumbled that he would see it tomorrow.

I should have followed his lead and gone to sleep myself. But I made the mistake of taking the dossier to bed. Propping myself up against the pillows, I began to read. The first pages contained Ovidio Díaz's account of Carlos's famous kidnapping of the OPEC representatives of Arab oil-producing countries in Vienna, in December, 1975. But the most frightening reading was Carlos's personal account of his first terrorist operation—obviously written to impress Waddi Haddad, his PFLP boss. Carlos had attracted Haddad's attention when he fought in Jordan with Palestinian guerilla groups against King Hussein's army. More than a million Palestinians—both indigenous and refugees—lived in Jordan by 1970, when Carlos joined the PFLP (the Popular Front for the Liberation of Palestine). Carlos had received his training in PFLP camps near Beirut. The fighting in Jordan that Carlos took part in later became known as "Black September," because of the enormous amount of blood that was shed that month. And later still, one of the most violent terrorist groups took the name, Black September, for itself.

Carlos's typed words were in perfect French (or else they had been translated by the French DST). They began: "I had hoped that day for rain. For its gray muting makes all figures vague and ghostlike. But the drenching downpour was an unexpected, good omen." The poetic, cultured language did not surprise me. Carlos had always struck me as a most sophisticated man. I continued to read, entranced: "I pulled my dark raincoat closer and looked down at the water seeping into my new black moccasins. I remember thinking that they would leave a discernible trail across the marble lobby of the apartment building where Edouard Sieff lived. He was vice president of the Zionist Federation in Great Britain and therefore a major enemy of the Palestinian cause. But then I realized that my footprints did not matter, because later there'd be enough other tracks to obscure mine—policemen, reporters, men from the morgue with their creaking stretchers. At every moment, I forced myself to control my emotions, to remain cool, as had been stressed in my training camp. Passion and nerves can doom an operation."

Luis was nudging me to turn out the light, but I paid no attention. Carlos's narrative read like a novel.

"I tilted my black umbrella, so I could scan the three darkened windows of Sieff's third-floor drawing room, overlooking the park. To my right, the guards were changing in front of the American Embassy. This was a recent security innovation, a marginal protection against terrorists. I laughed to myself, because I knew if I wanted to enter their precious embassy, such precautions would be useless. The rain was dripping in streams from the umbrella, as I watched the six Marines salute one another. I was shivering as much from the adrenaline surging through my body as from the chill and the wetness. Too bad, I thought, that my plans tonight were directed someplace else. And yet, I knew that tonight I would prove my courage and ability. Tonight was going to prove that I was worthy of the name terrorist.

"At a quarter to six, I saw the lights blink on in succession in the drawing room upstairs, splashing the windows with a muted yellow glow. I could even see the silhouette of a maid moving from one window to the other, drawing the drapes, probably heavy red silk, like my mother's. Then the maid's silhouette vanished. I imagined her lighting the fire, then placing ice and crystal glasses on a wallside table. As I stood there, I was saying to myself, 'But not tomorrow. There'll be no drinks then, not after what is going to happen tonight.' I felt as if I was waiting to step onto a stage . . . or into another dimension, where I would be huge, larger-than-life. And I knew that from tonight on I would be famous.

"I was so tense and exhilarated about what I was going to do that the thought made me giddy; and I had to take several deep breaths to restrain from laughing. What would my victim's laugh be like? Maybe he would merely smile. A hundred times, I'd imagined the moment and the scene. A telephone call I'd made to the man's office had introduced us and secured my interview. 'Mr. Sieff,' I said, 'did you receive my letter? You have been my hero since I was a teenager. I used you as an example in my thesis at the London School of Economics. . . . Yes, I'm a student there. Yes, I know Dr. Cohen. . . . But what I really want to know is how to best use my education to support Zionism. You are my inspiration.'

"Mr. Sieff was delighted. 'Most certainly,' he said. 'I received your letter and the thoughtful box of cigars. Not easy to get good Cuban cigars nowadays. They happen to be my favorites. I'm most grateful. All right, my boy. I am very busy, and I rarely receive people I do not know. But in your case, I will make an exception. However, your visit will have to be brief. Come to my apartment tomorrow night, about six. My secretary will give you my home address.'

"Obtaining the invitation was so easy, I could scarcely believe my luck. Frankly, I had given this approach only the slimmest of chances. Fortunately, I had already planned this operation and was well prepared."

For a moment, I stopped reading and looked at Luis, who was sleeping restlessly. A breeze from the open window rattled the papers in my hand, and again he asked me to put out the light. But I was engrossed in Carlos's story and continued to read.

"First," Carlos's script went on, "I had studied Sieff's neighborhood, every corner of it, until I determined my escape route. I would go diagonally across the park and around the corner. Then past the Connaught Hotel. I intended to amble, as if nothing was on my mind. Perhaps I would ask the doorman to call for a cab to take me to Heathrow. Once in Heathrow, I planned to get out and mingle in the crowds, then take another taxi back to Picadilly. Then I would change cabs again and return to my mother's house in Phillimore Court.

"As I stood there rehearsing each step in my mind, the process absorbed me so much that when I glanced down at my watch, I saw that it was five past six! I raced across the soggy grass toward the exit at the park's northeast corner. And then I stopped, forcing myself to walk slowly along the winding path, so as not to attract attention. Instead of a briefcase, I carried a student's satchel under my arm as I pushed open the heavy iron and glass entrance door to Sieff's building. I held it so tight that the gun was pressing hard against my ribs.

"As I entered, a doorman hustled down a short flight of marble stairs, 'Yes, sir, may I help you?' He said. And I told him that Mr. Joseph Sieff expected me.

The doorman stepped into a small alcove and telephoned; then he returned, saying, 'Very well, Mr. Steiner, I will take you up in the lift.' I was so exhilarated that for a moment I didn't recognize the name I'd given to Sieff. There was a moment of panic; I thought that things were off to a bad start. Maybe everything would spin out of control. But by the time the lift reached the third floor, I was in complete control again.

"The doorman in the elevator was an unforeseen obstacle. I had hoped for solitude . . . to check my gun. But now that was impossible. A young maid with a West Indian accent stood in the open door of the flat. There was only one apartment per floor, which was good. And I relaxed a fraction. The girl took my coat to a nearby closet, then led the way through a large hall to the drawing room. The drapes were nearly red, as I had imagined, a deep burgundy in fact; and a fire was crackling in a large marble manteled fireplace. The walls were covered in a cream-colored silk that looked like butter. The pretty maid stood with downcast eyes near a table stacked with bottles and glasses. When I coughed, she glanced up and smiled shyly. Despite the tensions of the moment, I found her strangely arousing.

"Then Mr. Joseph Sieff appeared in the archway. He looked at me and smiled. I think he was pleased with my appearance. He walked into the room and extended his hand to me in a pleasant manner. The moment for action was coming near. Sieff asked about my family, and I told him my mother was born in Greece, and my father was Polish and that I had spent two years on a kibbutz. I hardly knew what I was saying by this time.

"As I continued to describe life on the kibbutz, Mr. Sieff went to the table with the glasses and liquor. I was meanwhile scrambling for details I could barely remember from newspaper and magazine accounts. When Mr. Sieff asked me what I would like to drink, I thanked him and suggested a whiskey. Then I unzipped the satchel, explaining that I was going to give him the thesis paper I'd written. A stack of blank white sheets concealing the gun fell out when I opened the bag. And when my fingers felt the cold steel, I started to tremble.

"Mr. Sieff was asking me if I wanted water with my whiskey, and held up a carafe. In that moment, I had the gun in my hand inside the satchel. I managed to say 'yes.' Then he came toward me with a drink in each hand, gesturing to a leather sofa in front of the fire. Although I had practiced the next maneuver many times, now that it was actually happening, my moves were becoming awkward. I was also worried about the gun itself: Would it function properly? My hand was still in the satchel, while Mr. Sieff was standing patiently watching. When I pulled the gun from the bag, he looked completely stunned. Then he understood.

"As I pulled the trigger, I felt the recoil ripple down my arm. I was aiming at point-blank range. In that instant, which seemed an entire night, the drinks fell from his hands, splashing him with whiskey. The crystal tumblers rolled beneath our feet. Blood spurted from Sieff's head. A blotch splashed the pale-yellow wall with red.

"Despite the impact of the bullet, Sieff lunged at me. His hands pulled at my face with a force I couldn't have imagined. Frantically I pushed the man away, and he fell to the carpet.

"Moisture was trickling down my face, and I realized that Sieff's blood had spurted on me, too. I rubbed my face with my white handkerchief, and it came off red. The white sheets of blank paper that had scattered on the Persian carpet were also speckled red. But I was proud. It was a great moment for me, and the beginning of what I hope will be a long career.

"Then I realized I had to get out of there. I raced to the door and down the stairway, instead of waiting for the lift.

"It was a shock to me to learn the next day that Sieff had survived. It was hard to imagine how he could live, with all the blood he'd lost. Yet I was still proud. For I had proved to the PFLP that I could attack a man like Sieff and get away."

When I finished reading, I was exhausted, but I could not sleep.

To me it was unbelievable that this young man who seemed so affectionate and polite, was so totally lacking in normal feelings of compassion.

Luis would be astounded, too, I knew. But as I glanced at his sleeping form stretched out next to me, I realized I would have to wait till tomorrow to catch his reaction. Several hours later, when another early-morning phone call came from Jupiter, I was still staring bleary-eyed at the ceiling above my bed.

"I'm arranging for you to meet with Serge Lebedev," he said. "He's delighted to work with you again." In a few minutes we had decided on St. Moritz for our rendezvous. The place was convenient for Serge, and Luis had to be there for a special horse race in ten days. The race actually took place on the frozen lake. Jockeys would ride the horses, while professional skiers would be attached to each horse. And there was nothing like it in the world—one of the truly exciting racing events.

As I replaced the receiver in its cradle and turned over, streaks of dawn were filtering through the shutters. In the comforting daylight, I slept until noon. Then I started packing for Paco Cabanellas's shoot. We were driving to Paco's *finca* later that afternoon.

Chapter 11

S *hortly after I* woke that day, there was another call from Jupiter. This time he wanted to talk once again about Karl von Ridder's death. And he was characteristically blunt on the subject. "Poor man, too damn trusting. He should have changed his hours and route to work every day. That would have made it more difficult for the terrorists. I told you, Tiger, these people we're dealing with are killers." He made no reference to the obvious fact that von Ridder's death probably meant that his own cover was not blown.

"How convinced are you that Carlos could have been the one who is responsible?" I asked.

"I'm not at all convinced it was him; and we may never know who did it. But if Carlos was responsible, he was acting on someone else's orders and has been well paid for the job. And there's another thing, too, Tiger. I'm almost certain von Ridder had some sort of association with COCOM." Then he coughed into the phone, the sound reverberated over the wire, and then the line filled with static.

"John?" But he was not there—only the pulsing beep of a disconnected call. I put down the receiver and stared at it, as if willing the phone to ring again would put me back in touch with him.

After several moments of frustrating silence, I went back to the business of packing for Paco Cabanellas's shoot. With Karl dead, I was surprised that Luis was still willing to go. Karl's encouragement seemed to have led him to accept in the first place. The news of the murder had hit Luis very hard, for he had also been with Karl during what now seemed, quite obviously, a failed assassination attempt.

The phone rang again. Before the second ring, I jumped to grab the receiver. An operator with strongly accented English said I had a caller. And again Jupiter's voice came on the line. "Where are you?" I asked.

"Tripoli. Listen, Aline."

"Tripoli?" Hearing that, I was surprised that he had spoken so openly earlier, but I supposed he had put a "scrambler" on his phone, since he knew I had one on mine. Nevertheless, I was determined to be wary.

"Aline, I only have a second. This shoot at Cabanellas's. I want you to watch him, but also be thinking about 'negative space.'" Jupiter had adopted the phrase to mean: pay attention to the edges, not the center. Look for what isn't obvious. "The last time you saw Karl von Ridder alive, some of the people were present who will be there this weekend. While you're there, listen carefully and observe everything. And don't forget Luis; he may pick up some hint that you don't hear or notice. I'll be in touch." With that, the phone went dead. I knew that was all for now; and I went back to my packing, wondering if Jupiter had uncovered something more about Paco Cabanellas. As I draped a black silk blouse across the bed, I decided I'd better take a camera, as well as the supersensitive recorder Jupiter had given me.

I'D ONLY BEEN to the Fernández de León *finca*—estate—once before, but I never forgot the magnificent panorama of the Tagus River and of Toledo rising high above it, the thick crenellated walls and stone turrets of the ancient city etched against a deep-blue sky.

A bent, aged butler in livery shuffled before us, leading the way to our suite in the west wing of the rambling, luxurious old palace.

"Unfortunately," he said as he moved along, "the restoration of the house is far from finished, especially the electricity. El Señor Cabanellas was so anxious to have a shoot here this season, that he underestimated the time it would take to rewire the second floor. And so almost all the sleeping quarters have to use candles and oil lamps. We are very sorry for the inconvenience." He shook his head. "I've been caring for this house over forty years, and even in the beginning we had lighting here. Seems impossible that something like this could happen. But they tell us the old wiring could start a serious fire."

We proceeded along the corridor with difficulty; our steps resounding against the high ceiling and dark walls. Only dim inlets of light seeped through the small windows. And the floor of ancient wood was so uneven that we had to take care not to trip. Finally the butler pushed aside a heavy oak door, which opened inward with the sigh old wine casks give when rolled out of their resting places. To our vast relief, the room had large windows overlooking a sweeping park. The moment we were alone, Luis pushed aside the draperies, allowing a stream of light to enter, and I rushed to look at the glorious view of Toledo.

We opened the double windows wide; the slow crawl down the airless hallway had nearly suffocated us both. Outside, beyond the park, the country looked inviting. I couldn't wait to walk through the open fields . . . or indeed to explore the house and Paco's new gardens.

Luis became busy arranging his equipment for tomorrow's shoot, after which he intended to join the men downstairs, where they would be talking with the gamekeeper. Cocktails wouldn't begin until nine. So I had at least a couple of hours, plenty of time to carry out Jupiter's suggestions, and to enjoy the countryside as well.

The hallway was quite dark. But near a curve in the passageway, a sliver of light below the floor jam told me someone else was quartered in this section of the house. A cold draft slid through the corridor, and I realized it came from a window near that door. As I stepped ahead and reached up to close it, a low moaning sound stopped me from moving further. Then the moan came again, and this time it extended into a loud gasp of sensual delight. A man's sudden cry clinched what was already very obvious. And so I quickly scuttled away, embarrassed to overhear a couple's moments of privacy.

Reaching the first floor and buttoning up my jacket, I stepped out into the cooling, late-afternoon air. The sun had not quite gone down, and purple shadows played elaborate tricks on the landscape. I decided to head out toward the hills, where I could catch the best view of Toledo. Once past the formal gardens, the terrain became rough with sticker burrs and low scrappy nettles. For over an hour I walked around, observing where the butts had been placed for tomorrow's shoot.

And then I tarried for a while longer, because of the entrancing view of Toledo. Scarlet clouds were gliding over the medieval spires of the massive fortress on its pedestal of rock. I watched in awed silence as wondrous puffy clouds became pale salmon, then lavender, as they floated over the city, like ghost ships on a misty sea.

As I was about to turn back to the house, I bent down and picked up a twig of lavender, rubbing the wild, fragrant leaves between my fingers so they would give off their heavy scent. For a moment I closed my eyes and with delight sniffed the marvelous rich perfume. When I opened my eyes again, I had a shock. Not more than thirty feet in front of me, under a knarled old *encina*—live oak tree—a man was standing, looking straight at me. He was of medium height and dressed in the dark pants and blousy shirt of a country farmer. Although he had a clear view of me, I was unable to distinguish his features, since the shadows of the branches were shrouding his face. Normally, at such a moment, I would have said "Buenas tardes," or some such greeting. Or the man should have. But I was so startled that I said nothing. And he did not speak, either. Nor did either of us move for what seemed a long time. But then, as he finally turned to leave, I recognized the silhouette, the tilt of the head, the cropped curly hair, and the sunglasses: I was standing face-to-face with Carlos! It was already too late to react, because in that instant he vanished over the top of the hill.

It was only after he was gone that I became frightened—the unexpectedness of the encounter, the dangerous implications of his being here at all. Who was he going to kill this time? But I didn't want to fully consider such things until I was safely back inside the house. Jupiter had a hunch that this weekend was going to be interesting, and it appeared that he was not going to be disappointed. . . . The meeting with Serge in a week's time might not be soon enough.

Dropping the lavender, I turned toward the old *palacio*. It was then that I discovered another retreating figure; this time a woman. She was slipping beneath the shadows of the *encinas*. Obviously, Carlos, if it *was* him, and this woman had been together moments before. Right now, she was making desperate efforts not to be seen. But I had a pretty good idea that she belonged at the *palacio* and not in a farmer's cottage. The slim figure, the lines of the jacket, and the long, full skirt told me this was not a farmer's wife.

I felt a dryness in my throat and hesitated before plunging into the darkness of the trees between me and the house. Forcing my legs to move down the hill, all my senses were alert to any movement in the shadows. I felt caught between two perils, the terrorist who could be watching me from the hilltop and the unknown woman who'd melted into the woods—though it was the situation more than the woman herself that frightened me.

The low branches of the old trees formed dusty shadows; and I moved cautiously. Somewhere in this maze was the woman. She had undoubtedly seen me, and if she happened to be a guest like me, out taking a stroll before dinner, her normal reaction should have been to call out. Unless, of course, their meeting in the forests was for the sake of romance, I thought, remembering the couple I had heard making love back in the house. Then the woman might well want to avoid me. Of course, if their meeting was actually a romantic rendezvous, that gave a lighter slant to my darker considerations. Was Carlos having a love affair with one of the women in our group? And had he been following her around to the same places that I was visiting? That seemed a far-fetched idea. Yet, for the moment this was a comforting theory.

After what seemed an eternity, the woods came to an end, opening onto the formal park. The outline of the house against the darkened sky was clearly visible, and with relief I hastened toward it. The field was a broad stretch, and although the light was diminishing, as far as I could see, no one else was in front of me. The woman was either behind in the forest or had raced ahead and had already entered the house. I kept scanning the area in front of me, while repeatedly glancing back over my shoulder. Once I was out of the field, I ignored the circular garden paths and walked directly across the lawn to the sweeping terrace. Warm lights burned in the downstairs windows; and through the panes I could see the enormous salon being prepared for the evening ahead. One last time I looked back; then I slipped into a side entrance, determined to take careful note of all the women that evening.

The massive, rambling house was a fascinating place. On the death of its previous owner, the estate had remained fallow and untended, and the palace itself lay almost empty for several years.

And now, with Paco's acquisition of the estate and renovation of the *palacio*, some rooms had remained precisely as they'd always been, while others had been completely redecorated. Paco must have had crews working at breakneck speed to complete the rooms downstairs, for the contrast between them and those above was dramatic.

The side entrance led to a small office, where a heavy, carved black oak table stood at an angle in one corner, with a stiff-backed chair behind it. Covering one wall was an arrangement of various keys, hanging on hooks with spidery handwritten labels above them. When I opened another door, I found myself in a brightly lit hall opening into an enormous pantry. Servants were scurrying back and forth with large trays, wine glasses polished to a diamond glow stood in careful rows, thick ivory candles in elaborate silver candelabras waited to be carried inside. My sudden appearance so startled a serving girl that she dropped a tray; and several dozen tiny silver spoons clattered to the floor. I wanted to ask if someone had just entered before me; but the intensity of the preparations made me aware that the hour was much later than I'd thought; and I rushed ahead.

As I passed through the main entrance hall, the booming laugh of R. K. Rhodentus echoed from the large salon. Already people were gathering for cocktails! Fortunately, the circular wooden staircase that led to our wing was right there, and I bolted up it.

Just as I reached the top, I slipped and crashed to the floor, stunning myself momentarily. Only the rounded structure of the circular staircase kept me from tumbling all the way down. Slowly I pulled my aching body to a standing position, and gingerly stretched my limbs. Fortunately, nothing appeared to be broken. At first I thought that the bad lighting had made me miss seeing a loose plank in the ancient parquet. But then I remembered that I'd slipped on something. As I rubbed an ankle, my eyes fell upon a silk scarf lying across one of the top steps. Despite the dimness, I could see where my foot had slipped on it. I picked it up and held it close to the nearest oil lamp. But as I did that, my eyes were drawn to something else in the shadows. Again I bent down, and found a little leather case. When I opened it, I discovered inside a small electronic device of some sort. Perhaps, the woman I'd seen out in the fields had been racing so fast she dropped the leather case, and the scarf, too. The deep-blue scarf with a gold patterned border appeared to be from Hermès, and it was quite new. She must have been here only seconds before, hurrying to avoid me. That meant, in all probability, that she was staying in one of the rooms off this corridor—not far from Luis's and mine.

An uncomfortable thought crept over me then: Could this woman actually be helping Carlos stalk his next victim? Carlos, I speculated, was dealing with Paco. But could he also be dealing with one of Paco's guests as well?

The leather case and the scarf were both in my hands. I lifted the scarf and sniffed it. The perfume was unfamiliar; but I would remember it; and it would help me identify the woman later.

Luis looked at me in some astonishment when I limped into our room. While I told him about my fall, I dropped the scarf on the back of a chair and handed him the leather case. At first I didn't mention Carlos, for fear Luis would think I was obsessed. But since Carlos's encounter with the woman was related to the scarf and the electronic machine, I felt obliged to explain how I got them.

Predictably, my husband refused to believe me. "Now, Aline, your imagination is going too far. You're suffering from some sort of morbid fixation with that terrorist. I should never have told you anything about him in the first place. So forget the whole affair." He gave his head an indignant shake; his brows arched in disapproval; and his expression punctuated his conviction that my encounter with Carlos was unthinkable. "I can't understand how a woman as intelligent as you can indulge yourself in such fantasies."

Then he turned his attention to my physical ailments, running his fingers over my arm and shoulder. "Are you sure you haven't broken anything?" he asked, with warm concern.

"I'm fine. Nothing that a hot bath won't take care of. But open the leather case and tell me what you think."

Luis did as I asked and removed the electronic device, turning it over several times in his hands. "Why," he said looking up at me, "this is a very sophisticated miniature walkie-talkie—made in Germany. Someone else must have the matching one. What a great little machine—ultramodern!"

After we examined it, we both decided that someone inside the house was using it to contact someone outside. "However," Luis reminded me, "gamekeepers regularly use walkie-talkies to control the beaters. Still," he said as he turned the apparatus over again in his hand, "this machine is much too complex for such elementary work." Because of our suspicions about Paco, we decided not to tell him about my encounter in the field, or about the scarf and the walkie-talkie. And we also determined to wait and see if someone mentioned losing either of those articles. If she—or he—is on the

up-and-up, we reasoned, the person would certainly want to recover both expensive items.

By then, I was beginning to feel more than a little gratified. For
Luis's reaction to the German electronic device made me suspect
that, after all, he was putting more credence in my suspicions about
Carlos than he wanted to admit.

He wanted to stay with me until I was dressed, to make sure I
would be all right. But it was late, and I insisted he go join the others. That way, he could also keep his eyes open for my elusive
woman. She was sure to be late, since she would have to change for
dinner, and she would not have had time to do that yet. With luck,
we might be able to identify her and begin to understand the evening's mysteries.

I was one of the last to arrive in the large salon. Paco had expanded his party to include many others not invited for the shoot;
and who were, in fact, only there for dinner. Looking down from
the steps into the enormous room, now nearly filled with people, I
was dismayed. How could I hope to pick out my female target with
so many to choose from? Until that moment, I had assumed that the
scarf was the property of one of the weekend guests. But I now
realized that the woman could just as well be one of the many who
had come only for cocktails or dinner. After a second, I stepped into
the salon to join the others. It wouldn't help my cause, I realized, to
stand in the doorway so obviously surveying the group.

As I crossed the room, Luis caught my eye; I smiled to let him
know I was all right. And he gave me a slight, welcoming nod. I
already knew that he had not managed to discover who had
dropped the scarf and the walkie-talkie. If he had, he would have
instantly come to me. Meanwhile, he was seated on a small settee
with Nancy Rhodentus. R.K. stood looming above them, telling
some story, a process that involved huge sweeps of his ample arms.
Luis was laughing, and I could see he was enjoying our new American friends. The three of them made a striking tableau—my husband, very handsome in his smoking jacket; Nancy in ivory silk
slacks, with her taffy-colored hair, which gave her an ephemeral air;
and in complete contrast, R.K., huge and grounded, his thick legs
standing apart like tree trunks. As I looked at them, it occurred to
me that if everything had gone as planned, Karl von Ridder would
have been sitting with them at this moment . . . a thought that
brought back the plaguing worry that Carlos was now planning to
kill someone else.

Remembering Jupiter's directions, I studied the scene. As I did

that, Paco came to my side, delirious with the success of his gathering. "How am I going to seat all these people!" he wailed. "Three
grandees of Spain! And the daughter of the Head of State!" But I
knew his anxiety was for show. I'd seen the operations in the
kitchen. And it was obvious that he had the fine points down to a
science. I wondered if his girlfriend, Inge, had helped him put the
affair together, and assumed she had. She was a tremendous asset to
his social ambitions.

And then a moment later, there she was, shimmering at his side
in an exquisitely sequined navy-blue evening suit.

"Aline," she cried, a huge smile on her young, healthy face, "I
was so excited when Paco told me you had arrived. I went to your
room, but no one was there!" She gave me a brief hug then, to show
her delight in finally finding me. As she came close, a wave of the
same scent I'd noticed on the silk scarf enveloped me.

"I took a walk to see the *finca* in that lovely sunset this afternoon," I said.

"Oh, I wish I had known." She turned toward her fiancé, "Paco,"
she said, "you should have told me, I could have gone with Aline."
Nothing in her manner indicated she had recently been running
through the woods and up the back staircase.

"I wasn't aware that Aline was so enthusiastic about country
walks," Paco answered, but in a distracted tone that I was quick to
notice. And a second later I saw why. His attention was riveted on a
tall, dark-haired woman who was standing in the shadows with her
back to the room at a short distance from the animated group near
the entrance. Unlike every other woman in the room, she was
dressed quite simply, in an off-the-shoulder, long-sleeved black
dress. But it was cut strikingly low in the back, revealing beautifully
contoured shoulders. When she turned around, I recognized the
young girl I'd met at the wedding in Bavaria, Paco's sister Sofia.
Tonight she was as devastating as she'd been there. And several people had already turned to gaze at her. Meanwhile, Paco excused
himself and went over to her.

Inge noticed my glance. "Oh," she explained, with a resigned lift
of her brows. "There she is. Sofia. The crazy one."

"What do you mean?"

"She's difficult. And Paco feels obligated to take care of her." She
shook her head in charitable resignation. "The rest of his family
have washed their hands of her. And she's been living here since
Paco bought the *finca*. But she follows him wherever he goes. She

helped with the renovation; and fortunately that's still keeping her busy. She's quite harmless really; but she's still a great problem with her temperamental fits. And . . ." she shook her head again, in despair this time, "there's so much more I can't explain to you." And there was another shake of her head. "Paco's one of the few persons she'll speak to," she continued. "She treats me as though I carry bubonic plague."

"I met her during the wedding," I said, "and she was quite nice . . . if talkative."

Inge shot me a worried glance, but said quite normally, "I'm surprised Sofia came down tonight. Usually she stays up in her room if anyone is here other than Paco and the workmen. She lives up in the west wing where you and Luis are staying. But you won't hear a peep out of her, and you probably won't see her again after tonight. Usually she can't tolerate being near other people." This remark surprised me, especially after seeing Sofia with John Derby at the wedding—and with poor Karl von Ridder, too.

"Is her room at the end of the corridor near the stairway?" I asked.

"Why, yes. How did you know?"

"I pass it when I come downstairs." So Sofia was the one making love this afternoon, I thought. And that obviously means that Inge doesn't know that Sofia can tolerate at least one other person very well. As I was sifting through this thought, Paco and Sofia left the room together. Nervously, he glanced back, as if to make sure his exit wasn't causing a stir. Watching them disappear, I wondered if this "eccentric" young woman was the one who had dropped the silk scarf and the walkie-talkie on the steps.

Yes, "eccentric" is a good word, I thought. This strange beauty hadn't yet given me any reason to believe that she was crazy.

At that moment a butler came to have a word with Inge; and my husband signaled me from the other side of the room to join them.

R.K. greeted me with such a large wet kiss on each cheek that I had to laugh. I was totally charmed by this rugged bear of a man and his open, friendly American manner.

"Countess," he said, "I was just telling your husband how pleased we were that you two have come to this shoot. We were afraid you might not be here. Isn't that right, Nancy?"

Nancy looked up at me out of her wide blue eyes. "After Karl's death," she said warmly, "we weren't sure we would come ourselves. Since his wife is a good friend, we did what we could to comfort her. But now we are happy to be here, and especially since you two have come."

I, too, was glad to see Nancy Rhodentus again. In Bavaria I had grown very interested in her; but with my worries about Carlos, and after Karl von Ridder's death, I had forgotten we would be seeing them here.

Tonight she seemed less agitated than I remembered her. In fact, she seemed unusually serene. Then, as she was telling me about her new apartment in Paris (she was having it remodeled), for the first time I noticed a slight accent in her speech. When I asked her about it, she explained, adding a stronger emphasis to her accent, as though merely thinking about the country drew it out of her: "I was born in Venezuela. But I was only fourteen when we moved to Chicago. Although I did speak other languages, I didn't know English yet. So my classmates in Illinois didn't know what to make of a little convent girl who didn't speak their language. But I learned quickly. In fact, I'm disappointed you noticed an accent." She gave me a radiant smile. As she did that, my eyes were drawn to the scar I remembered seeing in Bavaria. But now, as this beautiful woman settled in the plump silk pillows of the settee, the subdued lighting made the tiny scar on her face practically invisible.

Meanwhile I suddenly realized that R.K. was talking about COCOM, of all things. So I hastily turned my attention to him. "Poor Karl," he was saying, "he was collaborating with the government in uncovering companies involved in illegal arms sales. In my opinion, that's the reason he was killed. Libya or Iraq, or who knows what crazy country, wanted to show that nobody could interfere with the imports they consider vital for manufacturing nuclear weapons.

"I told him not to be involved with COCOM. 'Why go out on a limb?' I told him. 'Why make yourself a target?' But that did no good. Karl simply felt that what he was doing was the only honorable course he could take." R.K. paused, and there was a large tear in his eye. "Jesus!" he went on. "You know? The guy was my best friend! And he was my financial advisor, too. Only a few days before Karl died, he advised me to cancel my investment in Reutger and Company. He believed they were making illegal exports.

"But, of course, the companies themselves aren't always guilty," R.K. explained, "even if their equipment ends up in the hands of some desert dictator. Sometimes an employee steals a blueprint or a technical paper and hands it over to the USSR or another Eastern

Bloc country. They manufacture the stuff there; and of course they have no conscience about selling what the West won't. All kinds of smuggling is going on, Karl told me. And it's difficult for a company to finger traitors. Today any dishonest employee can make a fortune."

So Karl was cooperating with COCOM, I thought. Somehow I was not surprised, for that explained a great deal. Did Karl suspect Paco of shipping illegal material, or of buying it for a third party? I wondered. Perhaps that was the main reason he had accepted Paco's invitation for this shoot.

Just then Nancy slipped closer to me. As she did so, I was again aware of the perfume I'd smelled on the scarf. Damn! I thought. If several women are using the same scent, how will I find the one I'm looking for?

"What upsets me," she said to Luis, "is that when my husband canceled that investment, he put his life in danger."

"Could canceling an investment put him in danger, Nancy?" Luis asked gently.

"I don't think that advice is what killed Karl, my dear," R.K. added.

Chapter 12

*D*inner was announced, which unfortunately interrupted the fascinating conversation.

Wild purple thistles and tangled vines comprised the centerpieces of the candlelit tables. The rich mahogany paneled walls gleamed, and a footman stood behind each of the three festive tables which glittered with crystal and silver. I was seated at a round table for eight, placed near a large, softly burning fireplace. When I found my place card, a short, dark-faced vaguely Arab-looking man was standing next to my chair, waiting to greet me. I hadn't noticed him in the salon before dinner, which wasn't especially astonishing, since the room was so crowded. He appeared too young for his dark greying hair brushed with wisps of silver, and his face was almost entirely dominated by a long elaborate nose. His eyes seemed barely visible in comparison—small, dark, nondescript. Still there was an exceptional alertness to their gaze. Although I am not easily made uncomfortable, I found myself glancing away as those eyes bore down on me.

Courtesy demanded that he kiss my hand in greeting, but I nearly pulled away as I watched his small, pursed mouth approach the back of my hand. Something about him sounded all my intuitive alarms. Yet on the surface, he seemed, if anything, quite ordinary. As his head hovered above my reluctant wrist, I stole a glance at the place card.

My God! I said to myself. So this is the desirable Nicky Maniatis. Could Nancy and Inge really have been serious when they raved about him? I thought. He's a creep!

Even the superb cut of his midnight-blue smoking jacket couldn't disguise a build that widened just when it ought to be tapering. Perhaps the two women had been playing some joke on me. But no, that's unlikely. They must be serious, I thought. Then what makes this unexceptional man so devastating to two quite beautiful women?

Nicky straightened to his full height, which was about the same as my own; and he assured me with some gravity that he had asked especially to be seated next to me and that we would talk privately as soon as he could politely release himself from the clutches of the woman on his right. I glanced beyond his shoulder to see whose clutches he was referring to and saw Nancy chatting amiably with a South African diamond magnate. What a rude, strange man, I thought.

On my other side was Inge's father, Hans. Since he and I had danced briefly at the wedding, I knew him slightly. Meanwhile, just before we took our seats, Inge dashed over and gave her father's arm an affectionate squeeze. "You see, Papa," she said. "I told you I would seat you next to a beautiful woman." And then she was off again performing her hostess duties.

"Inge seems very happy," I said to Hans Schmidt when we were seated.

"Oh, she is. Like a typical doting father, I never thought I would find any man good enough for her; but I'm glad to say that I believe Paco will make her the perfect husband."

Hans Schmidt was about sixty years old, though in many ways he seemed twenty years younger. He radiated strength and self-confidence; he was tall, like many Germans; and he had a strong and powerful physique—I imagined he'd been quite an athlete in his day. His silvery-brown hair gave him a distinguished air; and straight eyebrows framed two narrow slits of startling blue crystal eyes. "It's a pleasure to see you again, Condesa," he began. His voice was warm and friendly, his manner slightly formal. "I was delighted when Inge told me you might be here. She has said repeatedly how gracious you and your husband have been during her summers in Marbella. She admires you tremendously and regards you as a special friend."

"It's easy to be gracious to Inge," I answered. "She's utterly charming, and everyone likes her."

"Yes," he said, quite simply. "She's her mother's daughter. I had a wonderful son too, but he died several years ago. The experience almost killed me, but Inge gave me reason to live."

Before dinner Nancy had spoken to me briefly about Herr Schmidt. He was considered a wizard in Germany's business world, she said, but he'd had bad luck in his private life. His wife and brothers had been killed in the war; his only son died in an automobile accident; and he had no family at all, outside of Inge. "Though Hans Schmidt is enormously successful in business, he seems to have one of those jinxed personal lives, a man doomed for tragedy," Nancy said. "Yet he's indestructible. I'd love to be more like him. The smallest everyday setback sends me reeling."

Dinner was extravagant. Six menservants entered, bearing large crystal bowls of shiny gray caviar. As they served Paco's twenty-four guests, Hans mentioned humorously that he was pleased his daughter had not fallen in love with a pauper. The second course of salmon poached in exotic herbs followed. As we ate, Hans began to tell me of the odyssey of his early life. And I was captivated—as much by the charm of the teller as by the story itself. Hans had fled Lithuania with his mother, a concert pianist, and herself a very strong-willed person. Despite the difficulties of their escape routes, she had insisted on bringing her special white piano most of the way in a horse-drawn wagon.

Somewhere between the salmon and the delicious partridge baked in honey and herbs, I turned toward my other companion and found him waiting patiently to speak to me. As I met Nicky Maniatis's gaze, his small eyes flashed, as though I were the woman he had been waiting for all his life—a message he artfully expressed without moving a muscle in his face. The impact of his look was disorienting, and I found myself wanting to protest. He continued to pin me with his bold gaze for another moment. And then, like a stage actor's, his face softened . . . took on a less seductive aspect. Now I knew the real reason why the Duchess of Windsor disliked him: Disrupting his mother's household was only the tip of the iceberg. I judged him to be about thirty-five years old, though his confidence and the silver streaks in his hair made him seem older. I decided the best approach with him would be to meet his aggression head-on.

"You wished to talk to me, Mr. Maniatis. So what did you want to speak to me about?" I asked.

If he found my question disarming, it didn't show. On the contrary, he volleyed back, "I wanted to speak to you about yourself, Condesa. What could be more intriguing?"

"Only the topic of you, Mr. Maniatis, you are far more a mystery to me than I am to you."

"I would be exceptionally flattered if that were the case, but I am afraid you are merely trying to fend off my interest in you."

"You misunderstand me."

"Never, I assure you, Condesa."

This last statement was accompanied by a brief reappearance of his earlier gaze. And then, blessedly, Nancy leaned across and interrupted.

"Is Nicky telling you about his incredible boats?" she asked.

"I wish he would," I said, smiling at both of them.

"Well, he's just promised to deliver *La Sirena* by Christmas," Nancy said.

"That's wonderful," I said. "Nancy and R.K. both told me how remarkable your boats are." Nancy smiled and turned back to her other companion, but I clung to the topic like a life raft. "Tell me, do you see yourself as another Onassis?" I asked.

Nicky tossed his head back and laughed. As he did so he revealed a set of small, remarkably white teeth, so startling perfect that they looked like the creation of a Hollywood dentist.

"We all love the sea," he said still chuckling, "but not all Greeks are able to express their financial affinity as magnificently as Aristotle Onassis."

"Well, whom do you compare yourself to, then?"

"To you, Condesa."

"To me? That's preposterous. I have nothing to do with boats—or with business, for that matter."

"But you have everything to do with adventure," he said. This time, he had the good sense not to back up his ludicrous remark with a leering glance.

To my relief, Nancy broke in once again, with a breathless question to Nicky about *La Sirena*. Offering me a quick apology, Nicky gave Nancy his full attention. Hans was meanwhile engaged in conversation with the woman on his right; and so I was free to survey the room for a moment. Paco was seated at the table in front of me. But I was startled to see his sister presiding opposite him. Although I could only make out her lustrous black hair and bare shoulders gleaming in the candlelight, I gathered she was behaving, because Paco looked relaxed and delighted. Nothing about his manner suggested the murky world I thought he was involved in, and despite my suspicions, his loving and kind solicitude for his sister improved him in my eyes.

But don't be fooled, I told myself. People are not always what they seem.

"You look pensive, Condesa," Nicky said, nearly whispering in my ear. "Does Paco Cabanellas disturb you in some way?"

Nicky startled me, but I managed to smile. "It's not Paco, I'm thinking about. It's his sister. We met her at a wedding in Germany, and I was impressed with her beauty."

"Yes. There is no one more beautiful than Sofia," said Nicky, glancing in her direction. It was the first time I had seen his face free of calculation. Something about Sofia seemed to strip this complicated, devious man of his defenses. Up until this point, he and I had conducted our conversations in French; but now he switched to an awkward Spanish to tell me that Sofia was sometimes a *problema*, and that she was extremely *nerviosa*. As he spoke—with previously unsuspected sincerity—I wondered if this disturbing Nicky Maniatis was in love with Paco's sister.

So Nicky felt the same as Nancy and Inge about Sofia, I mused. However, intuition kept telling me that both women were jealous of the young beauty. I also sensed the topic of Sofia Cabanellas was a tender one with Nicky. Though he could be a most annoying man, nothing prompted me to touch so obvious a vulnerability.

I switched the subject.

"We were talking earlier about your love of the sea; and you said that comes from being Greek?" I said.

Nicky nodded. His eyes communicated that he was back on solid ground and ready to resume where we'd left off.

"But the Duchess of Windsor not long ago told me you are in fact from Palestine," I said.

"Did she mention me to you?" asked Nicky without missing a beat.

"Yes, she most certainly did." I stared at him, impressed by his self-assurance.

"I'm surprised," he said. "I didn't think she liked me very much."

"She doesn't."

Again Nicky laughed, his perfect teeth flashing. "Well, perhaps she's right," he said, "but I hope you won't be influenced by her."

"I generally like to form my own opinions," I said.

"I am sure that is true," said Nicky, smiling broadly. "And yes, my mother is Palestinian; only my father is Greek. But I love him dearly; and I identify myself with him and my Greek grandfather."

"Is your father called Nicholas also?" I wanted to know more about his background.

Nicky looked mildly surprised. "No," he said after a brief pause, "my father is called Herodotus. A terrible name! And my name also. Nicky is an *apodo*—a nickname I acquired in school because of brawls with my classmates. The teacher used to say I was covered with knicks, bruises, and scrapes. And so I became 'Nicky.' "

"Are you still so rough?" I asked teasingly.

"Aline, I am a lamb, I assure you." He had dropped the formality of "Countess." And there was no mistaking the intent in his dark eyes.

But by then, to my relief, dinner was over; and Paco had started to move people into the large salon for music and dancing. The Paraguayos, a small group of guitarists and singers who had been popular the summer before in Marbella, were already playing. The servants had rolled up one of the massive oriental carpets, leaving a large rectangle of gleaming parquet.

Inge grabbed Paco, and calling out to me to find Luis, she gestured for us to begin dancing. I realized she wanted help in getting the party moving; so I called R.K. and Nancy, who were nearby, to join us. For a woman of such natural grace, Nancy was an astonishingly poor dancer. She had absolutely no sense of rhythmn.

In no time, Inge got her wish; and many couples were moving about to the music. Early on, I noticed my obnoxious dinner companion wandering around looking for a partner; but I knew it wouldn't take him long to find one. Then Luis started to spin me. He was an exceptionally good dancer, and we both loved it. We swept happily around the floor for most of the first set. . . . Until I heard a snap: The tiny heel of my satin pump had caught in a small crack and had broken off. Fortunately, I had another pair in my luggage.

"I'll be back in a minute," I said to Luis.

"Wait," he answered. And with some difficulty he found the broken heel among the many dancing feet. He handed it to me, and I limped off the floor.

When I went from the brightly lit salon into the dim circular stairway, the darkness seemed greater than I remembered. A row of brass candlesticks was lined up on a table at the foot of the stairs, obviously to allow guests to light their way back to their rooms. I took one, lit it, and gripping the heavy holder firmly, started to climb, holding the candle aloft as I mounted. I kept a sharp eye on the floor. After my earlier fall and coupled now with my broken heel, I didn't want another accident. When we arrived that afternoon, we at least had the advantage of the light from the hallway's irregular window openings. But now long tapers in wall sconces cast uneven sputtering pools of light like dancing ghosts on the gray walls. My surroundings reminded me of a scene from a horror movie, and my own shadow huddled beside me, as if afraid of a specter I couldn't see. With childish relief, I finally reached our room. Instantly I relaxed. The fire had been replenished, our beds turned down, and a fragrant potpourri gave off a rich herbal scent. The room was deliciously cozy in the light of the blazing logs, and I thought how nice it would be to return later with Luis.

A maid had unpacked my bag, and I found my clothes. But search as I might, the shoes were not in the small salon, nor in the bedroom either. Then I remembered the large walk-in closet at the far end of the bathroom. Since there was no light in there, I took the candle with me and searched the closet. Still I could not find my shoes. Just as I gave up and stepped out of the closet, a sudden gust of wind blew out my candle's tiny flame. In that same moment, I heard a sound inside my bedroom, and realized someone had opened the door from the hall, creating the draft which snuffed out my candle. In total darkness, I stood paralyzed, listening to stealthy steps in the next room, then glimpsing the moving glow of a flashlight. "Carlos?" I asked myself. The name was like a shout inside my mind. I tried to calm myself. Perhaps it's Paco's sister, I thought. She lives in the room down the hall. Again soft footsteps tapped across the wood floor. The barely audible snap of the clasp of my camera case told me the person was standing at the desk. Then I heard the sound of my own voice, coming from my recorder.

Was the intruder armed? I asked myself. My evening bag contained a small gun. But foolishly, I had left my bag under a cushion in the sofa downstairs. When I was on an operation, I usually carried it and other practical objects like the recorder with me. If it was Carlos, he'd be apt to carry something silent, like a knife. Years ago, in the espionage training school in Washington, DC., Colonel Fairbairn, who was the best in the world with knives, had taught me how to kill silently with cold steel. I'd been especially afraid of knives ever since. But Carlos would certainly know how to use one. With my heart thumping, I decided I'd better not confront whoever was out there. Grasping the brass candlestick in my hand as my only protection, I remained motionless.

Whoever it was was moving around again; and the footfalls now sounded like a woman's. But to my horror they were coming toward the bathroom. A beam of light splashed under the sill of the door. The trespasser was a woman! I could smell her perfume, and it was the same scent I'd noticed on the scarf. Clutching the heavy brass stick, I was ready to spring. But after a moment's pause, the shaft of light moved away. A second later, I heard the turn of the latch and the soft whine of the door being carefully cradled shut.

With the heavy candlestick still in hand, I ran from the bathroom into the bedroom, where the glow from the fireplace vaguely illuminated the room. I went quickly to the door to the hall; and as silently as possible, I released the latch and opened it. The pale flickering light in the corridor made it difficult to see the entire hallway. I looked in both directions, but I could neither see nor hear anyone.

Frustrated and angry, I closed and locked the door. Then I looked around, spending some time going over the whole room (and yes, I found my shoes this time). But first I checked my address book; I was worried about the Agency numbers I had noted there. But that seemed undisturbed. In fact, only two items were missing—the small walkie-talkie and the silk scarf. And this confirmed that the intruder was the woman I'd seen in the fields. The walkie-talkie, I calculated, probably had come from Carlos. He'd doubtless given it to her so she could communicate with him. The awareness that someone in our group was involved with that man chilled me.

When I returned to the warmth of the party, Luis immediately saw that I was upset. He rushed to my side. And when I explained what had happened, he was shocked. "We have to be careful; we can't trust anyone," he said. Then we agreed it would be dangerous to mention the incident to anyone except Jupiter.

"This is becoming a crazy weekend," Luis went on. "Just a second before you came back, I was looking for a bathroom in a hallway behind the dining room. When I pushed open a door I thought might be the right one, I found—believe it or not—that Greek shipbuilder Maniatis and Nancy Rhodentus kissing each other." Luis raised his eyes. "Naturally, I was embarrassed and rushed out. I don't know if they saw who I was. But they were lucky. R.K. could have been the one to stumble upon them."

I was astounded. Until then I thought Nancy was a devoted wife. On the other hand, I could now eliminate one suspect. For she could hardly have been in Nicky's arms and searching our suite at the same time. Then I realized that twenty minutes had passed since the woman left my room. So the intruder could have been Nancy after all. Unfortunately, like the perfume itself, all my bits of evidence were useless. The intruder could be any woman in the house.

Later that night, shortly before the party broke up, Nancy asked me if I could loan her something that would make her outfit tomorrow more *campero*. I told her I'd brought an extra hat that she could have, and that I had an Austrian shooting cape that I probably wouldn't use.

"Wonderful," she gushed, clapping her hands. "You know exactly what one should wear to these shoots. I've never been to one in Spain before; and I have all the wrong things. I was originally going sightseeing in Toledo during the shoot, but I hate to leave R.K. I worry about him so. If you don't mind, I'll stop by your room tomorrow morning."

"Do you know where it is?" I asked.

"Oh, yes. Inge showed me the plan of all the guest rooms. I'll come by around eight-thirty. Is that okay?"

"That's fine," I agreed, wondering how she could act so attached to her husband after the scene Luis had stumbled onto.

Chapter 13

About nine the next morning, when Nancy knocked on my door, Luis had already left. She stood there in a blue plaid wool suit, beaming with her usual radiant smile. I invited her in and suggested she sit down, while I finished my makeup. She took a chair just behind my dressing table. Despite Luis's and my decision not to mention last night's incident in our room, and despite all the questions about her that Luis's revelation had raised, a sudden flash of intuition told me to risk telling her about the silk scarf (though not the walkie-talkie). I had a feeling that her answer would give me a lead.

Her eyes opened wide with innocence when I described the way the woman reclaimed it. "There's no doubt in my mind whose scarf that is," she declared. "Probably it's Sofia's," she said. "I was in her room earlier this morning, and a silk scarf like the one you describe was in plain view on a chair."

Now it was my turn to be surprised. "But why would that girl feel she had to come to my room like a thief to get it back?"

"For many reasons," Nancy replied. "First of all, she's off her rocker most of the time. I visited her a few minutes ago because she was crying her eyes out. I don't know how you didn't hear her wails. Our room is down the hall, and I heard her as I was coming to see you. That's why I'm late. For some reason, I seem to be able to calm her. But today she was more desperate than I've ever seen her. She's madly in love, and her boyfriend hasn't called her this morning. She's so childish. Can you imagine!"

"Who's her boyfriend?" I asked. My God, I thought, could that strange, gorgeous creature be sleeping with the world's most hunted terrorist?

Nancy shook her head. "Oh, he's no one you would know. No one of any importance at all. In fact, she falls in and out of love every other week."

"Maybe it's Nicky Maniatis," I suggested, curious to see how Nancy would react to that. "It seems everybody's crazy about Nicky," I continued pointedly. "Don't you think?"

"Aline," she said in a confiding tone, "I wanted to talk to you alone this morning about Nicky. I knew Luis saw me with him last night; and I'm sure he told you what he saw. I intended to explain what happened to you both before we went to bed, but that proved impossible." She sighed and crossed her long, slim legs. "Luis did tell you?"

I nodded.

"Well, I wanted you to understand what is actually happening. You should know first that Nicky and I had an affair. But that was some time ago, long before I met R.K. Now we are still friends . . .

and, well, you've met him. You know that sometimes he goes too far. Sometimes he goes too far with me. He tries to kiss me, and," she shrugged, "you know . . ." She opened her bag and fumbled inside. "I'm so upset," she went on as she dabbed at her eyes. "Nicky can be wonderfully sweet. But he's also a terrible problem; he'll cause trouble for me with my husband. R.K. is already jealous enough. It's hard for him to realize that Nicky is that way with every attractive woman; he's pounced on Inge just as often as he has pounced on me." Her eyes caught mine. "I just don't know what to do. He *is* an old friend; he has business connections with R.K.; and he's building our new yacht. We've paid for it in advance. And R.K. is so enamored with it, I'd hate to create an embarrassing situation."

She seemed so sincerely upset that I very much wanted to feel sorry for her.

"I don't want you and Luis to think anything is going on between us. I don't care about myself, but that would not be fair to R.K." She looked at me imploringly. "Will you explain this to your husband, and promise me not to mention it to anyone else?"

"Of course, Nancy," I said. "But can I suggest that you stay as far away from Nicky Maniatis as possible?"

"Oh, I wish!" she sighed. "But it's *so* difficult. During the past weeks, R.K. and I have seen him constantly. He and R.K. have been working closely together on some kind of terribly complicated business deal." Nancy closed her purse with a snap. And then caught my eye. "And you should keep an eye on him yourself, Aline. He tries to get every woman he meets in bed with him."

"Did he succeed with Sofia?" I asked. "A man was in her room yesterday. And it was very obvious that they were not having a serious, philosophical conversation. I could hear their cries in the hallway. Could the man have been Nicky?"

"Poor Sofia. They all take advantage of her. At what time?" Nancy asked.

"Just before I went out to the country for a walk."

Nancy paused a moment, thinking. "I didn't see you arrive, Aline," she said after a moment, "but that surprises me, because I was under the impression that Sofia was with Inge all afternoon, helping to decorate the dinner tables. They were out in the fields picking the lavender and the purple thistles that made the tables so lovely last night."

Nancy looked at her watch. "Oh, my God! We're late." I looked at mine. She was right. We had to rush, or we'd miss breakfast.

Nancy grabbed the hat and cape on the sofa, and we both ran out of the room.

As I hurried down the stairs, I wondered if Nancy was right about the scarf belonging to Sofia. If so, then Sofia might be a very bad girl. And what *was* Nancy's real relationship to Nicky Maniatis? Who had been the woman in the fields? What about Inge? She used the perfume, too. . . .

By the time we arrived in the dining room, the men were finishing their breakfast. Most of the women, however, were still asleep, and would be served in their rooms. The typical Spanish shooting breakfast was spread out on a buffet table: *Migas*—fried bread crumbs, fried eggs, assorted chorizos and all kinds of other sausages, fresh goat cheese, manchego cheese, sugary heavy cakes, red wine, and anise. There were other luxuries, too—French brioches, croissants, and smoked salmon. Paco was really making an effort to impress us.

Nancy chose an empty seat next to her husband. A moment later, Nicky sat down at her side. "I don't know how I dare show my face after the fiasco I made dancing so badly with you last night," she said to him.

"Nonsense," Nicky replied, as he dug into the *migas* and fried eggs. "You were just reinventing the rhumba, like Picasso reinvented painting."

She looked at him, momentarily abashed, not sure whether he meant to flatter or offend. I was surprised to see that Nicky's charm wasn't always foolproof, where Nancy was concerned.

Meanwhile, R.K. asked me if the group of men outside on the patio were the beaters for the day's shoot.

"Yes," Paco answered from across the table. "These *hombres* come from a town nearby. I've asked my gamekeeper to pick a good *cargador*"—loader—"from the group for you."

"Oh, that won't be necessary," interrupted Nancy. "R.K.'s valet will load for him."

AN HOUR LATER, Luis and I walked across the fields I'd crossed the evening before. In daylight the frightening shadows had vanished, and the fields lay before us in soft rippling patterns of gold and green. Halfway to the blind, the head gamekeeper appeared. "Excuse me, Señor Conde," he said, addressing Luis, "can you tell me where Señor Cabanellas went? I have to tell him we have at least one poacher out there already today."

Luis walked over to the man; and, while pointing to the jeeps that were pulling up under a tree in the distance, he and the gamekeeper continued to converse.

"What's so unusual about that?" I commented when my husband returned. "We often have poachers behind the lines in Pascualete."

Luis nodded. "Yes, but carrying a rifle. A rifle! Now what would a fellow with a rifle be doing at a bird shoot?"

"Perhaps the poacher is an assassin."

"Oh, Aline, don't overreact. I insist the man you saw in the fields is not Carlos."

I didn't dare contradict him. He'd only keep scolding me for imagining Carlos was everywhere. All the same, I was more worried than ever. The more I thought about it, the more certain I was that Carlos was the man I had seen and that he had an accomplice inside our group.

"Let's try to enjoy this perfect day," my husband said, squeezing my hand, which encouraged me to say nothing more about the poacher.

It wasn't until the third drive that anything unusual happened. Nancy and R. K. Rhodentus were about fifteen yards away. She was sitting peacefully behind R.K. on a small collapsible leather chair. The weather was warming up, the wind was subsiding, and the birds were plentiful. In fact, there were so many that both of Luis's Purdys were blistering hot. The racket from his rapid fire was enormous, and he was downing partridge right and left.

Then one of his guns jammed.

"*Maldito sea!*" he cried. "Now what am I going to do?" I knew that this was like losing a ski pole halfway down the mountain on a great run; yet he calmly continued with his one remaining gun, despite the loss of the birds that passed over while he was reloading. R.K. noticed Luis's difficulty and called over. "I've an extra gun here, you can have it if you want."

Since the drive was just about over, Luis waved to him not to bother. Nevertheless, because he was a generous man, five minutes later when the drive was over and everyone was still picking up his birds, R.K. appeared in our blind with a gun. "Here, feel free to use this one, Luis. I brought an extra in case something went wrong with one of mine. I see a lot of you Spaniards rotate three guns when there are this many birds; but two guns is all I can handle."

By then, it was already three o'clock, so we broke for lunch. Guns were put in cases, ammunition bags closed, dead birds handed to the gamekeeper, and we were directed to tables set up beneath a clump of *encinas*.

Sitting at the end of a long, narrow table in the shade of an enormous live oak tree, Nancy, R.K., Nicky, and Inge were enjoying the sweeping panorama of Toledo in the distance. R.K. was his usual gregarious self. "Aline!" he called with a friendly wave, "Over here."

Gradually the long table filled up; four menservants in high-buttoned grey-and-green flannel uniforms began to serve us. The enormous meal never seemed to end. Paella, seafood flown up from Málaga, *cigalas, chanquetes, percebes* (unusual barnacles found on ocean rocks), plus chateaubriand, cheeses, classic desserts like *brazo gitano* (gypsy's arm) and the unbelievably sweet *tocino del cielo*. Then cognac, coffee, cigars. . . . A banquet fit for a Roman emperor. It wasn't until four-fifteen that we rose from the table.

When we arrived at Luis's butt, he examined the weapon R.K. had loaned him. "A nice gun," he said as he turned it over, then lifted the shiny steel shotgun, broke it, and looked down the barrel.

"Well, well!" he let out a sharp whistle, while still peering inside the barrel. His face had changed color. "If I hadn't looked," he glanced back at the weapon, "this gun would have exploded when I pulled the trigger."

Luis handed it to me. "Fortunately, my grandfather taught me to inspect the gun barrel before each drive. Take a look."

About six inches down the right barrel was an obstruction. "Oh, my God!" I cried, astounded. "Your loader might never have noticed." I shuddered. "You're lucky, my darling. But R.K. is, too. The first person to shoot this gun would have had his face blown to bits."

Luis's loader was now examining it. He jammed a long, thin cleaning rod into the obstructed barrel. "Won't budge," he said. But he kept pushing, and eventually a small pellet fell to the ground. We all dove to pick it up.

Luis retrieved it and stood up, rolling the round, hard ball slowly between his forefinger and thumb. The three of us stared at the tiny object. "Amazing. It looks to me as if someone deliberately stuffed a pebble in there so tight that it wouldn't fall out." He passed the tiny stone to Gregorio. "What do you think, Gregorio?" he asked.

Gregorio rolled it between his two forefingers. "*Sí*. It's a small pebble, Señor Conde," he answered. "But it was in so tight, it's hard to imagine that it just fell in. I agree. Looks like someone jammed the damned thing there on purpose. A very dangerous game," Gregorio mumbled.

"Yes," Luis murmured. "I wonder what R.K. will think when I tell him."

"Luis, do you realize that R.K. himself could well have been the one who put the pebble in that gun?"

Luis shrugged. "He has no reason to harm me. If this was not an accident, it's someone after R.K. I'll have to show him this weapon, so he can be on guard."

As things turned out, Luis never had the opportunity.

Luis and most of the others kept shooting until it was too dark to shoot anymore (the fifth drive had to be abandoned). By then the Rhodentuses had already left for the house in one of the jeeps. Luis and I spent another half hour picking up his birds; and we were among the last to leave the field. Once back at the house, we went immediately to our room to rest and bathe before dressing for dinner. Later while Luis was zipping up my black velvet evening dress, he motioned for me to look out the window. "Look, darling," he said, and pushed aside the green silk draperies. A silver helicopter was lifting up into the dark sky. In the light from the house we could see the treetops fluttering as the machine hovered momentarily above the garden, then whisked off into the night, until only a vague hum and a light no bigger than a star remained. Then these, too, were gone.

At dinner we learned that R.K. had received an urgent call from Germany and had left abruptly. So Luis had no opportunity to mention the rigged gun to him.

As soon as we returned to Madrid, however, Luis sent R.K. a letter describing the incident. Surprisingly, he received no answer. Several weeks later, consequently, he tried calling. And he was finally able to reach R.K.

Though he was predictably shocked, and he apologized profusely, R.K. told Luis that he found it almost impossible to believe that the pebble had been deliberately placed in his gun. That would have meant someone wanted to harm him, and he didn't believe he had enemies that cared enough to go to such extremes.

"And yet," Luis told me later, "I could tell R.K. was protesting too much. Unless I am very mistaken, the man was seriously shaken."

Chapter 14

Several weeks later we left for St. Moritz and the Horse Race on Ice. Luis was representing an association there called "Gentlemen Riders" (he was president of the organization's Spanish branch). Although he had attended the Race on Ice before, this was to be my first chance to see that marvelous event. Normally I would have been thrilled, but by the time we left, my thoughts were focused on my reunion with Serge Lebedev.

I would never forget the time we had stood in the souk in Marrakech together, and Serge had bent his tall blond head low, trying to kiss me while he whispered words of affection. I had been stunned. The Russian was attractive to many women, but I was in love with my husband and placed our relationship immediately on a purely friendly basis. Fortunately, he understood that I was not interested in a romance with him, and we remained close friends. In fact, our friendship was a major element in his defection.

Of course, although I was going to be overjoyed at the chance to see my old friend again after quite a few years, his attraction today was that he was an expert on European terrorists. And he also knew much about one of my other "old friends," Carlos.

When Luis and I arrived at the Hotel Palace, the note I expected from Serge was not there. This worried me. Europe was a dangerous place for a KGB defector. As usual, Luis did his best to calm my fears. That evening at the opening ball I relaxed in my husband's arms and nearly forgot my concerns as we waltzed beneath the silver chandeliers.

When there was still no news the next morning, I really became alarmed. Luis left early for the races with the understanding that I would join him later. He kissed the top of my head as I was drinking my morning tea and gazing at the snowy landscape beyond our balcony.

"Don't worry, *guapa*, Serge has had more perilous destinations than a rendezvous in St. Moritz. He'll show up," said Luis, pulling on a heavy woolen coat and tucking a thick cashmere scarf into the collar.

"You're right," I said, forcing a smile. "See you later, darling."

After he left, I called down to the front desk. Still no message. Perhaps I had misunderstood the plans. But no, I remembered speaking to Jupiter after Paco's shoot: He set the date and the procedure—December 19, a note to be left with the concierge, arranging a meeting. Finally, unable to wait a moment longer, I dressed in my warmest clothes, a long muskrat fur coat and a bushy fur hat, and left for the races.

St. Moritz during a heavy snowfall in the dead of winter was a sight to behold. Like a frozen fairyland, its ornate, old buildings were wrapped in cottony swirls. Hunched figures bustled along whitened avenues, heads down and moving quickly from one place to the next. I began to descend the winding path that led to the oval lake where the race would take place. Despite the challenging weather, there was a sense of festivity, a holiday spirit that leavened my heavy disappointment. Skiers trying to walk in their clumsy boots slipped and slid down the steep street, keeping their skis in precarious balance on their shoulders.

Suddenly, I heard a strange commotion behind me. When I turned to look, I saw a man, swaddled in more fur than seemed possible, making a sharp, hairpin turn on a tiny sled. Then, careening down the path, making pedestrians leap out of his path, he yanked at the steering mechanism, uselessly. It was obvious he had lost control of the thing and was headed straight for disaster. There was no determining where he would end up, so instinctively I leapt toward a side path. But as if some inner radar had picked up my movement, the sled veered off its course and headed directly for me. With horror I watched as the huge furry creature loomed larger and larger. Then at the last possible second, the tiny sled did a backflip and the man landed at my feet, snorting and coughing and letting out a stream of American curses.

He stood up, kicked the sled as if that were the cause of all his troubles, slapped the snow furiously off the black fur of his coat, and then whipped off the coon hat he wore, whacking at it with his mittened hand. The removal of his hat let loose a wild bush of suspiciously dyed-looking blue-black hair. The hair framed a face pink with irritation and cold.

"God damn it to hell, Aline!" he bellowed in a thick Texas accent, "I thought you'd never leave that godforsaken hotel of yours."

Is this a bad dream? I asked myself. Who is this mad Texan on a sled? How does he know me? I looked at the man with frank astonishment, when a familiar light in his blinking blue eyes clutched at my heart.

"No . . ." I said slowly, staring hard, "it can't be."

"Bet your backside, Miss Aline, the one and only Steve Lederer. That's right, keep a grip on that name now." He reached into the jumble of fur for some inner pocket and extracted, with difficulty, a damp business card that pronounced him the travel editor and chief foreign correspondant for the *Austin Statesman*. I had to laugh. The transformation couldn't have been more complete. And it wasn't his body; it was his manner. I couldn't wait to present our old friend to Luis. He would be wonderfully amused.

I understood how necessary the change had been. Serge's KGB colleagues circulated everywhere in Europe, and Serge himself was still very much on their most wanted list. Having been a KGB agent for many years, he knew so many terrorists personally and was as familiar with their vicious operations. He believed that his personal knowledge was useless unless he was actually present on the scene. I admired his courage to risk encounters with the KGB and his old terrorist connections, and I was pleased to note that he had taken a few precautions at least.

"Serge, I mean Steve," I said quietly, but very, very happy to see him, "I've been worried about you." I reached out my hand and patted the bulky sleeve of his fur coat.

"Now, now, darlin', this is no time to be sentimental. I understand we have a horse race today! On ice no less. How d'you suppose those ponies keep their feet straight?"

This was too much. The last time I'd seen Serge—during his debriefing in Washington—he'd baffled his questioners with the gaps and strange leaps in his English. When things became too confusing, they had to resort to a translator. Now he was hurling words around like a crazed juggler.

"You mean you'd like to go to the race?" I was dying to talk to him; and the racetrack would be as convenient a place as any.

"Only if I can be your humble escort."

"My pleasure, good sir," I answered with a smile.

My gallant companion yanked his tiny sled out of the snowdrift where it had landed, hooked it under an elbow, and offered me his other arm. We had difficulty talking as we walked toward the lake; the snowfall had picked up, and the wind had increased. But from time to time, Serge would beam down at me; and in his twinkling face I caught the ghost of the lady-killer I remembered from Morocco.

"Your assassin friend, that man Carlos, is more dangerous than the guy I'm after," he said as we trudged through the huge drifts. "But the one I'm trailing—his name's Ali Amine—is no altar boy, that's for sure. He was a member of the PLO from the middle sixties. Then he had a falling out with Yasser Arafat and passed over to the PFLP. Politically, he's farther to the left than Carlos; and recently he's been forming a new radical group of his own. But he and Illitch have worked closely now and then. They've butchered lots of people together. Illitch," he repeated. "That's your friend Carlos's real name—Illitch Ramírez Sánchez. Carlos was a code name the KGB gave him. In Russian, it means 'young agent.'

"Perhaps it wouldn't be a bad habit to resume carrying your Baretta," he said then, changing briefly to French, the language he and I had always used with one another in the past. By switching to that tongue Serge confirmed what I already knew—that this meeting wasn't just a lark with an old buddy. It was an operational briefing.

"Knowledge is power, Miss Aline," he said in English, again with the flamboyant, Texas accent. I would have preferred that he had stayed with French, but I knew he was merely protecting his cover; someone was passing near us on the snowy footpath. "And that's what I'm here to give you—knowledge and power. You'll need plenty of both if it's Carlos the Jackal up there on that ridge."

By the time we arrived at the lake, a large crowd had already gathered. Stands for the spectators had been placed directly on the icy surface. And long stretches of pale-green canvas billowed out behind shelters that had been improvised to protect the fans from the harrowing wind. Every moment the weather was getting worse. Bad enough to make me wonder if the races would be canceled. Nevertheless, a small army of bundled sweepers was working hard to keep the ice clear.

Meanwhile, Luis, who was busy with the officials, waved and beckoned me to join him.

Though my husband was always the soul of courtesy, his jaw dropped open when he realized who my companion was. It was hard for him to see through Serge's Texas disguise and recognize the man who'd won his admiration for marksmanship during a shoot hosted by King Hassan in Morocco several years before. After the momentary shock wore off, however, he welcomed Serge and shook his hand with enthusiasm. Then he efficiently arranged seating where Serge and I could have an unimpeded view, as well as talk without being overheard.

Thoroughbreds in heavy blankets, their hooves encased in special shoes to keep them from slipping, were being led onto the track. Jockeys stamped their booted feet to stay warm. The ice looked especially treacherous. Blinding gusts of snow blew across the surface in tight swirls like miniature tornados. As we took in the scene, a man in a thick red parka arrived at our box with two steaming hot chocolates in plastic cups. Luis waved from below to let us know he hadn't forgotten us.

For a while we brought each other up to date. "You can't imagine the difficulties of those initial years of what I thought would be freedom," Serge said sadly, speaking in French. "I felt like a prisoner in the USA. Your chums in the Agency didn't believe anything I told them. It was a no-win life for me: They expected me to tell them everything I knew about all my old KGB friends; and they were generally disagreeable when I did not. I don't like squealers." Serge rubbed his hand over his mouth in a gesture I remembered. "But after a time, I guess, they realized that my story checked out. And I got some respect, too, when I explained why I had refused to talk about some KGB people whom I didn't want to betray . . . there are good people in any organization, Aline, as you know. And bad people. So finally, when I had been drained of all the information my poor old brain could hold, they set me loose . . . it was about two years ago. The Agency found me a job on a local newspaper where I cover foreign affairs, and which permits me to do odd jobs for them now and then. With my new name and a good job, I now have friends. And can go around without feeling like a hunted animal." He looked around thoughtfully. "That is, until today. I saw a couple of Soviet diplomats this morning whom I knew from my past life. You know the type, guys with beady eyes and titles like Assistant Commercial Attaché—low-level KGB officers looking for a way to make a score."

"And catching you would get them a high score?"

"Yeah," he sighed and gave his eyes an expressive roll, "it looks like that. It would be worth at least a promotion to them. And if they didn't recognize me this morning, I'd be very surprised. So please keep your eyes open for two fellows with black mink Russian hats and long heavy black coats. You can't miss them. They look like KGB heavies—just like you see in films."

The first race started up with a flurry of snow and flying ice, the thundering spectacle of thoroughbreds racing at top speed, as the ground actually seemed to slip away beneath them. I quickly understood why Luis thought so highly of this event. No other horse race was as dangerous as this one, or drew on such reserves of skill and courage . . . from both horses and jockeys. As I watched the beautiful animals and their riders grapple with the icy challenge, I thought, ruefully, how attractive danger could be, and how much of my life had been shaped by its seductive call.

That race ended without mishap. And after the cheering died down, Serge asked me to outline precisely recent events. I told him everything I'd seen and everything credible I'd heard, including the attack against Jupiter. And I spared no details. Experience had taught me that something that may seem insignificant to one person might be the precise key for someone else. I spoke quickly, and when I was finished, he sat in silence for a long time, deep in thought. Before he spoke again, the crew had swept the surface of the ice; and the next group of skittish horses was being led onto the frozen lake.

"Yes, that sounds like Carlos's style, all right," he said quietly, still in French. "As for the question of whether or not he mistook Derby for von Ridder, I have no information to give you. But I can tell you something about the beginning of his life to help you understand him." And as if to himself, he added, "What could that bastard want now?"

Serge sat back against the wooden seat, lifted the hot chocolate to his lips, and took a contemplative sip, "Imagine being fourteen years old, living far away from your parents in a foreign country, and being taught to kill your roommate with a knife. That was the kind of assignment they gave kids like Carlos in the training camps in Cuba. Carlos's Communist father sent him there from Caracas every summer, like American kids go to a Boy Scout camp. And Little Illitch was always the best at murder. From an early age, he excelled in handling weapons and explosives; and he became a crack shot. But he developed another side as well. At seventeen, he went to live with his mother in London, and he became a fullfledged playboy. His mother is quite attractive, so I'm told, and also a socialite . . . while his 'revolutionary' father lives an austere, simple life. The parents' marriage broke apart, apparently, because of this difference. Illitch, meanwhile, took after his mother; and they are still very close. She even seems to put up with his terrorist activities; and—oddly—he kept these secrets from his father, until they became public knowledge.

"Later, my former masters kicked him out of the Patrice

Lumumba University in Moscow, because he was too bourgeois for them (his Communist father sent him too much money to suit the Bolsheviks); and he was setting a bad example for the other students.

"Later still, he caught the eye of Waddi Haddad . . . that was in 1970 at the Chatila guerrilla training camp near Beirut . . . and Haddad brought him into the PFLP, the most radical of the Palestinian terrorist groups at that time."

"I know something about that part of young Carlos's life," I said. "I read a CIA background paper about him not long ago."

"Right," Serge said, "of course. But the one thing to remember about Illitch—this may or may not have been in the report—is that he enjoys killing. He loves it like a nymphomaniac loves sex."

In between races, I learned that in 1973 Carlos had worked for the PFLP in Paris. His job then was to establish a weapons and munitions depot for terrorist groups. He also supplied false identity papers and passports. He did the job well . . . so well that counterfeit papers became a Carlos specialty. "And another of his trademarks: Carlos often uses his women as accomplices."

"He goes through a lot of women?" I asked, thinking of Sofia Cabanellas.

"He likes loving women almost as much as he likes killing," Serge answered.

I wanted very much to raise the subject of Sofia with Serge, but the obstacle race interrupted our conversation. The wind had become so bitter by then that some of the jockeys were stuffing newspapers inside their jackets to keep warm. And then the flag went down and the pack was off. We watched enthralled as the horses took one jump after another. It seemed impossible that none of them fell on the slippery surface.

Even as we watched, the weather continued to grow colder. Serge bundled up more tightly and I pulled my fur up to my cheeks. But I managed to ask him, above the screaming of the wind, if he thought Carlos was pursuing Luis and me.

Serge became very serious. "You and Luis must take great care. It's always possible he's been studying your movements with the purpose of kidnapping you for ransom. He's also a mercenary, you know. A terrorist group could have hired him for that job." His eyes caught mine and held them. "Kidnapping is no joke, Aline. Even when the victim lives through it, the experience is shattering. Usually the person is held in something like an underground cell, measuring one and a half yards square. Food is dropped down once a day; a bucket for necessities is removed once a week." He shook his head in disgust. "It's even worse than I dare describe to you. The 'art' of the 'care and treatment' of kidnap victims is taught in terrorist camps in Cuba and Libya."

"Don't go on," I implored. "I've heard firsthand from families who've gone through this—in El Salvador, and in Spain, too," I said, then switched to another topic. "But what about Paco Cabanellas? I strongly suspect he was the Spaniard that Ava Gardner and I overheard talking to Carlos and the Arab that night in Bavaria."

"Have you investigated the source of Cabanellas's fortune?" Serge questioned. "He's a rich man, and his money is very recent. Who's paying him so generously and for what?" The wind was blowing the words into my ear. "The same goes for Carlos. Whatever Carlos is doing, you can be sure he's being well paid for his efforts. So who's paying him? Those are the things you have to find out, Aline. I happen to know that Carlos got five million dollars for his own pocket from two of those Arab oil magnates when he freed them after the OPEC hijacking a few years ago. Carlos handled that operation for the PFLP. And Gadhafi paid the PFLP fifty million for that job. Gadhafi denies this, but I believe it's true. Not bad, eh!" My Russian friend shook the snow from his hat and for the umpteenth time cleaned his glasses. "Easy money is a difficult disease to cure. That may be your friend Cabanellas's sickness."

As he spoke I remembered Carlos's gift to Cristina for her children's schools. Plainly that gesture had not been much of a financial sacrifice. At the same time, Alfonso Domínguez had told me that Carlos never had much money; and, though fastidious, he always wore the same suit to the office. No doubt he was maintaining a lifestyle to match his salary, so he would not endanger his cover.

Then I talked to Serge about Sofia. He smiled when I finished. "A fascinating young woman," he said, "and a mysterious one, as well. I'd like to meet her. As for your many questions about her, I don't really have any answers. There's simply not enough evidence. But did you ever think of some of the other possibilities? For example, perhaps that crazy girl might not be Paco's sister, after all," he mused. "And more to the point, she doesn't sound all that crazy to me. And further, Jupiter told you that there's a woman terrorist somehow involved in the activities you and I are concerned with. Do you think the beautiful and fascinating Sofia could belong to a terrorist group? . . . Could she be a trained terrorist herself? You should know that of the fourteen most wanted West German terrorists, ten are women. And in the United States, too, where there are also well-trained terrorist groups, there have always been as many women as men. The Weathermen . . . the Black Panthers . . . In all these organizations in your old country, women have proved to be tougher, more loyal, more fanatical, and to have greater perseverance and endurance than men."

"Perhaps, as a general rule," I said. "But no. That's not possible with Sofia." I was adamant. "This girl is very young."

"Don't fool yourself, Aline. Often the younger they are, the more radical they are," Serge said, making me feel like a novice. "You have to keep all these possibilities in mind."

The snow squall had passed. And looking across the *St. Moritzersee*, we now saw the horses being led onto the ice track for the feature race. A moment later, their blankets were being removed. Serge then explained that he would have to leave the minute the race was over. So we made a plan which would enable me to contact him later on from Spain if I needed to.

Then, with Serge at my heels, I rushed to join Luis, who I knew would want me with him to cheer on his entry. Since he was standing next to the track; Serge and I joined him on the ice. Assistants were attaching to the saddles parallel ropes that stretched out some thirty feet behind the horses. To these was attached a wooden handle. It was like the tow rope for waterskiing. But instead of a speedboat pulling a water-skier, the skier would be pulled by a horse. This unusual sport was called skijoring; and the race was about to begin.

And then the horses were off, lifting clouds of white powder that would have blinded the skiers if tarpaulins had not been stretched out behind their hoofs.

"Incredible!" Serge murmured, more to himself than to me. "Look at them go!"

Luis, on my other side, was absorbed in watching his horse. It lay third throughout most of the race. But coming out of the last turn, with our skier in a tuck. our jockey went to the whip and swung wide to take the lead. All three of us shouted with excitement as our horse pulled away from the field down the stretch. The race was ours, until half a furlong from the finish, our skier caught an edge of one ski and fell sliding along the track directly in front of the oncoming field. All we could see was clouds of snow, interspersed with heads of jockeys and horses. The crowd screamed. As the pack cleared the scene of our skier's fall, and bore down on the finish line, our horse, who had lost his jockey, too, kept running with the leaders, the skijoring rope and handles flying wildly. As the horses charged across the finish line, their icy spray made it impossible for us to see exactly what happened next. In the excitement of flying bodies and skis shooting through the air, I did not notice when Serge jumped out onto the track. Suddenly I saw him dodging horses and skiers; he seized the tow rope of our riderless horse and was dragged across the frozen surface, twirling dangerously as the frenzied animal continued running. The controlled weight of my friend gliding over the ice began to slow Luis's horse until it finally stopped on the far side of the track, frightened and dangerous. As Serge gently patted and soothed the animal, I marveled at his courage, just one more example of the outstanding abilities of this remarkable man. Then I remembered that Serge had been on the Soviet Union's equestrian team at one time.

Luis looked at me in amazement. "Your friend is incredible. That could have been a real tragedy. I'm always amazed how horses avoid fallen riders. And why another skier did not crash into him . . . hitting him with the tip of a ski at that speed! Thank God our skier is not hurt. It could have been fatal." He looked around. "Where is Serge now?" The horses and riders were at the opposite end of the track, and Serge had disappeared.

I turned to look for Serge, and was terrified to see just behind me two men in black fur hats and long black coats. With a jolt I realized that Serge must have seen them before he jumped into the tangle of horses and ropes. "Oh Serge," I said to myself, "you devil! It took a great deal of courage to do what you just did. But it wasn't altogether an act of pure heroism, either. . . ."

Chapter 15

Spring and early summer vanished like a desert mirage. Friends visited from America. Luis and I attended parties that started after ten at night. When there was flamenco, often we didn't get to bed until four or five in the morning. During the hectic bustle of weekend house parties in the country, trips to Paris, and guests coming and going, I hardly heard mention of Paco Cabanellas or his mysterious sister (Paco and Inge, it seems, were spending most of their time in Paris and Barcelona). At the Fair in Sevilla, however, I caught a glimpse of them, and Luis and I talked briefly with them early one morning while watching flamenco.

During that conversation, Paco dropped a tremendous bombshell: Nancy and R. K. Rhodentus had divorced. And now only God knew where R.K. was, Paco said. Nancy certainly didn't; R.K. had simply disappeared . . . though both Paco and Nancy suspected that he had gone off with another woman. In any event, Nancy was heartbroken. The news astounded Luis and me. For the Rhodentuses had seemed so happy. It also seemed odd to us that he left her; for, if either left the other, it looked to us as if she would have been the one to leave him. Later, whenever Luis and I chatted about the breakup of the Rhodentuses, we always commented on the very strange coincidence that von Ridder's and R.K.'s fate had taken such an abrupt change so quickly. Of those we'd met at that wedding, they had been the people we liked the most. And now, one was dead, we didn't know where the other was, and we would probably never see him again.

After that meeting with Paco, his path and mine did not cross again until August. Naturally, I wrote what I hoped was an affectionate note to Nancy, trying to cheer her up. And she wrote me back immediately to thank me and to reconfirm that she was terribly upset. She then went on to say that she still hoped to see us in the summer. That was the last I heard from her.

Meanwhile, Serge did not contact me; and I had no need to contact him. But as always, I continued to provide Jupiter with reports on various matters. During our first conversation after the Race on Ice, I asked if Serge had safely avoided the KGB officers we saw in St. Moritz. To my great relief, it turned out that he had.

As for my one-time friend Carlos Evertz, for a few hectic but blessedly unexciting months, he might have dropped off the face of the Earth. Foolishly, I came to think that he would never appear in my life again.

LUIS AND I usually stayed at our home on the southern coast of Spain during the month of August. Every year, we looked forward to the drive along the rocky, mountainous coast from Málaga to Marbella, and arriving at our house.

Luis and I designed the house ourselves, in Moroccan style. It was a whitewashed stucco building, with a lot of white marble stretching over the ground floor, and with a pair of Arabic domes above it. One was over our bedroom, the other was over Luis's study; and a terrace lay between the two rooms. Flowers grew luxuriously in our gardens; and they were especially brilliant in the closed-in patios of graceful alabaster columns and arched doorways. A large fountain splashed in the central patio. And banana trees and vines of jasmine grew in profusion. On the other side of the house, a lawn sloped down to a sandy beach. From the beach, the house stood like a rare, delightful shell, dazzlingly white, its contours and lines strikingly beautiful. Below the house, the Mediterranean was blue and placid, while the Rock of Gibraltar could be seen in the distance, looking like a prehistoric beast rising from the depths. On a clear day we could also see two low humps of Morocco's coast lying like a lazy camel in the far distance. Behind us soared the mountains, rocky and green, with the jagged peaks of the Montaña Blanca silhouetted against a sky of intense azure.

That August, we settled in quickly, and our vacation began in earnest. But our easy times were not to last long. Sometime that spring, John Derby had bought a small apartment nearby in the Port of Banus, and he made brief visits there now and then. Shortly after we arrived in Marbella, John called to invite us to the Marbella Beach Club for dinner. The sound of his measured voice made me listen attentively, as always. "It's important for you to come," he said. "I have a surprise for you; a friend I want you to talk to."

I wondered whom he could be referring to, but I sensed it would be no use to ask. "I'll check with Luis, John. But we are free; and I'm sure he'd be delighted."

"See you tomorrow then . . . at the Beach Club. About eleven." He rang off.

As offhandedly as possible, I told my husband, but he nevertheless raised an eyebrow. "Dinner with the boss, eh?" he joked. I knew he was remembering our bet from many months before . . . so long ago that I wondered if we still had a wager.

Marbella was discovered and then developed by Prince Alfonso Hohenlohe, who had the foresight to realize when he went there in the late forties that the beautiful little fishing village nestled between mountains, with groves of pine trees going down to the sea, had great potential for tourism. But now, unhappily, the new highway through the town, and the overabundance of tourists had greatly changed its sleepy, local atmosphere. Fewer fisherman now pushed their boats out through the low waves at dusk. Instead, many worked on the yachts that crowded the Puerto Banus harbor, like silent, elegant gulls. At night, the lights blazed till three in the morning—from the shops and the rows of frosty-white Andalusian-style buildings—illuminating the water like hundreds of brilliant moons, visible for miles.

Alfonso Hohenlohe's Marbella Beach Club was elegant yet picturesque, with low, red-tiled, white bungalows surrounded by tropical gardens of jasmine and banana trees. Alfonso had attracted a mix of wealthy aristocrats, movie stars, famous golfers, musicians and billionaires, converting Spain's relatively unknown southern coast into the most glamorous and exclusive summer resort in Europe. The Beach Club was the social hub of the town; and our dinner there that night with Jupiter, contrary to Luis's expectations—and, of course, my own—passed without incident. The friend Jupiter had mentioned on the phone did not appear.

The meal was pleasant. As soon as we were served, Luis asked Jupiter if he now knew whether the men who assaulted him in Germany had blown his cover, or if the attack had been a matter of mistaken identity. Jupiter merely shrugged, indicating he was still uncertain on that point. But I sensed that his mind was focused elsewhere. Afterward we walked down to the nightclub, which was built on logs suspended over the sandy beach. When the tide was in, small waves lapped at the pilings, making an agreeable rhythmic rumble. That night the yellow glow from the club's lanterns spilled onto the waves below, gilding the whitecaps and giving the surface a tortoise-shell sheen. Pebbles and sand along the shoreline tumbled back and forth as the low waves came and went.

Inside, the club was dimly lit, with candles on each table, and a pale glow from lanterns hanging over the open sides. A quartet of musicians was playing—guitar, piano, bass, and drums. And in a far corner, a bartender, surrounded by rows of gleaming, multicolored bottles, shook a silver cocktail mixer. As we sat down, the band finished their set and took a break; Luis lit a cigarette, and spotting a friend, excused himself.

When we were alone, Jupiter immediately told me part of what was on his mind. Since we had kept up to date through periodic telephone calls, I did not expect any really sensational news. "Today, this afternoon to be exact," John started, "I spoke to Jerry in Madrid. He has just received information about some crates that have been transported from German factories. According to their labels, they contain underground pipes for oil pipelines. These

crates are now in the port of Málaga awaiting shipment to Libya."
He paused dramatically. "Now there is a chance, only a chance, but
the shipment could be calutrons, not underground pipes! This
would be an exciting breakthrough, if it is true . . . just what we've
been looking for!"

"Oh!" I exclaimed. "That is great news! You've been working
since last October to find the people involved in this. Do you know
the name of the Spanish company that is handling the deal?"

"The transportation company is one we have been investigating.
Until today we had no evidence that the company dealt in anything
illegal; but now that we have these tips, we are very suspicious of
them, and excited. If the tips prove correct, it will be the first time
we've successfully tracked COCOM material into Spain."

"What's the name?" I repeated.

"You're going to be amazed and . . . pleased," Jupiter grinned. He
was taking his time. Impatiently, I resigned myself to wait.

"Is the name Transportes Inter-Med, S.A., familiar to you?"

"No," I answered. "As a matter of fact, I'm disappointed. I expected it would be Paco Cabanellas's company, and that he would
be the Spaniard you've been looking for."

"Well, don't jump to conclusions. This company uses a variety of
names. Each one controls a different business. There is one master
company controlling the others. You may be more familiar with
another name. This change of names on pro forma invoices and for
tax purposes has helped the owners to camouflage shipments. The
important detail, however, is that although we do not yet know the
buyer or the seller of the material we are watching, we do know the
name of the owner of the cover company."

By this time I was frankly annoyed and frowning. Jupiter noticed.
"As always your talent for detecting the guilty impresses me. You
were right again. The owner of Transportes Inter-Med is registered
as Cabanellas. Francisco Cabanellas."

A feeling of satisfaction swept over me. When months ago Jupiter
had told me that his investigations of Paco had not turned up anything unusual, I had not been convinced. He had said then that
Paco's transportation company, Exportaciones Mediterraneas, was
mainly involved in the shipment of automobile parts. So he had lost
interest in obtaining more information on him.

"But," he went on, "although Cabanellas owns the transportation company, as far as we know, it is merely a go-between. What
we're interested in are the names of other people involved."

"John, have you been able to find out if Cabanellas's other company has been shipping calutrons also?"

"No, we do not know that. This is the first time we were able to pick up anything suspicious at all. And, mind you, we're still not completely certain about our information. Those big containers have to be opened; but we have a reliable agent in Libya who'll confirm what's inside when the containers arrive there."

As he talked, Jupiter was focusing his attention across the room. When I saw who was there, I understood why. Inge Schmidt, Nancy Rhodentus, and Paco and Sofia Cabanellas were sitting at a table together. They spotted us as we were looking at them, and waved. And we waved back.

When we had first arrived in Marbella we heard that the Rhodentuses' new yacht had docked at the port of Banus some weeks before, and that the Señora would be arriving soon. So we were pleased to learn that R.K. had at least left Nancy well off. But I had not heard yet that she was here.

"I'm surprised to see Nancy," I said. "I didn't know she had arrived."

"She's been here for several days," John said, "keeping company with the others over there." He then made a gesture with his head. "I think they've adopted her. But who's the man joining them? I haven't seen him before."

I followed his glance. At first I didn't recognize the fellow. The sleek black hair was longer and thicker than I remembered, and I couldn't see the face at all. But by the time he sat down, I knew who he was. Tonight, as was his custom, he was well dressed, in a pale linen jacket, a pink shirt open at the neck, and a print silk foulard.

"That's a Greek called Maniatis," I answered.

John turned to me. "Now that it turns out your hunch about Cabanellas was right, I need you to get me more information on him. We want to know Paco's movements, who he talks to, something about his friends—you know by now what I want. What we're especially interested in is the person who buys the stuff in Germany, who pays the bill."

Suddenly John Derby stood up and waved to a new arrival at the door. A man dressed in an ivory-colored linen suit made his way across the room to our table. He wore slightly tinted aviator-style glasses, so his large eyes appeared like startled tropical fish. He had thick brown hair, severely parted on the right side and held in place with a considerable amount of lotion. Beneath a beaky nose, he sported a thick mustache.

Jupiter barely smothered a laugh as the stranger leaned over and with exaggerated courtesy explained how enchanted he was to meet me, in English with a slight Mediterranean accent that I placed as northern Italian. Baffled, I looked at Jupiter. Was this creature the old friend he had alluded to?

Without being invited, the man slipped into the chair beside me and signaled the waiter to take his order. All the while Jupiter silently watched the performance unfold. His attitude tipped me off. The stranger removed his glasses, rubbed hard at his eyes, and then turned to look at me full on before putting them back on again.

"Oh!" I exclaimed, half in delight, half in exasperation. "I can't believe you, Serge! What have you done to yourself?"

"Not so loud, Aline," said Jupiter, laughing.

Serge was absolutely delighted that I was unable to penetrate his new disguise.

The waiter arrived with Serge's Campari and soda, obviously a drink to match his new Italian identity.

"Who is that guy, Aline?" he said, nodding toward Nicky. "I think I've seen him someplace before. We bumped into each other outside, and I had the eerie feeling I was familiar to him as well. God forbid."

I explained what I knew of Nicky. Though both Serge and Jupiter listened carefully, my information didn't strike any chords. At one point Nicky turned his large lion's head directly toward me and stared. Though he couldn't possibly overhear me at that distance, something in his appraising expression chilled me to the bone. I remembered what Nancy had said about him at La Romana.

"He's a womanizer," I said, in conclusion.

Serge looked at me abruptly, and I knew I'd finally hit the right note. "Tell me more," he said quietly.

"Well, Nancy Rhodentus had an affair with him before she met R.K. And the affair may well have continued after their marriage. But she is not the only woman in Nicky's life." Then I told him about the incident at the shoot last November when Luis saw Nicky and Nancy kissing; and also about Nancy's somewhat questionable explanation of that event to me the next day.

One glance toward the party across the dance floor made Nancy's words to me then even more questionable than before. Nicky was seated between Nancy and Inge on the banquette. Both looked radiant. Nicky's arm rested affectionately around Nancy's shoulders, and she was talking happily to the two of them.

"Aline," Serge said, still staring hard at Nicky, "what you've said is a help, although I still can't place the guy. But something you described rings a bell. It will come to me." He glanced again at Nicky. I had faith in Serge's hunches and was curious to know what he would come up with.

"Anyway, I'm not here to quiz you about strangers. Has Jupiter filled you in?"

"Jupiter is having a very good time at my expense," I said.

"Sorry, Aline, I couldn't resist," John said. "Besides it's important to test Serge's cover. It helps to know you couldn't spot him even at close range."

"Yes, it's true," said Serge. "But I'm here in Marbella, tracking that major nasty, Ali Amine. As it happens, Ali is aware that I am on his case. An informer in Cairo turned out to be a double agent. And Ali knows me; he and I had dealings back in my KGB days. So it would be wise if I was not as instantly recognizable as—say—John Wayne.

"Anyway, my friend Ali is by all reports here on the coast, as we speak. And he's been very busy the last six months. He's formed his own faction of the PFLP, and we fear he is targeting Americans, and plans a strike someplace around the Mediterranean. He's here in southern Spain, buying weapons and explosives for that operation."

"None of our people knows this coast as you do, Aline," said Jupiter.

"And no one could be more helpful," added Serge.

I felt my stomach knot as I realized what they were asking. They didn't need to spell it out for me. I gave my husband a quick glance just then. He was joking with the musicians across the room. Of course, he would be far from happy with me if I agreed to help. But what else could I do? I looked at Serge, who politely examined his fingernails while I thought over their request. The musicians were meanwhile mounting the bandstand to start the next set. And Luis greeted other friends and was now joining them for a drink. He caught my eye, his glance asking, "Do you mind?" I smiled back, nodding, and feeling even more chagrined than before in the face of his consideration.

Serge excused himself and crossed the dance floor, presumably to find the men's room, while Jupiter and I sat in contemplative silence at the table. As I watched Serge's lean form navigate the tightly packed tables, I noticed that he walked with a limp.

"What's wrong with him?" I asked.

"He's had a pretty rough time. He didn't mention to you that he and Ali had an encounter in Cairo, and that bastard is deadly with a knife. He cut Serge pretty badly. There were complications. He almost bled to death. Ali didn't intend for our friend to survive."

"Now you tell me, John!" I cried. "Why am I the last to find out something like this?"

"Sorry, Tiger," Jupiter answered, "but I thought it was best not to say anything." His tone I knew well: "Don't bother asking for explanations," it said.

"Can't someone else track this Ali? After all, hasn't Serge been through enough?"

"Absolutely," said Jupiter, "as far as the brass is concerned he could retire and live comfortably for the rest of his life. But he insists on seeing this through. And there's not another agent who can touch him for knowledge and experience on this particular case, and he knows it."

"Sounds like a personal vendetta to me," I said, looking Jupiter straight in the eye. "Isn't that considered the best reason for an agent to be taken off a job?"

"Not in his case. You'll see when you talk to him. There's a shared personal hatred between those two. Ali is totally amoral, would sell his sister or cut his best friend's throat if the price was right. Serge considers his almost fatal wound part of his work. It's an attitude I don't entirely understand; but it sure as hell makes him a 'steely' agent."

There was another uncomfortable silence between us, as the band began to strum the opening bars to a breezy samba.

"He really needs your help," said Jupiter.

I gave him an irritated glance. I felt he was pushing harder than usual. Just then, Serge, who was on his way back to our table, was intercepted by Sofia Cabanellas. She moved close to him and all but wrapped herself around him. Then facing him, she began to move sensuously to the Latino rhythm of the band. Serge was flustered at first, but soon picked up the languorous beat and pressed his body close to hers. I was unprepared to see his easy vulnerability; his face seemed to crack open like an egg as he closed his eyes to the real world, totally absorbed by his partner. If the "steely" agent had an Achilles' heel, I thought, he was certainly displaying it now for all the world to see. But fortunately a dancing couple at this nightclub didn't attract much attention. And only one other pair of eyes seemed as concentrated as my own on that scene. Nicky Maniatis sat back against the banquette, oblivious to the animated conversation Inge and Nancy were carrying on across his ample chest. Steadily, he watched Sofia, following her every move, as if he was controlling her; as the puppet is controlled by the puppeteer. Had he sent her out to intercept Serge? I wondered.

Jupiter nudged me, and shifted his eyes in Serge's direction.

"All right, all right, I'll do it," I said, watching Sofia's bare shoulders pulse to the rhythm as her eyes drank up my friend.

Jupiter smiled and sat back in his chair. "I knew you would," he said.

Weaving my way between the dancing couples, I reached Sofia and Serge and joined in their samba, making a trio. Sofia smiled and continued her sinuous movements; and I gradually directed our little dancing circle toward her table. Before we arrived, Nicky was on the floor facing Sofia and moving to her beat. The tune had changed; now the band was blaring out a slow mambo. Placing my hands on Serge's shoulder, I directed him toward our table on the other side of the room. But to my surprise, he slid his arm firmly around my waist and began to move me sensuously around the floor. His long slinky steps amazed me; his body flowed with the beat; and his legs and hips hugged mine in a way that made me respond as theatrically as he. The two of us moved to the sensual rhythm as if we had been dancing together in salsa shows for years. I was having such a good time that I didn't have a chance to wonder how an ex-KGB officer happened to be such a fabulous dancer.

When we returned to the table, Jupiter kidded Serge that he had chosen the wrong career, and that he would get no more sympathy from him about his accident. "Your health must be excellent," John said. "I don't even know the names of the dances you and Aline did, but I can tell you that you two would be very successful running a dance studio."

Serge laughed. "Well, when I was a boy I wanted to be a dancer, even tried ballet; but they didn't let me continue." He turned to me. "My partner could also make her living dancing if other things fail. But look," he gestured across the floor. The orchestra had stopped playing, but Sofia had continued to dance by herself, swaying her lovely body with hands entwined over her head. She was such a splendidly exciting dancer that people had opened up a space for her so she could perform more easily. Nicky was clearly delighted, even though he had been shunted off to the side with the other observers. "I could lose my head over that woman," Serge added.

"Perhaps you don't realize that woman is Paco's crazy sister," I said. "It even occurred to me that the Greek might have sent her out to seduce you."

"Well, she succeeded," Serge mumbled, as he continued watching Sofia.

"I think Nicky is too interested himself in Sofia to sic her after Serge," Jupiter suggested.

Our friend did not seem to be listening. Then he interrupted us. "Yeah," Serge lifted a long finger, "now I remember the guy. He looks like a fellow I sold two Soviet helicopters to about ten years ago. He wasn't a terrorist, as far as I know; he wanted the helicopters for private reasons. Aline's information that he is a womanizer tipped me off. And now watching him on the floor, it came to me. If he's the guy I think he is, he was almost killed for fooling around with our Soviet ambassador's wife."

Serge's eyes continued to follow Sofia's dance; and Jupiter began to pull Serge's leg about her. He kept joking with him until Sofia was actually dancing directly in front of our table, swaying her hips, her pelvis, her legs to the edge of eroticism. Then she stopped and leaned over Serge, giving him a voluptuous kiss. Laughing, she returned to her table, leaving a speechless Serge.

"Ahem," said a chortling Jupiter. "Now that the charming Sofia has left us for the moment, can you give us an analysis of Ali Amine's plans, Serge? You said he's putting together a huge quantity of explosives? What for? Do you know?"

With visible effort, Serge switched his attention to Jupiter. "The supply of potential targets in Europe is virtually inexhaustible," Serge answered. "It only has to be very public, very visible, and offer a ready supply of casualties. And be aware that Ali is a man of demonstrated imagination . . . and ruthlessness. He does not think small. If he can bring this operation off . . . if he can set off all the explosives he is said to be assembling, then the result could be catastrophic, monstrous." Jupiter listened attentively. "To make my job of tracking the suppliers more difficult," Serge went on, "Ali Amine is almost impossible to recognize. And I'm afraid he knows I didn't die when he knifed me. I trust he won't recognize me before I find him."

"You're the only one we have who can recognize him," John said.

"It's not easy," Serge answered. "He's an artist at disguises, and he has become more daring than ever."

Just then, Luis returned to the table. And I was glad to see that he had as much trouble recognizing Serge as I did earlier.

The orchestra had returned to the small podium, and Paco and Inge rose to dance as soon as the band started to play. As I watched them, Paco's big, dark hand was like a tarantula creeping over Inge's naked back. My spine seemed to surge with electricity at the thought of her proximity to a man who might be dealing with terrorists. Yet I could not warn her. Meanwhile, his strong body dwarfed her smaller form, and their faces in profile were a study in contrasts: his dark features next to her pale porcelain skin. The band changed to a rhumba, and Paco glued his body to Inge's, their hips moving erotically together. Inge looked ecstatic.

A few moments into the new song, Nancy and Nicky joined the others on the floor. But even though Nicky's body pulsated with uncanny smoothness to the salsa beat, she was as awkward that night as she had been at the dance at Paco's shoot. Nancy's attempts to follow his lead were so clumsy that after a few minutes he led her back to the table and moved out again with Sofia in hand. The band was now playing a merengue. From the moment Nicky pulled Sofia close in a sensuous embrace, the two looked like professionals. His lithe form was twisting and moving suggestively; and Sofia swayed her hips with an abandon that again attracted glances.

Serge's eyes followed mine, and remained riveted on the couple. Then he asked me about Nancy, who was sitting alone at the table, and I explained who she was.

His eyebrows rose in surprise, when I told him about R.K.'s "disappearance." "That's an unusual twist. He skipped before somebody could get him. Sounds to me as if the people you met at that wedding are dropping off like flies," he said.

"You're exaggerating. Nobody killed Rhodentus; he just disappeared. Probably with another woman. That's usually the case when a man leaves his wife and pays her a good alimony."

He shrugged. "Any news of Carlos?"

"No. None, thank God," I said.

Paco and Inge were still dancing. As the band burst forth with the final crescendo of the set, Paco lifted Inge in his arms. She laughed with delight; the song came to an end, and they stood together, applauding the band enthusiastically.

As the dancers returned to their tables, Jupiter began to tell Luis about his golf game that afternoon with a close friend of ours. While we listened attentively, Serge silently rose from the table. I watched as he crossed the floor to where Sofia now sat alone. And a few moments later, I was startled to see Serge leading Sofia out the door. "Well," I wondered, "this doesn't look like a duty in the line of his work."

Later in the ladies' room, Nancy and I were side by side, looking into the long mirror while we refreshed our makeup. I was glad to have a chance to talk to her alone. Since my conversation with Jupiter in regard to Paco's company possibly being involved in smuggling and because of her close friendship with Paco, she had suddenly become a worthy target for my attention.

After telling her how sorry Luis and I had been to hear about her divorce from R.K., I asked what we should do with R.K.'s gun, which we had so far been unable to return. Her enormous blue eyes opened wide. "Oh, Aline, I'd forgotten all about that gun. What luck nobody got hurt that day! Well, just hold on to it in case R.K. appears one day. For the time being, I still have no idea where he is. He just vanished. Such an incredible thing for a man I cared so much about."

As she began to brush her hair, I told her that she was young and would certainly find someone else who would make her happy. She put the brush in her bag and laid her hand on my arm. "I thought he was absolutely perfection," she said softly, "but now . . ." she lowered her head expressively. "I used to find it difficult to talk about him; but now I find I can face up to it. I miss R.K., but life has to go on. Nicky helps me, and other friends do also." Her eyes met mine then. "On the other hand, R.K.'s two sons have been horrible. Have you met them?" I shook my head no. "Utterly horrible," she repeated bitterly. Then she took a tube of mascara from her bag and turned back to the mirror, leaning in close to color the tips of her lashes. "They hated to see what a good marriage we had. R.K. loved me and was wonderful to me; and nothing they did could change that. Now they are delighted that he's left me." For a moment, I thought I saw tears welling in her eyes. But then she replaced the mascara in her handbag, and the impression faded. "And they're constantly putting lawyers after me, to take away the part of R.K.'s fortune that he agreed I should have." She shook her head, making her taffy-colored hair swing jauntily around her head. "Life can be so difficult sometimes."

"When did Nicky arrive?" I asked.

"Tonight." She turned a smiling face to me. "He's the perfect medicine for me, don't you think? R.K. was always a bit jealous of

Nicky although he had no reason to be, from my point of view. But maybe I'm especially vulnerable, after having been divorced so abruptly. What woman could resist Nicky's charm?''

Though I was fully aware that my next question was far from charitable, in view of what she was just then implying about her relationship with Nicky, some demon pushed me to ask her anyway: ''Remember when you and I were talking during Paco's shoot, and I told you there were a man and woman in Sofia's bedroom making love? Did you ever find out whether Nicky was the man? It seems to me they must have seen a lot of each other to be able to dance like that exhibition they just put on.''

Nancy's expression clouded. ''Oh, that terrible girl. Nicky only puts up with her for Paco's sake. She has no sense of shame, and she makes a ghastly spectacle whenever she appears in public. Don't people realize she's utterly out of her head when they see her dance like that? Nicky tells me he's totally unable to talk with her sensibly, and he merely gives in to her whims now and then to keep peace. Sofia is a real problem for all of us.''

''Why doesn't Paco put her in an institution, then?'' I asked.

''He wouldn't hear of it. His parents and a brother have died. And the others are no help. He pampers her, buys her the most expensive clothes, and treats her like royalty. Inge is, of course, desperate. She even says Sofia will end up destroying her love for Paco, that he pays more attention to his sister than to her . . . that he claims Sofia is more intelligent than she is, of all things. Imagine! He calls Sofia his princess.'' Nancy shook her head in disgust. ''I don't like to even talk about that silly girl.''

If I had known then what the next day would bring, I would have gone back to Nancy's table with her and talked to Paco and Inge before leaving. But when Nancy packed her makeup away in her evening bag and left the room, I made no effort to go with her. In fact, I didn't see her again that night. But at least I had learned some important facts: Nicky was clearly more than a little smitten by Sofia; and that was the cause of Nancy's jealousy. Nancy must be in love with Nicky, and for a very long time. As for Inge, she hated Sofia because Paco devoted so much time to her. Maybe Sofia was even trying to break up their engagement. Perhaps the beautiful seductress was the smartest of the three women and not crazy at all.

Chapter 16

The next day was Sunday, and Luis and I went to the bullfight in Málaga. It was hot and the traffic was unbearable; but the difficulty of finding a place to park and then the discomfort of getting bumped and squeezed by the mobs crowding into the ring was well worth it. The greatest bullfighter since Manolete was making a comeback. Antonio Ordoñez, a close friend, had retired at the height of his career. Now, after enormous popular request, he was returning to the ring for one day—an especially risky move for a matador. Electricity filled the sticky, mid-August air—as it always does in the middle of August, when the greatest bullfights of the season take place in Málaga.

In our *barreras*—ringside seats—we stood and looked around, the usual pastime before a fight. It was almost six-thirty, the fight would begin then, and the mobs were hysterically pushing to their seats before the doors banged shut. The one affair in Spain that always begins religiously on time! Up in the balconies local beauties were wearing mantillas; and below, in *barrera* seats, were Peter Viertel with his wife, Deborah Kerr. Also present was Lola Flores, the great flamenco dancer and singer, in a white lace mantilla, flapping her fan energetically while her black gypsy eyes took in the scene. When she saw me, she made a friendly gesture. Smiling inwardly, I basked in the familiar panorama surrounding me, sharing the crowd's fervor and enthusiasm.

Just as the gates closed, I was about to sit down when my eyes were drawn to a man about fifteen yards away. He was among the women in bright silk dresses and the men in shirtsleeves still surging to their seats; and he was climbing the steps to the *tendidos*—the seats above. I recognized the curly black hair, the black curved moustache, and the sloppy beard . . . and a wave of fear pierced me! He was wearing well-cut beige slacks; he was so close that I could tell his yellow shirt was silk. Beads of perspiration glistened on his nose, so the usual shiny sunglasses kept wanting to slide down it. This time I had no doubt. Carlos! Only yards away. I yanked on

Luis's sleeve. "Luis!" I whispered, not yet turning my eyes away from Carlos as he sped up the narrow passageway. "I've just seen Carlos." I pointed.

"Carlos?"

"The terrorist." In my excitement, I was talking too loud.

"Where? Where?" Luis was alert, but by now I could no longer see Carlos. He had disappeared into the swarm.

"Really darling, you have a mania about that fellow," he said, with a shrug. "You think he's everywhere. He's not here. You can be certain of that. It would be too risky for him."

"But he is here!" I answered. "On one of Carlos's visits to our house in Madrid, he told me that if Ordoñez ever made a comeback, he would go to see him no matter where."

At that moment, the shock of seeing Carlos was interrupted by the blaring of trumpets announcing the entry of the matadors and their *cuadrillas*—assistants—into the ring. Crowds disappeared as by magic, suddenly everyone was seated, and I turned to sit down, too.

The plaza became silent with anticipation . . . the band struck up a pasadoble . . . the doors on the opposite side of the arena opened, and the parade began—*matadores, picadores, banderilleros,* and *peónes*—all dressed in shiny colorful satin, beads, and sequins. Antonio was at the front. Slung over one shoulder and wrapped around his arm was his heavily embroidered cape, sparkling brightly in the sun. The matador's black *montera*—hat—sat straight over his black eyebrows, and the handsome face was dead serious. The three front-row matadors stepped forward across the golden sand in unison. Their shocking-pink stockings moving in time to the music, they walked straight to the president's box just above us, where they bowed deeply.

My thoughts about Carlos faded as Antonio's *mozo de espadas*—sword man—brought his maestro's blue embroidered cape and threw it over our *barrera*. It was customary that the matador would show this attention to one of his friends in a *barrera* seat. The "man of swords" was the matador's valet, and principal assistant who helped him dress for the ring, and who was in charge of his cape and swords.

The matadors then executed a few test swirls with their yellow and red capes, until the clarion call of trumpets heralded the entry of the first bull. All eyes were fixed on the double doors where twelve hundred pounds of raging fury was about to invade the ring.

How the beast entered the arena would show if he was brave enough to create sufficient excitement for a good fight.

The monster black bull roared in, snorting like a locomotive as he stormed past our seats. The crowd emitted a murmur of approval. Before us was only the empty arena and that wild, ferocious beast racing around looking for a victim. Then, dramatically, Antonio appeared from behind a small enclosure, lifting his bright red cape high in the air, fluttering it to attract the bull's attention. The crowd was like one person—breathless with anticipation. Now the bull attacked. The beast was easily four times the size and ten times the weight of Antonio.

It appeared that the animal would plow right into him at a tremendous speed—all that great bulk and those sharp huge horns were driving to plunge into the man, to tear him to bits. Then, *swish*. The bull raced through the cape, raising it in the air as if it were chiffon. Antonio stood, his feet clamped to the sand, motionless as a statue. But in one split second, the animal whipped around and was after his quarry again, more ferocious, more determined than ever to tear him to bits. The moment was intense, compelling, hypnotizing.

As I had often been before, once again I was caught up in the incredible beauty of a man's courage in the face of violent death. Antonio pulled the cape closer to his body; and just as the beast reached the heavy cloth, the famous matador twisted, wrapping the cape around himself, leaving the animal plunging into open air. The crowd roared as one, "Olé!" I relaxed. But only for a second. Antonio made several more beautiful passes, the horns just grazing his body, all the terrible weight stabbing and thundering into the cape harmlessly. He initiated another pass—moving gracefully, with ease, as in slow motion, at just the exact moment to avoid the sharp points of the huge ivory-colored horns.

Then panic struck. As he passed the matador, the bull hooked him with one horn, just slightly. But Antonio was thrown into the air. The *peones* rushed into the ring, three of them at once, waving and tossing their capes to distract the bull from his prey. Meanwhile, the bullfighter lay inert on the ground, as if dead. Men groaned; women screamed. The strength of the bull was so great that one flick of his left horn had thrown Antonio like a rag doll. One bullfighter's black slipper was lying on the sand. Then to our amazement, Antonio staggered to his feet. A trickle of blood ran down his embroidered blue satin pants, an open tear split his sparkling jacket. But he had regained his composure and was moving toward the bull again with the red cape in hand. With a dramatic flourish, he waved off his *cuadrilla* who had come to protect him, and walked slowly toward the bull. With a gesture of insolence and indignation, he taunted the animal. This time, when the bull attacked, Antonio knew he hooked on his left side, so he pulled the cape close, very close, to the right. The crowd let out an agonizing "Aaaahhhhh" until the animal had stormed by. And then they let loose, screaming, jumping to their feet in a delirium of joy. Antonio made several more superb, classic passes, and then turned his back on the stunned bull and strutted toward the *barrera*. The crowd was enchanted.

Exhausted from the emotion, I remained seated. It occurred to me then that if Carlos was in the plaza, I did not care. After the incredible courage my friend had displayed, whatever danger Carlos might represent seemed minor. When the trumpets announced the entrance of the *picadores*, I grabbed Luis's field glasses to watch them enter the ring on their padded horses. There was always the danger that the bull might take a swipe at them before they were in place and before the *picador* was prepared to plunge the long, iron-tipped lance into the beast to weaken his neck muscles (a circular guard on the pole of the lance prevented the tip from penetrating more than four inches). Without this important action, the matador would not be able to bring his sword down over the animal's head for the kill.

As I swept the glasses around the ring, a face I recognized was suddenly caught in my vision. I felt a pang of apprehension. Serge was in a *barrera* seat about thirty yards away. Why was he here? He hadn't mentioned going to the fight last night. And was he aware that Carlos was also nearby? Probably not. At the moment Serge was concentrating on a woman in white seated next to him. Since her shiny black hair was blowing loosely about her face, it took me a moment to recognize Sofia Cabanellas. Even though the two of them were far away, I imagined that Serge had already seen me, for we were all seated ringside. So I kept looking at him, hoping he would glance my way, but he continued to be enraptured with his companion.

All eyes were now on Antonio's *mozo de espadas*, who was trying to attend the wound in Antonio's side. But Antonio disdainfully brushed him away and entered the ring again. Despite my preoccupation with Serge, my attention went to the matador. After the *picadores* had picked the bull—after the bull had managed to throw down two horses and their riders—the *banderilleros* came in and plunged three pairs of spiked sticks, decorated with colorful crepe paper, into the beast's neck. Now the final moments of the fight began. Antonio, as custom demanded, with hat in one hand and the red *muleta* in the other, walked up to the President's box and doffed his hat. Then he tossed the hat to the *mozo de espadas* and approached the animal very slowly. He began by drawing the bull close to his body, in a circle so small that the animal was almost bent in half, wrapped around the man's waist like a towel, the horns no more than an inch away. Every movement was a delight of elegance, lightness, precision. Now Antonio fanned the bull from horn to horn *abanicando*, directing the animal with a swing of the cape away from his body, and then close again. Next he stalked toward the audience, his back to the bull in another arrogant display of fearless disdain. Each time the people roared their pleasure.

Now, with the red cloth covering his sword, he approached the bull for the supreme moment of the fight, the kill. It must be clean, I knew, or Antonio's superlative comeback would be a failure. The crowd became deathly still, so still that I could hear Antonio calling to the bull, "Ah, toro, toro!" Lining the bull's front feet properly, Antonio took the classic killing stance, cape low in his left hand, the right elbow high, with the tip of the sharp blade pointed toward the bull's mortal spot—protected by those murderous horns. It was a tragic ballet. Swiftly Antonio moved forward and upward plunging the long silvery sword to the hilt. The bull dropped dead in his tracks. The crowd rose to its feet and exploded with emotion. Some screamed, others were slapping neighbors they did not know on the back, and a few were crying unashamedly.

After Antonio paraded around the ring, the bull's ears in his hand, his *peones* behind him, tossing back the flowers, hats, and cigars the enthusiastic public tossed to him, we were all on our feet again, gazing around the ring and stretching our legs. I took the opportunity to search for the bushy beard and the yellow shirt. But I could not find Carlos.

It was only at the end of the afternoon that I saw him again. When I did, it was hard for me to believe what I saw; for Carlos (if he *was* Carlos) was wrenching Sofia away from Serge. With one hand firmly on her shoulder, he turned threateningly to my friend. Then pushing Sofia ahead of him, he disappeared into the crowd.

Of course! I thought triumphantly. That settles it! Carlos and Sofia are lovers!

Unfortunately, by the time I pointed out the scene to Luis, all three had faded into the crowd. When we left the ring, Civil Guards were milling about the exits, but they were smiling, as carefree as the rest of those who had just experienced a supreme afternoon of bulls.

And I could only wonder: So what does my discovery—or at least my confirmation—mean? Sofia and Carlos? Lovers? Sofia and Carlos, the couple making love in the afternoon at Paco's estate near Toledo? Sofia and Carlos, the ones in the country later that afternoon? Sofia, the woman in my room that night? But I also had many other unanswered questions: Did Serge recognize Carlos? And, whether he did or not, where will all this lead?

Chapter 17

We were tired after the excitement of the dusty, crowded bull-ring. But before going to bed, we relaxed on our terrace, chatting about the day's events and admiring the shiny ribbon of moonlight on the water. The sweet, heady smell of jasmine blossoms mingled with the salty sea air.

"So what do you think happened with Carlos, Sofia, and Serge?" I asked. "I'm worried."

"Well, don't worry. You have only imagined that you saw Carlos. And if anybody knows how to take care of himself, it's Serge."

I leaned over to give my husband a kiss. "I hope you're right." I looked at the sky dusted with stars, and again I said something about how sure I was that I'd seen Carlos. The smoke of Luis's cigarette drifted among the flowers and dissipated into the darkness. "Why can't you forget that world of turmoil and enjoy all this," Luis accused gently, with a sweep of his arm. As he spoke, our butler, Andrés, materialized silently, a telephone in his hand. "Señora Condesa," he said in his soft voice, "the Señora de Ussia is on the teléfono."

"You take it, Luis," I said languidly. "I forgot to tell you that Casi called today just before we left for the fight." Casi was Luis's sister.

Luis reached for the receiver. Almost before his *"Sí,"* I could vaguely hear his sister's excited flood of words. As he listened, he grew instantly tense, threw his cigarette into a bowl of sand at his side, and then stood up. I knew something unusual had happened when he began to pace. The steady stream of words coming from the receiver continued. Once Luis interrupted with, "Who did it?" And this began to alarm me. But when he asked, "Are they both dead?" I jumped to my feet and ran to his side. Leaning close to the phone, I tried to make out the words buried in the blurred sounds coming from the receiver. Finally Luis hung up and placed the phone on a table.

Before answering my frantic questions, he calmly lit another cigarette. I was burning with impatience. "Luis, for heaven's sakes," I said, "Tell me what's happened!"

He raised his hand. "Inge is dead! Francisco Cabanellas and Inge Schmidt have been in a terrible accident." He spoke the words curtly. "They went out in Paco's Cigarette boat. There was some kind of gas leak in the engine compartment, or something like that. And it exploded. Evidently Inge is dead and Paco is badly injured. His body's a mess, but he's expected to live."

I was wide-eyed with horror. "Dead," I repeated incredulously. The splash and whisper of the waves on our beach seemed suddenly full of hidden dangers. "How does a boat explode like that? Isn't that unusual?"

"Casi said everybody is asking the same question. It's a strange accident. And since Paco is too seriously injured to talk just yet, he's unable to explain how it happened. Cigarette boats are so well designed and constructed that such an explosion never occurs."

"When did it happen?"

"Last night. But the news didn't spread around town until this afternoon."

"Do you suppose Carlos could have done it?" I asked.

"Please, Aline, don't go inventing things without evidence."

"Oh, Luis," I said, "I'm having terrible misgivings. I never spoke to Inge Friday night at the Beach Club. I should have taken the time to be more friendly."

I was also pondering whether it would be convenient to tell Luis Jupiter's news about Paco Cabanellas's company transporting illegal material. My position, as always, was difficult. Naturally, Jupiter preferred that Luis did not know about his work. In fact, Luis himself preferred not to be taken into Jupiter's confidence. On the other hand, Luis was my husband; and I owed it to him to be reasonably forthcoming about my "professional" activities. After turning the situation over in my mind, I decided to wait and say nothing for the time being.

"Well, it's too late now." Luis was referring to Inge. "And we will have to wait to see if Paco recovers." My husband sighed. "You know the fishermen here are superstitious about deaths at sea. And they're mumbling that it must have been an outright attempt by someone to get rid of Cabanellas."

Recalling that night in Germany with Ava, and the two men threatening the other, I still thought must have been Paco, I shivered. Did anyone besides Serge know that there was at least one terrorist on this coast?

"The police," Luis was reading my mind, "are already questioning everybody in the port. Of course, this is tricky business, because now and then sailors and fisherman are involved in contraband. Paco could be, too, as far as we know. You know I always wondered about him. Today, even minor smuggling is punished severely. The sailors will be reluctant to talk, for fear that whoever might have killed Cabanellas could take reprisals against them."

"Yes, I suppose everyone will imagine that Paco was involved in smuggling," I agreed.

"They certainly will," said Luis. "And you should try to forget the whole thing."

"Luis," I said, "how can you be so callous? Inge is dead, and Paco is seriously injured. The situation is ghastly enough to make anyone want to do something about it."

"I want no part of it. Your curiosity is a dangerous thing, darling. Don't go poking around. I know Jupiter will try to encourage you." My husband was just then lighting another cigarette, and I was relieved he couldn't see my face. "Realize, Aline, that whoever killed Inge, if such is the case, will kill anyone who gets in his way. Even if it really was Carlos who placed a bomb in Paco's boat, you will be in his way if you start nosing around, and he can do the same to you. So don't ask for trouble."

Suddenly I was exhausted. The strips of moonlight on the water no longer charmed me. I felt depressed and frustrated. "Luis, "I said, "let's go to bed."

INGE'S FATHER ARRIVED from Germany in a private plane before noon. I tried to reach him repeatedly, but the Hotel Los Monteros operator told me every time that he was unavailable. I left a flurry of messages. Remembering his pride as he entered the wedding reception with his lovely daughter, I realized this blow would be terrible for him.

I recalled then a moment on the night of the wedding. I was dancing with Hans Schmidt, and Inge whirled past us, sparkling in her embroidered gown, and he said to me: "When my daughter enters a room, she always lights it up like a chandelier." His daughter had been everything to him, and now, despite his success and enormous fortune, he had no family at all.

I was certain that the explosion on Paco's boat was not an accident . . . thinking, all the while, that the strange thing was that Paco himself, whom I had considered among the guilty, was now a victim. And there was another consideration, as well, for Inge's tragedy reminded me of Karl von Ridder's assasination. Now with her gone, two persons who had been at the wedding were dead, and only by a miracle it had not been three.

Meanwhile, I left a message for Serge, asking for Steve Lederer, of course. But so far no answer had come.

Chapter 18

The summer was becoming too hectic. Apart from my preoccupations with Carlos, and the horror of Inge's death, my two beautiful daughters-in-law arrived, each with two children. And my sons would be down for the weekend. We had been looking forward to their visit as the highlight of our summer. The grandchildren ranged from one to four years old, and they absolutely entranced us. So, although I wanted to be with them exclusively, when the call finally came from Serge, I agreed to meet him at the Hotel Los Monteros, which was just up the hill from our house. We could talk there confidentially. Fortunately, Luis was so completely absorbed with the small children that he didn't even notice when I left.

The side door of the hotel opened directly into the dim bar, and Serge stood up as I walked in. He looked almost ridiculous now, with hair sleek and dyed dark brown, a black jacket and tie . . . not the usual for hot, sunny Marbella. Contrary to our usual procedure, the meeting had a clandestine air, and I was immediately uncomfortable. I was not happy about the barman's puzzled look when I greeted Serge and sat down with him. The barman knew me well.

"Naturally, I saw you and Luis at the bullfight," Serge said, once we were seated. "But I could hardly do anything about it, since I had Sofia in tow. And then there was that scene with her boyfriend!"

"Did you realize that fellow was Carlos?" I asked.

Serge scowled. "That's serious. Are you certain? Even though I know his goings and comings almost as well as he does himself, I've never seen him." He paused a moment to think. "Well, if it was Carlos, at least he had no idea who I was." Serge took off his glasses and rubbed his eyes. "So . . . he's heavily involved with that girl. So heavily that his jealousy led him to take chances, yesterday. That may well offer us an opening. . . ."

Since we were both aware that our meeting had to be short, I wasted no time in asking Serge if he thought Carlos was the one who blew up Cabanellas's boat.

"You're right, of course," Serge answered. "That explosion could not have been accidental. At first I thought Ali Amine did it; he's an expert at car bombs. But now that you tell me Carlos is in the neighborhood, he could be the one. Carlos also has lots of experience with car bombs. Why not a boat bomb? It's the same idea. Whether it was Carlos or Ali—either way—it was certainly no accident."

Serge was not comfortable with this conversation, and so he spoke more quickly than usual. "If Carlos is on this coast, undoubtedly he is building up the same kind of arsenal here that he had in Villiers-sur-Marne in France. One of his surprising skills is that he's a damned good organizer and manager. His aim would be to provide a central supply depot for terrorist groups. So he's probably accumulating explosives and bombs of all types. And he could have a supply of submachine guns and assault rifles as well, like the AK-47 Kalashnikov, which is popular with the Palestinians. It weighs between four and nine pounds and contains thirty cartridges. Very practical for them. But Carlos usually manages to get a supply of antitank rockets also, like the Soviet RPG-7, a great land-to-air missile. These are shoulder fired and rocket propelled. And there's the SA-7, which is from two feet to three feet long and can be fired from a van. Terrorists used one of those outside the Rome airport. However, the end was seen sticking out of an ice-cream vendor's kiosk that time, and they were caught.

"But," he shrugged, then met my eyes with his, "all of these are tools of the trade. The most important thing to remember about Carlos is that he's very smart and incredibly unpredictable. If he just murdered one of your friends, he could kill you, too, merely for recognizing him in the bullring."

"I realize that, Serge," I answered. "But Luis still insists Carlos is a product of my imagination. However, now that it seems certain that Carlos has something going with Sofia Cabanellas, perhaps she is the reason they have been in so many of the same places at the same time."

"It's not that simple," Serge said quietly. "Last night she ended up in my room. She was afraid of someone—I don't know who—or at least she was putting on a pretty good act. At any rate, I'm taking no chances with her. Although she acts like an innocent, bewildered young girl, she could also very easily fit the profile of the political fanatic, indulging in the exciting game of terrorism. In other words, she could be playing a very clever game with me. But that doesn't mean I can't do the same with her."

Sofia had suddenly become another unexpected danger. The news that Serge had spent the night with her was disconcerting, to say the least. After all, he was human, and why should he be immune to her attractions?

Serge had no more to say then about the beautiful and mysterious Sofia Cabanellas. It was her boyfriend he wanted to discuss. "So, Carlos is almost certainly here to assemble an arsenal of weapons and explosives," he said thoughtfully. "And my Cairo police contact told me that Ali is in the market, which means he is probably here to buy."

The waiter appeared, and Serge asked for another double whiskey on the rocks. My eyes opened in amazement; and as soon as the barman left, he explained. "I need it. My concern is that Ali will find me before I find him. He can disguise himself in a hundred ways. I'm stuck with changing beards and . . ." He touched his glasses and ran his fingers through his hair. As he spoke, Serge's eyes roamed around the room. He was more uncomfortable by the minute, and so was I. Luis would be furious if he knew that Serge and I were conspiring together in such a public place.

"Ali and Carlos are old friends from 'Black September,' " Serge confided. "You know about 'Black September,' don't you?"

"A bit."

" 'Black September' members change frequently. They come from many different terrorist organizations, and they only work together for special operations. Right now Ali and Carlos are apparently working together once again. If that's the case, it would be most useful for me to learn what kind of weapons Carlos is selling Ali. That would indicate the type of operation he's plotting."

"What does this Ali look like?" I asked. "Is there any way I could recognize him?"

"He's small and wiry, not as dark as some Arabs, not bad-looking, no outstanding features, about thirty-four. And he's a master with knives. He can kill with one at ten meters."

I looked at my watch. "Serge, I have to go. Luis doesn't even know I left home."

"Yes, we'd better leave," he answered. "But before we do, let's clarify future plans." And then his eyes met mine. "Ever heard of a restaurant called Chez Jacques?" he asked.

I shook my head. "Never."

"Also I'm interested in a large estate, the Villa La Amapola. Do you know where that is?"

Much to my embarrassment, I had to say "no" again.

"Well, if there's any way you can find out, I'd appreciate knowing the general layout of both places—exits, entrances, windows—that sort of thing. Here's my new telephone number." He handed me a matchbook with Hotel Atlantico on the cover. It was a popular hotel in Marbella. "I move almost every day; but I'll keep you informed."

When I arrived back home, a small delivery truck was in the drive. The name of the local florist shop was inscribed in bright red letters on the newly painted white surface of the old van. The sight surprised me. Who was sending me flowers? I had not ordered anything; and no one I knew had reason to send us a bouquet today.

When I stepped into the driveway, I saw through the arched door of the patio a towheaded boy walking in the direction of my back door, carrying an enormous pink paper funnel filled with red flowers. On hearing my footsteps, the young fellow turned around. The fluffy crimson mass in his arms was so large that his face was almost invisible. On recognizing me, he changed direction and began to walk toward me. As the flaming bouquet moved closer and closer, I was suddenly fearful. My eyes remained fastened on the blaze . . . for it had suddenly become a blaze of warning. Dozens of huge, scarlet red carnations! It was as if Carlos himself was standing there. Few people knew how much I loved carnations.

"*Buenos días*, Señora Condesa," the young fellow chirped, breaking the spell. "Here I bring our largest most beautiful carnations for you."

Pulling myself back to reality, I made a proper comment on the lovely bouquet, and asked for the sender's card.

"There is no card," he answered. "These flowers were ordered by telephone and paid for with a credit card. The boss said the man insisted they be especially beautiful. Only red carnations; he didn't want any pink or white ones."

When I explained that I would like to thank the person who gave them, the boy shook his head. "My *patrón* also wanted to know who he was. But the name was unknown to him. It was a very common one—José García."

Of course, I realized, my question was useless. Carlos would never let anyone locate him. As I walked into the house, my arms heaped with huge red blossoms, I wondered what this gift meant. Was it a threat, or a warning? Or was it a request not to reveal his presence? In any case, after what I had learned about Carlos and his gifts, the glorious flowers left me completely unnerved.

Chapter 19

The following night our friends the Cocas gave a large dinner, with flamenco after. Ignacio Coca owned an important private bank, with branches all over Spain. He had also been one of the original developers of this part of the coast and had created an especially luxurious area called "Los Monteros." Of course, everyone at the party was stunned by Inge's ghastly tragedy; they spoke of nothing else. But Nicky Maniatis nevertheless brought some good news. For Paco was now out of critical danger; his chances for survival seemed good; and there was reason to believe he would recover without serious injuries. Nicky had been to the hospital early in the day, and the doctors had told him that Paco's prognosis was better than they'd thought possible earlier.

About midnight, the butler interrupted a conversation I was having with Silvia Coca to announce that Hans Schmidt was in the front room asking to speak to Mr. Maniatis. Silvia asked me to come with her to find Nicky. We went out of the house and crossed the garden to a clump of palm trees, where we both recognized Nicky's distinctive profile. He was wearing an elegant burgundy blazer.

Earlier in the evening, he had explained to me that the blazer was made by his tailor in Rome—a young man whom he had helped financially, whom he believed was destined to become famous as a menswear designer. No matter how much I disliked Nicky Maniatis, I had to admire his generosity. I'd also heard that he'd given Paco funds to start his business. Inge had mentioned this one night at La Romana in a burst of pride at Paco's success. If it weren't for Nicky, she had said, things would have been much more difficult for Paco, perhaps impossible. Though she was vague about what exactly Nicky had done, I assumed she meant that Nicky had provided contacts, and perhaps some financing.

Nicky stood up when his hostess approached, but looked disconcerted when he heard that Hans was there. "Yes, of course I will speak to him," he said. "But he will not find what I have to say very comforting. I know those boats inside-out. The chances of one exploding by accident are slim. I would guess that's why he'd like to see me."

We found Hans pacing Silvia's elegant foyer like a fox trapped in a cage. He only glanced up from the floor as Silvia greeted him. His eyes were red and swollen. Nevertheless, he stretched his hand out to me and then to Nicky. And then his first question was precisely the one Nicky had anticipated.

Nicky's reply was blunt, but expressed with surprising gentleness and concern. "Only a bomb could have created such an explosion," he said.

Hans stared at Nicky, and in a low voice said, "Yes, that's exactly what I think." He clasped his hand across his eyes; and his shoulders began to heave. We all understood how grief-stricken he was, but no one knew how to comfort him. After a moment, however, Hans regained his composure enough to say that though he couldn't reveal his source, he had reason to believe that members of an international terrorist group had arrived on the coast during the last few days. "I told the police this; but they wouldn't believe me," he said, becoming agitated again. "I know it's true. And I'll find them one way or another."

Just then, Nancy Rhodentus happened to come into the foyer. She explained that she was going home, because she didn't feel well. But when she saw Hans, she went over to take his hand. "Dear!" she said softly. "I'm so very sorry about Inge." She seemed able to connect with him in a way the rest of us could not. Noticing this, it flashed through my mind that perhaps some sort of romance had started up between these two after R.K. left her. After all, Hans was a widower; and she was divorced and lived part of the year in

Germany. It would certainly be possible. At any rate there seemed a special bond between them.

Hans looked at her for a long moment, then said, "Whoever did this to Inge will suffer." Nancy held his glance and didn't say anything. Finally he relaxed his grip on her hand and turned to us all, "If the police weren't so inefficient, they would know a lot more by now." Then he told us his own theory: In his view, someone sneaked on board and taped a small plastique explosive under the seat. The blast would have detonated the high-octane fuel and would leave little trace. He thought a tracking device of some kind must have been used. When the boat was near a deserted stretch of coast, the explosive was ignited by remote control.

"What did the police think of your idea?" asked Nicky.

"Not much," said Hans. "Their guess was that the gas tank exploded."

Nicky shook his head. "Not possible with that design."

Hans seemed to be on a talking jag. How terrible the last two days must have been for him, I realized. He was desperate to talk about what had happened. Meanwhile, Silvia suggested we all go into the library. But Hans told her he had to leave. Then, surprisingly, instead of doing that, he began to describe in lurid detail everything the police had told him—Inge's body floating in a life-preserver, both legs blown away. The fisherman who found Paco unconscious and nearly drowned. The botched investigation the following morning when it was too late to find substantial evidence. We all listened in embarrassed silence. "They didn't even call me until hours had passed. Yet they knew who she was. I don't understand it."

As he finished his account, Hans was becoming more and more agitated, intermittently wringing his hands and rubbing his nose with a hankerchief. Often it was almost impossible to understand him. Yet one thing was clear enough: He kept insisting over and over again that professional terrorists had been responsible for the tragedy, not mere run-of-the-mill smugglers. "But," he repeated, his face stunned and bewildered, his hands hanging lifelessly at his sides. "I'll find the killers one way or another. They're not going to get away from me." By this time Nancy was almost as distraught as he was.

With that he turned and left, so quickly the butler didn't even have time to open the door. We all stood helplessly by as he went out. But then it suddenly occurred to me that I might be able to obtain some useful information from him. I wanted to question him about the statements he had just made concerning terrorists. Coming to my senses, I ran to the door and out to the gravel entrance where the cars were parked. But the engine of Hans's car was already roaring. And he raced out the drive before I could stop him. When I returned, Nicky and Silvia Coca were out of sight. With mixed feelings, I left the party.

The next morning I called the Hotel Los Monteros, where I knew Hans was staying. But to my surprise the operator told me that Señor Schmidt had checked out. Then I asked to speak to the concierge, Javier de Sánchez, who often solved problems for us. When Javier came on the line, I asked him what had happened to Señor Schmidt and where I could find him. He told me that Señor Schmidt would not be returning, that his daughter's body had been released early that morning, and that the Señor had gone to the morgue with an ambulance to transport the body to Málaga airport. From there a private plane would take him back to Düsseldorf.

"I didn't know Señor Schmidt had a plane," I said, almost to myself.

"No, Señora Condesa, it belongs to a Mr. Maniatis," said Javier. "Yes, his pilot was here very early this morning with the release forms and customs papers. It's not a simple matter taking a corpse from one country to another. And poor Señor Schmidt was not in any state of mind to do much document work. I think Mr. Maniatis may have also arranged with the police to have the body released. Several times the police called, leaving messages for Señor Schmidt. They talked to me personally."

"But why didn't they just speak to him?" I asked.

"He wasn't here," Javier said. "He came in this morning close to five. The pilot arrived very soon after that. By seven, Señor Schmidt had checked out."

Javier went on to tell me that he didn't usually like working the night shift; but he was glad to be able to help a nice man like Señor Schmidt in a difficult time. I thanked him and hung up, thinking Javier wasn't the only one helping Hans Schmidt. Nicky Maniatis was certainly doing his part. Gradually my opinion of Nicky was improving.

Meanwhile, Hans's statement that Inge had been murdered by terrorists kept nagging me. Did Hans have a reason to consider Paco a likely target for terrorists? How many people knew terrorists were on the coast? Carlos had been at the bullfight, and according to Serge, Ali was also here. But how did Hans have his information? I couldn't help thinking of Jupiter's latest news about Paco's company transporting calutrons from a German factory to Málaga for further shipment to the Middle East. Did Hans know anything about this? After all he was a German manufacturer.

It wasn't until two days later that I received another call from Jupiter. His message was brief. "Could you be at my apartment in an hour? I would go to see you, but someone else is meeting us here, and I have to take a plane from Málaga at two."

We arranged that I would be there at eleven.

Puerto Banus at the peak of the season was like a carnival. Men and women wearing festive summer colors strolled in and out of side shops and cafés. Everything glistened in the sunlight. Massive yachts, sleek sailboats, racing boats, all were neatly ranged side by side. Tall masts vied with trim bridges to create a picturesque skyline. At this time of year, an empty slip was a conspicuous vacancy. But today there were several of these, with Nancy's yacht being among the most conspicuously absent. I walked past a Chinese junk tied up in front of the popular Bar El Duque and turned into the narrow street leading up to Jupiter's apartment building. Masses of red, yellow, and orange blossoms hung from flowerpots and window boxes on the walls and terraces.

The enchantment of the harbor was due not only to its location at the foot of dramatic mountains, but in great part to the architecture encircling it. Snow-white buildings, containing a myriad of small apartments, were perched in irregular fashion, like boxes, one on top of the other, creating the appearance of a fisherman's village.

Climbing the steps to the second floor, I rang Jupiter's bell. Manolo, his manservant, opened the door. *"Buenos días*, Señora Condesa. The Señor is waiting." Then smiling and chatting in his pleasant manner, he led me to the front room, which overlooked the port. When I entered, Jupiter and Serge both jumped up to greet me. So Serge was the person Jupiter had been expecting.

"Thanks for being so punctual," John said, as he put his hand on my arm and drew me to a comfortable chair. "It's important. Serge needs assistance. And I cannot help him, because I must leave the country for a few days."

Serge looked happy. "Finally," he said. "I've not only located Ali, but the place where he meets his associates as well. I hope to be able to obtain valuable information."

My chair was facing the harbor. A large sailboat was slowly moving out to sea. In the distance was the empty slip where Nancy's boat was usually tied up. "If you could accompany me," Serge began, "I should be able to get pictures, identify agents working with Ali, and even record conversations. The equipment I have is the very latest, but I can't handle it all alone."

"Of course I'll help," I said. "But what do you want me to do?"

"Serge would like to take you to a late dinner tonight," Jupiter interrupted. "Do you suppose you could get away? It's urgent, I can assure you." Both men were looking at me apprehensively, fully aware that Luis would not approve of what they were asking me to do.

"I'm flattered that my presence is considered so valuable." I smiled. "Probably, I could think of some excuse to get out of a dinner we have at the Stilianopouloses' tonight. Luis wanted to play poker with some friends, and I know he'd be delighted if I told him we were free. He's incapable of inventing an excuse himself." They were still observing me anxiously.

As I spoke to them, I had a few qualms of conscience about my bet with Luis. Only yesterday he was kidding me about it, slyly indicating that he knew I was deeply involved again, but that he preferred not to talk about it.

Nevertheless, I knew that their request wasn't a small one, as far as they were concerned. It was important to both of my old friends. "Yes, I'll do it somehow," I answered. "You can count on me."

"Good. What I might uncover this evening is well worth your sacrifice, Aline," Serge said. "Thank you very much. But at the same time I have to warn you. There is some danger in what I want you to do. Are you still willing?"

Jupiter laughed. "That's the right thing to say, Serge. Now you can be sure she'll go. It's going to be an exciting evening for you both. And I'm sorry I can't be with you."

The two men, I realized, had cleverly planned their strategy before I arrived. Serge didn't wait for my reply to Jupiter. "I'll pick you up about eleven. Be sure to take a handbag large enough to hold a camera, a tape recorder, and a small microphone. Don't dress in anything that will attract attention. The place we're going to is not elegant. No one you know will be there." He stopped for a moment to collect his thoughts. "And oh, do you have a small weapon?"

I nodded.

"Good. Bring it with you. But I'm sure you won't need it."

AT ELEVEN, WHEN I walked toward my car, Serge stopped me. "No, it's better we use my rented Renault. I don't want anyone recognizing your car and checking the plates." We piled into his black rental. "Before we leave here," he went on, "put this equipment inside your purse." He handed me a small recorder. "That has a microphone which you can manipulate from inside the purse and direct toward the next table. You'd better try it now. Put the earpiece of the mike inside your ear and hide it under your hair; then conceal the wire under your shirt." It took me a few moments to drop the wire inside my clothes. "That's fine," he said, as I showed him the jack protruding from under my jacket. "Leave the machine inside your bag, then place it on your lap once you are seated at the table. To focus it, twist this button," he showed me a knob. "You will hear the conversation clearly, but be sure to focus on the people we are interested in. Often it is not easy to mask nearby conversations. But you can control this somewhat by playing with that button. Practice as soon as we sit down." He waited to see that I had understood how the microphone functioned. "Now unplug that wire until we are inside," he ordered. "If properly focused, that machine will record every word." He stopped a moment to gather his thoughts. When he resumed, he was using a somewhat less commanding tone. "The men we're interested in are Ali—of course— and a German. They may speak English, or perhaps French. I doubt the German knows Arabic. Whatever we pick up will be translated later." He pointed to a button on his pocket and showed me the lens of a camera underneath. This did not particularly impress me. We had already used similar equipment years before, during World War Two. "I will be photographing the scene and the players. Hopefully we will go undetected. As far the restaurant itself, it's a good one. So we will order a delicious meal; and before we finish, we should have a wealth of information. All quite simple. But I couldn't do it alone." Then he turned on the engine, backed out and started up the hill.

"How did you locate Ali?" I asked.

"Well, remember that I asked you about Chez Jacques? I finally found it. It's a small restaurant in Puente Romano, and that's where we're headed." We'd arrived at the main road, and Serge slowed down, looking in both directions until there was an opening in the traffic. Then swiftly he pulled out among the maze of headlights onto the highway. "My Cairo police contact gave me the tip about Chez Jacques, and so I've been hanging out there since we talked. I couldn't call you because I was waiting for Ali to appear. Fortunately, he didn't recognize me when he did. There are a few highclass prostitutes peddling their business in that place, and I tied up with one. This made it quite normal that I spent some time there. As for Ali, he hangs out in the bar, but he also lives in an apartment above the restaurant. The owner of the building probably has some connection with Ali's organization. I suspect all kinds of illegal business is transacted in this place.

"At any rate, I had the good luck to meet a really *simpática* tart. I led her to believe I was a wealthy Canadian lumber magnate on vacation from a boring wife, and I gave her a sensational jewel, an excellent fake." Serge stopped speaking as he manipulated the car through traffic. Then he continued, "I have given her quite a few expensive gifts during these past few days. The manager of Chez Jacques is not stupid. The girls work for him; and check on the customers for him. Since this girl is making good money off me and wants to keep it going, I'm sure that she's reported that I'm a straight John."

"What's a John exactly?" I asked. "You know recent American slang, and I do not."

"A Canadian lumber magnate who gets taken for a lot of money by a call girl in Marbella."

We both laughed.

"Well," he went on, "through her I learned that there is a rich arms dealer who comes for dinner almost every evening and has a reserved corner table. Since Ali is here to get arms, I'm betting he has dealings with that guy. So I've reserved the next table for tonight. Ali's planning something big, Aline, I'm sure of it."

"We might even see Carlos," I suggested.

"You're right. But I've been asking this girl discreet questions about the people that hang out there, and she isn't aware of anyone that sounds like him. In any case, I'd prefer that Carlos doesn't see you, if he is around. Things might get too complicated. He might think you are following him, and that could cause us trouble."

"If there is an arms dealer there, do other terrorists—or representatives of other groups—go there also?"

"Oh, absolutely. You can be sure Gadhafi has somebody there negotiating arms deals for him. In fact, Ali himself has received training in Gadhafi's camps and could be filling orders for him as well. Be aware, too, that while Carlos is the star terrorist today, Ali is older and more experienced. So Carlos may be included in the operation Ali is plotting . . . not only because of his undoubted skills, but to give the plan class. Carlos is highly respected among his colleagues; and anything he does has very high publicity value, from a terrorist point of view. More than ever since he miraculously escaped death by not leading the Entebbe operation, where all the terrorists were killed by the Israelis. At the last minute his boss Waddi Haddad decided against Carlos taking part and that saved him. He seems to lead a charmed life."

As I listened, I realized how much Serge knew about my old friend Carlos.

He continued, "Carlos and Ali may be connected now with Abu Nidal, the code name for an up-and-coming terrorist who's organizing yet another radical group. All these guys have been in the PFLP, and they all participated in Black September."

We were now passing through the town of Marbella, where the traffic and crowds slowed us down, but soon we speeded up again. A little further on, Serge turned off the highway onto a dirt road. Soon we passed the brightly lit apartment buildings of Puente Romano. Then he turned into a still smaller road, more like a path, which ended next to a small two-story building, about two hundred meters from the water where a sign with an arrow pointed to "Chez Jacques."

About ten cars were parked under a few umbrella pines in front of the restaurant. The place had an unexpected air of romance that Serge had not warned me about. Soft sensual strains of guitars floated out to us, a row of lanterns cast dancing lights as they swung in the breeze. Serge studied the cars, then backed in close to the end of the drive so that we were headed out.

"Now, listen carefully," he said. "The table I ordered is next to the German arms manufacturer. I am counting on Ali joining him during the evening."

Inside the atmosphere had the feel of an Arabian Nights hideaway. The tentlike interior was draped in muted green silk, threaded with delicate strands of gold that caught and played with the candlelight from the tables. Banquettes piled with tasseled silk pillows and ottomans of colorful satin invited romance. The room was utterly sensuous and fascinating. Our table was next to one occupied by an elderly, overweight man. I presumed he was the arms dealer. He was looking extremely glum as he consumed enormous amounts of swordfish, then roast lamb, and finally couscous.

Everything went according to plan until Ali appeared. We had been finishing our couscous and were beginning to despair of ever seeing him, when we both noticed the arms dealer gesture toward the bar. Serge nudged me, and I realized Ali was there. His appear-

ance surprised me, a man one would never expect to be a terrorist.
He had an agreeable expression of kindness, handsome, regular features, neatly cut black hair; and he was immaculately dressed in
white corduroy slacks, a blue shirt, and a navy blazer.

But instead of Ali joining the German at the table next to us, the
arms dealer stood up, and without looking at Ali again, walked out
the front door. A moment later, Ali went out the back. Serge
jumped up. And the next second, he slipped out the front door,
without giving me any instructions. From my seat at the corner
table, I slid over on the banquette, nearer the window. Ali appeared
to be heading for a small pier about two hundred yards distant. I
assumed that the arms dealer and Ali would meet there. Unfortunately, the light from the lanterns outside was dim, and I had difficulty following his receeding figure.

At first I couldn't see Serge, either; but then I caught a glimpse of
him dodging through the cars parked between the restaurant and
the sea. Meanwhile Ali was fading into the darkness at the end of
the path near the waterfront, seemingly unaware that Serge was
following him. The arms dealer was already invisible, hidden by
shadows and low shrubbery. At the end of the path was a dock,
where the white hull of a medium-sized boat shone in the light of
the moon. Between the parking lot and the water was an area of
about one hundred yards that had no cover. I wondered how Serge
was going to manage that.

I finally saw the heavy figure of the arms dealer again, as he
reached the dock and continued to the boat. Serge had meanwhile
stopped to study the scene from behind a bush at the end of the
path. From the looks of things, I could see that he was already having problems. Picking up my handbag, I took out five thousand
pesetas, more than enough to cover our bill, and placed the money
on the table. As I did so, my fingers slipped over the cold steel of my
gun, and this gave me added courage. In another second I was outside.

Since the three men were in front of me, and no one else was
outside, I ran carelessly down the path toward the water. When I
reached the end, I saw that Serge was near the beach, but now had
some twenty yards of open sand to cross before he reached the
water. He was bent low but moving quickly. I gathered that he intended to swim underwater to the pier. Then from under the pier
hoped to listen to their conversation. I trusted there were no others
inside the boat. But that was clearly not one of Serge's main con-

cerns. To add to the risk, for all I knew, at any moment a cohort of Ali's might emerge from the restaurant.

Cautiously I remained in the shadow of the trees. Ali had now reached the pier, and was walking across the wooden planks, while the German had already entered the boat and disappeared. Just then Serge started to make a dash for the water, which was about twenty yards distant. "He's going to make it," I thought.

Then everything went wrong. Before Serge reached the water, a watch-dog started barking ferociously. Ali whipped around then and saw Serge. Now he knew someone was shadowing him. But at least he can't see Serge's features in the dark, I thought. It was important that Ali did not recognize Serge. Then a strong light flooded the area. The dog's raucous yelps must have alerted someone else. Ali could now see Serge more clearly. At that moment, Ali cried out something I couldn't understand. I took it to be a warning to someone inside the boat.

Just as Ali made his cry, Serge turned around and started to run back toward the cars, where I was standing. I expected to hear a gunshot, but there was none. Nevertheless Ali started chasing Serge. I remembered that Ali was an expert with knives and could throw one accurately at amazing distances. But the two men were now about fifty feet apart—too far for a knife throw yet. In another few seconds, though, he would surely be close enough if Serge didn't run faster.

In the distance, on the dock, I had the vague impression that two other men were emerging from the boat. I was now at the end of the path very near our car. And I knew I had to do something immediately or Serge would be finished. Ali was gaining rapidly.

I drew my small weapon from my bag, crouched, and pulled the trigger. I didn't try to hit Ali, but I wanted the shot to come close enough to rattle him. I got my wish. Ali dropped to the ground behind a bush. With a quickness I'd never known before, I dashed for the car, jumped in, and turned the key. Serge was nearing. Spurred on by the noise of the engine, he turned in my direction. Fortunately the car was placed parallel to the beach and all I had to do was move it forward so that the passenger seat was directly beside Serge as he came running up the path. When he jumped in, I stamped on the accelerator. Before he even hit the seat, we were speeding up the drive, with tires screeching. Serge kept looking backward as I swerved onto the road. Neither of us said a word until I had merged recklessly into the night traffic on the main highway.

Later Serge told me that his glasses had fallen off, and he had taken off his shoes to get in the water; so he was barefoot. In fact, when he looked at his feet, they were bleeding. But back on the beach, he said all he could remember being aware of was Ali screaming behind him. He still couldn't understand why the terror- ist had not pinned him with a knife in his back, or a gunshot. "For once he must have been without a weapon! To my good fortune," he added.

"Maybe I had something to do with that," I said quietly.

"What do you mean?" he asked.

"When I shot in his direction, he dove for cover."

"Well done, thanks, Aline," he said; there was nothing more elo- quent for him to say, and we both knew it.

After making detours and determining that we were not being followed, I drove home. "I knew you were going to be a help, but I never expected that you would save my life tonight," Serge said. "If you hadn't reacted so quickly, we might both be dead."

As we drove home, even though he had escaped, Serge grew de- pressed. For he knew that the evening's foul-up meant he would have to go underground for a while. "Ali may not have recognized me," he told me, "but he knows now someone is after him and he'll suspect me. That's enough. I'll be the last person to get close to him after this *fracaso*"—failure. Serge also worried that someone in the restaurant might have known who I was and that his blunder had put me in danger. "It's also a risk to you for me to remain on this coast," he continued. "So I will have to hide out for a time and find another disguise. Meanwhile, Ali is sure to alert the KGB, and they'll put two and two together. So Aline, in short, I've got to get out of here. Can you suggest a place where I could go right away?"

"How about my house in Madrid? I have a couple taking care of it, a new gardener and his wife. I think they're reliable."

"No, thanks. Cities are the best places to hide when you're being pursued, but your house in Madrid is too obvious. It's also known to the KGB, and too near the Soviet Embassy." Serge shook his head. We both remembered the tense night when he was defecting. Three cars full of KGB officers pulled up outside my house while Serge was inside. But we managed to keep them out that time. Thank God it was our country and not theirs.

I was about to say I couldn't think of any other place for him, when it occurred to me that during the month of August our ranch in southwestern Spain would be perfect. How stupid of me not to have thought of it immediately. When I asked Serge if a remote area would be satisfactory, a place where my servants and shepherds were the only occupants of thousands of acres, he grabbed my hand. "Even though we normally avoid remote places, at this moment your ranch sounds ideal. And my rented car will take me anywhere. I have several sets of license plates. I can change them, leave right away, and get out of this danger zone."

Even though the property was about six hours distant, and in a part of Spain he was unfamiliar with, Serge committed to memory my directions there. A minute later I was walking through the back patio into my house; and the sound of Serge's engine had faded away.

Chapter 20

When I told Luis that I had offered to let Serge spend some time at our ranch, he didn't mind at all. Of course, I did not tell him Serge needed it as a safe house to slip away from KGB agents and terrorists. Since we often offered the house to friends traveling through Extremadura, my husband did not find my invitation unusual.

The house itself was the central building of what had been a Roman latifundio in the first century A.D., and had been in Luis's family since 1231. It was a large, rambling medieval stone building in the middle of thousands of acres of rolling hills. The ranch produced merino sheep and wheat. I was pleased that Serge was going to be able to stay there; the sheep and the golden stubble fields of August would provide a peaceful retreat where I hoped no one would disturb him.

Though I was aware that Ali Amine and Carlos were probably still around, I had to give the impression of leading our usual busy life. Going out with our children to parties, or dining at the Puerto Banus at night and playing with the grandchildren on the beach in the daytime also served, I hoped, to mislead anyone who might be trailing me. I prayed that no one at Chez Jacques had recognized me and Serge or suspected that I was helping him. Many terrorists knew Serge from his assignment in Tunis working for the KGB. So for some days it would be necessary to put preoccupations about bombs and terrorists out of my thoughts and to try to live with complete normality. Fortunately, our social routine did not include the exotic Chez Jacques restaurant, nor did I hear anyone mention the name.

However, the calm did not last long. About a week after Serge departed for the ranch, while Luis and I were dining at the Marbella Beach Club, Hans Schmidt reappeared. He was leaning on the railing near where I was dancing, staring absently out at the sea. It seemed strange, improbable, that he had returned so soon to the scene of his daughter's tragedy. Less than two weeks had passed.

I was crossing the empty dance floor, and the band was on break, when his sad face caught my eye. He seemed utterly out of place amid all the usual merriment of the peak of the summer season. His suit was rumpled, his silvery hair was disorderly—almost humorously messy. If it had not been for his constant ravaged gesture—his hand dragging again and again through the tangles, as though to dislodge a thought he couldn't bear, he might have looked comic . . . or drunk.

I hadn't seen Hans Schmidt, of course, since the night at the Cocas. Inge's funeral had taken place in Germany, and I had written him at the time. But I was not surprised that he hadn't replied. As I approached him I was even more struck by his pained expression. His features were drawn, his cheeks hung in loose folds, and his eyes glistened like wet azure beads, their gaze fastened on some point beyond me out at sea.

Tapping lightly on his arm, I hoped not to startle him, "Good evening, Hans," I said.

He looked at me, straightening up, bowing with his usual courtesy, "Oh, I was distracted. Very nice to see you, Aline."

His excellent self-control and manners helped him mask his sorrow.

"I'm surprised to see you here, Hans," I said.

"Well, yes, I suppose it appears unusual, but it seemed to me that Inge found her happiness here. So I thought I would come and spend some time in the place that she loved so dearly."

Perhaps, I thought. But I suspected his purpose in coming to Marbella was not entirely sentimental.

"You're still not satisfied with the official version of the accident?" I asked.

"You are clever, Aline. No, I'm not. There are so many gaps in the police reports that even a simple businessman like me can see more behind this."

I smiled, recalling the industry he had nearly single-handedly re-created after World War Two. He was one of the major rebuilders of the economy of his defeated country. "Are you staying here at the club?" I asked.

"Actually, no. I'm staying at Los Monteros as usual, but not past tonight. My friend Bastiano Bergesi has loaned me his lovely villa. His other house guests leave in the morning."

I knew the villa well. It was one of the most luxurious on the coast, with gardens stretching down to the waterfront, and a cement wall overlooking a steep drop to the sea. Below that, a small floating dock jutted out into the water. Luis and I had been impressed by the house ever since Bastiano bought it. There was one drawback to it. It had no beach at all, only a treacherous wooden staircase that clung precariously to the cement wall gave access to the water.

"I would like to say hello to Luis," he said, "but I see there is quite a group at your table." Bowing quickly and awkwardly, he added, "Can't face up to all those people—they're apt to mention my daughter's accident. Sorry. I must say good night." And he rushed off. As I watched his retreating back zigzagging between the white-draped tables, sparkling with crystal and candlelight, I felt sorry for this kind man who was so haunted with the terrible death of his daughter . . . a death we both knew might well have been murder.

TWO DAYS AFTER that, in the late afternoon, and with no previous notice, Hans Schmidt appeared on my terrace. I was stretched on a deckchair, though I was about to go upstairs in order to avoid a strong wind that had just risen. He entered my back patio and walked through the open door to the salon without my hearing a sound. How easy it would be for someone who was not so friendly to get into my house, I realized as he approached. But that thought quickly vanished when I saw Hans himself. For his cheeks were flushed, his manner agitated.

Despite his visible anxiety, he politely and even somewhat graciously begged me to accompany him in his car. "It's absolutely essential," he said, "to show you something very interesting . . . and important. And I desperately need your—or Luis's—advice." And that was all he said.

By chance, none of the family was around. Luis was playing golf

160 / ALINE, COUNTESS OF ROMANONES

with Guy de Rothschild. And my children and grandchildren had left that morning for Jerez de la Frontera. Very aware of his depression, and that he was suffering terribly from Inge's death, I found it heartless not to do as he asked. Ordinarily, perhaps, I would not have been so willing, but I was also affected by Inge's ghastly accident, and I felt sorry for him. So I grabbed a sweater and went with him. Moments later, we were barreling along the coast road in his midnight-blue Porsche convertible.

It was almost dusk, a time more suited to curling up with a good mystery novel than to taking an eighty-mile-an-hour romp along the dangerous coastal highway. The wind was now blowing stronger than it had been earlier; the waves rolling up the beach to the left of the road were a scowling, foamy gray; and the horizon bore a dark slash of black: clear signs that a storm was fast approaching. Gusts of wind tore through my hair, and the car jolted over the uneven pavement. But Hans was a superb driver; and I had confidence in his skill. He held the wheel lightly between his fingertips, adjusting the car to the demands of the road and weather as sensitively and confidently as a surgeon performing a delicate operation.

Soon we were making the sharp left turn into the villa of Bastiano Bergesi. Pulling up beneath the portico, he leaned over and opened the door on my side, then jumped out himself.

"Thank you for coming, Aline. I think I've discovered something related to my daughter's accident, and I'd like a second pair of eyes. I feel that you and Luis are my only friends on this coast. Unfortunately, I've always been too busy with my own affairs to spend time here in the summer with Inge.

"In any event, now that she's gone, I fear I might be too eager to produce explanations for her death; and I don't entirely trust my own perceptions."

Luis would disapprove of what I was doing. But I would deal with that later. Right now I was helping a friend; and that, I soon realized to my dismay, involved scaling Bergesi's cliff down that treacherously shaky staircase I'd hoped never to see again. We'd come here last summer in a friend's boat; and while climbing the stairway, I'd cut my leg badly. I was astonished that Bastiano hadn't replaced it.

Despite my fears, Hans was clearly headed in that direction, moving with surprising agility for a man his age (he was well past sixty). When he reached the uppermost landing and grabbed the railing, it swayed with his weight.

"Come, Aline, this way," he waved his free arm in a looping gesture to encompass the wind, the mounting sea, the ominous sky, and the horrific stairway. By the time I reached the balustrade, Hans was already twenty feet below me and descending rapidly. He seemed like a man possessed. I couldn't imagine what he hoped to show me. But you only live once, I said to myself as I placed a reluctant foot onto the first rickety step.

As I climbed down, I noticed that many steps were loose, clinging to the memory of nails and bolts. Others were dangerously decayed, eaten away by the salt air. Meanwhile, the closer we came to the sea, the more violent it became, as though mirroring the anger of an old man haunted by the death of his daughter.

When Hans reached the floating dock, it was rocking alarmingly. Standing like a lusty pirate, legs strong and feet spread wide apart, his ability to maintain his balance was remarkable. He was obviously shouting to me; but his cries were almost impossible to hear above the drum of the surf.

Edging my way down the final flight, clinging to the jagged rock wall with both hands, I realized that following Hans had been more than foolish.

A thunderbolt crashed, it sounded just above our heads, to announce the storm was in full fury. Rain poured down with such sudden ferocity that I nearly lost my hold on the rail, and my feet could find no traction on the slippery planks. By the time I actually reached the floating dock, I was drenched. When I stepped onto the thing, Hans caught my wrist and pulled me to his side. His strong arm wrapped around my shoulders and held me steady in the onslaught.

"Aline, look!" he cried directly into my ear.

Look where? I could barely see a foot in front of me; but now Hans was pointing out to sea.

"Look, do you see them?"

"Hans, what? I don't know what you're . . ."

"Lights . . . flashing lights."

"I don't see anything . . . nothing. I'm sorry."

"This is the hour they're usually out there. Just wait. Keep looking." Hans was still pointing. "There . . . now. Don't you see them . . . now . . . ?"

And then I saw them. Lights that were blinking in staccato flashes, like the Morse code which I had been familiar with years ago.

Though I had given him no answer, Hans knew that I had seen

them. So far away. Yet, despite the darkness and the driving rain, every few moments a small flash shot through the dense blackness surrounding us.

"Now turn around. Look to your left. Do you see? There? Beyond the curve of land? Just behind that dock jutting out from the curve? A villa! La Amapola! Do you see lights flashing on the shore there! And there!" He pointed again at the sea. "More lights!"

"Yes, it's true. I see them. Must be fishermen." But I remembered Serge mentioning that name, the Villa La Amapola. He had told me no more about the reason for his interest in it. But here it was again.

"No!" he cried. "Not fishermen! Signals. That's what they are. They're a code. A code! No one would be out there fishing on a night like this. Damned smugglers. Cabanellas got in their way, so they destroyed his boat. I'm sure of that. Keep your eyes on those lights."

"Did you ask Paco if he saw anything that night?" I yelled. But because of the noise of the storm, Hans seemed not to hear me. He then indicated that we should go back up the stairs where we could talk better. He led me back across the pitching dock to the stairway.

Then one of the two lines securing the dock parted, causing the floating dock to swing away from the staircase. A gaping stretch of rough water instantly formed between our heaving dock and the questionable safety of the stairs. Meanwhile, the dock was half-submerged, tossing, heaving against the one remaining line. If that one tired rope broke, we would be swept out to sea . . . or else thrown up against the cement retainment wall. And nobody knew where I was.

"Sit down, Aline," shouted Hans. I didn't want to do anything like that. I wanted to keep holding on to his strong hand. But then I understood what he was doing. He was about to let go of me, and I wouldn't be able to stand alone.

"What can we do?" I shouted back.

"I'm going to try to retrieve the broken line. I'd like you as close to the edge as you can get, but sitting!"

With that, he let go of me; and I sat down abruptly and shimmied my body close to the edge of the plunging dock. Hans then dove into the raging waves, got his bearings, and dropped under the angry sea. For a long moment, I waited.

Then Hans finally bobbed up with the lost rope in his hand. He was a strong swimmer; and soon he was hoisting himself up on the ramp. Once he was there, he looped it through the dock ring; and with incredible strength—or maybe will power—he pulled the dock back to the staircase platform. At last, he reached out a hand, and I jumped to the small ramp. Then carefully mounting the steps, we slowly made our way to the top.

I HAD ALWAYS admired Bastiano Bergesi's *chilabas*, but I never thought I'd be wearing one like the one his manservant provided. It was made of luxurious soft indigo cashmere. Hans had also gone to change, and the butler was preparing hot tea. Logs crackled in the massive stone fireplace, giving the narrow room a cozy feeling. The leaping blaze enlivened the atmosphere, dispelling the gloomy chill of a few minutes before.

The lights that Hans had showed me, in my opinion, were not necessarily proof that he was seeing smugglers. I was anxious to tell him that I'd seen lights like these many times, looking out from my own house. Hans's lights could easily be fishing boats signaling each other because of the storm. They were perhaps even using some kind of a code. Then I recalled the other lights, the ones that came from the land around the corner—from the Villa La Amapola, according to Hans. Could these be coming from boats near the beach? I mused. Or was something actually going on there. In either case, the truth was clear: Nothing could change the fact that Inge was dead; and that was Hans's basic problem. Whatever I told him would make slight impact on him. He was consumed with the idea that his daughter had been murdered; and he was looking for conspiracies to explain it. He would jump from one to another, no matter how irrational. I knew, consequently, that I had to be patient with him.

The rain continued to stream down in dense gray sheets over the windowpanes. Hans was taking too long to change. Nearly half an hour had passed since he had waved companionably from the archway, promising to return in a moment. As I waited, it occurred to me that Luis would be wondering where I was. I had raced out of my house, without saying anything. Now I was anxious to end this evening's adventure and get home.

I searched for a telephone and found an old black one with a long extension cord on the floor beside the sofa. I went across the room and brought the phone back to where I was sitting. I intended to ask my husband to send someone to pick me up.

As I lifted the receiver to my ear and put my finger on the dial, I realized that the phone was in use. Instead of hanging up, however, I kept the receiver at my ear; for the distressed voice I heard was one I knew well. The first words shocked me to immediate alert.

"Weapons . . . money, that's all they ever want." The anguished voice seemed to cry through the line. It was Paco Cabanellas!

"Weapons cost a lot; and they're going to kill me because I can't deliver." He went on, "If you don't do it for me, do it for Inge."

"Calm down," Hans answered. "My daughter's dead, and you're alive. And if you hadn't been mixed up with those people . . ." He left that thought unfinished.

Paco spoke then, more hysterical than before. "The police question me every day . . ."

"Should I care? What difference does it make to me now?"

Paco came back with a blast, "You're involved, too, Hans, no matter what you say. And how do you know they're not out to kill you as well? Now that you know what you know. They're going to get all of us . . . one by one."

"Control yourself, Paco." Hans's tone was icy. "Watch what you say on the phone. And tell your problems to your boss, not to me. And you can also tell him I intend to bring him to justice—him and everyone else connected with Inge's murder . . ."

"Are you serious? Justice! Justice!" Paco seemed to spit into the phone. "These people are beyond justice! Justice doesn't touch them. And don't feel so sorry for yourself, either. I'm the one who has lost everything—Inge, my business, and my life isn't worth a peseta now, too. So don't teach me lessons . . ."

My ear echoed with the bang of the receiver slamming down. For a moment I held the phone, afraid to breathe. Then I heard the phone click. Hans had waited before he replaced the receiver. Did he suspect that someone had overheard his conversation? I knew there was only one telephone number at Bastiano's house, but there were certainly many extensions. And if Hans felt someone else might have been listening, I prayed that he would think it was the butler or some other servant. I carefully replaced the receiver.

Hans's and Paco's conversation had left me confused and apprehensive. What did it mean? Was Hans involved with terrorists? That didn't seem likely. But what *was* he up to? That was by no means clear. Meanwhile heavy footsteps were sounding in the long corridor. Hurriedly I placed the phone on the nearest table and tried to compose myself, leaning back into the embroidered pillows, opening a magazine. Hans would return at any moment.

A second later he entered. I gazed up with what I hoped was a casual happy smile. But my thoughts continued to spin.

"Aline, you are lovely sitting there," said Hans, "precisely what's needed in this room."

"Hans, you were sensational out there in the water. Were you a sailor?" I asked, hoping to draw attention off myself.

"Not at all; but I am a swimmer. Was on the German Olympic team many years ago." The big man slumped into one of Bastiano Bergesi's leather armchairs. His face now regained its care worn expression. "In fact, I blame myself for Inge's passion for those damn Cigarette boats. When she was a little girl, I used to take her out in a speedboat on the lake near our house in Bavaria. The faster I went, the harder she laughed . . ." Hans's face crumpled then; and he covered his eyes with his fist. After a time, he called the servant to bring him a whiskey.

"Hans, have you talked to Paco about the night Inge was killed?" I asked, hoping my voice sounded as controlled as I intended.

"Well, yes. I even asked him about the lights that I showed you. But he claimed he did not see any lights. The night was dark; he was going very fast. His Cigarette boat was making a deafening noise as it banged down over the waves. There was some wind. Paco says he never saw another boat, or anything else out there. As far as he remembers there was no moon; and there were no lights on the water outside his own. The explosion came as a total surprise. An earsplitting blast; the flash of flames. He thinks he must have been knocked out for some seconds, because he knew nothing more until he found himself choking and floundering in the water—with his boat in flames nearby.

"He tried to find Inge, but only got a glimpse of her head; and realized she was dead." Here Hans paused and wiped his forehead. Then he went on, "As he struggled to get to the shore, he said, his thoughts were with Inge. He was also trying to understand what had happened. But only later did he suspect that someone had planted a bomb. The engine and the fuel system of his boat were always in perfect condition, he's an excellent mechanic, so there was no natural cause for the explosion."

"What do you think really happened, Hans?" I asked.

"Paco and Inge took the boat out almost every night. That night, someone was waiting with a remote-control device as Paco raced by on his usual route along the coast. He would have been in a boat nearby—or on land for that matter. When he pushed the button.

Inge took the brunt of the explosion—she happened to be steering the boat; Paco was next to her—and the explosion threw him into the water." Hans sighed dejectedly. "Paco told me that it was just bad luck that Inge was driving, but she insisted."

"But what did the police ask Paco? Did he tell them his suspicions?"

"I don't know exactly," Hans said. "But Paco told me that the police were still insisting that the accident was caused by a mechanical defect—a spark that ignited the fuel."

"Did they say they would investigate further?"

"Oh, yes, half-heartedly. And they had the same attitude when I spoke to them. I suggested that the explosion was very likely the work of terrorists involved in some kind of smuggling. But they told me that the only smugglers they catch coming across from Morocco are small-time hashish dealers. As far as the police are concerned, no smuggler that they know has the ability or training to blow up a boat. So they promised to keep their eyes open, but would not believe what they consider my paranoid suggestions." Hans sighed again. "But neither the police nor the Coast Guard will find the killers. These bastards are experts, well trained, with significant financing behind them. And they are handling more than minor drugs, I am sure. I intend to get them, one way or another."

He picked up his whiskey, while I sipped tea. "The lights we saw tonight," he went on, "caught my attention two days ago, in the evening around ten o'clock. Looked like a code to me. But the first time I saw them, I couldn't see anyone answering. When the same thing happened the next night, I went down to the dock and walked out where I could see around the curve of the land. There I saw lights answering from another point to the north of us but closer to shore. Later, I realized that the lights on land originated from somewhere near the Villa La Amapola. I decided then that I needed help."

"But why me?" I asked.

"Because the police pay no attention to me. Also you know the coast; and you and Luis are my closest friends here. At least you could tell me how you understand all this . . . or if I'm going mad."

In my most diplomatic manner, I told him again that I'd often seen fishermen's boats out at night with lights like those we'd seen.

He shrugged at that, and pressed on: "I have reliable information that high-level international terrorists are active in this area. There are also drug dealers."

The butler entered, bearing a silver tray with several decanters on it. Hans once again became the bustling, considerate host. As soon as the man left, Hans went on. "There's nobody I can ask to help me discover who killed my daughter. But I have my own ideas. Nearby there is a center for some kind of international illegal traffic. Either traffic in drugs, or traffic in something else. Have you ever been to any of those houses up on the hill in the Arab section?"

He was referring to El Ancon, a new development next to the Puente Romano. Many wealthy Arabs had built large mansions there. A mosque had been constructed at the entrance; and one wealthy Arab had even built an exact replica of the American White House high on a hill next to the highway. At night it was illuminated by strong spotlights. It was quite a sensation to pass by at night and see the White House on a hill in Marbella.

More to the point, however, La Amapola was in El Ancon.

"No, I don't know anyone who lives there," I answered. "Do you suspect an Arab drug dealer placed that bomb? That seems farfetched to me."

"I'm not thinking of just any Arab smugglers. Remember, out on the dock, I pointed out to you the Villa La Amapola?" His eyes caught mine. "Did you know that place has an exaggerated number of armed guards surrounding it, day and night? The property is enormous and goes right down to the water. Nobody is allowed near the house or the grounds.

"I'm sure the place is a center for international crooks," Hans went on. "Englishmen, Germans, and Americans have been seen there. Yes, don't look so surprised. Americans, too. They come and go; and nobody who does not belong there can get near. The armed guards carry weapons . . . and not your average handgun."

I nodded, but I did not have a reply to offer him. At the same time I made a mental note to find out who was the current owner of La Amapola. Only the night before someone had mentioned that the house had been there quite some time. I had listened attentively when I heard the name, The Amapola. Evidently, early on it had belonged to the Marbella Club. Then it was sold to a German. That was over five years back, way before Arabs began to construct their own sumptuous estates in the neighborhood.

"Tried to look around the place," Hans went on, "but it's impossible to get near. It's protected on three sides by high walls; and only the beach side is open. When I was walking along that beach, two guards appeared almost immediately; and I was forced to get back in the water. The guards threaten anybody who approaches the place. But I have been able to learn that the owner is Arab, and he has friends in the police force." He sighed and took a sip of his drink. Then Hans shook his head, "Whoever owns that place has something to do with my Inge's death. And I intend to find out more about what is going on there." He picked up the teapot and looked at me. "More tea?"

"I should be getting back."

"Of course. You've been too kind as it is. I'll drive you immediately."

The wind was howling through the chimney; and I didn't relish the idea of a return trip in the little Porsche.

"It's too much trouble, Hans. My driver can come for me. I just have to call."

"Yes, perhaps you've had enough of a sad old man for one day." I was taken back by the self-pity in his voice. With that he reached down for the telephone which, before I had moved it, had been on the floor next to his place on the sofa. "What's your phone num—" and then he paused. My heart nearly stopped as his hand searched the floor at his side; and then I saw him bend over, looking for it. Slowly his eyes glanced around until they rested on the phone now sitting on the table next to my chair. Standing up, he took three steps and reached out for it. He completed this action with such concentration that I had to make an enormous effort to maintain a serene appearance. Then he looked up and asked, "Were you just using this phone?"

Foolishly, I answered, "No."

His glance became icy, his voice lost the warmth of a minute before, as he asked, "Your number?"

At that moment, the butler who had been doing something at the bar and had overheard the conversation, offered to drive me home. Casting a grateful smile in his direction, I jumped up and, after a quick goodbye, hastened to the front entrance where the butler was already waiting. Paco and Hans's words to each other still rang in my ears as Bastiano's old BMW merged into the traffic. My awareness that Hans suspected I had lied about the phone did not soothe me either.

When I arrived home, to my surprise I found Luis having a drink in the salon with Nancy Rhodentus. "Where have you been?" he asked, staring at my still damp stringy hair and Bastiano's *chilaba*.

After I explained that I'd been with Hans and got caught in the storm, Luis told me that after the golf game, he had gone to an art exhibit at the Hotel Los Monteros, found Nancy there, and brought her home for a drink.

"When I left my house, it was raining, but not like this," Nancy said as she gestured toward the sea, where the waves still thundered as they crashed on the beach.

After we settled down, I told Luis and Nancy my story about Hans and the lights. And they were as baffled by it as I was. "He's convinced that the lights are signals made by smugglers of some kind, and he paid no attention to me when I explained that we see lights like that from fishermen every night. He's also suspicious of the people who own that big house in El Ancon—the one called La Amapola. He told me the wildest stories about the place." I purposely avoided mentioning the telephone conversation I'd overheard between Hans and Paco. I wanted to tell Luis about that when we were alone.

"No doubt Inge's death has knocked a few screws loose," Nancy suggested, pointing a finger at her forehead; and Luis nodded in agreement.

By then, dinner was about ready. Though the storm had subsided while we were talking, I convinced Nancy to stay. This was really the first chance we had to spend some private time with her; and I was glad for that. She was an interesting young woman whom I wanted to know better. During our chat we learned that she'd attended the University of California at Berkeley, graduating in 1965 with a degree in Social Science. "For a while," she went on, "I was very involved in social work in and around Los Angeles, and later in New York, but I couldn't get along on the salary. And when I realized I had a future in modeling, I made the career jump. In fact, that's how I married R.K." There was a flicker of irritation in her eyes as she mentioned his name, and I realized she was still upset about him. Luis tried to change the subject; but she went on, explaining that she'd been sent to Paris on several modeling jobs and had settled there. She met R.K. in the Champs Elysées Drugstore one afternoon when he was trying to buy a razor. He couldn't speak a word of French, so she translated for him. Eight months later they were married.

"I never knew anyone could be so wonderful—so good," she went on. "Before R.K., I'd been married for six months to a monster, so I really appreciated every minute with R.K. But now, after both experiences, I have a very bad opinion of men. I don't think I'll ever marry again," she added, maintaining a normal voice with difficulty.

Before that evening, I had had some suspicions about Nancy. But her very evident sincerity was most convincing. It looked to me then that she had been truly fond of R.K., and that she really missed him.

By the time dinner was over, the rain and wind had stopped and we were able to walk out to the terrace. Enough of the clouds had passed by to allow us to see a few stars. And we could also see in the distance a fishing boat bobbing up and down on the still rough water, its lights like a giant firefly fluttering in the shiny blackness. "You were right," Nancy said, "those lights come from the fishermen trawling for squid."

Andrés interrupted to announce that Nancy's driver had arrived. We walked with her to her car; and as we watched it pull out of the drive, Luis turned to me, "You know, darling," he said, "Nancy's quite a girl after all. I can't help liking her." That was just the way I felt, too.

We turned around. And on the way upstairs, I told Luis about the telephone conversation between Hans and Paco. "Well," Luis said, shrugging his shoulders, "sounds like trouble. You know, I never trusted that Cabanellas. I'm not surprised to find out he's got himself caught up with bad people. He's that kind of man. As for you, my darling, I can't think of any good reason for you to involve yourself in either Hans Schmidt's or Paco Cabanellas's affairs. What could you possibly accomplish? Who could you help? I want you to avoid them. Don't poke into their business.

"As for that house in El Ancon, I do believe what Hans told you about it may be true. Somebody else commented only the other day about the protection around that property. So much security just doesn't make sense. Smugglers don't want anything that looks out of the usual. If the house is a cover, exaggerated security would attract the attention of the police."

As we parted to change for bed, my husband grumbled, "This coast is filling up with dreadful people."

Chapter 21

The next morning, the events of the previous day still made me uneasy. I wanted to consult Jupiter or Serge, but that was going to be difficult for the time being. Jupiter was traveling someplace outside Spain, and he had not mentioned where he was going. And there was no telephone at our ranch, or anywhere else within kilometers. Lines had not yet reached many areas of rural Spain. So I could not contact Serge either. Usually we telephoned the operator in a small town about five miles away; and she would send a message into the *finca*. But this was not practical now, since I didn't want to draw attention to Serge.

The relentless hot sun that came after the night's storm made me restless and increased my curiosity about the mysterious house, La Amapola. It seemed odd, I reflected, that Hans was so familiar with the place. I was dying to learn more about it, and wanted at least to see the property myself.

Even though I was well aware that the wisest thing would be to sit tight until Jupiter returned, I found myself in my small red Seat on the road from Los Monteros to Marbella, headed for El Ancon. My plan was merely to drive through the village, pass the entrance to La Amapola, and form some kind of impression of the place.

Ten minutes later I was in El Ancon. Although I passed this road many times every week, I had not noticed how much the area had grown. It covered most of a hill that sloped down to the sea. On the hill, El Ancon spread before me; huge new mansions surrounded by bushy gardens covered the entire slope. Further on, rose a graceful white mosque, its dome brilliant with luminous mosaic tiles. Their blazing colors, saturating the eye with their radiance, were an ostentatious symbol that after hundreds of years the Arabs had returned to this coast. On the other side of the highway, stretching down to the sea, a twisting road circled pyramid-shaped apartment buildings, lines of luxury shops, neon signs, and beyond in the distance more mansions and gardens. When Luis and I had first built our house, Marbella was barely more than a sleepy fishing village with a few stores; and the surrounding area was made up of a few simple farms, where groves of umbrella pines led down to lovely peaceful beaches. But now El Ancon, like other nearby developments, had a pompous entry gate, and its streets were flanked by impressive homes. The sweeping entrance avenue, curving down to the beach, was heavily planted with palm trees. Directly ahead, on a spotless stretch of blue-green grass, lay the entrance to La Amapola.

I turned the car toward the gate. The street was virtually deserted, and as I drove toward the closed wrought-iron entrance, I saw the high stone wall that isolated La Amapola from the world outside. The dark outlines of two men were visible through the windows of the guardhouse, and parked next to it was a small delivery van belonging to Antonio's Specialty Shop. This did not surprise me at all. Antonio had the best selection of gourmet foods on the coast.

I had an idea about chatting with the two guards. At least I would have something to tell Jupiter. I could always pretend that I was lost and looking for some other house. But as I slowed down, I noticed a surveillance camera on top of the guardhouse, slowly panning the area. The last thing I wanted was my face and license plate on videotape. Immediately I braked, turned around, and drove away.

Heading back into the main village, I felt frustrated that I hadn't been able to learn more, but the camera was a significant deterrent, as far as I was concerned. Without my cover, I was useless to Jupiter. And more important to me, without my cover, my life and the lives of my family members were at risk.

An hour later, after taking care of some necessary shopping, I was passing Antonio's Specialty Store, when I once again noticed his delivery van, this time parked in front of his shop. At the same time, I remembered that Antonio carried a cheese that Luis was particularly fond of and which would be perfect for a small group of friends who were coming for lunch. So I pulled into a parking spot and went in. The place had originally been a tackle shop for local fishermen, but it now catered to the wealthy and anyone else with a taste for exotic foods. When he took over the shop, however, Antonio had made few changes, for the original decor gave the store a rustic charm its clientele enjoyed. Exorbitantly priced champagne was stacked on wooden shelves originally built to support rods and reels.

Antonio himself greeted me and prepared to take my order. I was about to ask him for Luis's cheese, when I noticed he was packing a basket large enough for a sizable picnic. Among other things, it contained at least two dozen smooth metal canisters of a rare and very fine Iranian caviar.

"Pepito," he called to a tall lanky boy who was busy stocking shelves in the back of the store. "Take this over to La Amapola."

"Where?" said Pepito as he stepped forward. I recognized him from the times he'd delivered things to our house.

"Where do you think?" asked Antonio and gave the boy an affectionate swat on the shoulder. "The usual." He nodded toward the basket.

"I was just there," Pepito said. "Don't they ever know what they want?"

Antonio mumbled between clenched teeth some words that were barely audible. "It doesn't matter, you *idiota*, as long as they pay."

Casually picking up a jar of honey, I looked away from him, to give the impression that I was uninterested. But "La Amapola" was still ringing in my ears, a name that had been spinning through my head all morning.

Antonio closed and tied the top of the basket and then turned to me, "Perdón, Señora Condesa, how can I help you?"

"I'd like Pepito to deliver one of your Camemberts to my house. It's not a big order; but my husband is having friends for cocktails before lunch and would be grateful. I would take it with me, but I'm on my way elsewhere."

"Señora Condesa, for you we would deliver a parsley twig. Of course, right away." He turned around, "Pepito," he said to the delivery boy, who was carrying the heavy basket out the back door. "Wait. I want you to take some cheese to the Señora Condesa's house before you make that other delivery." He moved over to the cheese section; and as he reached for the wheel of cheese, I was already on my way out the door.

As I drove home, I gathered my thoughts. And by the time I pulled into our drive and parked under the green awning, I had a plan. I knew I had to rush, though, if I was going to make it work, since Pepito should arrive in a few minutes.

When I heard the crunch of his small van on the gravel by the delivery entrance, I was just slipping on a pair of dark slacks and a black sleeveless top. Tearing down the stairs, I managed to sweep up my purse from the hall table in passing. And as Pepito raised his hand to knock, I opened the back door. He was startled to see me standing there breathless.

"*Buenas*, Señora Condesa," he said with a shy smile. His hair was oily; he had acne; and he had a boyishly timid manner; but his eyes had an interesting light in them. At first I took this to be intelligence; but a moment later I realized it was only the sharp look of a young, would-be hustler. That gave me a moment's pause, in view of what I wanted from him. But then I realized I didn't have to trust the boy very far.

"*Buenas*, Pepito," I said, and made way for him to come into the kitchen. He carried the round white package stiffly in front of him and placed it gingerly on the tiled counter.

"Pepito," I drew him aside where the cook could not hear, "I was wondering if you might do me a favor." At this point, I opened my purse to find my cash, indicating I intended to pay him. Glancing back at him to gauge his willingness, I saw the boy looking eagerly at the bills in my hand.

"*Sí*, Señora Condesa?" he said.

"Pepito," I said, making an effort to convey a sense of gravity, "For important reasons I must visit La Amapola without anyone there observing me." His eyelids fluttered a little as he waited for my next words. "And so I would like to accompany you in your delivery truck now when you deliver the champagne and caviar. It is extremely important for you not to mention this visit to anyone; and for that reason I will pay you one thousand pesetas. Do you suppose you can let me go in your car with you?"

"Oh, yes, Señora," Pepito answered, his eyes narrowing as I handed him the one-thousand-peseta note.

"Do you pass through the gate, or do you deliver to the guards?" I decided to get to the point immediately and to encourage him to realize he should do exactly what I told him.

"Always through the gate, Señora Condesa. There is no other way." His voice was cheerful, and I knew he was delighted with my tip.

"Pepito," I went on, "once we get inside the property, do you think you will be able to handle what I ask of you?"

"*Sí, sí*, Señora Condesa."

And so the tall skinny boy and I walked together to his van. The vehicle was perfect for my purposes. It had originally been a small, open delivery truck. But a tin roof had been added, the sides had been closed in with divided wooden slats, and the back was now covered with a canvas flap. Unless the guards were very thorough, I would enter the grounds of La Amapola undetected.

The old van was not a pleasant vehicle to ride in, however. The worn shock absorbers made for a rough ride to El Ancon; Pepito whistled tunelessly the entire way; and the heat in the back was stifling. Through the narrow openings in the old wooden slats, I could see the countryside whizzing by, so I knew pretty well where we were all the time.

"Señora Condesa, *ya estamos*," Pepito whispered so loudly I nearly groaned. If the guards were paying attention, they would wonder whom he was talking to. But Pepito's truck was such a common sight, they probably didn't give it another thought. And then the next thing I knew, he accelerated the engine. We continued up the drive which, thankfully, was well paved. Compared to the highway, it felt as smooth as a china plate.

Soon the van pulled to a stop, and my hideaway was steeped in shadow. Pepito lifted the basket with the champagne and the caviar from the passenger seat and opened his door.

"I'll be right back, Señora Condesa," he said in a stage whisper over his shoulder. He had parked the little van beneath the portico, which protected the back entrance from the strong sun. I peeked over the top of the front seat and watched Pepito climb the four steps to the back door, rest the package at his feet, and knock loudly. I was very curious to see who would answer. But no one appeared. And then, after a moment, Pepito opened the door himself and disappeared into what I assumed was the kitchen. A minute later he was out again, tripping down the stairs, still whistling loudly and tunelessly. He popped into the driver's seat and began to start the engine.

"Wait, Pepito," I said. "Why didn't anyone answer the door?"

"Oh, it's often the case. Usually nobody's in the kitchen, not even the servants. But today I could hear them all out on the terrace. They talk a lot, and the servants are busy serving drinks out there. The guards are careful about letting me into the grounds, but I could go all through the house without anyone stopping me, if I wanted. I know where to put the caviar. There's a large refrigerator. I put the package inside, and leave the champagne on the table."

"They were expecting you?"

"Yes, I come during the week with other things, but on Fridays they make a larger order. That's usually when they have lots of people here."

"Pepito, could you go back inside and tell me who's there today?"

"Oh, I already know that. It's like I said—the usual. They're all outside on the terrace. The couple who takes care of the big house, then el señor, the owner. I don't know his name. He only comes here now and then. And the others—many foreigners. That's why they have so many rooms, I guess, sometimes the same people, sometimes different people. And a lady. She's new."

"Why are they all outside?"

Pepito shrugged. "That's where they have more room. He—the boss—talks to them. Sometimes two guards I know from the port are there also. Those guards have nice boats. I had a ride in one once."

As Pepito spoke, a daring idea was forming in my mind. "Pepito," I said, "do you think I could go inside without anyone seeing me? I would like very much to see who those people are."

Pepito's eyes opened wide, wonder was all over his face. "Sí, sí, Señora Condesa. You'll have no trouble. But it would be easier to see the people on the terrace from there." He pointed to a decorative white trellis covered with moonflowers that ran parallel to the house. "Inside is a clothesline; the gardener had that made to hide the laundry when it's put out to dry. But you can walk up and down inside it and see into the house very well. And that trellis goes right up to the terrace, and you can hear what they say there. Usually they're speaking Arabic. I never can understand them."

Obviously Pepito had gone eavesdropping himself more than once.

"But what if the guards at the gate come looking for me?" he went on. "I don't like them."

"Look, Pepito, it'll only mean a few minutes more. I tell you what. Just take a few steps around the corner where you can see the guardhouse and keep your eyes on them. If you think they're coming, all you have to do is whistle to me and I'll run back to the van. It'll take them at least five minutes to walk up that winding drive to the house. We'll be able to leave before they reach us."

He didn't look convinced. "But when we go through the gate again, they may ask me why I took so long," he said, still anxious.

"Tell them you lost something."

"But what could I have lost?"

I thought for a moment. It would have to be something plausible. "No, wait," I said. "I have a better idea. Let me get out of this thing, first." I then squeezed out of the tight quarters in the back by climbing over the front seat instead of opening the back canvas flap, since that would have made me more visible. After that, I slipped out of the van's driver's side. Through the open slits in the side, I had determined on our way into the grounds that the guards view would be obstructed by the parked van. Also I had surveyed the area in case a camera was set up above the entrance or anyplace on the side of the house. I hadn't spotted one. And I prayed there were none hidden inside the trellised enclosure. The house was surrounded by a magnificent garden with flowery bushes, banana and palm trees that could easily hide a video camera. I knew I was taking a chance, but I also knew that Jupiter would be disappointed in me if I missed this unique opportunity.

"Come with me," I ordered, and Pepito followed me to the front of his van. "Now open the hood, will you, please." When he had done that, I reached inside the engine compartment, found some barely visible wire or other, and gave it a strong pull until I felt it give. "Now you have a good excuse for a delay," I said.

"*Sí*, Señora Condesa," he answered, with a sidewise, knowing look.

Running close to the ground, I reached the trellis in seconds. The long clothesline down the middle was heavy with thick linen sheets, which were waving in a strong breeze coming in from the sea. With so many sheets obstructing my view, I couldn't see the end of the small enclosure. As I cautiously proceeded, I prayed that there was no alarm system. Then it occurred to me that servants would have to pass through here to hang and collect the wash, and I felt slightly safer.

As I moved along, I peered through the trellis and saw that the vines in some places were so thick I could not see through them. I carefully lifted a few leaves with my hand; and, to my surprise, I found myself looking into a large, Arabic-style dining room, with light-colored banquettes lining the walls. Some of the blue moon-flowers were pressed against the pane of the dining-room window, so close was the trellis to the house.

But what gave me a real jolt was my proximity to two men seated in wicker chairs on a terrace which opened from the dining room. I was standing only three feet from the house; and the men were seated half facing me only two feet beyond that, not far from the open door. They were so close I could see the detail of the embroidery on their Arafat-type headdresses. Their thick black beards and heavy black eyebrows gave their faces a threatening expression that sent chills down my spine. If someone were to discover me now, I would have no plausible explanation to give them.

Beyond the Arabs, a long terrace stretched across the entire front of the house; and glass doors opened along the length of the facade. Carefully, I inched a few meters further, until I was parallel to the terrace. Meanwhile, the wind was blowing the sheets around my head and the thick vines made it impossible for me to see. Now with still more care, hoping no one on the terrace would notice, I lifted some leaves. The seated men were now so near that again I was startled and dropped my fingers from the leafy wall.

A flicker of motion sent shadows into my hideaway. I froze, not daring to move. Gazing intently, I saw a quiver of white dancing through the leafy pattern of the vines in front of me. Through an open space in the trellis, I could now see a man about ten feet away on the terrace. He was dressed in a long frosty *chilaba*, and he was facing a group of perhaps a dozen people, all of whom were listening to him. It was the reflection of his voluminous white clothing that had penetrated my enclosure. As for the two other men, they were now only three feet away.

Of course I was desperate to get a closer look at the man in the white *chilaba*. But at the moment his back was to me; so I could see only the faces of the others. But I recognized none of them.

At the far end of the terrace were two men in olive cotton khakis with submachine guns slung over their shoulders. Both were attentive to something going on farther away, in the direction of the sea. So near to me were the two men at this end of the terrace, that I feared my slightest move would give me away. I wondered if they also had weapons, smaller ones perhaps, and were acting as guards.

As I was calculating the many risks, a branch crackled behind me. One of the Arafat Arabs turned his head in my direction. My heart stopped. I waited for the prick of a cold blade penetrating my back, or the sound of a shot. Paralyzed, I turned around. Pepito was at a slight distance, looking at me with a pained expression. Making an effort to keep my breathing soft, I gestured for him to go back. And I silently retraced my steps to join him. What had happened? Was a guard already coming up to the house?

As soon as we were at a safe distance from the people on the terrace, I motioned for him to speak. He whispered, "I fixed the wire. Are you ready yet?"

I shook my head no, and as softly and firmly as I could, I whispered, "Pepito, calm down. Go back and keep your eye on the gate. I'll be here three or four minutes. If, by any chance, the guard gets to you before I'm back, don't look for me. Tell him the story about the loose wire. Then get in the van and leave. There's no way anything can happen to you. Don't speak when you get in. Just drive away. All right, Pepito? However, if you leave without me, no extra tip. You realize that?"

"*Sí*, Señora Condesa."

I glanced at my watch. Two precious minutes had passed, while explaining to Pepito. Silently I went back to my position at the end of the trellis. Now I tried to get some idea of the interior of the house. I could make out through the small wooden slats two doors leading out of the kitchen toward the main part of the house. One had a round glass window that allowed a small view of the dining area. As I took that in, it also occurred to me that someone could go into the kitchen and see Pepito's van from there. And if they investigated, they would see him spying around the corner down the driveway. The other rooms that opened onto the terrace all had many windows; and shafts of sunlight danced on their white marble floors. Listening carefully, I crept a few steps forward to get a better view of the house, and of the people on the terrace.

This action brought the two men quite close again, which made me terribly aware of every breath I took. Even moving a leaf could be a reckless act. The large main salon beyond the dining room was huge and bright, its cathedral ceiling had a carved-wood design, as in Arabic palaces. Though it was warm on the terrace, and the house was surely air-conditioned, the meeting was nevertheless being held outdoors. Still, there was a breeze, and the terrace's canvas cover kept it shaded from the sun. The breeze was, in fact, a problem for me, since the laundry blowing around me kept obstructing my view. I was also afraid that the two guards near me (if that was what they were) would hear even the slight noise of my disengaging my head from the folds of a sheet or towel.

From where I stood, I could see that the gathering was certainly not a party. Everyone was listening with careful attention to the words of the speaker in the white *chilaba*. In fact, the churchlike quiet of the whole scene was eerie. The sea was too far distant to hear, and not even birds were singing. I was so close to the group that I almost felt vertigo, as if my slightest move might throw me into their midst. All the same, I carefully moved an inch further, trying to get the best possible view, and praying that no one's eyes would explore the trellis. The uncomfortable thought that my shadow might be visible through the vines plagued me. And despite knowing that Pepito would be hoping for more money from me, I also worried that he might get cold feet and skitter off. I was sure I would never get out of here, without the protection of his van.

Meanwhile, the man in the frosty white robe had begun to pace back and forth, and he was now walking in my direction. So his voice came to me quite clearly. But as Pepito had explained, he was speaking in Arabic, and I understood nothing. About that time, I noticed that some of the men were obviously not Arabic; and I wondered how they understood. This meeting must have a special significance, I concluded. I looked at my wristwatch. Time was running out, and I'd failed to discover anything important. I gave myself three more minutes. I couldn't give up now.

A moment later, the leader stopped to say something to a man seated on a canvas hassock; and as he did, I heard the screech of an iron chair being pushed against the stone floor of the terrace. Then one of the Arafat types nearest me stood up and lurched toward me.

I nearly gasped. He was headed for me. I stopped breathing. He had seen me!

Then, just as he came close to my feet, he spat on the ground. I looked down and was horrified to see that the trellis did not reach to the earth. Perhaps my feet were visible through the slim stalks of the vines? I asked myself. But the man had returned to his seat. He hadn't seen my feet after all!

My sigh of relief could have given me away. But no sooner had that crisis faded than I heard the confident click of high heels tapping across the terrace. A woman, whom I had not noticed before, had risen from a chair. Her back was to me, so I could not see her face. But she was dressed in Western clothes, and not a *chilaba*, though the significance of that was not immediately clear. She strode into the cavernous main salon and passed out of view.

What is immediately clear, I thought, is that if she goes to the kitchen, she can see Pepito's van. And if I return now, and she's in the kitchen, when I run for the van she'll see me. To my heightened nerves, the sound of her heels on the marble floor felt as violent as the spray of a machine gun. And then, gathering myself together, I tried again to make out her face. But I feared betraying my position if I took steps to follow her movements inside the house. So I could only make out the back of a blue dress on a slender shape.

The woman vanished into the dining room, in the direction of the kitchen, perhaps blocking my escape route. I decided to stay just two minutes more. Creeping closer to the end of the trellis, I tried to see the face of the speaker. Here there were fewer flowers and vines, and the sun was shining in my direction; so I could go no further. I tried to calm myself, struggling to keep my courage. For the place I'd picked was more exposed than the ones I'd watched from earlier, but from it, I could view the entire scene.

Rapidly, I scanned the servants. All of them were dressed in gray *chilabas*, and they were standing at a respectful distance near a long table bar. The breeze wafted to me the smell of fried fish and other foods on the table. Among the servants was an unveiled woman. And this led me to conclude that the servants must be Moroccans. For Moroccans were now working in many houses on the coast; and Moroccan women were rarely veiled.

After that, I looked again at the men gathered for the meeting; and I began to get some sort of a picture of who they were. For instance, a pair of dark-skinned men standing at the far end appeared to be local fishermen. And to my initial surprise, I recognized a policeman who had been helpful when Luis's wallet was stolen two years before.

All were still listening attentively to the leader, who continued to pace as he spoke. Their faces followed him like spectators at a tennis match. I waited anxiously until his restless pattern would bring him nearer. But that happened sooner than I expected; for before I knew it, he had taken several long steps toward the Arafat-type men closest to me. Then he turned in midstride and glared directly at me. I was petrified. I had seen that face before!

Through the patterned trellis, I was staring into the eyes of a strikingly handsome man with dark, Arab coloring, thick black eyebrows, and a small Omar Sharif moustache. For a heart-stopping second I waited for him to call out a warning; but then I realized he did not see me. And at that moment, his head turned, and a beam of sunlight hit his cheek. My astonishment was complete—a long, deep scar slashed down his lower right cheek—not a tiny, almost invisible line like Nancy's scar, but a deep, wide laceration. This was the man I had seen with Carlos the night before the wedding in Germany!

He said something to the men in the fancy headdress. And abruptly the Arab seated closest to me got up from his chair. My God, I thought, he's coming to get me! They've seen my feet. They've seen my shadow. I felt as if I were standing before them naked.

Before I could budge, the man made a sudden, dramatic gesture with his arm. And with relief I realized he was only asking a question. Still, it took all the self-discipline I could muster to keep from bolting. But the Arab with the scar was still only ten feet away; and any sudden movement might catch his attention. I tried to calm my breathing enough to be ready to move out at the best moment . . . aware that when I did leave, the woman in blue might be in the kitchen. Maybe she'd already caught Pepito and had warned the guards. At any rate I knew he would be beside himself with anxiety by now. I prayed he hadn't left. I was again terribly certain that without the cover of his van, I didn't have a prayer of getting away safely.

The man with the scar again spoke to the Arab near me, scowling as though he was admonishing him. But the other wasn't intimidated. On the contrary, he waved his arms more violently than before, and said something in an angry voice. Then he spat. To my surprise, the leader didn't respond to this insulting gesture. Instead, he turned on his heel and continued talking to the others.

This time I didn't waste my chance. As soon as the leader's back was turned, I moved quickly and silently down the small enclosure. When I reached the spot where I could see into the dining room, I had a dilemma. If the woman was in the kitchen, she would be able to see me as I left the protection of the enclosure. Yet no other exit was available.

Toward the end of the trellis, I cautiously lifted a sheet and peered through the small triangular holes into the kitchen. To my vast relief, the room was empty. Just one more second and I was free. I didn't lose a moment moving the last few feet. But when I got to the end of the thin wooden structure and once more peered through, my heart caught. Not only was the woman standing in the doorway, but Pepito was there as well. And if his expression was any indication, his excuse about the loose wire was not working.

I had no choice but to make a dash for it the minute her head turned away from me. Thank God, the old van was only twenty feet away. Pepito was all this time pleading with the woman. I could hear his plaintive tone, but I didn't have time to wonder what he was asking for.

I glanced at the kitchen door. Now both the woman and Pepito had disappeared inside. The van was facing down the drive, and the passenger door was open wide. I thought Pepito must have left it open for me.

I was about to make a lunge for the car, when I realized the door was open because someone was sitting inside; his large feet were hanging out. Just then, I heard the back door of the kitchen swing open; a woman's voice called to the person in the car; and a man, who looked more like a gorilla than a human being, squeezed out of the tiny van. In his arms rested an automatic rifle, cradled like a baby.

He lumbered up the steps; and I heard the kitchen door slam and nothing more. So, I dashed for the van and entered it by the door the guard had left open. I dove into the back and had barely time to pull the smelly old blanket over my head and flatten myself against the metal floor when the entire vehicle listed with the weight of the huge man stepping back inside. A moment later, the driver's door opened and Pepito slid into his seat. "Move it," said the heavy man.

"*Sí, sí. Ahora mismo!*" Pepito managed to squeeze out of his throat; I wondered if the man was pointing the gun at him.

He called Pepito a name too hideous to repeat. But Pepito did not reply. Meanwhile, the stench and the heat of the blanket were suffocating. I wouldn't be able to bear it much longer. The van moved slowly down the circular drive. It was becoming nearly impossible to breathe. My mouth pressed against the metal floor, the blanket weighing down on top of me reeked of machine oil.

The brakes of the van finally whined, and the machine came to a halt. The passenger door banged open; I heard a loud smack, followed by Pepito's sharp cry of pain; the man had slapped him. With a curse, the man pulled himself out of the narrow front seat and slammed the door hard. So hard that I nearly slid across the metal floor as the van bounced up and down.

"Your last delivery was short, you little f——ing pig," the man said. "Do it again, you crook, and I'll scrape your face off your skull," he added for emphasis. Then I heard the loud impact of his gun against the metal door. Pepito cried out again as the glass in the window rattled from the force of the blow. The old van again rocked back and forth like a tiny boat tossed in the waves. And I nearly screamed, too.

As the rocking stopped, another harsh voice called something sharp. Pepito ground the gears, found first, and the van moved forward with a lurch. In a few seconds the ride turned rough. Never have I been so happy to feel a bumpy road! We had cleared the entrance to La Amapola! Pepito was clearly upset; he was barely keeping us on the road.

I threw off the odious blanket to get my bearings. I saw that Pepito had made it as far as the mosque near the entrance of El Ancon.

"Pull over, Pepito," I said. We were well out of sight of La Amapola. Hot air rushed through the open windows. Pepito's face was red; a welt was visible on one cheek, and there was a bloody scratch across his forehead. Except for these minor wounds, he seemed unharmed. "Pepito, please pull over, it's safe now."

He yanked the wheel to the left and pulled the car close against the curb. And then he started breathing heavily, and raggedly. He was only eighteen at most, and he'd been badly frightened. I climbed into the front. "Let me look at you, Pepito."

The boy showed me his bloody face. The scratch was superficial, nothing that would be visible in a few hours. "I'll drive," I said.

Pepito was still too dazed to move, so I ran around and indicated to him to slide across to the passenger side. After he did that, I crawled in and took the wheel. Fortunately the traffic was light and soon we were at my house. Once there, I carefully washed Pepito's wounds with cold water. He seemed calmer once we were seated in my kitchen.

"Did you recognize that woman in the blue dress?" I asked.

"Yes, Señora, I saw her there two days ago, but I don't know who she is."

"Why was the guard so angry?"

"Well, he asked me to get him some special stuff," Pepito said with a frown, "cigarettes a friend of mine brings in, hidden in his knapsack. He has a job on a boat that touches in at . . ." he indicated with a shrug the direction of Morocco.

"Only cigarettes?" I asked.

"Well, sometimes . . ." he shrugged again. "Well, sometimes there are other things. You know, Señora Condesa. . . ." his voice trailed off.

"I understand," I answered. I wanted to laugh. Pepito had more nerve than I'd given him credit for. "But why was the guard angry?"

"Because the guards like very strong dope, Señora Condesa. And the last I gave them was . . . well, they didn't like it."

"All right, Pepito. I can't help you with that problem. Although I must tell you that it would be wise if you stayed away from your Arab friends for the time being. If that proves to be a problem with Antonio, I'll see if I can talk with him and see what I can do. As for now, take this. You were a help to me, and I am grateful." I then handed him four thousand pesetas from my purse.

"Thank you, Señora Condesa," he answered. "Thank you very much."

And then Pepito left, whistling his awkward tune, with five thousand unexpected pesetas in his pocket.

Chapter 22

On the day Pepito and I went to El Ancon, Luis was getting ready to leave for San Sebastián, where he was attending the Copa de Oro, a prestigious race in which his favorite horse was entered. Before he left, I told him as much as I dared about my visit to El Ancon—even admitting that I'd hidden in Pepito's truck to get a better view of the place. Of course, I did not mention that I had entered the grounds. Luis looked at me skeptically, shaking his head; I could see he was annoyed. Oh well, I thought, but his mind was on the forthcoming race. At least my guarded admission relieved my conscience a bit.

Shortly after he left, Jupiter's manservant called to say that Mr. Derby had an important message for me and that he would like to stop by that night on his way home from the airport. Manolo also explained that Mr. Derby regretted he would be late—perhaps after eleven—because the plane would not arrive in Málaga until nine-thirty.

But, it was almost midnight when I heard the squeal of tires, the slam of a car door, and running steps. Jupiter burst into the room, his pale-blue eyes squinting with exhaustion. Yet rarely had I seen him so keyed up. "Sorry. The plane was late!"

After making himself a drink at the bar and selecting a comfortable seat on a sofa on the terrace, he sat down. "I apologize for coming here at this hour, but there's so much to tell you that could not wait."

"Before you go on, John," I said, "I think I should tell you a few things." And then I briefly summarized what Paco and Hans had said over the phone the other evening. Jupiter listened in silence. And when I finished, he made no comment. So I continued with my news. I told him about Serge's and my sticky experience together at Chez Jacques; about Hans's theory that the lights at sea were a code used by smugglers; about my visit to La Amapola, and the meeting I witnessed there. "And," I concluded, "the man who is probably the owner looks very much like the same person who was with Carlos in Germany that night when Ava Gardner and I hid outside Paco's window."

"Yes," Jupiter nodded thoughtfully. "This is all interesting and important. Now, let's combine our information.

"You will remember our suspicions that Cabanellas's company has been shipping calutrons camouflaged as oil pipes to Libya and the Middle East?" John said, looking at me inquisitively. "Well, our COS in Bonn called me urgently last week . . . that's why I could not accompany Serge to the restaurant. It's why you had to go instead." He looked at me for a moment, and then continued, "I was obliged to rush to Bonn. When I arrived, our people told me they now had confirmation that the suspicious crates were definitely carrying calutrons; and that Transportes Inter-Med, S.A., had been acting as go-between for over a year. From Bonn I went to Washington, where we had another consultation, the upshot of which is that the Agency wants information about Francisco Cabanellas. We have orders to investigate him in depth—and secretly, of course. We want him to continue his business transactions long enough for us to uncover the other players." John sighed. "That includes learning everything we can about the recent murder attempt. I want to know what really happened, and why." Jupiter spread his hands wide, "And his conversation with Hans Schmidt is obviously an important piece in the puzzle, though I don't know yet how it will eventually fit. Also, I don't think Schmidt's theories about the lights at sea are completely mad. But for the moment, it is Cabanellas himself that I am most interested in. He is the key to the whole thing . . . unless I am very mistaken.

"And this man Hans Schmidt . . ." John continued, "I don't know what to make of him. It's anybody's guess whether his daughter knew about Paco's clandestine activities." He took a silver case from his inside jacket pocket and removed a cigarette.

"John," I began, "I told you I saw Hans Schmidt only a few days ago. . . . Do you actually suspect his company has been one of those that are exporting illegal material?"

"Not yet." Jupiter made a grimace. "No. I don't really have any reason to suspect him. But one of his companies manufactures calutrons; and other companies he's connected with produce the kinds of modern weapons that interest terrorists."

At that moment I interrupted him, "In other words, you are talking about the kinds of things that interest Carlos especially, and I . . ."

"I don't want you to get distracted with Carlos," he broke in. "We must concentrate on finding out more about Cabanellas and Schmidt."

"But," I insisted, "it seems to me Carlos must be mixed up in these transactions. After all if he is building an arms depot on this coast . . . or at least according to Serge. And since the companies that produce calutrons tend to produce weapons as well, Paco's company could be transporting both. In other words, investigating Carlos should give us other worthwhile information. In fact, I find it hard to understand why Carlos is not a concern of yours. Have you decided that he wasn't involved in the assault against you in Germany?"

"No, Aline. Actually, I'm virtually certain he was involved. But he's a hard man to investigate, as I'm sure you know by now. And a dangerous one, too. But more importantly, right now it just happens that following up on Cabanellas is much easier. We know where he is, he is a friend of yours whom you can talk to, his business is here. In fact, he can lead us to the whole group of COCOM violators. And if we get lucky and manage to catch your Venezuelan friend in the process, well, all the better."

What John said was of course true. He went on, "Whether Hans Schmidt breaks COCOM laws or not, I bet he has a pretty good idea about which German manufacturers do. And, of course, given the products his companies make, we feel quite certain he has been approached by illegal buyers at one time or another. In other words, Herr Schmidt has been faced with a great deal of temptation. Though I don't know whether he has yielded to it, I can tell you, I find him very suspicious." John raised his hands in the air. "And if Schmidt is one of the COCOM violators, the killing of his daughter as a result must be especially painful for him. In which case, he'll probably give himself away sooner or later. So he may already have a pretty good idea who his daughter's killers are, and who is behind the whole deal."

Jupiter went on to tell me that sometime during the past month—before Inge was killed—the CIA people in Bonn spoke to Hans. And he appeared to cooperate then. He maintained that he had never sold any of his products to Libya or Algeria, or to any Middle Eastern country. He claimed he only deals with reputable customers. He also claimed that he knows no German companies who violate COCOM regulations.

As John spoke, I became aware that all along he had known more than he'd told me; and I wondered if he was being completely open now.

At any rate, what he did tell me was certainly fascinating: For instance, he mentioned that Bonn suspected that a one-time member of the recently diminished Baader-Meinhof group (seven had committed suicide)—a specialist in making car bombs—was in Spain and had prepared the bomb that blew up Paco's boat. But Jupiter disagreed. He told our people in Bonn that others on the coast could have handled that bomb. Ali Amine, for instance, was an expert at making bombs; and Carlos was also apparently nearby. Jupiter found it more likely that one of them was responsible than some vague Baader-Meinhof person.

As I listened, I recalled Paco Cabanellas's tortured voice on the phone. More than ever I was determined to use my friendship with Paco and Hans to find at least one COCOM violator. I then got up and made John another drink. As I handed it to him, he said, "I still haven't told you my main reason for seeing you tonight."

I went back to the bar to fill my own glass. I felt fatigued. Actually John's news had bothered me. . . . The fact that our people had talked with Hans Schmidt and that John had not told me about that until now was irritating.

"Maybe you'd better sit down to hear the rest," John said. "You look tired." I gave him a long, slow nod; then I went over to the sofa and collapsed.

Jupiter took a sip of his drink, and began. "We've found out a few more things about Cabanellas. His father and grandfather were farmers in Guipúzcoa, near Oyarsum. When he was very young, he went to Barcelona and worked in a garage where he learned about engines and cars. He is a superb mechanic—another reason why the Cigarette explosion could not have been an accident. We don't know why he moved to Marbella. But once there, his industriousness and mechanical skills helped him to get a job in the best garage on the coast where he made contact with many wealthy owners of Bentleys, Porsches, and Ferraris. About seven years ago, he began a transportation and shipping agency."

Jupiter leaned back and spoke more slowly, "Cabanellas met Inge in Marbella; and his connection with her father probably followed that. Though Paco must have become involved with weapons smuggling several years ago—shipping the material to Libya and other ports in the Middle East, and I wouldn't be surprised to discover that he was collaborating with one or more calutron buyers early on, either—when he became intimate with Inge, more extensive possibilities obviously developed. Her father happened to be a big producer of precisely those things Cabanellas's principals were interested in. In fact, that may well be the reason Paco Cabanellas cultivated her in the first place. If friendship later developed into romance, all the better." Jupiter stood up and went to the bar for some ice.

John lifted his glass. One question after another was taking shape in my mind. "John, why do you think those men were threatening Paco that night in Germany?"

"That's anybody's guess," John answered. "Perhaps when Inge agreed to marry him, Paco no longer needed his illegal business to support himself in style. Perhaps he wanted to get himself untangled from a very messy and dangerous situation." Jupiter kept shaking his head. "These are bad people, Tiger. Terribly bad people.

"And again, what do we make of Hans Schmidt? When did he find out about the mess Paco's in? Did he try to help him with one or two shipments of calutrons? Was Paco aware from the beginning that his big buyer had connections with terrorists? There are many questions to be answered. If Paco was trying to get out of his mess . . . well, it's not easy to find transportation for illegal material. The buyers were not going to let him off the hook."

Jupiter went on, "You should be reminded of how COCOM offenders ship the goods. Sometimes these things are trucked out of Germany under the guise of perishable goods like fruits and vegetables, which are sent through Czechoslovakia, Romania, or Bulgaria to the Middle East. This enables the shippers to operate quickly at frontiers. They camouflage shipments through Spain more often as antiques and furniture. It also happens frequently that illegal shippers take arms to the East and bring drugs back to the West.

"Cabanellas's company transports all kinds of materials by truck to Barcelona and Málaga, and then by ship to countries around the Mediterranean. We need more detailed information on his shipments. For instance, most ships that dock in Málaga also stop in Barcelona. The office in Málaga must have files that would show what merchandise is being loaded in Barcelona as well."

Jupiter stood up and began to pace the room. I sensed he had still not told me the purpose of this late-night meeting. "Aline," he began again, "most businesses in Europe give employees the month of August off. Is that correct?"

I nodded, waiting for the other shoe to drop.

"We need to uncover Cabanellas's buyer. To do this we need details about sources, quantities, and destinations of his shipments. And, of course, we do not have a search warrant; and we do not dare go to the authorities for one."

"Yes?" I asked.

"If we could latch onto the Trans Med files, they would provide valuable data which we could follow up on. And we would find out what Paco's role in this business is. So far, much of what I have told you is supposition. By investigating his files, we might discover the identities of his associates, and get to the actual buyer."

"I hear you suggesting a break-in, John," I said with a nervous smile.

"Something like that, yes," he answered.

"And you want me with you?" I asked. Much as I agreed with him about the need to learn the identity of those behind Cabanellas, I did not see that I had—or should have—an active part in the investigation. I wasn't eager to become the Spanish counterpart of a "Watergate Burglar."

"You are the best person for the job—the only person, really. You're the only one who knows this part of the world so intimately." He looked closely at me; he could not fail to see my skeptical expression. "And no one will find out," he went on. "I wouldn't even suggest it, if there was any danger of that. Also, there's no time to discuss this with your husband. Didn't you tell me he's in France and not back until next week?"

"No," I insisted. "I told you Luis is in San Sebastián and will be back day after tomorrow." I waited a moment, thinking hard. "Look, John," I said finally, "I could help set up this break-in, but I'm not going to risk embarrassing my husband by getting caught. The scandal! The newspapers!"

"Oh, come on," Jupiter was impatient. "There's no way I can do this alone. It's a job for two people, working as a team. If the entry is well prepared, we could pull it off with no trouble at all. You know that by now. The only one who could possibly recognize us is Cabanellas himself; and in the state he's in, he's not apt to be going to his office at all—much less at night, and especially on a Sunday. Now," John's tone indicated that he had dispensed with my foolish fears, "we have some serious planning to do."

"All right, John," I sighed. My agonizing about accepting had more or less faded away. I knew John couldn't do the operation without me. His Spanish was appalling. He would not even be able to read Paco's files if we found them. And obviously there was not time to find a reliable, bilingual agent to go instead of me . . . especially to go with Jupiter, whose cover had to be carefully protected. So I listened as he went on.

"There'll obviously be a guard at the building, probably at the front door. I know a clever and good-looking prostitute in Málaga whom I can pay to bribe or trick him into leaving his post for a couple of hours on Sunday night. That would be the best time, because I'll be leaving here beginning of next week."

Jupiter smiled. "And if we are surprised by someone, we can practice our skills."

I laughed. "You enjoy this, don't you?"

He cocked his head. "And, Aline, so do you."

As I handed him the bowl of nuts, I said, "But didn't you say this will be almost too easy. Frankly, for me . . . your plan isn't risky enough to be fun."

Fortunately, for us both, we had no idea how hazardous the visit to the transport office would turn out to be.

Chapter 23

L uis usually called me at night when he was away. So on the Sunday evening when Jupiter and I planned our break-in of Paco's offices, I left word at home that I would be dining in Málaga. Luis would be taking a plane back to Marbella the next morning; and I knew I'd be seeing him at lunch, by which time the whole ordeal would be over. Meanwhile, my mind was made up not to say anything to him in advance about the break-in. I now agreed with John Derby. This was a routine investigation—no need to worry Luis. After it was all over? Well, perhaps I'd tell him then.

That Sunday, stormy weather returned, quite unusual for this time of year. The day was cloudy; and by nightfall, a steady rain drummed onto the streets and rooftops. I grabbed a raincoat, and as I drove my car down to Málaga, peering through the rainswept windshield, I couldn't help but be apprehensive. To John Derby these operations might be routine, but for me, such things were far from normal.

Ever more anxious, I parked at a safe distance from Cabanellas's offices and walked two blocks to a building opposite that gave me a view of Transportes Inter-Med's front door. Though lights were on in the lobby, there was no guard there; and the building appeared deserted. I stood under the roof overhang waiting for Jupiter. It was exactly midnight when he appeared.

The lights of ships in the harbor flickered dully through the downpour; and the sea was indistinguishable from the streaming sky. The rain slid off the overhang in a transparent sheet and cracked into shards on the pavement. My feet, despite rubber-soled shoes, were soaking. A voice in my subconscious kept murmuring, "Aline, you foolish woman, you can be caught before you've discovered anything worthwhile. You are endangering the reputations of your husband and children for nothing." In front of me the long, low office building loomed like a crouching beast; and the steady pounding of the rain drowned out other sounds and did not improve my pessimistic mood. I jumped as a hand touched my arm. Jupiter had emerged out of the torrent. He whispered to me, "Everything's fine, Tiger, and on time. I've checked the lobby; and there's no guard." His words were encouraging. So was the sound of his voice.

After he'd shaken his umbrella and brushed off his raincoat, we walked across the street. Neither of us said a word as Jupiter's pick rotated in the double locks of the old door. It caught in the top lock, and at first didn't budge. But then slowly John turned the doorknob, and we were inside. Once we were in the lobby, Jupiter removed two cloths from the pockets of his trench coat and silently motioned for me to dry the soles of my shoes. He did the same to his; and he dried his umbrella and trench coat as well.

The lobby smelled of stagnant air and stale cigarette smoke. The night guard's shabby table in one corner was deserted.

"Cabanellas's office is upstairs," Jupiter said, indicating with a wave of his hand the building directory on the wall, his whisper resounding in the cavernous room.

Jupiter led the way to the stairs. As our footsteps echoed in the stairwell, I caressed the Baretta in my right pocket, and then the minature camera and small flashlight that were in the left. I usually kept a small automatic hidden in our house. And although Jupiter had not asked me to bring a weapon, it had certainly come in handy the night I dined with Serge at Chez Jacques, so I brought it tonight as well. I was also sure that Jupiter was armed. Nevertheless, I was nervous. Anything could happen.

We stepped onto the second floor; and luckily, the lights were on here also. Side corridors shot off in several directions; and before us was the long, main corridor, with several openings to offices and other corridors visible. I had a sudden panicky vision of myself lost all night in a maze of hallways. I took a deep breath and followed Jupiter's lead.

Jupiter set off down the hall on the left. We turned a corner, then another, and went through a short hall and an entryway to a set of double doors. "Paco's office," said Jupiter. He spoke at normal volume, and I jumped. He gave me a disapproving glance, knelt down, inserted another pick, and gave a slow twist. The tumblers turned and the door opened. We slipped in and Jupiter relocked the door.

Noticing my questioning look, he murmured in a schoolmaster's tone, "When you unlock, relock."

Inside, the room was completely dark; our flashlights barely penetrated the blackness. Jupiter shone his light around the walls, and when he pressed the wall switch, the room leapt into focus. "Fortunately," he said, noticing my questioning look, "my good friend Carmen, who is baby-sitting the guard tonight, has orders to keep him out of this part of the building. But even if he, or someone else, happens to come this way, we'll hear them long before they arrive. Anyone walking on the tile floors of the corridors will make enough noise to give us time to cut the lights."

"Good," I said, relieved. I was grateful for the lights.

The first thing I noticed was a large framed map of the Mediterranean on the wall. For a moment, Jupiter stared at it. Then he went to the sides of the frame, fiddled a bit, gave a lift to the bottom, and the map slid up vertically, revealing a similar map underneath. He turned to me with a grin. "We have the same fancy frames to shut out prying eyes. But look at this one—a lot different from the one that masks it." This map was covered with colored pushpins, with the heaviest concentrations of these in Libya and Lebanon, while others were at several ports in the Mideast. Green pushpins marked certain European cities; blue pins marked others, while red dominated the Mideast and North Africa. I assumed that the pins represented clients and shipping routes. Jupiter studied the map for a few moments, and then carefully pulled the original map back in place. He turned to me with a broad smile. "Always pull down what you pull up."

Filing cabinets lined an entire wall and rose to the ceiling. An aluminum stepladder, for access to the files, stood in one corner. A long massive desk, with large built-in drawers at each end, dominated the room; and there was an empty metal waste basket on the left side. The shiny metal door of an antiquated wall safe faced the filing cabinets. Apart from the desk, which was a magnificent thing, nothing in the office indicated the taste of the wealthy shipping company owner, especially one so fond of luxury as Paco. In fact, the only items on the vast desktop were a large old-fashioned wooden index box for eight-by-twelve cards, a pad, an ashtray, and an expensive gold and silver pen from Cartier. I had given Luis a similar one for Christmas two years ago.

"Well, we have our work cut out for us," mumbled Jupiter, chuckling and indicating the wall of files.

"I would guess," I whispered, "that the contents of the safe might be worth studying, too."

"I have a feeling we'll have to go through those files carefully. And that will not be as easy as cracking the safe," he answered.

The safe had a combination dial lock and was relatively small. Again the lack of expensive furnishings struck me as being out of keeping with Cabanellas's well-cut suits and lavish lifestyle. While Jupiter twirled the combination lock, I rolled the stepladder over to the file cabinets and climbed up for a quick check. The metal frame files were quite new; and the drawers opened smoothly on their tracks. I pulled out the first folder, marked "A–Am." Papers, documents, and records crammed every millimeter. In order to search properly, I would have to take out every piece of paper, and then replace each one in its original position. The task was daunting. Hastily I glanced over all the folders up to the Gs. All were bulging with documents dating back to 1970: old business cards stapled to sheets of paper, shipping invoices, employee information. None referred to shipments from Germany. I looked at my watch. 1:08, already! It was useless to continue here. Hoping for better luck, I decided to investigate the desk.

Jupiter, meanwhile, was making notations in a small notebook and trying various numerical combinations. Surprisingly, his task of breaking the combination had become as tedious as my search through the files. But he continued, unruffled and serene. Perhaps because he sensed me watching him, and he knew I would be upset that time was passing, he looked up and spoke, "Aline, this is an old-fashioned safe; but it has been upgraded with a modern lock. Don't worry, though, I'll get in. Even you could do it if you had kept up the training they gave you at The Farm. The trouble is the skin on my fingertips is not as sensitive as it used to be." The Farm was our old spy-training school outside Washington, DC.

Though he didn't say much, his words calmed me, and I went to the desk. There were two drawers, one on either side, leaving ample space for the heavy, comfortable, old-fashioned armchair. I was surprised to find the drawers unlocked. Concluding that there would be nothing important inside, I gave them a quick check—pencils, colored pushpins, stationery, Spanish-French dictionary. I then took three steps over to the other side of the huge, period desk and found the drawer filled with letters from various companies, the first concerned a convention taking place in October in Munich.

Jupiter was still working on the safe. The fluorescent lights were drenching the room with a sallow, blue glow. And I stood in the close, heavy air, wondering what to do next. The building was absolutely silent, except for the occasional soft click of the dial on the safe. Suddenly the windowpane rattled noisily, and the hair on my arms stood on end. Then I realized that was caused by a strong gust of wind. The storm outside was still going strong.

Still wondering what to do next, I decided to check the desktop, and my eyes fell on the card index next to the empty pad of checked paper. I picked that up and lifted the first sheet to see if the impress of what had been written above might be visible. But nothing was discernible.

Well, I thought, even though the card index is the most obvious, unconcealed object in the room, it might be worth investigating. The minute I picked up the first card, however, I realized I had hit onto something important. The cards were in a personal code. But it didn't look to be a particularly difficult code to crack. In fact, it was a type that had always amused me. "Grève," was the first word I saw. The next was "Dormir." The other code names were also all in French—"Perle," "Manier," "Cauchemar."

Which was the one hiding illegal shipments? Did the code names represent illegal material, the sources, the ultimate buyers, or all three? For a time I simply stared at the words. Nothing came. No answers.

Then a sudden flash went off in my brain. My heart beat faster; I took a deep breath, and picked up the top card again. "Grève," the word in French for a "labor walkout," "a strike."

Jupiter's voice interrupted me. He was still bent over the safe. "I'm having a hard time here," he groaned. "A pity we can't use an explosive."

"I've got my problems, too." I answered. "This card index is in code." But I was not as discouraged as my remark, since I knew I was close to breaking it.

"That should be no problem for you," he joked in his caustic way. He must have picked up my excitement. "Weren't codes your hobby years ago?"

But I didn't answer him. I had just remembered the French-Spanish dictionary in the drawer, and dove for it. The word "grève" was marked with a tiny dot. "Of course," I muttered under my breath, "how stupid of me." Hurriedly I climbed the ladder again and looked for "huelga," which is the Spanish word for "grève."

The "Hu" file contained an invoice, which at first glance was innocent enough. But then my glance came to the third paragraph. There the paper read: "Cabanellas—Private Shipment." The contents of this shipment was referred to as "matter," "origin Munich, compagnie Reutger." The destination was Libya, and it was scheduled for June 12. The freighter carrying the "matter" was called *La Martina*; it was scheduled to take on cargo arriving June 11 from Munich by truck; and it was to depart Málaga at six a.m. the following day.

"I found it," I hissed. Jupiter hurried to the desk and looked over my shoulder. His sharp intake of breath convinced me that he agreed that I had indeed been successful.

A few moments later, we discovered invoices referring to previous shipments. Rapidly I photographed each one. The cargoes were unidentified, but we both realized that if Cabanellas had gone to so much trouble to conceal them, they wouldn't be innocent. The list I was compiling showed three other shipments, two for Libya and one for Iraq. I worked fast, trusting that the photographs would reveal the information we needed. After I reached the final coded words and the corresponding files, Jupiter went back to the safe.

After replacing each invoice so that no one could tell they had been touched, I tidied up the desk. "John, our time is already up," I warned.

"You're right," he agreed, still manipulating the dial. "It's not really necessary to open the safe now, but I would like to know what's here." He raised his eyebrows speculatively. "It may be that Paco has more up his sleeve than we suspect."

"The incriminating data in this office was not well hidden, was it?" I said. "Paco must have felt pretty certain that no one would search for it."

"He's probably just careless," Jupiter speculated. "The colored pushpins and French words—they're almost playful. That Cabanellas is real cocky."

"That'll make catching him even more satisfying," I said with relish.

"You bet," Jupiter answered softly, without looking up from the safe as he spoke. His patience and cool head, as much as his formidable intelligence and intuition, had made him a brilliant agent. What he was doing now was rote tedium, of the kind that would drive me crazy, yet he continued to steadily turn the dial.

Finally: "Aline," he said with a grin, "watch." And the safe door swung open.

At that moment, we both heard a door slam somewhere in the building. The sound rattled through the long passageway outside. Jupiter and I stared at each other, frozen. His hand was inside the safe; mine held the camera and the index box. A more incriminating picture could not have been imagined. In one motion, Jupiter turned from the safe, I jammed the cards back in the file box, he switched off the lights, and we both dove for the only possible hiding place in the room, the large open space underneath the enormous desk—which, happily, was closed in front, and wide enough for both of us. My ears rang with the steady heavy beat of approaching steps, each time louder. Whoever it was was coming our way without suspicion. He didn't realize we were here.

The footsteps resounded through the empty hall. Sharp, determined, heavy heels were striking the ancient tile floor in steady rhythm. They approached the office door, and stopped. A hand gave the locked door a firm rattle, then paused. The pause gave us time to settle deeper into our tiny pit. And I remembered Jupiter's words about locking what you unlock. A key was inserted into the lock, and the door swung open. We huddled helplessly. The lights then flooded the room; but there was no sound. Whoever it was must hear the pounding of my heart, I thought. The lights flicked off, the door slammed shut, and the key turned in the lock. Then the footsteps continued down the hall, slowly fading away. What had happened? Carefully we backed out of our cramped cell and stood up. The guard, we realized, was making his rounds. He'd returned forty minutes before we expected him back.

"Okay," John said, "all clear for the time being. I'll bet he's going to make one go-round and go back to his desk downstairs."

I was trembling, but gritted my teeth and stood up. Jupiter switched the lights on and started twirling the dial of the safe again. Silently, I sat, aware of someone in the building with us. How would we get out without being seen? Why had the guard come back early?

"Look!" He exclaimed as the safe door swung open again. "Look what's inside!" Stacks of neat, new paper money, not pesetas but U.S. one-hundred-dollar bills! This was all we could see. Silently we shot glances of wonder at each other. Again Jupiter's hand probed inside, this time deeper into the depths of the safe; and he extracted a few wrapped stacks of Spanish currency. Then he plunged in again and removed a small box with a hinged top and a clasp, which he snapped open. Inside were bundles of cash of different countries, plus two green Libyan passports. When opened these contained no photos, but there were names. "We'll have to leave those here, or it'll be obvious the safe was opened. Just get the addresses and names of . . ."

He was listening to the faint sounds of footsteps coming up the staircase. We looked at each other, the same question in our eyes. We stood paralyzed, as the sounds became stronger. This was obviously a different person—the tread was lighter, the rhythm quicker. Jupiter grabbed the passports from my hand. In one brief gesture, he rearranged the interior of the safe, leaving the stacks of new bills in the front as before, and closed the door, giving a twist to the dial. I rushed to the switch. Out went the lights. Once more we dove under the desk to doubtful safety. The footsteps were now in the corridor. Then there was a pause just outside the door.

Huddled in utter silence under the desk, we listened as a key rattled in the lock. Then the the door opened, and the lights went on. I almost cried out as I remembered: I had left my flashlight on the desktop! How could the person entering miss it!

With growing difficulty, I controlled my breathing—trying not to make a sound. Surely we were lost! Jupiter's breath was coming in small short gasps; and for the first time, I knew he, too, was worried. My own fear jumped a hundredfold.

Every muscle in my body was taut. We waited helplessly. I hoped Jupiter had his automatic handy. Foolishly I'd left my Baretta in my pocket and dared not reach for it. Suddenly, I became aware of the smell of a vaguely familiar cigarette odor. Where had I smelled that before? It was a sweet, pungent scent that was easily recognizable as Turkish tobacco—something none of my friends used. And not Paco either, as far as I knew. So whoever this was, it was not Paco, I realized.

Meanwhile, the light, quick steps on the tile floor broke the silence like shattering glass as he moved quickly across the room toward us. A bang on the desk informed me that he had put down something, perhaps a briefcase. He's found the flashlight! I almost screamed. But the steps moved away. Then I heard the clicking of the dial on the safe. Obviously the hand was accustomed to the settings. Next I heard the door opening, and the rustle of the paper bills. I wondered if the intruder could hear the beat of my heart.

"*Maldito,*" the person muttered, and then he cursed again. He was obviously irritated. I held my breath, waiting for him to come to the desk again . . . or behind it to sit down! The logical thing to do.

I braced myself and sensed Jupiter doing the same. From the front we were not visible, but if he decided to step behind it, we were lost.

Menacingly it seemed to me, the sharp steps moved quickly toward us. Then they stopped. Had he seen us? Was a corner of my jacket visible? The resounding thump of something again being dropped on the desktop was like a blow rattling through my tense body. Then the footsteps returned to the safe and back again, and this was followed by the rhythmic sound of flipping bills. The man was obviously removing the stacks of money from the safe and counting it. Again sharp, fast steps to the safe and a return to the desk, with another sound of stiff new paper bills being rapidly turned and counted. The process was repeated twice, three times. The moments lagged as the sound of paper bills being flipped and counted dragged on.

Meanwhile, I grew aware that the man's cigarette was now in the ashtray on the desktop—he'd left it there while counting the money—and the smoke was drifting down to us. Who smokes Turkish tobacco? I kept asking myself. At the same time, the cigarette was giving me an almost irrestible urge to cough.

The footsteps came and went from the desk to the safe and back again, while the pungent smoke continued to tickle my nostrils. Then I remembered Carlos lighting his cigarette at our house the first time I met him. His cigarette was Turkish, I remembered, and very pungent. . . .

I almost screamed. Could it be Carlos here? If it was, Paco's connection with him was absolutely certain. If Carlos was taking money from the safe, obviously he was being paid for something. What for? Probably arms. The minutes dragged on; and the intruder continued to go back and forth to the safe. Finally I heard the click of a small lock. The stranger had counted the money and had put it in the briefcase on the desktop. Another five footsteps to the safe. It was always five going and six returning. The bang of the metal door. My knees were both numb, my wrists ached, my back was one long pain. Now the scrape of the briefcase lifting from the tabletop, eight footsteps to the door. And with a wave of relief, I heard the knob turn. The lights were switched off, two more steps, and the door was slammed firmly shut. The man's retreating footsteps sounded down the corridor, and then more faintly from the stairway.

Wordlessly John Derby and I remained in the small dark space until we could no longer hear any sound. "So far we've been damn lucky,'' Jupiter murmured as he started to squeeze out. "I don't think the guy noticed anything unusual—he was too preoccupied with the money—but we've got to get out of here in a hurry. He might come back."

"The flashlight," I cried. "I left it on the desk!" Still on my knees, I ran my hand over the top of the desk. Just next to the large card box, my fingers grazed the small flashlight. Had it been partially concealed there? Had the man seen it? Had he left to call the guard? And what about the guard coming back early? Or would the guard and others be waiting to catch us red-handed as we left the building? If the man had been Carlos, he would surely kill anyone who got in his way. The memory of Inge's ghastly death swept over me like a fever. All these thoughts raced through my mind before I could say a word to Jupiter.

He was already on his feet. When I stood up, the blood flowed back into my numb legs with a prickly rush. I welcomed the discomfort. At least I was still alive. "Let's get out of here," I whispered.

"Not until I take another look in that safe," Jupiter responded. "Where's your flashlight?" In the darkness, I handed it to him. In a moment he was in front of the metal door and turning the dial. This time, he was swift, and the door swung open, revealing a now apparently empty interior. The stacks of one-hundred-dollar bills were gone. But then I realized Jupiter was extracting a paper and reading it. He turned it toward me flashing the light on the words.

The page was almost blank. There were only three words: "Falta cien mil"—one hundred thousand missing—in a hasty scribble, and two inky fingerprints, but no signature. There was no doubt that message had been left by the visitor. I whipped out my camera and took a shot of the entire page, then a close-up of the prints. Then I remembered the old glass, metal-topped inkstand on the desk; and when I directed the flashlight there, I saw that its top was open. Next to it was the ashtray and the cigarette stub. Taking a step, I grabbed the stub and put it in my pocket. I would explain why to Jupiter later.

"What do those fingerprints mean?" I asked, but Jupiter had already closed the safe door and was indicating that I should follow him.

Silently, we moved toward the door, and put out the flashlight before opening it. Gingerly he pulled me behind him as he stepped outside, and then motioned for me to follow down the long hallway, now almost dark; there was only the low glimmer in the distance of an exit light near a stairway. Whoever had been there had put out the lights, and Jupiter was cautious. I had to be very careful so that my steps would not sound on the tile floor. Jupiter stopped. I felt his hand touch my feet; and I realized he wanted me to remove my shoes. Evidently he had already done so. Thus we moved, two shadows, silently through the semidarkness, feeling our way along the wall. Was the intruder lying in wait for us, with the guard to help him? Maybe he didn't want to face us alone. Anything was possible, but we had no choice. We had to move on. Meanwhile, my Baretta was cocked and ready; and I relied on Jupiter to give the signal.

Jupiter reached the stairwell; and slowly, silently, one step at a time, we crept down, hugging the inner wall, pausing now and then to listen. At the bottom, Jupiter stopped and murmured in my ear, "This is the only way out." I nodded in comprehension.

Ever so carefully, he opened the door facing us just a crack and peered through. The lamp at the guard's desk lit the entrance hall with a bright white glare. The sound of a radio tuned to a music station was barely audible. Jupiter shut the door. "The night watchman's there," he whispered. "He's facing the entrance. Can't get out that way without being seen. There's no fire escape either, and the windows are covered with iron gratings.

"There's one possibility," he continued softly. "We could go down to the basement. There may be a window."

So we crept down another flight, then entered the musty, cavernous basement. Jupiter's flashlight tunneled a path through the thick, dead air, past old filing cabinets, boxes piled to the ceiling, broken chairs and desks, and the boiler. As we moved forward, cobwebs brushed my face, clinging to my hair and eyelashes. We proceeded through a series of low-ceilinged rooms, each piled high with storage, each windowless. A large rat scuttled out from a pile of boxes . . . and only by a miracle did I not scream. Unidentifiable objects on the floor pressed into my feet. Then a box nearly toppled as we passed by. Involuntarily I flinched, thinking someone was hiding behind it; but John caught it before it fell; and with a minumum of noise set it back in place. I imagined Carlos everywhere. In the shadows, behind every corner; and I winced every time we took a slight turn.

Only in the last room did we find a window, high up in the wall, a small square shape that looked as if it hadn't been opened in years. John found a chair and stood on it to push the window open. "Don't know if even you could squeeze through this, but it's our best hope," he muttered. There was no way Jupiter's husky frame could fit through it.

The window would not budge. Jupiter stepped down and searched the dirty floor for a bar or a piece of metal to use as a pry. "This is taking too long," he said. "I'll have to smash the damned thing and pray to God the guard's radio blots out the sound." Expertly, he rolled up a wad of old newspapers and climbed the chair again. A moment later, there was a faint tinkling of glass. I waited impatiently for him to climb down. "What are you doing"? I cried.

"Picking out the rest of the broken pane from the sides. You could badly cut yourself. And better put your shoes back on, too." Jupiter finally descended. A cool, fresh, salty breeze flowed in; and I breathed damp, rainy air, relieved and encouraged for the first time in what seemed like forever.

When I climbed the chair, however, I could not reach the sill.

"Get on my shoulders," Jupiter commanded, stooping down. I stepped carefully from the chair to his shoulders, then felt his hands grabbing my ankles.

"Hold on," he said, "and straighten your legs. I'm going to give you a shove. Lean as far out as you can."

I did as ordered; and he shoved me up and forward with such force that I was halfway through the window. I wiggled through the rest of the way, cutting my hands and knees from small shards of glass. But I was out! Then I crawled to the protection of the wall of the building, stood up, brushed myself off, and looked around. The parking lot was deserted. Thank God! There were two cars which I could barely see through the fog. Then I bent down to tell Jupiter what I could see.

"I'll never fit through," he said. His voice sounded small and hollow in the airless room below. "But one of those cars doubtless belongs to the guard," he whispered from his stand on the chair. "Wait for two minutes, then break a window of one of them. Be sure you make a lot of noise and honk the horn. I want him to think you're a thief. Then drop low and run to the west side of this building and hide there. If we're lucky, the guard will come out to investigate. The most direct way for him is around the east side, so you'll be safe. While he's dealing with the car thief, I'll run through the front door and come around to where you are."

"What will I break the window with?" I asked.

"Well," came the voice from below, "find a good solid Iberian rock." Jupiter sounded almost jovial. I realized that he'd been trained all his life for operations like tonight's, and he was actually enjoying himself.

Looking at my watch, I was shocked to see that it was 2:14. Terribly fearful that Carlos could be waiting nearby, I stood in the shadows and looked around. There were no trees or hedges to hide behind. If someone was watching, I would be on center stage. And my appearance would cause instant suspicions—my torn dress, my wet hair, my stockings in shreds, and blood oozing from the cuts on my left knee. For a moment I continued to study the two cars. Which one was most likely to belong to the night guard?

I remembered that Jupiter was waiting, probably already at the stairway to the main floor, expecting to hear window glass shatter. I glanced at my watch; it was almost 2:16. I had to hurry.

By then the rain had finally stopped, and the night gleamed. Light from the streetlamps lay like yellow oil on puddles. The briny smell of the Mediterranean drifted to me, redolent of the squid and shrimp that unloaded on the docks every morning. I drank the air in huge gulps. Ten seconds to go. I looked around until I found a likely stone.

The cars were in the brightest spot on the lot. Taking a deep breath, I scurried across the open space and up to the nearest car, which was also the smallest one. Recklessly I struck the windshield as hard as I could with the stone. As the ugly sound shattered the heavy night's stillness, I jumped. Then I pressed the horn, long and loud, as if I had mistakenly fallen upon it.

A loud call boomed through the night. *"Quién va?"* The night watchman was already standing in front of the building entrance. Even in the dim light I could see the glint of his weapon.

I started to run. I knew he was aiming at me. Heading for the shadows by the building, I raced faster. Suddenly, a blast broke through the air, and a rain of bullets hit the cement. One whined past so close to my ear that I wondered if I'd been hit. With all my force, I bounded into the shadows, the ring of gunfire sounding in my head. Keeping within the murky darkness, I continued to flee, but the staccato bark from the guard's firearm still chilled my senses.

Wildly I ran toward the west corner and kept on going. Knowing the guard had seen where I was headed, I feared he would come after me. Peering back as I ran, I saw the outline of his body coming full speed toward me. Then I almost screamed as another body slammed into me, hurling me to the ground. Next, a strong hand picked me up. Jupiter's voice was urgent. "Keep running. The guard will give up if we're fast enough."

It seemed that my chest would burst. My feet splashed through one puddle after another. With Jupiter in front of me, I simply followed, ignorant of where we were or where we were headed. Darting away from Paco's building, we passed two warehouses, then left the docks and entered a narrow street. Slowing down to a walk, Jupiter indicated for me to follow. But it wasn't until we were safely in his car with the engine running and the doors locked that he said anything. As he spoke he put the car in gear and we raced off.

"Well done, Aline," he began, "but are you all right? No harm from those bullets?"

I assured him I was fine. "Thank God that guard wasn't a professional. He could have gotten me easily."

"Right." Jupiter sighed. "It wasn't as simple as I'd hoped, but we did what we came for."

"Do you think we have all we need?" I asked.

"Not yet, unhappily," he responded. Then seeing the disappointment on my face, he continued, "What we really want is the big wheel in these deals. Cabanellas is a go-between; but who supplies the money? The money we saw in the safe is probably not Paco's. So whose is it? No, we don't have enough yet." Jupiter shook his head. "No, we need more."

As he was speaking, while we idled at a stoplight, another car pulled around a corner and waited, engine running, about a block behind us. I turned around, still jumpy, since we were yet quite near the dockyard area. "Jupiter," I said calmly, "I wonder if that's one of the cars I saw in the parking lot." I peered intently through the gloom. "It could be," I said.

Jupiter put his foot on the gas and expertly turned a series of corners, navigating a complicated path. A moment later, he pulled up, turned off the engine, and waited. The other car never appeared. "We're safe. That guy was not following us," he said, with a sigh. We waited a minute more before he drove to the side street where I had left my car. My little blue Seat was the only car in sight.

"Aline," said Jupiter, "I don't want you driving home tonight alone. Give me your car keys. I'll drive you home in my car and have yours returned to you tomorrow."

Then I remembered the cigarette butt in my pocket. So I told Jupiter about the only man I knew who smoked that kind of tobacco.

"Carlos?" he answered. "Yes, perhaps. But many people on this coast smoke Turkish tobacco. That cigarette bothered me, too. Made me suspect the guy could be an Arab. All that money in hundred-dollar bills, the Arab connection . . . I was beginning to sense that the business we witnessed up there in Paco's office smelled more of terrorists than smugglers. This case is not turning out the way I thought it would."

He kept his eyes glued to the road as he talked. "Yes. . . . Who knows, maybe it was Carlos up there. Better give me that cigarette stub now. I'll have it analyzed. We may be able to tell if that particular cigarette is sold in Spain—or what country manufactures them."

"One thing I'm sure of, John," I said. "The man in the office was not Paco Cabanellas. He doesn't smoke Turkish tobacco; at least I have always seen him with American cigarettes."

"Whoever it was doesn't know we were there. If he did, he would not have let us get out. And I doubt the guard will want to admit that someone entered the building without his knowing."

While he spoke, I was digging into my raincoat pocket for the cigarette stub. My fingers first touched my still very damp gloves. Under them was the cigarette, which I handed to Jupiter. He made no further comment as he drove. He was exhausted; and so was I.

When he pulled into my drive, John restrained me while he surveyed the area. Then he got out, came to my side, opened the door, and accompanied me as far as the arched entrance to the patio. There he touched both my shoulders gently. "You were a real pro tonight, Tiger." Then with a quick kiss on both cheeks, he turned around and left.

When I closed the door to my house, I clung to the knob to steady myself. After the tension of the past hours, the relief I was experiencing made me weak. I staggered up the stairs to my room and drew a bath, while I stared at my reflection in the full-length mirror. My hair was matted and clinging to my head like seaweed. A large dirt smudge was under my left eye; and the rest of the face was splattered with mud. The right shoulder of my raincoat was badly ripped. Both knee caps were covered with blood, and my hands were caked with black mud.

Thank heavens, I thought, Luis can't see me.

Despite the sharp stings of the cuts, I gratefully sank into a hot tub. Later I lay for hours in bed trying to sleep. Each time I drowsed off, I would see Carlos's face. Or else the Arab with the scar. Or else cobwebs brushing my face. Twice I sat up with a start and looked around, trying to reassure myself. This went on almost until dawn. The birds were calling to each other in the trees outside my window when finally, completely exhausted, I fell asleep for good. I slept for ten hours straight.

Chapter 24

The next day I did not awake until two. When I drew the heavy curtains, lined with metallic material to reduce the heat of the sun, I could see that the rain of the night before had given way to one of Marbella's perfect days. And I could hear people splashing in the pool. Out beyond, small boats with striped yellow-and-blue sails skimmed the gently rolling Mediterranean.

Meanwhile, Luis had sent a message that he would be staying another day in San Sebastián. Fortunately lunch was never served until after four o'clock, so I would have time for a walk on the beach and a swim.

I spent the rest of the day thinking over the developments of the night before, hoping some of the information we had gathered would help Jupiter find the people he was looking for.

In the midst of these thoughts, a call came in from Suzanne Blum, the Duchess of Windsor's lawyer. The Duchess had been hospitalized, she said. Would I be able to come to Paris to cheer her up? After reaching Luis in San Sebastián, he and I decided that I would fly to Paris the next day and stay at the Georges Cinq rather than at the Duchess's house in the Bois. It was more convenient to the hospital; and I wasn't happy with the idea of spending the night at that beautiful house at 4 Rue du Champs d'Entrainement without her.

As for Jupiter, he was flying to Washington in a day or two with the photographs we'd taken the night before; he would not learn how successful our work had been for some time. He also had the cigarette butt; a specialist in Langley might determine where that unusual type of tobacco came from.

DESPITE THE NECK collar supporting her head, the Duchess seemed to be resting comfortably when I arrived at the British-American Hospital the following afternoon. Her secretary was in the room with her, and she did not leave when I drew up a chair next to the bed. "Tell her to go, dear, so we can talk," my sick friend whispered as I sat down. When he picked me up at the airport, Martin, the chauffeur, had warned me that he and his colleagues did not like the secretary and that the Duchess seemed to be afraid of her. Indeed, I was surprised to notice that sickness had so weakened my friend that dealing with the secretary had become an effort. Usually, she had no reticence about that sort of thing.

The room itself was filled with orchids, which I assumed Georges, her butler, had brought from the Duchess's own hot-houses. So I asked the secretary if she would be kind enough to get some water to freshen them up. I was relieved to see her awkward figure stamp out the room and down the hall, calling rudely to a nurse. As soon as she was gone, I shut the door.

"You know, dear," the Duchess began, "if I weren't so weak, I would have fired that girl. I've never liked her, and now less than ever. When I'm stronger, that's the first thing I'll do. Everything about her rubs me the wrong way. Even the way she walks. Wouldn't my 'romance,' " her favorite term for her late husband, "have been horrified by the way that girl moves?" Her sapphire eyes danced with humor. "David loved being around graceful women. He was always so fond of you, Aline, for that reason— among others."

She turned to settle herself more comfortably in bed. "My neck is so stiff," she complained in a tired voice. Then more energetically, she added, "You're sweet to come. I certainly hope you didn't make this trip just to see me, dear."

"Oh, no. I had some shopping to do; and when I called your house to say I was coming to Paris, Georges told me you were in the hospital."

"Now you mustn't worry. I'll be all right in no time. My ulcers have been bothering me again. That's all. Well, now that you're here, my dear, tell me what you're up to these days." And without waiting for me to answer, she added, "We did have an exciting time with our spell of cloak-and-dagger work, didn't we?" The Duchess had helped me uncover a mole in the NATO offices in Paris some years before; so she was one of the very few persons who knew about my undercover work. "My heavens, that must have been al-most ten years ago. How time flies when one is getting old! Do you know, everything gets better with age except women? Gardens get better, wine gets better.

"However, we are what we are, aren't we, dear? So there's a little frivolous errand you could do for me," she said, changing the subject.

"Of course," I said.

"Well, it's a dress I saw last week at Givenchy—stunning, but all wrong for me. I can't seem to get away with the cuts I used to wear. It's not that my figure has changed."

I thought, as she spoke, that in fact it had. She was even thinner than usual. And I was worried that she was not recovering as well as she would have me believe.

"I want you to take a look and tell me if I'm imagining things, but I think it would be fabulous on you."

We had always shared an interest in beautiful clothes. Her taste was extraordinary; and I was touched that she would think of me when she was ill. I would certainly look in at Givenchy and told her so.

We chatted for a while. And then, after a time, she pointed to the American *Herald Tribune* on the table next to her bed. "Do you remember the last time we were together? There was another murder like this one. These things depress me so. Just look at that terrible photograph. Why do they publish such horrors?"

Under a grisly photograph in the upper corner of the page was the headline: GERMAN INDUSTRIALIST SLAIN. FAMOUS TERRORIST SUSPECTED. Impulsively I grabbed the paper and spread it out on my knees. The lurid photograph showed a man slumped in the backseat of a taxicab. The rear door was open as though he'd been about to exit, one lifeless leg dangled in an interrupted step. His head was turned, arched against the seatback, the eyes were two gaping holes with black trails leaking down his cheeks. Obviously shot at close range through both eyes, he looked like a hideous, modern day Oedipus. The rest of the face was so deformed that it was unrecognizable. Was the grotesque body once Hans Schmidt? I asked myself. What other German would Carlos have assassinated? Under the banner headline, the story explained that Carlos had not actually been identified as the assassin; but he was suspected, because the weapon, a .36 caliber submachine gun, was a type he had used before, and the manner of the attack was also typical of him. The victim's name was not mentioned. I wondered why.

"Aline, dear, what fascinates you so much in that dreadful story? I could barely look at the picture."

So I told her how I happened to know Carlos, the terrorist mentioned in the article, and how I had more than once run across him again . . . or at least, I may have run into him, if I wasn't imagining things. As soon as I finished my Carlos story, her face lit up and her voice rang with a burst of enthusiasm. "Oh, how I would adore doing another job with you, Aline. I still think of Claudine de Jorans now and then. The poor woman. Do you know, Edouard de Jorans was released a couple of years ago, but he disappeared. No one I know ever saw him again."

She was referring to friends who used to come to her dinner parties. The wife was murdered, and the husband was imprisoned for helping a NATO mole. "I would hate to discover that any more of my friends were crooks. But that was an exciting time for us, wasn't it? Aline dear, I do hope you are careful. Terrorists are much more dangerous than NATO moles, I believe."

As I recounted more details about my recent adventures, her violet eyes flashed with an almost youthful brilliance. "Oh," she said, "you are so lucky. I'd really like to meet this man Carlos. He sounds fascinating. At least a terrorist isn't boring. Nothing is worse than a bore, my dear."

Then we talked about less dramatic topics. The Duchess was worried, for instance, that her hothouses would not be properly cared for while she was in the hospital. She was a born worrier. And yet as she talked on, she laughed at her own exaggerations. "You see how ridiculous I am. Forgive an old lady for talking about such boring things. Do you know sometimes I spend half the night awake after a dinner party, worrying if the servants have broken or chipped any of the dishes."

But eventually she became restless and turned her head sideward on the pillow. "My dear," she mumbled in a weak voice, "I'm afraid I must rest now."

Back at the Georges Cinq, I sank into the thick brocade armchair in the salon of my suite. Luis sometimes stayed here when he came to Paris for the races; but for me it seemed strange to be in a hotel in Paris. For over twenty years, I either stayed with the Windsors or with Guy and Marie Helene de Rothschild at Ferrieres.

My visit with the Duchess had of course saddened me, and yet at the same time I was extremely anxious to find out if Hans Schmidt was the man murdered in Rome. My intuition told me it had to be him. And so I placed a call to Jupiter; and another to Luis, to whom I also wanted to talk.

As I waited for my calls to go through, I ordered a cup of tea and sat for a bit, thinking of happier times the Duchess and I had spent together. Even in a setting as unappealing as a hospital room, her usual elegance had been undiminished. The embroidered pink Porthault sheets had been brought from home, her blue silk, lace-trimmed bed jacket was obviously handmade. On the table next to her bed was her favorite snapshot of the Duke, a photograph someone had taken in Houston when the Duke had been there for his aneurysm operation. Clearly Alexandre had visited the Duchess in the hospital and had done her hair just as he did every other day. I smiled at her fastidiousness; but recalled that her impeccable appearance had always been a source of pleasure and satisfaction to the Duke. "David would want me to look my best," she had said to me, when she described what she had worn for his funeral, as though no one else's opinion could ever really matter.

When the operator informed me that the lines both to Jupiter and to Luis were still busy, my mind circled back to the office only two nights before. I saw myself again beneath the desk, I smelled again that Turkish tobacco, saw again the shoes as the man approached the desk, his legs just inches from my face. I remembered the shoes were wet but polished, the damp cuffs of the trousers that broke perfectly across the instep of the elegant Italian loafers. Whoever the intruder was, he liked expensive clothes—just as Carlos did. My call to Luis finally came in; but Jupiter was traveling and unavailable.

The next day, after another visit with the Duchess, I went to the airport for the Iberia flight back to Spain. Since there was no direct flight to Málaga, I had to change planes in Madrid. As I moved to my seat, I picked up the Spanish newspaper, *ABC*. Skimming through the editorial on the first page and the pages of photos, I kept turning until I found the black letters I was looking for at the bottom of one page: CARLOS EL JACKAL SUSPECTED ASSASSIN IN ROME. My eyes rushed down the column. I was hoping they had captured him. I continued to read; but I already knew the answer before the article informed that the assassin had not been apprehended. And there was another gruesome photo of the victim. This one focused on the stricken faces of the pedestrians gaping at the scene before them. Some had closed their eyes, some had their mouths open in frozen screams.

Still, there was no mention of the victim's name. Nevertheless, I felt it had to be Hans Schmidt. Yet, as I considered the killing in Rome, I hit a major catch: How could Carlos have been in Italy and in Málaga at the same time? If he was the assassin in Italy, he could not have been in Paco's offices. . . .

Chapter 25

*A*s I rushed from the international terminal in Madrid, I heard a woman cry out my name. Looking up, I was astounded to see my old friend Salima Karam, an incredibly beautiful Moroccan girl I had not seen in years. I'll never forget the first time I met her at a party in Rabat—tall and very slim, long graceful neck, thick golden-brown hair hanging loose down her back, flawless skin, as creamy-white as seashells, large pale-blue eyes, unusual for an Arab woman.

Salima had spent quite a few years in the United States, where she attended Vassar, graduating with honors. Later she had been involved in a public relations agency which specialized in business between the U.S. and Morocco. Later still, she had married disastrously—a marriage that her wealthy Moroccan father had annulled. She had also lost a child, dead at birth. Both the end of the marraige and the loss of her child had affected her deeply. But her luck seemed to change when she married the perfect Moroccan—only to have him killed a few months later in a plane accident.

Salima had always been the wild member of the Karam family; and she had seemed destined for tragedy. I hoped that now she had found a calmer path. . . .

Salima and I rushed together and hugged like children; and when she learned that I was on my way to Málaga, she offered me a ride in her private plane. Two Arabs in dark business suits accompanied her, bodyguards. I wondered why Salima now had bodyguards.

Forty minutes later, the tiny plane made a rough, jagged landing on the not quite completed new landing strip of the Málaga airport. The pilot had swung down over the mountains, made a turn over the Mediterranean, and circled back to the unfinished strip. We bounced, dragging screeching wheels. Dirt flew in spurts across the windows. And I swore to myself as I walked across the open tarmac to the terminal that I would stick to Iberia's Madrid-Málaga flight the next time I was offered a ride on a private plane to the coast. My legs still trembled from the harsh landing. At the same time, I was feeling a mixture of delight and apprehension after the half-hour's chat with my old friend—her main news being that she had remarried, and she was ecstatically happy, she told me again and again.

Salima continued to chat happily about her new husband as she led me from the terminal to a car he had sent. He was a wealthy man named Jamal Abad; and he had swept her off her feet. Jamal adored her and she was divinely happy, Salima declared yet one more time with a wide smile that sparkled with a confidence that I did not trust. I remembered how susceptible Salima had been in the past to the allure of an exciting and attractive man. Her romantic words continued to show that she had not changed—at least in that regard. For there were other changes. She had maintained her soft voluptuous curves; and her smart Parisian suit lay flat on her narrow hips as before. Yet even though she was just as slim and chic as ever, her nervous manner today made her seem older, and she had lost the unique expression of innocence that had been so appealing. She was not the carefree Salima I had known. I suspected she had problems.

She waved a bejeweled hand to a bodyguard to take care of my luggage, and then beckoned to her chauffeur in a Mercedes a couple of hundred meters away to come pick us up.

As I watched her, I couldn't prevent the dark thought these gestures sent fleeting through my mind—the image of that lovely hand dispensing a lethal drug. Back when I first knew her, Salima had been only too capable of handling her problems. If pushed to desperation, she could well have solved her problems in a particularly dramatic and effective way—such as murder. God knows, she had reasons to want to. The man she was in love with turned out to be a KGB spy who was using her for her contacts in Morocco. Not only was he using her, but I suspected he was also secretly having an affair with her sister. But Michel de Bonville, aka Dupont, was found dead one night, murdered by poison, in a Paris bistro. I never quite shook the impression it might have been one of the sisters that killed him. Both had a motive.

"I never would have believed love and happiness were possible for me," she told me one more time, as we settled into the luxurious seat of the car. "Up until last year, I was sure that part of my life had died with Ahmed." She bowed her head for a moment as if to dip just briefly into her reservoir of grief. Even now, so many years later, her face altered dramatically at the mention of her second husband's name. I remembered her ecstatic happiness on the eve of her wedding to Ahmed nearly six years before. He had been a good man, and an officer in the Moroccan Army, and I had liked him very much.

Just as the car pulled into the entrance to my house, Salima reached across and took my hand. "I so want you to meet my new husband, Aline. Promise me you and Luis will be our guest this week, perhaps Thursday? Jamal has a friend with a marvelous restaurant that's quite near."

"I would love to meet your husband," I declared. "What restaurant is that?"

"Chez Jacques. It's very nice, and it's Jamal's favorite place here in Marbella."

As the name rang through my mind, excitement ran through me. This could be dangerous but interesting, I thought. But I was also immediately on guard. Since I had never told Luis about the evening I had spent there with Serge, I had to maintain my ignorance of the place. "That's odd," I said. "I've never heard of it."

Salima smiled. "It's not well known. But the food is delicious. Please say you'll come?"

"Well, I'd love to; let me check with Luis, and I'll tell you tomorrow." I took a pen from my bag and asked her for her telephone number. She waved the pen aside. "Please, Aline, I'll call you. I don't even know my number, but I do know yours."

I was astonished.

She giggled like a shy girl, "77-70-88. Correct? Jamal wanted me to have friends here; he got it for me as soon as we knew I would be coming. You see, even if I hadn't bumped into you in the airport in Madrid, I intended to call you as soon as I arrived. I tried several times to phone you from Algiers before I left this morning. The proof is I still remember the number."

I wasn't laughing. The number she'd reeled off was new and non-listed. How did Jamal get it?

"My goodness," I said, struggling to match her light tone. "You do have a good memory. Tell me, exactly where is this fabulous restaurant?"

"In Puente Romano. You must know the area?"

"Quite well, but I've never heard of a restaurant called Chez Jacques there. Are you and Jamal staying in Puente Romano?"

Salima shook her head. "I just don't know what that place where we're staying is called. I travel so much lately, I can't keep up with the addresses." She gave a weak laugh; and I thought I saw a trace of fear travel across her face. I decided not to press her further on that point.

Then she flashed a smile. "Oh, Aline," she gushed, "I'm so happy to find you again!" She seemed overcome with emotion. As I kissed her thin, smooth cheek, I felt almost certain that luck had nothing to do with my sudden reunion with Salima.

Chapter 26

A s I opened our front door, Luis came charging across the salon. "I've been worried out of my mind," he said. "Where have you been?"

"Darling, what's wrong?" I asked. This was not Luis's usual manner.

"I sent Julio to Málaga to meet you. When you didn't show up, he asked at the counter; and the Iberia manager said you were reserved on the flight but had never boarded the plane. I've been calling everywhere. I even spoke to the Duchess of Windsor in the hospital in Paris, praying you were just delayed."

"But . . ."

"Wait, Aline. When I read about the assassination of a German industrialist and that the assailant could be Carlos, I was afraid you might have offered to help John again and have put yourself in danger. Then, this afternoon a boy was found shot through the head, sitting in a delivery van near the entrance of El Ancon." He gave me a hard look. "He was shot very near the place you went to. . . . Aline, I don't know if the two things are related and I don't care. What matters to me is this: You are not to involve yourself further in any way with John Derby's business. I don't care what you have promised him."

"But, Luis . . ."

"Don't interrupt me, please. I don't want to know what you've promised, but as of this moment, it is a closed case for you. Do we understand each other?"

"Yes, darling," I said and shrugged out of my jacket. There was no point discussing the matter right then. "Who was the boy?" I asked. But as I did that, I knew; and my heart sank.

"Aline," said Luis. His voice held a warning edge.

"All right, all right!" I said, "I'm going upstairs to change."

"But how did you get home?"

"Believe it or not, I ran into Salima Karam in Madrid. She has married a very wealthy man with a private plane. She gave me a ride to Málaga in it; and then by car here."

"Salima? What a surprise! How is she?"

"She says she's dramatically happy with her new husband; and she wants us to meet them for dinner Thursday night."

"I'd be delighted to see her."

THOUGH IN THE morning this day had promised to be a simple one, it now felt as if it had stretched on for several grueling weeks.

I took a brief swim before dressing for dinner. As the cool water refreshed my body, I felt a momentary release from the pressure that had been building in my mind since reading about the German's murder in Rome. And now Pepito! Of course it had to be him. I wrapped myself in one of the huge white terry cloth towels we kept near the pool and stretched out on a *tumbona* to watch the stars above the water. I stared straight up, wondering if their orderly constellations could show me the pattern in the confusion of recent events.

Meanwhile, I was curious to find out what the Rome police would discover about the murder there. Another headache was going to be the tracking down of Jupiter. My intuition told me things were developing quickly. I wished he were nearby; but God only knew where John Derby was just then.

And then there was the death of Pepito. First thing in the morning I would find out that story. I didn't like to think of the implications for me. Did the people in La Amapola kill him after discovering he'd smuggled me inside? Or was he more involved in selling drugs than he had let on to me?

As for Salima, well, she gravitated toward dangerous men. Something in her manner as we talked made me suspect that there was more than deep bliss in her life right now. No doubt about it, she was frightened.

Luis and I had a quiet dinner together at the Marbella Beach Club that night. By then he seemed more relaxed than when we had met earlier; and after dinner he suggested a quick dance before heading home. I always loved to dance with my husband; and we ended up staying until the band finished for the night. Though we chatted with various friends, we mainly focused on each other, which was a delightful reprieve from my anxieties.

The following morning at ten, I parked my car in front of the little specialty store off the Málaga-Marbella highway. As I pushed through the old door, still hoping to see Pepito's skinny frame stacking bottles on a shelf, the owner, Antonio, emerged from the back of the shop. Apparently he didn't see me, because he absently began wrapping and putting away a variety of cheeses. I noticed, with apprehension, that he looked utterly dejected.

"Señora Condesa! Buenos días. How can I help you?"

I took a deep breath. I felt my method was blunt; but I couldn't think of a delicate way to do what I had to do. "Could Pepito deliver some things to my house today, Antonio?" I asked.

The man's stricken expression told me I'd hit my mark. My face must have paled as well. "What is it, Antonio?"

"It is too terrible, Señora Condesa." His eyes were wide and heavy.

"Please, what's happened? Perhaps I can help, Antonio."

"Pepito is dead, Señora Condesa. Killed by sick animals."

"What do you mean?" My heart sank. Poor Pepito!

"Shot through the head, in the middle of the day, opposite the mosque at El Ancon." Antonio's face was filled with grief.

"But why?" This was the answer I was most afraid of hearing.

"I'm ashamed to tell you. I knew about it, but couldn't stop it. It was drugs. He was delivering for drug dealers."

"Are you sure?"

"Completely. Often I found him with inexplicable amounts of money. Only a few days ago, I caught him with a quarter kilo of cocaine and a roll of large bills. When I asked him where it came from he refused to answer me!" A righteous anger came into his eyes as if he was scolding Pepito all over again.

"Were there many times?"

"Excuse me?"

"Many occasions when you found him with such things?"

"No . . . but now and again." At this, Antonio's eyes began to fill with tears.

"You must have been very fond of him," I said.

"He was my nephew, Señora Condesa."

"Antonio, do you know whom he was working for?"

At this he seemed to gather himself up, as though I'd crossed an imaginary line. "Señora Condesa, that is for the police to find out."

"Yes, of course," I said in a conciliatory way. Then to change his train of thought, I added, "What about that marvelous pâté Señora Coca said she found here last week. Do you have any left?"

The shopkeeper was grateful for the distraction and began pulling out various delicacies for me to taste. After I'd placed an order, which I promised to have Julio pick up later, I gave Antonio my condolences and bid him farewell.

"You know, Señora Condesa, Pepito admired you very much."

"He did?"

"Yes, he said you were a brave lady."

"How kind," I made an effort now to keep my tone normal.

"I thought it was an odd thing to say, though very nice," Antonio smiled and shrugged. "Adios, Señora Condesa."

Although I had no real hope of recovering any evidence that the police had not already found, I wanted to take a look at the place where Pepito had been killed. So I drove directly to El Ancon. Fortunately most of the visitors who flocked to Marbella in the summer started their days late, and the road was clear.

The first thing I noticed as I passed through the entrance of the development and stopped opposite the mosque was that there were no signs at all that a tragedy had occurred. No security fence, no tape, no patrolman. The place looked as if nothing had happened. Was someone in this development so influential that he could arrange to have the "eyesore" of a police investigation avoided?

I parked the car beside the mosque and walked a few feet up the hill, scanning the area. This was actually the spot where Pepito and I had traded places behind the driver's wheel. The thought gave me a sickening feeling.

As I gazed at the spot, I tried to suppress the possibility that I might have had something to do with the boy's death. On the other hand, if he was involved with drug dealers, perhaps his death had nothing to do with me.

With my head bent low, looking at the concrete roadbed for tire marks, I must have been an odd sight. Luckily the street was deserted. I was studying the surface of the curb, where Pepito had pulled the van into the dirt, when I heard the distant purr of a high-powered engine. Quickly I straightened up, put my hand over my eyes to cut the glare, and observed the low shape of a blue Porsche take the curve and come straight toward me at a high speed for a residential street. As it bore down on me, I leapt up onto the lawn that surrounded the mosque. The driver slammed on the brakes with a shriek, opened his door, and stepped out.

Standing before me now was the imposing figure of Hans Schmidt! Three long strides brought him to my side.

"Aline, what an unexpected pleasure," he smiled and bent to kiss my cheek.

I could barely control the urge to recoil from his touch. My feelings were so confused. His frigid stare after the telephone conversation with Paco was still fresh in my mind. Also, the realization that the man was alive made me aware that I was making too many incorrect deductions lately.

"Are you sightseeing?" he asked, a bit too facetiously.

"Yes, Hans, as a matter of fact I am," I answered; for I could be facetious, too. "Luis has been telling me for months that I must take a look at this mosque. You are aware, I'm sure, of its historical significance?"

"No, I'm not," a glint of uncertainty in his hard eyes.

"Since 1492, when Isabel the Catholic Queen signed a decree exiling all Moslems and Jews who did not convert to Catholicism, no mosques have been built under the blue skies of Spain—until this one. So you see," I explained, "this mosque represents the beginning of a new era. Not to mention its architectural beauty."

"Well, that's interesting. I wish I had the time to explore it with you."

"Hans," I asked, changing the subject to something more serious—and closer to what I thought was his real reason for being here just then, "have you learned anything more about those mysterious lights?"

"No, I'm afraid I've given up the project. I return to Germany tomorrow. In fact, I must get going, I've a great deal to do before then."

"Well, I'm glad I saw you before you left. I hope you'll be back soon," I said awkwardly.

"I hope not," said Hans, completely dropping the facade of social conversation. "I hope I never see this place again." He looked me in the eye with a severe coldness that gave me chills. What had made him change his attitude? What had happened to his obsession about Inge's death? "Goodbye, Aline," he said. Then he turned his back, slipped into his powerful car, and sped down the street.

This German was a deeply disturbing man. So disturbing that I began to wonder if he might not really be insane. It was terrifying the way his face could change expression so abruptly.

I wondered more than ever whether Inge's death had unhinged him.

Chapter 27

Driving back along the highway, I felt my spirits flagging. I was depressed about Pepito, worried more than ever that I might have been to blame.

In this frame of mind, I noticed that I was approaching the entrance to Puente Romano. On the spur of the moment, I flipped my right indicator and turned down the narrow entrance. I wanted to see what the area around Chez Jacques looked like in daytime. Now that Salima and her new husband had joined the list of interesting people who had connections there, I was still more anxious to get a better sense of the neighborhood.

Unlike the Puerto Banus and El Ancon, Puente Romano was small and enchanting, with picturesque balconies overflowing with red geraniums. In the daylight, the development was not much more than a long Andalusian-style building stretching toward the waterfront, and containing many small apartments clustered together. Driving slowly past the apartments, with their luxuriant hanging gardens and flowering porches, I found the side road Serge had taken the night he and I were there. Then I spotted the small sign of CHEZ JACQUES. An arrow pointed to an entrance on the sea side of the building; and I drove to the parking area I remembered. Today only a few cars were there, and one small delivery truck. Evidently the place was not as busy for lunch as for dinner. I got out and walked down the same path Ali Amine had taken that night. As I did so, I turned around and looked back up at the restaurant building. It had a second floor, which seemed to house two apartments, for there were two identical terraces on either side. The porch of the restaurant was half obscured from my vision by large bushes and flowering plants. Looking toward the water, I saw a shiny, luxurious cabin cruiser at the end of a long narrow dock. This, I decided, must be the same boat that Ali and the German were headed for that night. The shiny white hull rose at a dramatic angle above the gentle stirrings of the water. With its sleek lines and elegant prow, the boat was arresting. Clearly it was designed for more challenging weather than this perfect day with a sea as smooth as a table.

Barely visible from where I was standing was a silver star on one side of the stern. This reminded me of Paco's cigarette boat and made me wonder if this vessel, too, may have come from Nicky Maniatis's shipyards. I walked down to the pier to investigate; and as I came nearer, I verified that it was indeed Nicky's silver trademark sparkling on the stern. My curiosity satisfied, I was about to leave, when the voices of two men reached me from one of the portholes. Embarrassed that the owners might appear and think I was trying to eavesdrop, I hastened to get off the dock and back to my car. My footsteps must have alerted those inside, because the voices ceased. Running as quickly as I could, I reached the corner of the restaurant building. When I glanced back, a man in a white *chilaba* was on the aft-deck, squinting in the sun and looking in my direction. The sun was in his eyes, and I was standing in the shadow, so I hoped he could see no more than a silhouette. My relief only lasted until I saw the black shoulder strap of a gun holster cutting into the soft fabric of his Arab robe.

As he stood there, a woman in a bright-red skirt and a frilly white blouse came out on deck, her thick curly red hair was blowing in the wind and almost covered her face, so I got only a brief view of her features. As I darted around the corner to my car, I saw her withdraw from her pocket what appeared to be sunglasses. Fortunately, a second later, I was out of her vision and into my car. Thankful for the quick start of the engine, I backed down the narrow path as swiftly as I could. It occurred to me as I did so that there must have been three people in that handsome yacht, because I had heard two male voices; and only one man and a woman came out on deck.

And then I had another surprise: Just as I was about to regain the access road, I noticed the unmistakable front end of a blue Porsche, parked by the roadside. Suddenly Hans Schmidt was like a popular song, he was everywhere.

How I longed to talk to Jupiter just then, to tell him that.

JUPITER'S MANSERVANT MANOLO called that same afternoon to tell me that the señor would not be back in Marbella until the following week. Unforeseen matters had postponed his return; but he would contact me as soon as he arrived. It was exasperating to have to wait so long to talk to John Derby.

On the other hand, since today was Thursday, my curiosity about meeting Salima's husband was going to be satisfied. However, I was experiencing misgivings about going back to the mysterious Chez Jacques. I worried that someone might remember seeing me— someone like Ali, who might connect me with Serge.

I had just finished dressing and was looking down from our upstairs terrace, when I saw the long black Mercedes that had driven Salima and me from the Málaga airport sail like an ocean liner into our drive. I rushed down to welcome our guests, whom I had invited for a drink before dinner; but only Salima stepped out onto the gravel.

The heels of her black kid shoes were high and narrow. At first I thought that was the reason she seemed to have trouble keeping her balance. But as I gave her a quick hug, I realized that something was upsetting her.

"Buenas noches, Aline," she said, her voice unusually flat and without animation.

"Salima," I said, "What is it? Aren't you feeling well?" For a moment I had the impression she had taken some kind of drug.

Gathering herself together, she gave me a wan smile. "Only a bad headache, but it will pass."

"Is this usual?"

"Recently it is. I think my constant traveling is affecting my health. I'm anxious to be in my own country. I'm sick of London and Geneva. Back and forth. It is exhausting. Last week I was in South America, and in Panama also, for only a day! Can you imagine?"

She went on to explain that she traveled everywhere with her husband, and that his business obliged him to be constantly on the go.

"What business is he involved in?" I asked.

"Oh, primarily investments. His interests are very wide. I shouldn't complain about the travel, really. It's just this headache. I'm actually thrilled to be with Jamal so much."

I knew Salima well when she was "thrilled" about someone; and this wasn't the way I remembered her. As we spoke, we walked through the salon out onto the terrace where the new moon was just coming up over the silvery Mediteranean.

For a time, Salima stood on the terrace without speaking, simply gazing out to sea. After perhaps a couple of minutes, she threw her arms skyward, and then let them fall around her body. "Oh Aline," she cried, hugging herself tight, "it's so beautiful here!" It was the first time I felt as if I were with the old Salima.

"Marbella resembles the northern coast of Morocco at night," she continued softly, "especially when the wind ripples the sea as it is doing now." The anxious furrows in her forehead had relaxed.

As she spoke, I couldn't help but notice her exquisite earrings, an irregular gold figure eight with tiny pear-shaped cabochon emeralds, like beads of water along the bottom curve.

"Salima, what magnificent earrings! They must be designed by Fatima. Tell me how she is."

Salima's sister Fatima was a world-class jewelry designer. I had met her years before her success, when our small sons attended the same school in Madrid. Unlike her sister, Fatima was successfully married to one man, Raul Aziz, a diplomat. Indeed, her calm, controlled manner and stability were a marked contrast to Salima's unpredictability.

At my prompting, Salima chatted amiably about her sister, telling me proudly that Fatima was still in Paris, where her jewelry continued to be a marvelous success. But when I asked if Fatima returned often to Morroco, a small frown pulled at her mouth.

"I'm afraid I can't tell you that, Aline. Fatima and my husband, unfortunately, do not get along. Since my marriage we have only seen each other once, briefly in Paris last winter. That's when she gave me these earrings."

"I'm sorry to hear that," I said, not knowing quite how to respond. I knew there had been tension in the past between Salima and Fatima and hoped this feeling between the sisters didn't cast a shadow on Salima's new marriage.

Luis, who had taken his time with dressing, now joined us, followed by Andres carrying a tray with drinks. Luis greeted Salima effusively. He had always liked her.

"I hear congratulations are in order. But where is the bridegroom?" he asked.

"Jamal sends his apologies. A business associate just arrived from Germany; and the meeting could not be delayed. But he assured me that he will be at the restaurant before we arrive."

TO MY SURPRISE, at least twenty cars were jammed into the tiny space in front of Chez Jacques, twice as many as the night I went there with Serge. And what had looked like a simple terrace in daylight, now had lanterns circling it, illuminating flowerpots I hadn't seen before.

Once we were inside, Salima giggled happily when Luis looked around the crowded oriental room and told her that he liked the Arabic atmosphere and the smell of sandalwood.

We had been standing in the doorway only a moment, when a tall man dressed in a flashy white suit embraced Salima. When I saw him, I recognized him immediately. And I was terrified. This was the same man who had walked past me that night in Germany with Ava. And the same man I had watched from my hiding place in La Amapola only a few days before. The scar running down his left cheek made him unmistakable. Sensing my gaze, he turned his head toward me. Good heavens, I reflected, Salima's husband is not only a dangerous man, he's also associated with Carlos, who was there with him that night in Germany! A shiver went down my spine as the mocking black eyes glanced at me. Did he know I had been here at Chez Jacques only a short time ago with a KGB defector now working for the CIA?

As these fears hit me, the man with the scar continued to embrace Salima; and I felt a shudder of concern for her.

A moment later, released from his arms, excitement flushed Salima's cheeks; and oddly, for a second, tears quivered in her eyes. Then with a wave of her long elegant hand, she introduced her husband. He bowed dramatically as he turned toward me again, raising his head slowly, like a dancer. His piercing eyes disarmed me with an almost hypnotic effect; and a sudden broad smile magically changed the sinister face. In that brief moment, I understood how Salima could have fallen for him. All the same, his emotional intensity was unsettling.

I looked at Luis, knowing that his clear common sense would restore my calm. Gratefully, I watched as he reached out his hand to greet Jamal, and effectively broke the spell Jamal's entrance had created. This was going to be a strange evening! I wondered if Luis would believe me when I told him this was the Arab I'd seen with Carlos that night in Germany.

Waiters dressed in blue caftans and red fez hats and carrying large round gilt trays moved between the tables, while a dark-skinned, Hindu-looking maître in a bright-pink turban led us to ours. We settled in a corner on a deep-green banquette steeped with cushions of all colors and shapes. And the men faced us on ornately designed leather ottomans. The round, low table glowed with candles inside blue crystal flutes. Very soon Luis and Jamal found they shared an interest in racehorses. Jamal, it turned out, had recently bought a famous stable in Morroco. Although he admitted he was not a specialist in thoroughbreds, he claimed he had a passion for racing.

Meanwhile, the waiter brought small, delicious wafers with a tart, spicy flavor; and Jamal began to order the dinner, which we were happy to have him do.

Salima leaned back against the cushions, and I imitated her gesture, trying to appear equally relaxed. But actually I was scanning the room for Ali Amine. He was not present; however, nor was the German who was with him the night Serge and I came here. On the other hand, if Salima's husband remembered me, he gave no indication of that. After gazing lazily in my direction when he first sat down, he directed much of his attention to a table with three men across the room.

The creamy silk of Salima's dress stood out against the elaborate patterns behind her. Her eyes looked dreamy, focused on the candles on the table, as though she had passed through some kind of tension which was now over. I then looked at her husband, who was chatting amiably enough with Luis. As if trying to counter my earlier impressions of him, he began to speak lovingly of Salima, then told the story of their first meeting. It was in Paris, just a year and a half ago. They met at a dinner.

"Oh yes, it was lovely!" cried Salima.

"It was boring," said Jamal, "only Salima's beauty made the evening tolerable."

Luis, who'd suffered his share of boring dinners, said gallantly that I had rescued him in the same way from many tedious events. But Jamal's attention was suddenly attracted by someone across the room. I followed his gaze and saw that he was staring at a strange-looking woman with shoulder-length, wavy red hair. And it seemed to me that the redhead looked back at Jamal with equal concentration. Immediately I was reminded of the woman I had seen on the boat. This woman was the same size, and had the same abundant red hair. Salima, meanwhile, didn't seem to notice this exchange; she was busy talking to Luis. Her husband's gaze continued to follow the woman's awkward stride as she crossed the room to the table he had been watching since the beginning of the evening. None of the men there rose to greet the redhead. In fact, they did not in any way acknowledge her. Perhaps this was one of the tarts that according to Serge frequented the place.

After the redhead was seated, Jamal excused himself and walked directly to the table, which was about ten yards away. No one shook hands or smiled when he sat down. His stay there was brief; and before Salima had had time to comment on his absence, he was back. Jamal returned pleased. And his expression—which I was beginning to feel was capable of infinite variation—now appeared open and guileless. I glanced back at the other table and was surprised to see the redheaded woman staring at me with intense concentration. Could Jamal be keeping a mistress? Of course, it was possible, but why would he choose such an ordinary-looking woman when he was married to someone as lovely as Salima?

Despite my doubts about Jamal's character, I couldn't fault the menu he'd selected. The food was sublime—each dish with its delicate spices was more tasty than the last. The restaurant's cuisine was essentially Moroccan. But the courses were more varied and much more complex than one normally found in Morocco. Jamal explained that since he was Iraqi, he had chosen a menu that included Middle Eastern, and especially Lebanese, delicacies. Lebanese cuisine, he said, is the most refined of all Arab cuisines. During desert and after, while the waiters came to the table with perfumed tepid water to wash our hands, Luis kept us amused with humorous stories about our experiences in Morocco with Salima's family, but when he mentioned Salima's sister Fatima, I noticed Salima glancing uncomfortably at her husband. Though she took part in embellishing Luis's stories, she never mentioned her sister's name. Jamal listened quietly, without comment.

During this time, I had the sensation I was being observed. My first instinct, of course, was to look for the redheaded woman, but she was no longer there. However, near the table where she had been sitting, just about to push his way through the swinging door to the back of the restaurant, I saw a man who made me catch my breath. The glasses, the dark curly hair, the familiar gesture as he became aware of me looking in his direction. Carlos! Here in this restaurant!

This time I was going to be sure, so I could prove it to Luis.

Too suddenly perhaps, I stood up. Luis gave me a puzzled look. Smiling I asked Salima the way to the ladies' room. She began to rise to accompany me, but Luis restrained her. "Salima, Aline can find the place alone; you can't leave before you finish your story." Without suspecting it, Luis had helped me more than he knew.

Less than a minute later, conscious that I had no weapon with me, I was following the man I believed to be Carlos. The swinging door opened into a short hallway, which went almost directly into the huge kitchen. Spirals of steam rose from an old-fashioned stove in the middle of the room. In the thick kitchen fog, phantomlike figures in long, dirty rags milled about, some supporting stacks of dishes, others bending over pots on glowing burners. In the background, carcasses of baby lamb sputtered and shot off tiny orange sparks over an open fire. The heat was almost unbearable.

A cook with a particularly dirty turban looked up from the huge pot he was stirring and frowned at me as I rushed by. The discolored cotton turban wrapped low over his forehead barely absorbed his sweat; and beads of water were running down his cheeks. The smoke, the steam, the heat, the many men moving through the haze made it almost impossible to see if Carlos was there. In my haste to find him, I bumped into a waiter in a blue *chilaba* balancing a huge silver tray; and he almost dropped it. I apologized as best I could, then scanned the room and rushed out, mumbling to no one in particular that I'd taken the wrong turn. Obviously, I'd lost the man I was looking for.

As I retreated from the kitchen, my mind was filled with what was becoming a familiar dread. Carlos seemed to be everywhere . . . or else I was losing my mind.

The ladies' room was immediately in front of the kitchen; and it was as elaborate as the main salon. When I entered, I saw my own image repeated again and again before me. Mirrors placed above skirted vanity tables reflected everything in countless mutiples, creating something like an infinite mozaic. Suddenly, in the midst of the complex pattern, I saw a hand—or rather a thousand hands— lifting the pink fabric of the vanity skirt and dropping a shiny metal object, much too large to be a compact or a lipstick case. The mirrors were so disorienting that I couldn't identify the real hand until I heard a deep cough from behind and to my right. I stepped farther into the room and found myself with the redheaded woman I'd seen earlier. In the strong light her complexion was rough; her flamboyant curly hair did not enhance the heavily made-up face. Impossible that Jamal would have an affair with this woman, I thought.

I smiled and said good evening. She nodded, passed a large hand through her curls, and left the room.

As I took a seat at the same vanity she had just left, I looked down and saw a basket at my feet. In the basket was the object she must have dropped there. Intrigued, I bent over and picked up what appeared to be a very sophisticated miniature recorder or transmitter.

At one end was a small mesh circle, which looked like a microphone with a tiny on and off push button. Since my experience with the walkie-talkie at Paco's shoot, I was especially sensitive about the use of small electronic devices for clandestine purposes.

Not until I'd turned the device over several times did I become aware that the thing was not a communications device but a very sophisticated electric shaver. And it was still warm!

Abruptly, the door to the room opened again. I stuffed the shaver into my purse and bent over the table, applying lipstick as though that were my only concern. In the mirror I recognized the same woman. She took a quick look at me and left.

Had she come back to retrieve her shaver? I wondered. Quickly I took the razor out of my purse and dropped it back into the basket. Never had I known any woman to carry a razor with her makeup. As I considered that, I noticed a small electric outlet in front of me. She must have been using the shaver here only minutes before.

Jamal was not at the table when I arrived, while Salima and Luis were still absorbed in conversation. But as I took my seat, Luis gave me one of his wry glances, "I hope you weren't getting yourself into trouble, darling."

"Not in the least," I said with a smile, "but I did come across something strange. You see the woman over there with the long red hair?" I turned to point out the woman.

"You can't miss her," laughed Luis, following my glance.

"She had a small electric razor with her in the ladies' room."

"Well, who knows what crazy things women do these days!" he quipped.

Salima listened, but made no comment.

"What were you saying you stumbled on, Aline?" Jamal had approached the table without my noticing, and now hovered uncomfortably above me.

"My love, Aline was telling us about her visit to the Duchess of Windsor in Paris," Salima said so cooly that Luis and I were astounded.

Though he had never met her, Jamal was interested in the Duchess and pressed me for anecdotes about her. So I told him about the Duchess's fondness for pugs; and Luis aided me with colorful details. But as we spoke, I was thinking of Salima's smooth lie. Deception seemed to be a part of her life. I wondered why it was necessary. Why would she not want Jamal to know I had discovered that the redheaded woman used a razor in the ladies' room?

A little later, Salima left for the ladies' room, and Jamal excused himself to greet some friends. While they were both away, I quickly told Luis that I was certain Jamal was the man I'd seen with Carlos in Germany. He rolled his eyes, as he often did when he thought I was overimaginative. Of course, I dared not add that I'd also seen Jamal at La Amapola. If Luis knew how risky that visit had been, he'd be furious. I had only told him Pepito had driven me inside the gate, and that I had remained in the van.

Leaving the dining room, we bumped into the Cocas, who were just entering. "We called your house," Silvia Coca said. "When Andres told us you were dining here, we thought we would try the place. Neither Ignacio nor I ever heard of it." Ignacio kissed me, and Silvia continued, "Aline, one of the reasons we came was to give you the incredible news!"

"What is it, Silvia?" I could barely phrase the question my mind was so caught in the mystery of the redhead, and of Salima and her husband.

"Nancy Rhodentus is getting married again!"

"She is?" I was startled. It seemed incredible—especially after our last conversation. "I'm astonished."

"Aren't we all," said Ignacio, "but wait until you hear who her fiancé is!"

At that same moment, I noticed the redheaded woman; she was seated at the bar not far from where we were standing; and she was laughing with a short man whose heavily scented cigarette smoke swiveled in the air like thick unraveling yarn. But when she saw me, the woman stopped smiling. And when I looked back at her, her eyes had the same intense expression I had noticed earlier.

Unfortunately, the Cocas had moved on to their table before I could find out whom Nancy was marrying. And I found myself being propelled to the door by Luis, while Jamal held it open for Salima and me. When Salima passed him, he kissed her gently on the cheek.

As I passed Jamal, my thoughts were in a turmoil. For he was a double-faced mystery. I was also worried, of course, about Carlos's presence—if it was Carlos whom I had recognized. And I worried, too, that the redhead's intense gaze had some special significance I did not understand.

As we went to the car, I looked toward the sea. A path led to the dock where I'd seen the white boat. But now the slip stood empty. There were no lights down there, only a few small skiffs and several fisherman's boats illuminated by the moonlight were bobbing along the shoreline. The sound of the rolling waves mingled with guitar music that drifted from the restaurant.

We rode the short trip home in fragile silence. Somehow a tension had formed between Salima and her husband. Something she'd said—something about the redhead, I sensed—had clearly turned his mood into smouldering anger. As we proceeded, Salima rubbed her forehead, as though her earlier headache had returned. I was so struck by their tension that I couldn't think of a diverting topic of conversation. Luckily, as we approached the port, Luis began to talk about his friend José Banus who had conceived and developed it; and blessedly, a comfortable conversation followed.

When we finally pulled into our drive, Luis invited Salima and Jamal to have a drink. To my relief, Jamal declined, while Salima sat in a kind of sullen stupor. I couldn't imagine what was bothering her.

Before I stepped out of the car, I leaned across the seat and kissed her cheek, "Salima, come and see me while you're here. When do you plan to go?"

"I'm not sure; but I would love a chance to spend some more time with you. May I call you tomorrow?"

"Yes, of course." I said good night and left the car, hoping that she would indeed call the next day. I was worried about my friend.

Meanwhile, Luis and Jamal stood talking in the drive. For some reason Andres had not left the outdoor lights on; so only the entrance door was lit, and the car was in relative darkness. As I approached my husband and Jamal, they both stepped forward into the headlights, whose harsh beams seemed to magnify the scar on Jamal's cheek. Jamal then said good night; and in a few moments the long car eased out of the drive and up the hill.

The next day, I hoped for a call from Salima. It did not come.

Chapter 28

The next evening, Luis decided to cancel all our engagements so that we could be together and rest from our harried schedule. That night Felisa prepared a special dinner that we both enjoyed, with swordfish and *chanquetes*—which are crisp, tiny fried fish, found only on the coast of Spain. We were happy just to be alone. And he wanted me to forget about Carlos, terrorists, and assassinations. The bright-orange cloth draped over the table rustled with the ocean breeze. Candles in glass encasements gave a soft, gentle glow; and as Luis leaned back into the white canvas chair, I forgot my worries and was caught by the thought of how lucky we were.

"What are you smiling about, darling?" Luis asked as he tapped his cigarette into a silver ashtray.

"Just thinking that I have more fun with you than anybody. This is what I really like."

"Well, then, why don't we do this more often?" he answered.

Andrés came out with the delicious *higos con crema*, Luis's favorite dessert. My husband looked at the large serving I took for myself and raised his eyebrows. "I'll never understand the appetites of American women. Don't you worry that someday it will all march straight to your waistline?"

"I'll risk it," I said, after the first bite. The figs were pure heaven.

Then Andrés appeared again. "Señor Conde, la Señora Rhodentus," Andrés pronounced it RRRRo-deen-toos, "on the telephone."

While Luis went to the phone, Andrés began to clear the table; and I walked to the edge of the pool that separated the terrace from the wide lawn spreading down to the sea. The salty air was mixed with the odor of jasmine. The rumble of the waves on the beach was soothing, and the open view gave me—as always—a feeling of freedom and bliss. I continued standing there, entranced by the shiny ribbon of light the moon was casting on the sea's surface. Many fishing boats were bobbing up and down on the waves, reminding me, unfortunately, of Hans Schmidt.

"Are you in the mood for a cruise?" Luis said when he returned, interrupting my thoughts. "You look like you might be." He put his arm around my waist, and together we watched a pair of sleek speedboats come out of nowhere and careen too close to shore at a fantastic speed.

"Not in one of those, thank you," I answered. "I think of how Paco Cabanellas used to flip around in his. It's a wonder he didn't have an accident sooner."

"I thought you were going to forget about that," said Luis, sternly.

"You're right," I said, and gave him a hug. But I was still watching the aft-lights of the boats as they zigzagged into the darkness. It was hard to entirely forget that tragedy.

"Nancy called to invite us on a cruise to celebrate her engagement."

I interrupted him. "Whom is she marrying?"

"When I asked her who was the lucky man, she said, '*Un norteamericano*. His name is Jack.' So I don't know much more than I did before. She's decided to celebrate with a house party on her yacht instead of a dinner in Marbella. It means a trip to Tangiers, leaving tomorrow," Luis paused, then went on. "Naturally, I said no."

My curiosity about Nancy's fiancé was enormous, and that alone would have made me eager to make the trip. When I first heard she was engaged, I suspected she might be marrying Nicky. So, of course, I was surprised that it was an American. Someone she must have met in France or Germany, because I'd neither seen nor heard of her dating an American in Marbella.

But I was also eager to accept Nancy's invitation for other reasons. For one thing, I was intrigued by the two days of close contact with the other people she was sure to invite—like Paco, who was now able to move about, and Jamal Abad, who had mentioned her name. Thus, as far as I was concerned, Nancy's invitation was irresistible. But I knew it would be difficult to change Luis's mind. Though at the moment he rather liked Nancy, he was not anxious to be in any group which included Paco Cabanellas. No, Luis would not be easy to convince.

The telephone rang again; and since it was now on the table next to Luis, he picked it up. A moment later I could hear him talking with Silvia Coca, who evidently had been asked by Nancy to convince us to go.

"Well, if my sister is going, too," Luis said, just before he hung up, "I'll talk to Aline about it." Then he looked at me. "There seems to be a plot to get us to go," Luis explained. "Casi will be the next to call trying to convince us. The trouble is I can't possibly go tomorrow, you know that; but you could go without me."

I had completely forgotten Luis's plan to go to Málaga for some business meeting.

"Oh, I don't think I would enjoy the trip without you," I said. And then after a moment I added, "But if I were to go, I could pick up that screen you bought at the antique dealer's. At least it would arrive intact if I brought it home on Nancy's boat. If we trust it to shippers, it could be a pile of splinters by the time it reaches here." Luis had been especially enthralled with a delicate oriental screen when we were in Tangiers a year ago. Only a few weeks ago, he had telephoned the dealer to tell him he had decided to buy it. His love of beautiful objects and his anxiety about this piece would contribute to his willingness to let me accept Nancy's invitation. "We're also out of Moroccan tea glasses," I added thoughtfully. And continued: "Naturally I dislike the idea of accepting this particular invitation for the same reasons you do; but Lord knows when I'll have another chance to go to Tangiers this summer and pick up that screen."

"Aline, I can't help but feel that Paco Cabanellas brings trouble, and that we would both be better off if we'd never met him. But if my sister and most of our friends are going, and if you are willing to go without me, it might be a good idea to join them."

So Luis convinced me to go without him.

EVEN AMONG THE many important yachts docked at the port of Banus, Nancy Rhodentus's was by far the largest and the most spectacular. On deck were two sleek white Cigarette boats, similar to the pair Luis and I had seen the previous evening. I wondered if the crew sometimes took them out for a spin when Nancy wasn't around, which was most of the time. Luxurious yachts were a familiar sight in Marbella. And at night, with their riggings decorated with hundreds of tiny lights, these large boats added to the festive atmosphere of the port. Tonight, *La Sirena* easily outdid all the others.

As the Cocas and I approached the elegant white-and-blue boat, my eyes were drawn to a blue Porsche pulling up near *La Sirena*'s slip. I watched with much curiosity—and some astonishment—as Hans Schmidt stepped out. His driver handed him a small suitcase; and he began to walk toward Nancy's yacht. This is going to be a fascinating voyage, I thought, in more ways than one. How is it Hans is not in Germany? The last time I saw him, he had sounded so fed up with Marbella that I never expected to see him here again.

When he reached me, he greeted me quite pleasantly although he was less exuberant than when we had first met months ago. He then stretched out his hand to Ignacio and Silvia Coca; and together we mounted the gangplank. A steward with gold-braided epaulettes, who spoke French but had the warm smile and black eyes of a Moroccan, led us to our staterooms.

Ignacio and Silvia's stateroom came first. After we left them, Hans was silent as he and I continued to follow the steward down the long corridor. As we walked together, I recalled how distant

Hans had been during our last meeting, and his smouldering hostility then. This time he was not much different, merely nodding coolly when he was directed into the stateroom immediately facing mine.

Inge had told me weeks before, with some awe, that Nancy's ship had been decorated by the famous Mongiardino, and that the staterooms were more like luxurious suites in a French château than the cabins of an ocean-going yacht. In my own stateroom, a French eighteenth-century bed was heaped with silk pillows, crimson damask draperies covered the portholes, and a small Louis Seize armchair faced a lovely nineteenth-century English writing table. The coziness and beauty of the room made up for my discomfort at finding myself quartered so close to the enigmatic German.

After freshening up, I left my suitcase open for the maid to unpack and crossed several corridors and winding stairs to the top deck. I was finally going to meet Nancy's fiancé, and I was extremely curious to learn who he was. When I arrived in the salon, the two of them stood greeting guests in the midst of a babble of voices and the clinking of champagne glasses.

To my great surprise, the groom-to-be was a man I had met many years before. His name was Jack Wilmington, and he was an American financier with significant connections in the Middle East. Though Jack Wilmington was at least as powerful and important internationally as R. K. Rhodentus, nothing about him indicated that he could produce the kind of great passion I'm sure R.K. could inspire. I always felt in R.K. an almost boundless energy and charisma. Jack was short and plump, with pink shiny cheeks. He was a fine man. Yet—no matter how hard she tried, and she *did* try her best to show it—it was impossible to imagine Nancy being in love with him.

As if guessing my thoughts, Nancy entwined her long, slender hand around the back of Jack's neck, and to his embarrassment, kissed him on the ear. His cheeks instantly flushed red.

When Luis and I met him briefly years ago, Jack was married. After that meeting, we had not run into him again until today. Looking now at the two of them, Nancy purring like a leopard and Jack blushing like a little boy, I wondered what were Nancy's reasons for marrying him. Maybe she was lonely? Maybe she was broke? Neither seemed likely. Certainly with her alimony from R.K., she should have no need of Jack's fortune.

When it was my turn to greet the couple, I smiled and reminded

Jack of our former meeting. He answered me pleasantly; but he was not a man of many words. However, Nancy made up for his quiet manner with an enthusiasm and wit that outshined her normal gaiety. To all appearances, she was a happy bride-to-be.

The walls of the salon were covered with eighteenth-century Italian paintings. Adjoining the salon was a smaller room with magnificent antique tapestries draped over the walls, where dinner was to be served. In a corner of the dining room, guests were milling around Paco Cabanellas, who had just arrived. This was one of his first times out since the accident. He was alarmingly pale, with a bandage over his left eye; he had lost considerable weight. It was clear as well that his wounds were spiritual as well as physical. For he had the manner of someone who isn't quite able to withstand the usual hustle-bustle. There were crutches leaning against his chair; and I heard someone say that the operation on his eye had only partly restored his sight. As I greeted him, I wondered how long it would take before this snake was uncovered publicly. The truth about him would certainly shock most of our friends, if they knew.

"Lucky to be alive," was the standard comment of those around him.

"Lucky not to be in jail," went through my mind. I realized I held Paco completely responsible for Inge's death. Hans and I had something in common after all.

Paco's arrival seemed to distract Nancy. She unceremoniously dropped her fiancé's arm and kindly went over to welcome the sickly, gray-looking man, who was coughing raggedly as she approached. When the bout ended, Paco settled back into his chair, like an old man. It was hard to realize this was the same man I had seen dancing so happily with Inge only a short time ago. I wondered how Nancy would react when she learned that this friend was actually an international crook.

After Nancy left us for Paco, Jack and I struggled to resume our conversation. I attempted a few words more, but his attention was riveted on his fiancée across the room. Actually I was also more interested in Nancy, too. She was just then doing her best to make Paco more comfortable; and she had pulled up a small footrest for his bad leg. She spoke to him for a brief moment, then went to the bar and poured something from a bottle she took from under the counter. She carried the glass, now filled with a deep-red liquid, over to him. When she handed it to him, he tried to refuse it. And after taking the glass in hand, he continued to hesitate until she finally persuaded him to lift it to his lips. Nancy's kindness did not impress him, and I thought that the reason must be that he was still in pain. His expression as he drank was so unhappy that I had to laugh. "One would think Nancy was giving him poison," I commented to Jack.

That apparently most-conventional man surprised me by answering with more humor than I had credited him with: "He looks so miserable, she might do him a favor if it were poison. But I doubt Nancy would be likely to poison him in the middle of our engagement party . . . not with fifty witnesses." We both laughed at that, as we continued to regard Paco, who was now scowling at Nancy as if she actually had made him drink poison.

The evening passed quickly, for everything went particularly well. During dinner I was seated on a banquette between Nicky Maniatis and Mike Stilianopoulos. Mike, a handsome Filipino of Greek descent, had recently been the Philippine Ambassador in London, and he was a charmer; for some time I didn't turn to my other side. When I did, I saw that Nicky was busy talking to Salima Karam, whom I had not seen since the night of our dinner together at Chez Jacques. As always, Salima was ravishing in a sensational beaded two-piece gazar suit from Valentino's last collection. She had taken off the jacket, revealing a smooth suntan and a daringly low décolletage. Jamal was in another room, where other guests were dining; and it seemed to me that his absence might have been the reason Salima appeared more relaxed than the last time I'd seen her. On the other hand, she was basking in Nicky's attention, which sent shudders through me. Salima certainly had a penchant for dangerous men.

Eventually we joined conversations, and I made a few jokes about Mike's and Nicky's Greek names, despite their different nationalities. Nicky answered that though he considered himself Greek, he sometimes felt closer to his Arab relatives. Since I wanted the conversation to continue in an "Arab direction," I mentioned that the entire crew of *La Sirena* appeared to be Arab, yet it was a pity they weren't dressed in Arab clothes, like Alec Guinness and Omar Sharif in *Lawrence of Arabia*.

Salima was listening and leaning across Nicky, when I asked her, "Salima, do the Arabs in El Ancon wear *chilabas* and fezes?" So far, Salima had avoided mentioning where she and her husband lived— for a reason I failed to understand—so I thought this would be a good chance to tease the truth out of her.

She seemed unperturbed by my question, though, and answered unaffectedly, "I'm afraid you'd be very disappointed. For the most part they wear bathing suits and Western slacks. Only a few wear *chilabas.*" At least, I thought, she is now close to being as open and natural as she used to be.

"Tell me, Salima," I went on, "why do they have so much security there? Some of the most beautiful houses on the coast are in El Ancon, but no one can get a look at them."

A flicker in Salima's expression showed me she was uncomfortable with my question, but Nicky quickly answered for her. "Many Spaniards have security, too, nowadays. Especially bodyguards. Why should it seem strange that Arabs do the same? Unfortunately security has become necessary in our troubled times."

"And do not think that all the people in El Ancon are Arabs, Aline," interrupted Salima. "For instance, Nancy's fiancé has been thinking of buying a house for her there. A large one called La Amapola. He intends to build a dock in front of it, so she can go back and forth to her yacht in a small motorboat."

Amazing! I thought. Jack Wilmington is buying La Amapola? Mike Stilianopoulos, having overheard, asked, "Why don't you tell Jack to buy my house instead? We want to move further up the coast."

Nicky laughed. Mike had an easy humor that most people found delightful. And he continued to joke about how happy Nancy and Jack would be in his house. The four of us were still giggling over that, when Nancy suddenly appeared next to the table, her face clouded, her tone chilly. "Nicky," she said, "I need your help. I have a small emergency. Could you come with me for a minute?"

Nicky rose and excused himself; we all sensed he followed her out of the room reluctantly.

"What could that be about?" mused Salima, almost to herself.

"Maybe Nicky is going to sell her my house," said Mike hoping to revive our previous hilarity, but Nancy's cool interruption had punched a hole in our high spirits.

As she and Nicky departed, I suddenly had a curious insight. Could she be jealous of Nicky? Did it bother her that he and Salima were having such a good time together?

I knew that made no rational sense, since she was supposedly falling blissfully into the arms of another man. But all the same . . .

· · ·

WE WERE A long time at the dinner table; and then gypsies appeared. Over half the guests had come only for cocktails. And these had disembarked when we left port before dinner. But it seemed there were still more people on board than the yacht could hold. When the gypsies entered, we stood up and moved out of the way so the furniture could be moved to make space for the flamenco. Chairs were placed in a semicircle, and tables disappeared. As I was wondering where to sit, Hans Schmidt, who had been dining at the far end of our table, took my arm and led me across the room. I was more than a little surprised at this attention, given the stiff reception I'd been treated to earlier.

I was about to ask him about this newest change in his mood. But before I could do that, he leaned closer, hissing into my ear. "Aline, there's no time for light talk. A killer is on this boat. I'm sure. The bastard who killed my daughter. And I intend to capture him." While I digested this amazing statement, he patted his jacket in a way that could only mean he was armed. He's totally crazy, I thought.

"I overheard some of your conversation during dinner about the Arab development in El Ancon and about the villa La Amapola," he continued, flashing me a meaningful glance. "Too bad you didn't ask about the people who arrive at that house by boat, and by helicopter."

I knew from my experience with Hans that no matter how exaggerated his statements, there was some factual basis to what he said. The lights he had been obsessed with *had* been there. And the explosion in Paco's boat was surely not an accident. It was on my lips to ask who he had in mind, when a disturbance on the dance floor demanded our attention.

The great Lola Flores had begun dancing a rumba *gitana* and was encouraging guests to join in, the sway of her hips catching the beat with a sensual rhythm. But few of the guests were aware of her; for a woman on the other side of the floor was attracting everyone's attention. Hans pointed, and I turned my eyes toward the woman who was creating the excitement—Sofia Cabanellas, definitely more beautiful than I remembered her from the shoot. Sofia's long black hair flooded down her back; and she wore a pale, sheer blue slip, nothing more. Her feet bare, her eyes closed, as if oblivious to everything except the music, Sofia was dancing. I hadn't known that she was on board; and it was a shock to see her the way she was, barely dressed and completely given over to the ecstasy of her dance. When Sofia first appeared on the floor, the musicians faltered; but then with a nod from Lola, who seemed to understand something the rest of us did not, the guitarists picked up Sofia's rhythm and continued the melody.

Sofia was spellbinding, moving tauntingly to a tarantella, a priceless gem of the most pure flamenco. Our little group was mesmerized. The thin slip barely concealed her beautiful supple body. Her hips, arms, and legs moved langorously to the sensuous rhythm; her head was thrown back, her full lips parted. I recalled that Nancy had once told me that Sofia was part gypsy; and it occurred to me that generations before, in the white caves of Granada, she must have had a very gifted ancestor.

Just as Sofia was lifting her arms in a slow arc above her head, while her body twisted in sensuous pleasure, Nancy and Nicky entered. When they saw her, their expressions were a study in contrasts. Both stopped dead, Nicky stared, totally enchanted. But Nancy's glance was indignant. She took a step forward, and for a moment I thought she was going to slap Sofia. But then she retreated, watching the performance with an annoyance she could not hide. When Sofia's performance ended, a storm of shouts and applause went around the room. She gave a shy smile; then Lola Flores embraced her, crying, *"Chiquilla, es tu sangre gitana"*—it's your gypsy blood.

Nancy, meanwhile, affecting the attitude of a solicitous friend, put an arm around Sofia's shoulders and walked her off the dance floor and out of the room.

There was a stunned stillness for a moment, accompanied by an enthusiastic murmur. Then the party recommenced, filling the space, growing loud with talk and laughter and music.

I saw Paco Cabanellas hobbling across the cleared space about that time. He lowered himself with difficulty into an overstuffed chair. If he had witnessed his sister's performance, he did not acknowledge it. I hadn't seen him during dinner and assumed he had been in the other dining room. But he didn't appear to be a man who had just completed a satisfying meal. On the contrary, he looked even more ravaged than before; and again I remembered our jokes about the poison. Even if Nancy had given him something harmful in that drink, he could hardly have looked worse.

Hans, who was also looking at Paco, turned to me. "I must speak to him. The little bastard has to help me." Looking at his icy blue eyes, I was startled by the anguish and suffering I saw there. He seemed to perceive my compassion, because calmly, he said: "Aline, would you please help me?"

Naturally, his question surprised me; but I was even more amazed to find myself nodding assent. Hans's complete dedication moved me, I couldn't help it. Despite my questions about him, I had to admire his determination to uncover his daughter's killer. When I accepted, Hans's smile was the first sign of hope I'd seen illuminate his distinguished face all evening. "What I want to ask you, my friend," he began, "is important for many reasons. Mainly, I need you as a witness, so that I can use your testimony in court later. And although what I want to do may sound daring, it is quite simple. Without your help, however, it would be impossible.

"I intend to find the man who killed my daughter . . . the terrorist who murdered her. There will be risks, I must tell you," he went on, "but not for you. I will be the only one taking chances."

Hans then began to explain, "Unfortunately, my plan requires you to be up in the middle of the night. So I will knock on your door in about two hours." He looked at me questioningly.

I nodded.

"Could you put on something practical, and dark-colored?"

I told him that would be simple.

"And do you have a watch that you can read in the dark?"

Again I nodded.

"And do be careful if you see a crew member or a ship's officer. I have reason to believe that *La Sirena* is not the pleasure craft that it seems to be. I don't trust a soul who works on this boat."

"Yes," I said, "if you say so." What can he mean by that? I wondered.

"And finally, I don't have the entire plan worked out yet, but I'll explain it to you when I pick you up later. By that time I'll know exactly what I need from you." Again his lips curled in a sad smile. "I can't thank you enough, Aline. You are indeed a friend. Inge was right when she told me you were a fine person."

Then he formally bowed and left me. For a moment I wondered if I'd been foolish to agree to help him. But at the same time I knew that if I wanted to get to the heart of the mysteries that obsessed both of us, he was as direct a path as I could find.

Chapter 29

The party lasted well into the night, long after Jack Wilmington fell sound asleep in an armchair and his bride-to-be had disappeared with Sofia. Nicky only paused in the salon for a moment after their exit; then he, too, slipped out and never returned. After their departure, Paco and Hans had a heated discussion that perhaps no one but myself noticed; for Lola Flores had regained the dance floor and absorbed everyone's attention. As I talked to friends and pretended to enjoy the music and the dancing, I kept Hans and Paco in the corner of my eye. After a time, Hans stood up and wandered away, leaving the sick man nearly collapsed in his seat. It was painfully obvious that whatever Hans had said to him had left Paco Cabanellas extremely upset. Hans was now standing with his arms folded across his strong chest, watching Lola's dance with the kind of concentration I could imagine him giving a balance sheet. His face was utterly blank of expression, his pale eyes as sharp and unrelenting as an eagle's. I watched him with curiosity. He was such a strange man, unfathomable in many ways—yet a man of stubborn determination, and unveering passion for his daughter.

He must have sensed my look, because he gave me a barely perceptible nod, which I took to mean "my plans are almost ready." In the moment it took Hans to communicate with me, he held my gaze, and then he abruptly exited the salon. A prickle of fear alerted me. Hans was unpredictable. What would he do next? What was I getting myself into?

Not long after Hans left, Nancy appeared at my side. Surprisingly enough she had changed out of the clothes she'd been wearing earlier. The lovely short robe she now had on was a cool blue chiffon that caught almost precisely the shade of her eyes. Her taffy hair was loose on her shoulders, and she was still wearing the diamond necklace she had on at the beginning of the evening. It was difficult not to comment on the irregular starbursts of perfect diamonds cascading across her low décolletage.

"Nancy, your necklace is stunning," I said.

"A present from Jack," she said smugly. "He thought an engagement ring didn't really express his excitement about our marriage." She touched the large diamonds in the middle with long slim fingers.

"I'm fortunate, too," I said. "Luis loves jewels. Often he surprises me with something I wouldn't dream of asking for."

"Frankly, I think women should be open about such things. Many men don't have your husband's sensitivity for jewels," Nancy said. "In my case, I know how to be persistent." She patted the massive necklace again. "Usually how much I want something has a direct impact on my chances of getting it."

Her eyes wore a candid, almost doelike expression, but her words were typical of another kind of woman, a kind of woman that I did not like. The combination left me confused; I didn't know what to make of her. This confusion bothered me perhaps more than it should have, because I truly liked her.

One thing, however, had become very clear: Nancy was marrying Jack for his money. Why? She had money of her own from R.K.'s alimony. And if—as I suspected—she was in love with Nicky Maniatis, he was certainly wealthy enough to satisfy Nancy's requirements. She didn't need Jack for those. So what kept her from marrying Nicky? Maybe he already had a wife, but if that were the case, he never mentioned it.

Although Nancy had considerable charm and was fun to be with, I was discovering a woman of many faces. I decided to continue playing her game.

"What would you like to get now, Nancy?"

She looked at me with cool blue eyes. Then a beaming smile spread across her face as she reached out an arm to someone behind me and said, "Only my beloved's happiness."

Jack Wilmington had awakened from his nap and was joining us, smiling awkwardly, as though he still couldn't quite believe the passion this beautiful woman felt for him. There was a clumsy pause in the conversation, which I did nothing to fill in. Then Jack offered me champagne, which I took, and toasted their mutual good fortune.

Meanwhile, a commotion was taking place around Paco as he indicated he was ready to retire. Several friends surrounded him; and a few minutes later two of them accompanied him to his room. As he left, I decided his departure was a good time for me to do the same. Although the party was still in full swing at two a.m. I wanted to prepare myself for the night ahead, so I said a round of good nights and returned to my cabin.

I took off my evening dress and changed into black stretch pants and a thin black turtleneck sweater. Then I collapsed on the beautifully embroidered sheets, let my head sink into the massive feather pillow and inhaled its gentle fragrance. That's the last thing I remembered until I was startled awake by a rapid knocking on my door. Jumping out of the bed, it occurred to me that someone else might be there instead of Hans.

"Who is it?" I asked, in what I thought was a normal tone.

"It's Hans, Aline."

I opened the door; and before I could say anything he was thrusting a flashlight into my hands. Then I tiptoed out into the corridor, locked my door, and put the key in my pocket. Hans was already walking toward the stairs. As I passed the staterooms where my friends lay sleeping, I couldn't help but wonder if this strange vocation of mine was worth the sacrifices.

When I caught up with Hans, he whispered, "Paco has agreed to be the bait. He will lure Inge's killer onto the upper deck. Then he will give me the signal—he'll drop a crutch. And I'll deal with the killer. Meanwhile, you will need the flashlight I gave you to let me know if anything unforeseen comes up. My only worry is that someone else may appear on deck unexpectedly. I don't anticipate this will happen; but if it does, use the flashlight to warn me. Don't worry. I'll place you so that you can direct the light to the best spot for me to see it."

All the while he was talking, my intuition told me that even though I had no evidence so far that he was aboard La Sirena, Carlos could very well be the killer he hoped to catch. The possibility made me tremble.

"Aline," he whispered, "just follow me to the bow of the top deck."

Everything was in darkness, only a low glimmer from tiny floor lights enabled us to see our way. After we reached the end of the long empty corridor and climbed the stairs, we entered the large salon. I followed him as he walked toward a door across the room. When he reached it, he placed his hand on my arm. Then he turned around and bent down to my ear. "When you go out there," he murmured, "I would like you to hide directly beneath the rigging of the Cigarette boat on the port side. You won't be visible there, and you will have a clear view of the entire bow. If anyone else approaches besides Paco and whoever may be accompanying him, flash the light once into the Cigarette boat's stern reflector. The light will deflect from that, and the source will be impossible to detect. No one will know where you are. Just flash once, for a second. That's all. Then leave immediately."

He lowered his head to glance at his wristwatch, and then whispered. "Wait exactly two minutes before following me."

The words had barely tumbled out of his mouth when he turned and slipped through a door to the outside. In the silence that followed, I stood suspended in indecision. Then I turned my attention to my watch.

Outside, the night was so black on the main deck that I had difficulty finding the bow. Only the port and starboard lights shone dully, and one large beam illuminated a path on the water, which showed me that the yacht was barely making headway. There was not a speck of the morning dawn. And the stars seemed more distant than ever, tiny, fading dots in the dark sky.

I inched forward silently along the deck railing toward the bow of the boat. Fortunately, as I crept ahead in my bare feet, some intuition made me aware that a person was crouching on the deck not ten feet before me. My heart jumped. By a miracle, I saw the silhouette before falling right over him. The dark outline was too small to be Hans, but beyond that I couldn't make out a single detail. Not wanting to advance or retreat, fearing any movement might expose me, I remained like a statue.

Almost immediately, the figure scurried forward in a crouch. My breath was short now, and I had to make an effort to keep quiet. Since I couldn't see Hans or Paco, I did not know if this was the person who would be joining them. The figure then moved again to a spot beneath the left Cigarette boat, precisely the spot Hans had chosen for me.

That was when I realized that Paco had betrayed Hans. That this person was not supposed to be there, I was certain. Whoever crouched there was someone who intended to attack Hans. Hans was going to be ambushed.

My priorities were clear. I had to signal Hans. Voices ahead were now audible. Men were speaking English—Hans did not understand Spanish. But all the speakers had accents. Paco was laughing in the high nervous way I remembered from La Romana, and with the same almost hysterical tone that I had perceived in the intercepted phone call with Hans. Then I recognized Hans's voice. A second later, I heard someone else. The crouching figure before me was definitely someone Hans did not expect.

But I couldn't warn Hans; for the other was occupying the only place where I could safely aim the light at the rear reflector of the Cigarette, which was about fifteen feet above the deck. I kept my eyes on the crouching figure. Finally, he moved forward to the bow of the small racing boat. I took two careful, silent steps to put me in line with the reflector. With any luck, the beam should pass over the intruder's head unseen, and land directly on the target. I lifted the flashlight and lined it with the port riding light, then pressed the switch. The beam shot out, shockingly bright, and hit the reflector. At the same instant, the crouching figure leapt from his hiding place.

Hans had told me to disappear the second after I flashed the warning light, but I was too worried about him to move. A moment later I heard men fighting. There was a loud groan, and the ugly, soft sound of blows smashing flesh, men pummeling each other.

I had no doubt who was being beaten. Yet I could not help, but I could not leave either. I peered through the shadows along the railing, trying to see what was happening. But it was too dark, and all I could make out were dark silhouettes of interlocked bodies.

Then I saw a terrifying spectacle. Two men were lifting another off the deck. To my horror, as I watched, a man was thrust over the side. Since the boat was hardly moving, I clearly heard the splash as the body reached the water.

This all happened so quickly that for a moment I was incapable of registering what I had witnessed. Then suddenly I became terrifyingly aware that Hans had been thrown overboard. Whoever the others were, they had murdered him. And they would kill me as well if they knew I had seen the crime. At the same moment, it also hit me that Paco was just as guilty as the people who committed the act. Even though he was not physically capable of attacking anyone, he had set up the meeting, and he had betrayed Hans.

Then the idea flashed through my head that perhaps Hans was still alive, struggling in the water. As that thought hit me, I turned around and plowed recklessly through the darkness toward the stern, using instinct and memory to find my way back as fast as I could. The terror of being caught by Hans's attackers pushed me on. Shoving through a door, I entered the deserted large salon. Chairs had been left strewn helter-skelter throughout the room. So I was in danger of jarring against one and creating a noise which would reveal me. Like a slalom racer, I dodged through the semidarkness, and somehow missed the obstacles. When I finally found the long corridor I had traversed with Hans only minutes before, my heart was throbbing. Now it was without light. For a moment I paused in the blackness, heaving to catch my breath, desperately trying to decide whom I could turn to for help.

I was afraid to call out, in case Hans's attackers should hear me. And I was equally afraid to go to a ship's officer, in case Hans's earlier warning was valid.

At any rate, I had to take the chance that Hans was still alive and find a way to help him.

Scurrying down the stairway, I entered the corridor that led to my stateroom. All was silent, but a dim light made it possible for me to read the name cards on the doors. My first thought was to go to Nancy. But I knew her stateroom was not on this hallway; and I had no idea where it was. On the other hand, I knew the Cocas were quartered only two doors away from me. A few seconds later, I was knocking lightly on their door. I prayed that Ignacio would open quickly.

In a moment, Ignacio opened the door just a crack. He was rubbing his eyes, and his hair was disheveled. Ignoring explanations, I pushed into the room and closed the door behind me. His eyes blinked in surprise when he recognized me. And Silvia was sitting up in bed, looking equally astonished. My face must have been a study in anguish, and my black tights and black sweater were a strange outfit for four-thirty in the morning. Intelligent as always, both of them held their questions as I tried to briefly explain the problem.

I kept my story simple: I'd seen a man fall overboard. Without explaining why I couldn't do that myself, I begged them to tell the yacht captain immediately, and not to mention my name to him. Ignacio immediately went to the table and picked up a phone. The skipper answered right away. And almost immediately, bells began to ring all over the ship. Soon the boat, which had been barely moving, began to power forward. I hoped the captain would have strong lights now sweeping the water.

Once Ignacio had alerted the captain, I explained that I'd felt sick and had dressed in something warm to go up on deck to get some air. Just as I had arrived there, I saw and heard a man fall overboard. Of course, I could only wonder how my friends would interpret my reasons for going to them and not directly to the captain myself. But

I was an old and trusted friend, and they sensed my urgency, so they said nothing. In fact, Ignacio let me know he would protect my identity. While the two of them quietly donned sweaters and robes to go up on deck to watch the rescue proceedings, Ignacio told me he would explain that he had been walking on deck when he heard a man scream and a splash. When he said that, I gave him a quick, grateful kiss on the cheek, wishing I could tell my friend the whole story.

After waiting in my own room for several minutes, I undressed and put on a robe, then went up on deck to join the others who had been awakened by the clanging of the bells. For over an hour I stood next to Ignacio and Silvia, leaning over the railing watching the search. But when the first rays of the rising sun sent a shimmer of gold over the sea, Hans had still not been found, and the search was given up. I knew he was dead.

The general opinion was that whoever had fallen overboard had had too much to drink. "Probably one of the Arabs in the crew," someone suggested. And the captain decided that since there was nothing else to do, he would wait until the morning to find out who—if anyone—turned up missing.

And so with a heavy heart, I put my key in my door and opened it, glancing cautiously inside before I entered. It was still possible that one of Hans's murderers had seen me flash the warning light.

That I slept at all is nothing less than a miracle. But I did sleep—a long, black, dreamless sleep. I fell onto the bed and clutched a pillow to my stomach and plunged into unconsciousness. When I awoke, it was close to noon. The boat was motionless. A bright Mediterranean sun sparkled through the lace curtains covering the portholes. From the relentless hum of distant sounds and the clatter of voices, I knew we were in the port of Tangiers.

Achingly, I pulled myself out of bed. I took a long, very hot shower until the worst clouds left my mind. After I finished, my next move seemed clear: First I called the chief steward, to find out if anyone had turned up missing. But he had no word on that. Some of the passengers were still sleeping, he claimed, and no one thought there was any reason to wake them. (This was very sloppy procedure, I realized; someone should have been trying to account for everyone on board. But there was nothing I could do about that.) Next, I thought I would tell Nancy that I had tried to waken Hans, and there was no reply, and that I was afraid he could be the one who fell overboard.

But when I called her stateroom, she had already left the ship.

Jupiter would be my best help, I knew. But how was I to reach him? His advice would be invaluable, but telephoning him from the yacht would endanger his cover as well as my own. Then I remembered that the antique dealer I planned to visit had a phone. I decided to attempt a brief untraceable call from there. Dressing quickly in bright colors, to mask my dark apprehensions, I prepared to negotiate breakfast.

When I opened my door, the corridor was silent and deserted. Then to my surprise, I noticed that the door to Hans's stateroom was ajar, and I could hear someone moving around inside. I tapped lightly and then pushed the door open.

Sofia Cabanellas stood there, startled as a deer, frozen midmotion. She had a large briefcase propped open on the bed and was in the act of pulling out a sheaf of documents. Other papers lay scattered across the dark, plum-colored spread.

"What are you doing, Sofia?" The words burst out of me before I could think. Fortunately, I was so genuinely perplexed that my tone was not accusatory. She stared at me for a moment, like a child caught in a forbidden act. Her stunning dark eyes held mine for a time, and then she answered, "Why, Aline, Hans Schmidt needs these papers. He asked me to bring them to him at the Minzah Hotel. He wants me to meet him there at two this afternoon."

This incredible response nearly took my breath away. I thought for a moment, then asked carefully, "But, how did he let you know he needed them?"

Again she stared at me with utter guilelessness. She was so beautiful. The black hair piled haphazardly on top of her head had gleaming blue lights. When she found her answer she smiled, "He called me!"

"On the telephone?"

"That's right."

I nodded and said, "I see. Well, perhaps we'll run into each other later." But Sofia had apparently forgotten me and had returned to her task.

Incredible! I thought after I left. Could Hans be alive?

But in the back of my mind a darker voice prompted, "If Hans were alive he would have found a way to let you know."

But then, I asked myself, why is Sofia going through Hans's papers? Is she doing this for her brother? Or for Carlos?

A vast buffet was spread out in the large salon. Although only two other people were there (they were seated at a corner table), every serving dish was full and fresh. There was a mixture of Mediterranean delicacies—fruit juices of every variety, dates, raisins, smoked eel, honeyed cakes, wines, anise, thick chocolate, black coffee. But there were American favorites as well.

When I recognized my dining companions—they were Paco and Jamal—I trembled. Paco was as guilty as the men who had thrown Hans overboard. And Jamal, I suspected, could have been one of the guilty also. Only the bright sunshine pouring through the glass, and the two stewards standing there, gave me the courage to face them.

But the two were deep in conversation, and neither realized I was there, until the steward brought my plate of pancakes to their table. So I had no choice but to join them.

Paco looked visibly worse than he did the night before. His unpatched eye was ringed with dark circles; and his mouth was a white stripe across a stubbled chin. His clothes looked slept in. Still, I could not forget that this man had stood by and watched someone being thrown overboard.

Paco hardly greeted me. But Jamal more than made up for Paco. He jumped to his feet, gave a deep bow, and then leaned forward as though he wanted to give me the classic kiss on both cheeks. I drew back, however, before his face reached mine.

And then, not very subtly, I asked him where Salima was.

"Ah, you wish to know about my elusive bride. Well, that is an interesting question. I myself prefer the morning hours, the most delightful and productive time of day. But my beloved prefers the darkness. I think it appeals to her romantic nature." He smiled at me knowingly, as if his words had a secret meaning.

I despised this man.

"Tell me, Condesa," he continued, "what is your formula? Beautiful at night, beautiful at noon, but most beautiful just before dawn."

I felt my throat go dry and stared for a moment, waiting for my mind to spin out an answer. Jamal had seen me on deck last night!

"My formula?" I said, testing my voice. To my surprise it held its normal register. "Well . . ."

But Paco interrupted harshly. "Don't be an ass, Jamal. Do you think last night was the first time Aline went to a party that lasted so late? We all do in Spain. There's no formula."

Jamal sat down next to me, leaning back against the banquette. Impulsively, I said, "I was up much later than four. In fact, I was on deck until five-thirty at least, watching them look for the man who fell overboard." And looking at Paco, with what I hoped was an innocent expression, I asked, "Do they know yet who fell overboard?"

"Nobody," Jamal answered instead of Paco, who was in the process of stuffing a large piece of toast in his mouth . . . to give him time to think of an answer, I thought. "Most likely one of the crew threw something overboard—garbage, or empty cases of champagne, or whatever," Jamal went on. "The man who was walking on deck interpreted it wrong. He thought he saw someone and heard a splash. That's all. No. No. Fortunately everybody on the ship is safe and sound."

Paco looked relieved. "Did you enjoy Lola Flores last night, Aline?" he asked, rather lamely. I nearly leapt at this crumb of conversation that was not steeped in innuendo. I looked at him and then at Jamal for a brief second before answering, but I could not tell if either suspected I had been on deck last night when Hans was thrown overboard.

Jamal soon tired of our company and stood up, explaining that he intended to awaken his wife from her beauty sleep. "You must tell her your secret, Condesa," he said with a bow.

He gave Paco a curt nod, which was cooly returned, then left. Paco slumped against the banquette, as though his last bit of strength had given out. For a while he was silent, and I continued to concentrate on my pancakes and hot honey sauce. But after a while, the silence became unbearable. Finally, I said, "Paco, are you all right?"

Rubbing his unpatched eye as though it pained him, he didn't answer immediately. At last he said, "Aline, you have put me in an awkward position."

Wondering what he meant, I didn't answer.

"I think we both know what I am referring to," he said.

Still I didn't answer.

"The others know there was a witness; they just don't know who it was. But I'll warn you, be careful. Your name has been mentioned."

I took a sip of coffee.

"Hans told me his plan," said Paco. Then added significantly, "All of it." He paused and looked at me hard. "I had no choice . . . or rather, I had a choice: Hans or me."

I stared at him. What a coward, I thought.

"And I guarantee that if I'm given a choice between you and me, the decision will be the same. But it hasn't come to that yet," he said quickly. "So listen carefully. Spend as little time as possible in your cabin. You must leave this ship and not come back. A maid can pack for you. For your own safety, you should not be alone. That's all. I've risked enough for you. Good luck." Painfully, he struggled to his feet and arranged the crutches beneath his arms.

"Why are you telling me this, Paco?" I said at last, fully realizing he didn't have to do that.

He stared at me blankly, then turned as if to go. But after two steps, he looked back over his shoulder, his face suddenly slack with sadness. "Because Inge cared about you," he said. Then he hobbled slowly out of the room.

Damn you, Paco Cabanellas! I wanted to scream at him. But I held myself in. There was too much left to do.

And damn you, Hans Schmidt, I thought. Why did you have to tell that snake Paco that I was helping you?

TODAY'S SCHEDULE, ANNOUNCED yesterday, was to leave the day free for shopping in Tangiers. *La Sirena* was to lift anchor for Spain that afternoon around four. On the return voyage, dinner would be served; and the ship was expected to dock back in the port of Banus during the night. As I went down the gangplank, I asked a steward to tell the maid to pack my things while I was gone. Looking at my watch, I saw it was almost two. I knew there wasn't much time, but I couldn't resist peeking into the Hotel Minzah on my way to the antique dealer. I was curious to see if crazy Sofia was making her fantasy appointment with Hans.

Out on the pier, dark-skinned men in bloomers and turbans, screaming children, and veiled women in long dusty *chilabas* created a cacophony of sound and color that provided a welcome respite after the horrors of the night before. Several other yachts were moored in the harbor, as well as a large passenger ship, two merchant ships, a coast-guard vessel, and a flat, broad barge transporting coal. In the distance, the sun glistened on tiny whitecaps. At the end of the pier, two rickety old taxis idled. Their drivers waved and beckoned to me; but I could see the roof of the Hotel Minzah ahead on the hill, and decided to walk.

Two tall doormen in white *chilabas* opened the heavy double doors. Countless times Luis and I had been here; and I knew that to the right of the old-fashioned lobby of blue and yellow tiles and ancient silks, there was a small room where mint tea was served at any hour. I directed my steps there. And when I passed through the archway, the sight that met my eyes made me stop in my tracks.

Had I seen Hans and Sofia in the tearoom, I would have known I was hallucinating, but to see Nancy seated there, alone at a corner table, was nearly as startling. Instinctively, I drew back. This was fortunate, because a moment later someone brushed passed me and walked straight to her. I didn't need for the tall, exquisite figure to turn around to know it was Sofia.

Sofia bent her lovely head and dug through the enormous shoulder bag she was carrying. A moment later she withdrew a stack of documents and offered them to Nancy. But Nancy, shaking her head sharply, rejected them. She seemed to be asking Sofia for something else. But the young girl merely shrugged and continued to hand over documents. Nancy looked unhappy; but finally she accepted a few. She looked at them lazily, flipping through one page after another. Then abruptly, as if disgusted, she tossed all the pages on the table. Meanwhile Sofia drew up a chair and sat down, while a waiter proceeded to place a glass in front of her and pour the steaming mint tea. She then concentrated on a silver platter of sweet cookies, while Nancy, with a resigned shrug, retrieved some of the papers and listlessly began to study them. Sofia still didn't speak. She stared absently off as she nibbled on a cookie.

So, Hans was dead, and Nancy was going through his papers. What did this mean?

For one thing, that Sofia had lied to me. She had not received a call from Hans, but from Nancy. They both knew Hans was dead.

Though I wanted to stay and watch this scene play out, I knew I hadn't much time. For Rashid, the antique dealer, often left his shop by three, and if I hoped to catch him I would have to leave immediately. I hastened back through the lobby, directing my steps to the souk. As I walked along the winding streets, I was consumed with confusion about Nancy's interest—or lack of it—in Hans's papers.

Along the way, vendors pestered me with their wares, "Madame, s'il vous plaît." And I was sidetracked by some lovely hand-carved bracelets, then by a display of carpets—I needed one badly for a new guest room. So it must have been almost an hour later when I came near the area where Rashid's small shop was located. Meanwhile my thoughts kept returning to Nancy and the dead man's papers. What is going on? I kept asking myself.

After several more winding turns in the narrow dirt street, I arrived in front of the small shop where Rashid conducted his business. With something close to pleasure, I opened the flap, and entered the quaint little room. Blessedly, Rashid was still there. And, though he was with another client, he excused himself to greet me. Then, seating me in a comfortable antique chair, he asked an assistant to bring me a cup of mint tea.

While I waited for Rashid, the assistant insisted upon pointing out the most important new additions to the shop's collection of beautiful objects. All the while, I was getting nervous. Time was passing; and I was still weighing the advantages and disadvantages of telephoning Jupiter. I didn't need Paco's warning to realize I was in danger, and I felt I needed Jupiter's advice. At the same time, I would never be able to tell Luis what was happening. If I did, he would force me to give up espionage forever.

Meanwhile, Rashid was taking too long. I was about to leave to look for a telephone elsewhere, when he finally made his appearance, asking kindly for Luis as he approached, then expressing his pleasure at my visit.

As soon as I could interrupt the man's gracious remarks, I asked if he had a private telephone.

"But, of course, Madame la Comtesse," he said. "But not here. I have one in my other shop, which is nearby. We can go there immediately." With the intuition that made him such a superb antique dealer, he sensed that my call was important. And with no questions asked, he said, "Allow me to escort you, Comtesse."

Stepping ahead, he drew back the curtained entrance. The blue silk gave way to reveal the narrow street. I followed him. The entrance was cluttered with porcelains, hand-carved lanterns, silver teapots, and antique perfume burners; and I had to weave my way through the helter-skelter to gain the narrow passageway behind the shop. To our right was a dead end. To our left was the street where I had been before. Rashid indicated a small door beneath an arch directly in front of us.

"This way, Madame la Comtesse. It's a shortcut that will take us to my shop, and a telephone."

Barely had he spoken when I heard someone say in heavily accented English, "Telephone? That won't be necessary, Countess, will it? Nancy Rhodentus has a superb communication system on board," the voice went on. "You can call anywhere, anyone, directly from the boat."

What happened next is difficult to explain, because I never saw exactly how or from where the large white-clothed figure appeared. He was suddenly there, confronting us. From seemingly nowhere, the voice rang out, "Good afternoon," Hans Schmidt said, immediately absorbing our total attention. As I looked at him, I truly wondered for a moment if I had lost my mind. He was standing there before me, hale and hearty, dressed in a white *chilaba* that reached down to his moccasined feet.

He continued to speak, ignoring Rashid's presence. "In fact," Hans declared, "you just have time to get back to the boat. I will take you personally to *La Sirena*. You can make your call from my room, if you do not have a phone in your own." At which point he reached out and grabbed my arm, his strong fingers wrapping around me like tentacles. Instinctively, I yanked my arm away. Rashid stepped forward.

"Hans," I said. "I would like to introduce you to an old friend." Bending my head I indicated Rashid. "Luis's favorite antique dealer. He has searched for special pieces for us for years."

"Ah," Hans said. "Delighted." But he did not release my arm. "I was hoping we would run into each other," he continued, turning to Rashid. "Monsieur, do not worry about this lady, I will take her back to the boat. We are friends."

As I looked at Hans, he winked, and gave my arm a reassuring tug. Somehow he transmitted a comforting message; and whether warranted or not, I experienced a wave of relief.

Poor Rashid still did not understand what was going on. He only knew I wanted to make a call; and so he still struggled to help me. "Before you leave, Madame la Comtesse, will you please sign a receipt for the screen, so I can have it delivered before the ship leaves?" Saying that, he politely directed me to his shop through the opening across the street. But Hans had his own reasons why I should not be left alone; and though by then he had released my arm, he followed. And then a moment later, when Rashid asked me to sign the paper, a telephone was close at hand, but I decided against using it while Hans was nearby. I didn't want to risk violating Jupiter's cover. So I merely signed the invoice and tucked the copy inside my handbag.

As we said goodbye, Rashid bowed and smiled at me, glancing suspiciously at Hans. I felt a rush of gratitude toward the elderly man as I stepped away from him to join Hans, who was silently waiting, as grim as a prison guard.

I wasn't pleased with the idea of going back to *La Sirena*, which seemed to be Hans's intention. But I thought it best to go along with him for the time being . . . since he was the only one who could clear up the mystery about what happened to him last night. Meanwhile, Hans was busy glancing from side to side, preoccupied with something I did not understand.

As soon as we were out of Rashid's hearing, my companion turned to me, his hand again on my arm. "Please forgive me for treating you so harshly, Aline, but I was worried about that Arab— and relieved to find you. I don't trust anyone anymore; and I feel responsible for your safety." He paused to draw in a breath. "I'm certain there are several people who would like to have you disappear." He drew another, longer breath. "You cannot go back to that boat, Aline. Look, while you were signing those papers, I made plans. You'll take a plane to Málaga, all right? And whatever you do, you must not return to *La Sirena*. Even the slightest possibility that the men who threw me overboard could suspect you were a witness would put you in danger. And if anything happens to you, I would be to blame. You can make a call to the boat from the airport, saying you are remaining here for dinner with friends, and that you will send your chauffeur tomorrow to the yacht for the screen and your luggage."

During the hour's wait in the terminal, we had time to talk.

"What happened to you, Hans?" I asked him. "I saw two men throw someone overboard. Naturally, I knew it had to be you; and I was devastated that I didn't flash that light in time to warn you."

Hans laughed. It was rare to see him so pleased.

"They wanted to kill me all right, and they nearly did," he said gleefully, as if telling a great joke.

"That much I know," I said, trying to match his high spirits, though in truth I felt confused.

"There were two men struggling with me. You were right about that. And they did toss me overboard," he continued in his laughing voice—which I now realized carried a hysterical note. "But more important than any of that, now I know who killed my daughter." He raised a hand up to stop the question that leapt to my lips. "However, I'm not going to put your life in danger by telling you who he is. Not until I've finished with him." Hans's voice was now very low, and hoarse with emotion. "Paco set me up, of course," Hans continued, switching back to last night's events. "And he's up to his eyeballs with a crowd of very nasty people. Yet even he does not know who put the bomb in his boat. The ass is still in the dark about that." Hans's expression darkened.

"But how did you survive?" It was a strange sensation, sitting there speaking to a man who I thought was surely dead. And now he was so obviously alive that it seemed we were speaking of an incident from the distant past.

"Well, luck is the most of it; but that's not the only reason."

"So then what happened when you went overboard?" I asked.

"That is when my luck began. I flipped over and over. It's a long drop from the bow. By sheer fortune my legs entered the water first, and that cushioned the impact. I didn't sprain anything. No contusions. A miracle in itself. Next I was afraid I was going to be drawn into the ship's propellers. But the boat was barely moving—perhaps it was ahead of schedule and they didn't want to dock until morning. It was moving enough, however, to pull away from me."

"But I alerted the captain to look for you."

"Yes, I guessed that when I saw the lights. But it was dark, and by that time I was too far away. Anyway, I told you I didn't trust the crew; and from where I was, it looked as though the floods and spots were all shining in the wrong direction. However, I know a lot about swimming. I took off my shoes and trousers, which had become like lead in the water, and floated, treading water, doing what I could to conserve my energy. After I was more sure of myself, I looked around, and I was surprised to see the lights of the shoreline. I was closer than I expected. Though it was too far to swim, that knowledge gave me tremendous hope." Hans paused for a moment and shook his head. "I'm not a religious man, but the Lord was certainly on my side. I just tried not to panic. At least the water was warm.

"Daybreak encouraged me, and the shoreline was closer then. The tide was pushing me toward land. And when the sun began to rise, I spotted a small fishing boat at some distance, say half a kilometer. I figured it was my best chance, so I started swimming toward it. Fortunately they spotted me almost immediately, and rowed over, hoisting me aboard. Naturally, they were amazed—as amazed as I was to be living.

"The fishermen were very accommodating; they gave me warm wool blankets and drams of a Moroccan liquor. They would not bring me to shore, though, until they had completed their day's catch. Which was actually for the best. I was warm and dry enough, and it gave me time to devise a plan. We didn't dock in Tangiers until eleven in the morning. And it took me until noon to reach Nancy Rhodentus by telephone."

"Nancy?"

"Yes, I called Nancy. But I got Sofia Cabanellas. So I asked her if she would be kind enough to find my briefcase and bring me some clothes. I badly needed clothes; and I knew it would be hard to find anything my size in Tangiers. But the poor girl must have misunderstood me. With my accent, her bad English, and my bad Spanish, she ended up bringing all the papers and documents I had in my cabin, but no clothes at all."

"So that explains one mystery," I said greatly relieved. "I saw her going through your papers in your stateroom."

"Yes." He smiled. "I asked her to bring my things to the Hotel Minzah, and to tell Nancy to go there, too. In fact, I've just come from there."

"Did Nancy know you had been thrown overboard?" I asked.

"Not until about an hour ago. She told me about the excitement last night; but the captain thought that must have been a false alarm: The crew was intact and no guest was reported missing. But when I explained what really happened, she was horrified, as you can imagine. Nancy is a wonderful girl, and a really good friend."

"But did you tell her that I helped you last night?"

"No. I prefer not to mention your name. But I did warn her that she has a killer on board. And I asked her to keep that knowledge secret, since by doing that she can help me." Hans looked worried, and paused. "I didn't tell her the killer's name—for the same reason that I can't tell you. But like you, she deserves to be alerted to the danger, even though I know this particular person won't harm her." Hans stopped speaking again. Obviously he was weighing something in his mind.

"Hans?"

"Yes, sorry," he said, shaking his head; then he looked at me frankly with those intense eyes of his. "Aline, did you see Paco this morning?" he asked. "I assume you did."

"Yes, he looked awful, worse than before."

"Well, it's not because the little worm has a conscience, I can assure you of that. More than anything, it's his stupidity that killed my daughter. What did he say to you?"

"He implied that he—and others—suspect I was a witness to the attack last night. He gave me a warning, told me to leave the boat, not to trust anyone, not to talk to anyone alone . . ." As I said this, the words caught in my throat. What was I saying? I felt suddenly that it was impossible to know whom to trust. Maybe Paco knew that Hans had survived and that he was precisely the person I should be avoiding.

Apparently my thoughts telegraphed across my face; for Hans burst out laughing. "Aline," he said almost tenderly, "you have been kind enough to help me more than once. I don't think I will repay that kindness by killing you." He laughed again; but I was unable to join in. I felt I was swimming in a situation that was becoming murkier by the second; and I didn't have the slightest idea who might be a genuine ally. Not even Hans.

"Hans," I said, hoping to begin to clear up my growing apprehension, "what can Nancy do for you if someone wants to kill you? And what are you going to do about Paco? Does he know who else was on the deck with us last night?"

"Paco is nothing more than a puppet, Aline. He is irrelevant. As for Nancy, she is an old friend, and a most courageous woman. She also knows several important people who can help me."

"You mean her connections through R.K.?"

"Something like that," said Hans. "Let me put it this way. I will need proof against the man who murdered Inge—proof that will stand up in court. Now that she's aware of the problem, she has promised to do her best to help me."

"Hans," I said, "I want to help you, too. Please trust me enough to tell me who this man is."

"Sorry, no. I can't do that. I can't risk you the way I've had to risk myself. No. To tell you would neither help you nor help me."

I felt he was being purposely obtuse, and it annoyed me.

"Why are you returning to *La Sirena*, then?" I asked, continuing to press him. "Can you be certain that nothing will happen to you on the trip back?"

He met my question with silence. Not a cold silence, just a deliberate choice not to answer. Finally he said, trying to be lighthearted, "Look, Aline, Nancy is our hostess. It would ruin her reputation if someone was killed at her engagement party. She was terribly upset when I told her about my adventures last night. Don't forget she's had her share of scandal. If she intends to marry Jack Wilmington in the near future, she has to keep her guests happy and healthy, don't you think?" He smiled a disarming smile. "She is determined to do whatever she can to protect me, at least on her boat. And after we return to Málaga, she's ordering a complete investigation of her entire crew—to protect herself, and her guests."

This was as much as Hans was going to reveal.

Hans did not leave me until he saw that I had boarded the Iberia flight to Málaga.

Chapter 30

The next morning my spirits were still very low, but I knew I had to conceal that fact from Luis.

I found him at his desk, reading reports from the administrator of our ranch, who he'd seen in Málaga the previous day. The first thing I did was set up the antique screen which Julio had already picked up. Then I settled in a comfortable armchair next to him and gave him a brief account of what happened on *La Sirena*, omitting, however, the major events. And, of course, I didn't dare tell him that my own life might be in danger as a consequence of what happened.

As I expected, Luis was delighted with the antique screen. After admiring it for a time, with his usual grateful enthusiasm, he went back to reading his reports; and I did my best to relax and collect my thoughts.

A few minutes later, he said, "Good news, darling." He waved the sheet of yellow paper he'd been reading. "They're finally going to start repairs on that blessed roof at Pascualete." In the early spring, a windstorm had torn away half the roof tiles; and then the resulting leaks had ruined two valuable paintings, not to speak of damage to rugs and furniture. "I'd love to go there," he said, "to make sure they do it properly. But Blanca is arriving from Madrid tomorrow; and of course I must be here." Blanca was Luis's stepmother.

"Let me go instead," I cried. "I hate to miss Blanca; but one of us should supervise the repairs!" Pascualete! Of course! Why hadn't I thought of it? This would be a way to spend time with Serge and get his advice. And it would also be a perfect way to "make myself scarce," as they used to say in old crime movies. If Inge's killer suspected I might know too much—as both Hans and Paco feared—then it would be wise for me to put myself out of the way for a time.

"What?" said Luis, startled by my sudden enthusiasm.

"I'll go to Pascualete and make sure they're doing the job right."

"Darling, it's hot as blazes there now. I wouldn't dream of it."

"I insist, I'll leave after breakfast tomorrow, have lunch in Sevilla or Jerez with Beltrán and Ann Domecq. It'll be fun for me. Also Julio can help with the driving, if that makes you feel better."

"Are you sure you want to go?" Luis still seemed doubtful; but I knew it would relieve him if I was in Pascualete to oversee the job.

"Absolutely. Don't give it another thought," I said.

Luis stood up and put his arms around me, gently kissing the top of my head. "I'll miss you," he added.

He went back to his report, and I went upstairs to put through a call to the village nearest our ranch, asking them to send a message to the *guardesa* that I would be arriving the following evening.

SINCE IT TURNED out that Jupiter was expected to return to the coast at any moment, I left a note for him at his apartment in the port, written in our private code, letting him know why I was going to Pascualete, and explaining that I would contact him in two days, when I returned to Marbella.

The trip to the ranch was beautiful.

The last rays of the sun were just hitting the tips of the crenellated walls of the majestic medieval city of Trujillo as I approached. This was a view that thrilled me every time I saw it. Often I tried to imagine what joy must have filled the hearts of the conquistadors when, on their return from the New World, these same stone turrets and towers came into their line of vision. Francisco Pizarro, Hernán Cortés, and Francisco de Orellana had been born nearby and had often viewed what I was now seeing. High on the hill was the Roman castle and the thick wall they had built in the first century. Embracing that was the Arab wall, built in the eighth century. The narrow winding cobblestone street had been there for centuries, as had the great plaza, where storks' nests crowned every palace tower and church steeple. Little had changed in Trujillo since the sixteenth century, and it always appeared to me a small miracle that I could enjoy today a scene typical of the world of hundreds of years ago.

Ten kilometers further on, as I entered our property, the feeling of peace and contentment continued to accompany me. My eyes took instant delight in our racehorses grazing in the golden fields, in the rolling hills of live oak trees, and in the open expanses of stubble fields. Then I drove the car under the thirteenth-century arch with the carved but weathered stone family crest and pulled to a stop in front of the entrance. Twenty-five generations of our family had given us a special attachment to this land, to the stone, and to our almost two-thousand-year-old home. Although the place had *only* been in our family since 1231, the first floor of the building was constructed by Romans in the first century, and was still livable.

Faustino and Manoli, our *guarda* and *guardesa*, were waiting in front of the large double doors; for they had heard the car pull up. By now it was almost dark. The air was hot and dry outside, but inside the thick stone walls, the house was cool. By the time I entered the old *palacio*, my peace of mind was almost complete.

And yet, I couldn't wait to see Serge. The thought that he would give me professional advice was comforting—and exciting. Unfortunately, that wasn't going to happen just yet, since "the Señor guest was riding and had not yet returned," Manoli informed me. So I went directly to my room and she drew a bath for me in the deep old-fashioned tub. Afterward, without meaning to, I fell asleep. And it was dark when Manoli awakened me to say that dinner would soon be ready.

Summer evenings at Pascualete are delightful. As soon as the sun goes down, the earth cools off, the stars come out, and the fragrance of jasmine fills the air. So, tingling with anticipated pleasure, I went looking for Serge. But when I ran down the back stairs to the garden, where I thought he would be waiting for me, he was not there. Returning upstairs to the big salon, where flickering candles made shadows on the ancient tapestries, and where an old-fashioned fan in the high ceiling whirred and cooled the air, I called Serge's name. A moment later I heard steps; and glancing up, I saw him peering over the railing of the balcony at the far end of the room. "Aline, you're here!" he called out. "I'm coming right down."

As he hastened down the steps, I was astonished to see the change in him. His head was now completely shaved, and he had put on perhaps five or ten pounds. Life at Pascualete clearly agreed with him. Even more significant to me, his eyes sparkled with a characteristic mischief that shone through any superficial disguise. How revealing eyes can be, I thought, as I recalled Carlos's penetrating dark eyes and Hans's icy blue slits.

"Oh, Serge, I was really anxious to see you," I said as I greeted him. "I fell asleep after I arrived. I hope you haven't been waiting a long time."

"Not at all," he said. "After my ride, I was glancing through some of the old manuscripts in your library. Many of those documents are from the fourteenth century. I wish I knew more Spanish."

"Luis has family manuscripts in the archive in Madrid that date back to the ninth," I answered. "You're welcome to take a look at those the next time you are in the city. The scribes of all the great families maintained a detailed account of money spent, illnesses, purchases. I've spent many hours with them; they're fascinating. What stories they tell, behind the bare facts."

As we sat down, I couldn't keep my eyes from his shaved head.

"My god, Serge, is that a new disguise?"

Serge rubbed his hand over his head. "Well, I had to get rid of that dyed hair and change as much as I could."

We both smiled, but our smiles were more than a little forced. Neither of us had a mind for light talk. Serge was anxious to know if I had seen Ali or Carlos again. And I was anxious to tell him all my news. I filled him in on everything that had happened since we last spoke. "You know, Serge, all this has me frightened," I confessed as I finished briefing him.

"You should be." Serge's expression had become deadly serious. "There is a network of some of the world's most dangerous people involved in a variety of illegal transactions around Marbella. You've begun to see some of the links in that network. But in doing so, they may have become aware of you, which means that they may now see you as an obstacle which they must remove.

"My best advice to you would be to stay out of the way for a few weeks. Stay here at the ranch, or spend some time in the States. You've done what you need to do for Jupiter."

"Well," I answered, "none of that is exactly practical."

Serge smiled. "In other words, Aline, you're frightened," he went on, "but 'damn the torpedoes and full speed ahead' as your Admiral Dewey, or someone like him, is supposed to have said."

I had to laugh at that. He smiled with me, and then he went on, "Now about my own personal obsession, Ali Amine. Ali's not hanging around Marbella just for the fun of it. But I'm not completely certain what that good, sweet man is up to." He stopped for a moment and rubbed his hand thoughtfully over his Yul Brynner skull. "I wouldn't doubt he's still living at Chez Jacques, but it will be difficult to recognize him. He changes his appearance almost daily. That's his big defense." He stopped again. "You know? I suspect Hans Schmidt has dealings with Ali or some of the others. If he is not one of the COCOM violators, I would be very surprised. Otherwise why would he fool around with assassins?"

"But if he's involved with them, why would they try to kill him?" I asked.

"That's hard to answer. Ali wouldn't be in one place for this long unless he was planning something big. And that means he needs large amounts of explosives. Hans may be one of the suppliers. Perhaps he demanded too much money? Or didn't deliver as promised?" Serge shrugged. "It's a guess."

"Do you really think Hans Schmidt could be selling weapons to terrorists? That seems terribly unlikely to me."

"Why not? His companies produce the things that terrorists most want," Serge replied.

"Why doesn't Ali get his explosives from Carlos?" I asked.

"He does. But obviously he needs more than Carlos can provide. Ali's project is LARGE." Serge spread his arms globally. "He's been doing the 'normal' terrorist thing for the PFLP for years. Now that he has his own more radical group, he probably wants to make a bigger splash."

"It sounds to me as if Ali is more important than Carlos in the terrorist hierarchy," I said.

"No, he's not. Carlos is the big star in that world. But Ali is completely without human feeling. Compassion? Forget it. And he's capable of anything." He gave a little laugh as he said that. "Did I tell you about the time I ran into Ali in Rome, earlier this year?" he continued. "He might have killed me that time; but he was in one of his crazy disguises; so I'm alive today. He couldn't run because he was dressed like a woman, wearing a long skirt and high-heels. If it hadn't been for those high-heels, I would have had his knife in my back."

"Oh?" I said, for his words had opened a fascinating possibility. "Tell me, Serge, what is Ali's hair color when he disguises himself as a woman?"

"Depends on which wig he has available, I guess. He must have a large wardrobe, dresses, skirts, and blouses, with shoes to match. But he dresses like a woman often. That's why it's so hard for people who don't know him well to recognize him. I've often wondered if he's a homosexual."

"Have you ever seen him with a red wig?"

"Yes, in fact, the one he was wearing in Rome was red."

"Well, I'm sure Ali was at Chez Jacques when we went there last week. And now I understand the electric razor!"

"What's that?" Serge looked at me with a puzzled expression.

I told him about the woman in the ladies' room. "Of course, if a man's stubble begins to show," I said, "he'd need a razor to smooth if off. Ali probably has to do that frequently when he wears a female disguise. He's like a transvestite—like Gadhafi."

"Gadhafi doesn't dress like a woman," Serge said.

"Well, I heard he wears heels and makeup!" I laughed.

"Even if he does, he doesn't dress like a woman," Serge smiled. Then he explained that he'd met Gadhafi often when he used to go to Libya for the KGB. "He's pretentious and affected," he said, remembering. "A visit with that pompous fool is something you don't forget. But, no, he's no transvestite.

"Usually," he continued reminiscing, "I was picked up by a helicopter and taken to a military compound guarded by tanks and jeeps mounted with machine guns. Pictures of Gadhafi in his fanciest uniform are everywhere. He always made me wait, even though we were in the same room, anything to demonstrate his superiority. The dark-green uniform and all that gold braid, plus the high-heeled shoes and the sunglasses, made him look like a comedian in a movie about a banana republic. And while he talked, he'd often take a Napoleonic stance, or throw his hands in the air to show off the gold rings and emeralds on his fingers. It's amazing how overwhelmed he is with his own importance. Though his officers wear elaborate green uniforms, too, his own is more fancy than anything dreamed up by Hollywood—gold cording, gold epaulettes, stars everywhere.

"During one of his temper tantrums, I saw the makeup and black mascara running down his cheeks in rivulets." Serge stopped, then shook his head. "He's the worst kind of despot—erratic, emotionally unstable, grossly insecure. And unfortunately, he's building up more training camps for terrorists all the time. In fact, your friend Carlos has been one of his favorite consultants."

Just then, Faustino appeared silently on the stairs, spiffed up and proud in a starched white uniform, and announced that dinner was ready.

Faustino had set our places on either side of the long, narrow table; and he had decorated the center with long branches of jasmine and bougainvillea from the garden. High candles cast a soft glow on the blue and yellow Talavera plates. Dozens of candles in wall sconces sent flickering shadows over the ancient *reposteros*—tapestries—emblazoned with the family crest. These had been stolen during the Civil War; but by a miracle Luis found them years later in the *rastro*—flea market.

The first course was gazpacho served with *tropezónes*—stumbling blocks, as Spaniards call the tiny pieces of chopped cucumbers, onions, and green pepper that garnish that classic soup. Every cook in Spain has his or her personal gazpacho recipe. Manoli had several. Sometimes she made gazpacho with almonds instead of tomatoes, sometimes with beets. But tonight it was a classic tomato gazpacho, cool and spiced to perfection.

Serge's remarks about Chez Jacques led me to the subject of my old (and now desperate) friend Salima Karam. "You know her well from your days in Morocco, Serge," I said. "Salima. Remember Salima Karam? The sister of Fatima Aziz?"

"Of course. I remember beautiful Salima Karam. You say she's married?"

"Her husband is a monster; and I think he makes her miserable. He has her surrounded by bodyguards. In fact, I'm sure Salima's husband is the man Ava Gardner and I saw with Carlos in Germany. Which means that he must be collaborating in some way with Carlos."

"What's his name?" asked Serge.

"Jamal Abad," I replied. "He's odious."

Serge put his spoon down. "I've known about Jamal for years. He's a drug dealer. One of the big ones. And you're right about his nastiness. Even the people who work with him don't like him. And he has the nasty habit of turning his girlfriends into junkies, a detestable man."

I thought about that for a time. That Jamal was a drug dealer didn't surprise me. But had he made Salima a junkie? Very possibly. Those vacant stares, her strange moods, the stumbling walk?

"I'm afraid he's done just that to poor Salima," I said.

"Well, if she's married to that guy, it's more than possible. It's his way of keeping control. I'm sorry for Salima. She's had nothing but bad luck with men."

"I have to find a way to help her."

"Aline, Jamal knows both Carlos and Ali. They're doubtless working with him right now. To get mixed up with Salima would be to endanger yourself even more. It's not even a risk. If they suspect you of meddling in their business, it would be suicide."

"But maybe Salima could help us, she could give us information!"

"Salima's in no position to help anyone. Leave her alone."

Serge was absolutely closed on the subject. Even so, I was determined to bring the matter up with Jupiter as soon as possible.

As Faustino served the *pichónes*—baby wild palomas in a sauce of tiny onions and mushrooms—another detail was puzzling me—the villa La Amapola. After I briefly told Serge what I had learned about that strange place, I said, "Why are these drug dealers and international terrorists interested in Marbella?"

"That coast is strategically located between Europe, Africa, and the Middle East, convenient for drugs, convenient for weapons, and for all sorts of other illegal traffic. Terrorists and drug dealers can often help each other. They use the same routes and shipping facilities. And terrorists who are moving arms often make extra money to finance their operations by working with drug dealers. It's not uncommon that they will trade favors. For instance a drug dealer may need protection. Terrorists will provide it—for a fee. In this way terrorists can fund their training camps, and build their arsenals, and so forth. Carlos is very likely doing something very much like this right now. Terrorists are sometimes surprisingly sophisticated businessmen.

"And speaking of businessmen, I wonder who is providing financing for Ali and Carlos? Someone is backing their current operations. I wonder who?"

We were now consuming Manoli's watercress salad and homemade goat cheese. After that, we ate raspberries in silence. We both were thinking about our unsolved mysteries.

A FEW MINUTES later, we were sitting in the garden, sipping coffee. Serge had just poured himself a Carlos Tercero brandy.

"What about Jamal?" I blurted out suddenly.

"Excuse me?"

"Jamal Abad," I said. "I bet he's the man behind Carlos and Ali."

"Aline," Serge answered, "you give him too much credit. He's no more than a drug dealer. As I tried to tell you, nobody trusts him. He's unstable. He's amoral. He likes sex with young boys and girls. He's a voyeur. He takes pictures. I shudder to think what he's done to Salima."

"All the more reason to try to help her," I answered. But before he could reply to that, I went on, "And who do you think owns Chez Jacques?"

"Possibly Jamal," he replied. "He always liked good food and wines. On the other hand, the restaurant may be totally legitimate. Even though the spot seems to be a rendezvous for all that's bad around Marbella, that doesn't mean that crooks and criminals don't enjoy an excellent restaurant."

Just then, Faustino handed me a note scribbled in the childish scrawl of the telephone operator in Santa Marta. "Señora Condesa, Juan has just come in his motorcycle to deliver this telephone message," Faustino said. "Eusebia says it is important, and it's from the Señor Conde."

I took the note, then asked Serge to excuse me as I read it. And then for a long moment, my breathing stopped:

Terrible news but thought you'd like to know. Hans Schmidt has just been found dead. Come back soon. Love, Luis.

Chapter 31

All the way back to Marbella, I thought about the mysteries of this strange summer. Even though Hans Schmidt's life was in danger from the moment he started investigating his daughter's murder, Luis's message was still a shock. Poor Hans, I thought. Nancy was right when she told me his life was jinxed from the beginning. As I observed the breathtaking landscape gliding by on either side of the road, I wondered how such ghastly events could happen in an otherwise lovely world. Endless fields of yellow sunflowers, like happy smiling faces, gleamed in the morning sun. In the distance, cool green mountains were etched against a purple sky. On a nearby hill, small whitewashed cottages clustered around an ancient octagonal church. A man riding a donkey on the roadside waved at me. Everything bespoke beauty and harmony.

Nevertheless "Paco Cabanellas is the most despicable character I've known" kept running through my head. And also: "Was Hans shipping calutrons through Paco's company? Or was their relationship based exclusively on Paco's relationship with Hans's daughter?"

And damn it, I kept thinking, I liked Hans—even though I sometimes didn't understand him, even though he was sometimes exasperatingly strange.

And now that Hans was dead, I hoped he was the honorable man that I believed him to be, and that we would learn he was innocent.

I wondered how the assassins finally killed Hans. It was probably someone who had been on Nancy's ship with us. Maybe Ali. But possibly Carlos. And yet, I certainly didn't see either one of them on the cruise to Tangiers. However, they were both masters of the art of concealment and disguise, I remembered.

To change my train of thought, I turned on the radio; and I was lucky enough to find a station that was playing Beethoven's Fifth Symphony, which is my favorite piece of music. It is exciting, dramatic music, yet it calmed my spirits. And for the remainder of the drive, I concentrated on the beauties of the countryside.

Sevilla, as always, was a thrill. I followed the Guadalquivir River through the town, passing the "Torre de Oro" built in the fifteenth century to hold the gold arriving from the New World. Then about an hour further on, in the exquisite Moorish town of Arcos de la Frontera, I lunched with the Marquesa of Tamaron in her beautiful ninth-century castle, so high on the mountain that eagles soared below us. Finally I was on the road from Ronda to Marbella, winding through the steep mountains down to the sea.

When I drove into the back of our house, a large black Mercedes parked under the shade of our awning told me we had visitors. Andres appeared to take my bag. As I walked through the patio into the house, I noticed two strangers seated on the terrace, talking with my husband. How annoying! Now I would have to wait to ask Luis about Hans Schmidt. As I came closer, I saw that they were young and in business suits. They must have just arrived in Marbella, I concluded.

The young men stood up when I entered; they were both tall, and quite good-looking. And despite their business suits, they had the look of men who had spent considerable time out of doors.

"Darling," Luis said, "here are two charming fellows I know you will like to meet. Bob and Alex." We shook hands, and Luis continued, "Bob is the son of R. K. Rhodentus; and Alex is the son of Karl von Ridder. You must remember their fathers talking about them. They told us that the boys were diving for Spanish gold and sunken galleons in the Caribbean?"

"Of course I remember," I said. "And I'm delighted to meet you. What an exciting life you both must lead!"

"You see, Countess," began the taller of the two, Alex von Ridder, "before he died, my father said that you and your husband were the only Spanish friends he had. So we took the liberty of telephoning your husband to ask if he would be kind enough to receive us. We've only just arrived from Munich, so here we are imposing on you."

I assured them they were not imposing, then begged them to sit down again. Once they were comfortable, I sat next to Alex on the sofa.

Luis explained, "These young men have a problem, Aline. It seems that they have not been able to locate Bob's father since he divorced Nancy. Just before the divorce, R.K. put several of his holdings in his sons' names, among them the yacht. They want to get Nancy to leave the boat, so they can take ownership."

I must have looked puzzled, because Bob Rhodentus interrupted. He had the physique of a wrestler, and he was only slightly shorter than Alex. He also appeared to be a few years younger. "My brother, Rick," he said, "has not yet arrived. He and I do not want to put Nancy off the boat by force; and we hope to avoid lawyers and courts, if possible. But my father gave us the boat last Christmas, before he left Nancy; and we have been trying to take possession of it ever since, almost eight months. Now we need the boat badly for our work in the Caribbean this winter."

"Can you imagine?" Luis interrupted. "These fellows have made a great discovery. They believe they have finally found the wreck their fathers started searching for years ago."

The boys described their underwater discoveries, explaining that at this stage of their work they needed a larger boat and that *La Sirena* was perfect. They were thrilled to have finally begun to conclude a search that their fathers began twenty years before.

"But Nancy insists she must have the boat another three or four months," Bob said. "This goes on and on. We ask her to hand it over, and she tells us we have to wait. This has been going on ever since my father left her. So we thought it might be helpful to talk to you and your husband and get your advice on how to proceed. I certainly do not want to create a scandal. But we must have that boat."

"In Marbella," Luis added, "most people believe the yacht belongs to Nancy. It is taken for granted it was included in whatever settlement R.K. made with her."

"It may seem strange to you, Countess," Bob said, directing himself to me. "And it did to me also; but last Christmas, my father asked us to spend some time with him. That was unusual; we've hardly seen him over the years. Once we were with him, he turned over a certain number of assets to us which were formerly in Nancy's name. When he left her a few days later, she discovered this, of course. That must have been quite a blow to her." Bob looked embarrassed. "You should know—and probably you've guessed—that Rick and I never got along with Nancy. But you should also know that we have never been close to our father, either. In other words, the choice in giving us those things was entirely his. Neither of us put any pressure on him; we didn't try to persuade him. In fact, we said nothing to him. We didn't expect him to do what he did."

No one said anything for a moment. I was astounded, as I knew Luis was also. What a bit of news! Now I understood why Nancy wanted to marry Jack Wilmington.

My husband began to speak. "It might clarify things, and reinforce what Bob just said, if I told you what Bob told me earlier: Until last Christmas, R.K. had given his two sons nothing. Nancy had signature authorization for R.K.'s bank accounts, and some shares and assets had been put in her name. But when the properties Bob mentioned were transferred to the boys, they realized that the marriage had turned shaky."

No one said a word. But probably we were all wondering the same thing. Why did R.K. lose faith in Nancy? The instant that question floated up in my mind, of course, I thought of Nicky Maniatis. What a pity if she lost a fine and decent man like R.K. for the sake of that contemptible fellow, especially when R.K. had been so obviously in love with her. If that was the case, it must have been a hard blow for R.K. Now Nicky was evidently a thing of the past. . . .

Bob Rhodentus interrupted my thoughts. "My father's change of attitude toward Nancy was sudden, but Rick and I are not as surprised as others may be. My father's not like most people. We have seen little of him, but we know one thing about him. When he starts to lose faith in someone, the loss is not gradual or tentative, it's total and absolute. And practically instantaneous."

Luis then asked the boys if they had ever met Jack Wilmington.

"Oh, yes, I know Mr. Wilmington well," said Bob. "In fact I've been dating his daughter. . . ." He grinned sheepishly and I gathered he was quite seriously interested in the girl. "Jack was a close friend of my mother; we have known him forever."

"Well, Jack Wilmington is here in Marbella," Luis continued. "Perhaps, you don't know that Nancy and Mr. Wilmington are getting married in two days. We've been invited to the wedding, which will take place here in Marbella."

Bob frowned, and then looked confused. The news obviously surprised him. The two boys glanced at each other, as if wondering what to say next. "Do you know where Mr. Wilmington is staying?" blurted Bob finally.

We told him we thought he was staying at the Marbella Beach Club. In any case, the club would know where to reach him.

Both young men jumped up at the same moment. "Well," said Alex, taking the initiative, "we've taken up enough of your time. We must be going. We cannot thank you enough."

We repeated our offer to help them in any way we could. But they were in such a hurry to leave that their original intention, to talk to us about taking over *La Sirena*, remained forgotten. There was no doubt in my mind that the news that Jack Wilmington was about to marry Nancy had changed their plans.

We didn't spend much time speculating on that, however, because as soon as they left Luis gave me the gruesome details about Hans Schmidt's death.

"His body was brought up in a fisherman's net yesterday. The skull was fractured. The coroner's report has not been released; but the paper today claims he probably committed suicide; and that's what most of our friends think."

"But I'm sure that's not true," I interrupted. "He was trying to find who put the bomb in Paco's boat. He thought that same person was on *La Sirena* the night we went to Tangiers. I wouldn't be surprised if he was right, and that person killed Hans because he knew too much."

"You'd better not say that to anyone," Luis warned me. "I don't want you muddying the waters and getting into danger yourself. This has been a miserable summer. I'm almost thinking of going back to Madrid. You've never been so nervous. All these killings, and all the mysteries that surround them, have obviously affected you. I also suspect that you are working with John Derby much more than you let on."

Despite Luis's warning, I telephoned Paco Cabanellas as soon as I was alone. Paco told me he was very upset about Hans. But he had nothing to add to Luis's story. Even if he did know more than he let on, I knew Paco would never tell that to me. He was too afraid of meeting the same fate as Hans.

The official reports on the death of Hans Schmidt affirmed a suicide verdict. But I never believed these for a second.

In order to reach their conclusion, the investigators had to ignore the blow to his skull. The generally accepted theory was that Hans, driven mad by grief, threw himself into the sea and drowned. But this theory did not explain the blow above his right eye that crushed half his forehead. . . . Driftwood, the police decided. Or else he hurled himself off a cliff and struck rocks on the way down.

Not likely.

When I learned that Hans's body was still at the morgue, I went down and tipped the guard so I could take a brief look. Luis would have been horrified if he had known. It was the first time I'd ever seen someone who had spent many hours in the water after dying, and it was far from a lovely sight—certainly not the best way to say goodbye to a friend. The right side of his forehead, as well as his right eye were totally crushed. Shards of his shattered skull protruded from the vacant socket. But it was clear to me that the gash in that bloated face was most certainly made before the body went into the sea. Besides, I knew well what kind of swimmer Hans was. If he wanted to end his life, I doubted if drowning would have been his method of choice. A former Olympic swimmer would have to work hard to drown himself.

Chapter 32

The next day, I invented an excuse to go to the port. It was my intention to get more news about Hans's death. But I told Luis I wanted to shop for a wedding gift for Nancy.

As it happened, when I drove into Marbella and continued on toward the port, I ran into Antonio, the owner of the shop where Pepito worked. He pulled up next to my car at a red light. We waved at each other, and he rolled down his window. "Ah, Señora Condesa," Antonio called out, "please come to my shop. Some special Brie has just arrived. The kind Señor Conde likes."

This would please Luis. So I followed Antonio's old delivery van into the side street and up to his shop. We chatted as we walked across the small plaza. Once inside the shop, he went directly to the cheese counter to find the wheel of Brie. I followed him. "Tell me Antonio," I said in my most casual manner, "have you been delivering any special orders lately to La Amapola?"

"Strange you mention that, Señora Condesa. I just came from

there." He handed me my package of cheese and leaned against the counter. "Most amazing thing I've ever seen. Two women were in the kitchen when I entered. They were fighting . . . hitting each other. And then one grabbed the other's hair, and it came off in her hand. And underneath she had a man's haircut!"

"What do you mean?"

"The woman was a man!" Antonio scratched his head. "The hair was a wig. I realized that when I saw it in the other woman's hand. She threw it on the floor and stamped on it. Without the wig, the woman was obviously a man. Strangest thing. The guy wore lipstick and a dress. When they realized I was there, they both left the room. The things that happen nowadays in Marbella!"

Before he told me more details, I realized that the man in the wig had to be Ali Amine. I also knew that it was more than possible that the other person might be my friend Salima; and that worried me very much.

Antonio stood shaking his head. "I suppose he's what they call a transvestite, but I'd never seen one before." Then Antonio explained that since Pepito's death he'd been afraid to send anyone else to deliver orders to that house. He also felt that if he handled the deliveries himself, he might find out who had shot the boy. "But," he added, "no one talks to you there."

"Who owns the house, Antonio?" I asked.

He shook his head. "I have no idea, Señora Condesa. Maybe Señor Abad, but maybe not. The bills are paid by a secretary once a month, and always punctual. This past month many people have been staying there; and I get big orders all the time. Sometimes I've been making daily deliveries. The thugs who guard the entrance are all nasty, unfriendly. But I have a feeling they treat me better than they treated Pepito. He was such a kid. They must have had him delivering dope for them. They wouldn't dare ask me to do such a thing. They know I won't put up with that.

"You know, Señora Condesa, I don't like the people there at all. But I can't afford to lose such good clients. Nobody buys as many expensive things."

"Have you ever seen Señor Cabanellas there?" I asked.

"Oh, el Señor Cabanellas is not one of them. El Señor Cabanellas is a nice man, and I don't think he's a friend of theirs. No," he shook his head, "not Señor Cabanellas." Then he returned to a subject he had touched on a moment earlier. "Lately there's much going on at that house," he said thoughtfully. "But come to think of it, there is a man there I can talk to. A South American, I would think, a well-mannered fellow with a beard, and he always has something pleasant to say. Saw him yesterday, in fact. Trouble is I've only seen him twice. Thought that maybe on one of my deliveries I could strike up a conversation with him and ask about Pepito.''

"How do you know he's South American?"

"By his soft, slurry accent, Señora Condesa. Those South Americans sound more like us *Andaluces*''—Andalusians, southerners—''than you *Madrileños*.''

Carlos! I thought. And Antonio saw him yesterday! So Salima probably knows Carlos as well! What greater confirmation did I need that Jamal and Carlos were the two men Ava and I had observed in Germany?

Just then, the telephone rang; and Antonio excused himself to answer it. "Oh, I'm sorry to hear that, Señora Rhodentus," I heard him say. Though I was about to leave, I was curious to learn how this exchange would turn out. As I watched Antonio, his face fell. "But the order is already being prepared, Señora," he said sadly. "I don't know what I can do."

"Excuse me for eavesdropping, Antonio," I said, when he hung up and walked toward me, "but that sounded like bad news."

"Mrs. Rhodentus has canceled the wedding," he announced.

I'm sure my face must have dropped more than Antonio's just did, though I doubt that he realized what a jolt his news was for me. So Bob Rhodentus and Alex von Ridder must have said something to Jack Wilmington, I concluded. I wonder what.

Meanwhile, I tried to cheer Antonio, who was downcast about the money he was going to lose. However, my own worries had increased considerably, and I was anxious to leave. Ali and Carlos were still on the coast.

And what was going on between Nancy Rhodentus, Jack Wilmington, and the two boys Luis and I met yesterday evening?

Chapter 33

The setting sun was illuminating the whitewashed walls of my house with an iridescent pink glow when I returned after an afternoon at the Marbella bullring a few days later. I was still obsessed by Hans's and Pepito's deaths and the mystery of La Ampola.

Though I had expected a call from Nancy to apologize for the wedding cancellation, I had not heard from her, nor from Bob Rhodentus or Alex von Ridder.

However these thoughts were now taking second place; for guests would be arriving for cocktails in a half hour; and I was not going to be ready! I hastened through the patio, across the front room, out onto the luminous, rosy glowing terrace. Almost every sunset in Marbella had this magic; and it always filled me with wonderment.

Then my eyes were attracted to a beach chair in front of the pool, where two small feet in white, high-heeled sandals were all that was visible of a woman reclining there. She sat up and called my name. When I saw who it was, it seemed that indeed the moment was magical, because the woman in front of me was Fatima, Salima's sister.

Fatima had been a friend of mine for over twenty years; yet it had been some time since we had last seen each other. And now this afternoon, it seemed to me that she had dropped from heaven. She was the one person I could talk to comfortably and with confidence about Salima and Jamal. We kissed and hugged. Fatima looked as lovely as ever. She was not as tall as Salima; but she was slim and had a great figure, with broad shoulders and lovely legs. Her lips were full, and her perfect teeth gleamed startlingly white, in contrast to her olive skin. Where Salima was blond, Fatima was more typically Moroccan, with masses of shiny thick black hair, which she usually wore in a chignon. Everything about her was harmonious and elegant.

Fatima had made a name for herself as an outstanding jewel designer. For this reason, and for the overall success of her private and public life, I had always considered Fatima the more mature of the two sisters. And indeed, whenever Salima found herself in a bad situation—and there had been many of these—it was Fatima who invariably came to her rescue.

After Fatima and I embraced and blurted out our usual warm and joyful greetings, her next words to me were about her sister. She told me she had come to Marbella to see Salima. At which point, I almost laughed. "For at the precise moment I saw you," I told her, "I was wishing I could telephone Salima to invite her to the cocktail party I'm getting ready for. But I don't have her number."

"Oh, my poor sister," Fatima blurted out, her expression changing completely. I thought for a moment that she was going to cry.

"You must help me, Aline. She's in such a mess. Our poor dear Salima . . . always in trouble."

I waited for her to continue with that thought, but she was too moved by emotion. So I asked her to accompany me to my room while I dressed, and I told her we could talk there. She sat down on my chaise longue in the corner, staring despondently out at the sea. I went to my dressing table, from where I could see the last rays of the sun illuminating the crest of Montaña Blanca.

At first Fatima continued her silence, and I did not press her. While I refreshed my makeup, she continued to stare silently out the window. In the distance, the outline of her country was still visible in the dimness of the sunset. Then abruptly, in brief, impassioned sentences, she began to tell me that her father had sent her to find out what was happening with Salima. This was not surprising. Their father always held Salima in a deep place in his heart—especially when her life took one of its many downward turns. Salima was his "Prodigal" daughter. "I know he will only be happy when she returns . . . ," she said in a sad voice.

Fatima went on to explain that her father's health was now failing and that he was tortured by the fear he would never see his youngest daughter again. "Before the marriage, my father investigated Jamal and received a very bad report," Fatima explained. "Jamal Abad is an Iraqi and very wealthy; yet the source of his fortune is murky. Now my father has learned that Jamal's business is drugs and that he has all sorts of international criminals working for him.

"So my father sent me here on a 'mission.' " Her eyes met mine, and she took a long, slow breath. "I'm supposed to more or less kidnap Salima and bring her home."

"That won't be easy," I said. "She seems to be very much in love with her husband."

"Not at all, Aline," Fatima hastened to interrupt. "She merely pretends to love him. She hates Jamal. She's terrified of him. She's afraid he'll kill her. I saw her today, Aline. She was in the most desperate, helpless state. . . ." Fatima herself now looked so distressed that she seemed to have aged ten years in a minute. "She desperately wants to leave Jamal. But she is convinced that if I, or anyone else, tries to help her, Jamal will have me or them killed. She begged me to forget her, to leave as fast as possible, so nothing would happen to me."

"To tell you the truth, Fatima," I said, turning around from the mirror and putting the comb down, "I've been very worried about your sister. Jamal is repulsive; and Salima is no longer the woman I knew and loved. And since you should know everything that I do, I am also aware that Jamal is a drug dealer. In fact, I'm virtually certain that he is giving Salima drugs to keep her under control. Getting her away from him will almost certainly save her life. God only knows what she'll suffer if she stays with him.''

"Yes, I know. Especially after what I saw today." The voice I heard was hard to recognize as Fatima's. "I went to the house where she lives, a huge house behind high walls, with TV cameras all over the place, and guards carrying machine guns. I'm still shaking from the experience.''

Trying to compose herself, she went on, "As you know, my father has important contacts in the Arab world. So we knew the location of Jamal's house on this coast; but we could never discover a telephone number. I flew to Málaga, hired a car in the airport, and went there unannounced. Though the house is quite lovely, Jamal has made it a prison. I was greeted by a surly guard, who waved a weapon at my driver and in filthy Arabic ordered him to leave and to take me with him, which the driver was all too willing to do. But I refused. I told the brute who I was and I insisted on seeing my sister. He gave me an arrogant stare and sauntered back to the guardhouse, where he made a phone call. When he finished, he slammed down the receiver, came back, and demanded my passport! After examining it, he returned it to me and walked back to the guardhouse. The heavy iron gates opened and he gestured us through. I have never seen such security! At the house, a properly dressed butler greeted me politely enough. Then I paid my driver, and the terrified man left as quickly as he could. The butler led me into a sparsely furnished salon and said that he would tell Madame Abad I was there.''

Fatima was becoming more upset as she talked. And for a moment she had to stop. Then she asked me if she could have a cup of tea.

"Of course," I said, and called Andrés to order that. Then she resumed.

"Aline, you would not believe how terrible Salima looked as she walked into the room. Her frightful husband, all contrived and mocking smiles, was supporting her. When I first met him, a year ago, I did not like him. And I begged my sister not to marry him. But you know how stubborn she can be, especially with me.'' Fatima grimaced sadly, and continued: "Salima was well dressed, her hair was carefully coiffed, her makeup was perfect; but under that mask was the wreck of a beautiful face. You remember how lovely she was. Now her eyes look glazed under the heavy makeup. Her skin is sallow and puffy. She seems out of contact with the world, as if drugged." She looked at me fiercely. "She has been drugged, hasn't she?"

"Yes," I answered. "I think so."

We were interrupted as Andrés brought in the tea. I poured it, and Fatima, after taking a sip, went on, "Her grinning, despicable husband told me how delighted they both were to see me! What a slimy monster!"

Fatima replaced the cup on the tray and continued. "Of course I asked to talk to my sister alone. But he looked at me as if he was deeply surprised and offended. Then he said something about my not considering him part of the family, that he should share the confidences of his wife and sister-in-law. I wanted to vomit. He went on to tell me about how much he loved Salima; and then right in front of me gave her a sensuous kiss. Then he had the nerve to say, 'Oh Fatima, we are so in love, aren't we, darling?' And all my sister did was nod dumbly."

Fatima shuddered. "Since I still wanted to talk privately with Salima, I suggested that we go outside. But that reptile said, 'Why of course. Come see our beautiful garden.' He took Salima firmly by the arm and led her. She was so unsteady she almost fell down the steps. As we walked down a path toward the ocean, he kept taunting me—asking about my father and the rest of the family. How he hates them. When we reached an umbrella and some chairs in the garden with a view looking out to sea, Salima stumbled. But Jamal eased her into a chair, saying: 'Oh Fatima, my poor darling has not been feeling well lately. Let's sit here.' Then he settled down himself and said, 'Now, what shall we talk about?' "

Fatima picked up her teacup with a shaking hand, took another sip, and then continued. "Fortunately, a fat pig of a guard with an automatic weapon ran up to Jamal to tell him that the important message he was waiting for had arrived. Jamal rose, told the guard not to leave us, and hurried toward the house. The guard stood close enough to hear everything we said." Fatima shook her head. "We had been speaking Arabic. But when we changed to French the guard objected. Then I remembered something. When Salima and I were children visiting my uncle at his palace in the mountains of Morocco, he taught us an amusing game where you would juxtapose the ends of words. It was something like what Americans call 'Pig Latin.' I spoke a few words that way. They sounded like Arabic; and of course they were Arabic, but turned around. The guard said nothing; he just looked puzzled. And I figured that to cover his ignorance he would not say anything to Jamal.''

Fatima's voice became more excited as she continued: "For the first time there was a flicker of interest and hope in my sister's eyes. In our private language, I asked her to tell me quickly the truth about her situation, since Jamal could return at any moment. That's when she admitted that she'd come to hate him. These last weeks, he had kept her a prisoner in their bedroom. He had spells when he turned cruel and perverse. Jamal would tie her hands together and run a rope through a bolt in the ceiling. He would pull the rope until she was on the tips of her toes, then strip her and whip her naked body with a long, thin leather rod. She had to make a great effort to tell me all this, without letting the guard see her getting hysterical. I don't know how she managed . . . she's a strong girl, deep down.

"Jamal sometimes brought in drunken friends to watch those performances. And with the threat of more whipping, he would force her to perform unnatural sex with him, and sometimes with another man and woman, as well.''

Fatima put her hands to her face and broke into sobs. I went over to her, and kneeling, I put my arms around her. After a time, she continued her frightful story. "As I said earlier, Salima told me to leave, to forget about her, that it was hopeless to try to rescue her. The house was like a fortress, and Jamal would kill her.

"At which point, Jamal came loping back. Before he spoke to us, he and the guard exchanged a few words. Then he laughed uproariously. Still chuckling, he sat down and shook his head. 'The guard told me you were talking like little children,' he said, 'and that women are only good for one thing.' As he said that, his eyes slowly traveled over my body, hungrily. And I wanted to vomit again.''

Fatima took out a handkerchief and wiped her eyes while she tried to compose herself. "I rose then, and Jamal accompanied me to the front portico. A car was waiting there, with a chauffeur and a guard in the front seat. As I climbed into the backseat, Jamal held my hand. How gallant! Then he ran his hand up my arm and tried to fondle my breasts. 'Your sister is a marvelous bed companion,' he said. 'But you are older and surely more experienced.' I shoved him aside and slammed the door, shamed that the grinning chauffeur and guard had seen his disgusting advances. I left with the sound of that filthy man's laugh ringing in my ears." Fatima shook her head in fury, then continued. "After the driver dropped me off at the Hotel Los Monteros, I remembered that you lived nearby. So I pulled myself together and came here. I doubt that Jamal is having me followed. I don't want to drag you into this mess."

With compassion I looked at my old friend, but also with fear. I was, of course, greatly concerned about her sister; but even if Jamal did not have Fatima followed, he would surely learn that she had come to my house. Nevertheless, I wanted to give Fatima all the help in my power; and in a sense I owed her this favor. For Fatima had helped me in Morocco, six years earlier, when I was almost killed in a plot to assassinate their king.

Chapter 34

As I was drinking my morning coffee on the terrace the next day, Andres appeared with a note from Jupiter. He had finally returned to the coast and wanted me to lunch with him in the port. What great news! There was so much to tell him, and I was desperate to hear his report about the material we had gathered in Paco's office. We set a date to meet at Menchu's bar, which was the most popular spot in the port, and then have lunch at Pepe's.

At two o'clock, I was already dashing along the walk beside the marina. Today it had more schooners, sailboats, and skiffs than ever. And in the distance *La Sirena* presided majestically over the scene. The weather was perfect, dry and sunny, but not too hot, just a slight breeze. On the landside of the boardwalk were shops of all kinds. Under canvas awnings their wares were displayed—colorful skirts and blouses swayed in the light breeze. Other shops were selling pottery, local handwork, and frequently fishing and diving equipment. There were also many little restaurants and bars, with porches facing the sea, where people sat long hours observing the boats and the passersby. Rising behind this panorama, clustered and piled one on top of the other, were little houses and apartments, where red and orange geraniums tumbled out of window boxes, their colors dazzling against the white stucco. And above that the jagged peaks of the Montaña Blanca rose high into a deep azure sky.

As I hastened along, I saw in the distance out on the placid Mediterranean a large transatlantic ocean liner on its way to the straits of Gibraltar and the Atlantic Ocean.

Jupiter liked to lunch early, much earlier than our customary summer hours. But today I did not mind, since we had so much to talk about. When I arrived, he was talking to Menchu. Then, after exchanging embraces, we had a drink. The place was decorated with fishermen's nets and scuba-diving equipment. At this early hour, no one that I knew was about; there were only tourists. Once we were alone, John set the pace of our meeting in his usual calm fashion. When he was assured no one was observing, he reached into his pocket and withdrew a small brown packet. Opening it, he poured the contents into his hand.

"This is Turkish tobacco like the kind from the stub you pocketed in Paco's office. Notice how the leaves are fine and curly."

He watched me as I poked a fingertip into the stuff. "Still smells as strong as it did that night," I said.

"This is not from the stub you picked up, Aline." He looked at me and grinned. "I've been doing my homework also. The day after we checked out Paco's office, I picked up a few Turkish cigarette stubs myself before I left Marbella. You'd be surprised at the collection I have." He paused, "And some come from several of your friends, I might add."

"Who, for heaven's sakes?" My astonishment amused him.

"You'd be amazed. But for the time being, the important information for you is that the person smoking the cigarette in the office that night was not Paco."

"I knew that, but who was it?"

"Identifying this man was quite simple. Mainly because he has the unusual habit of signing his notes and documents with his fingerprint. He makes this arrogant gesture to be sure no one doubts who he is."

"Well?"

John Derby kept on speaking. "The note left in the safe that night stated that he was still owed a hundred thousand dollars, and it was signed, as you may remember, with two fingerprints. That custom is typical of Carlos the Jackal, a fact confirmed by our people in Washington. So as it happened, although pocketing the butt was a good idea, it wasn't necessary."

"I suspected it was Carlos all along," I interrupted.

Ignoring that, he went on, "With one notable exception, the butts I picked up turned out to be of little consequence, since it has turned out they contained other kinds of Turkish tobacco than the one you took. Carlos's cigarettes are quite unique. The tobacco is a blend made only in Damascus, and it is not easy to find on the open market. So if you notice it again, pay attention."

Jupiter's news hit me like a blow. My worst worries were confirmed. Carlos seemed to be always nearby!

Meanwhile, I had important news for Jupiter, but before I could tell it to him, he suggested we continue on to Pepe's restaurant. On the way we met people who stopped to chat, so we had no chance to continue our discussion.

Pepe came personally to direct us to a table under a green-and-white-striped awning facing the port, a spot which happened to give us an excellent view of *La Sirena*. Looking at the sleek lines of the gigantic yacht, it was easy to understand how Nancy would hate to part with it. I told Jupiter that she had canceled her wedding plans, and asked him if he knew Jack Wilmington. He did not know him personally, he answered, but like everyone else, he had heard of him. There was a nice breeze, and it was cool under the awning as I brought him up to date on the momentous happenings since he left.

John listened attentively and then suggested we order a shellfish paella; and although I complained that a paella took too long to prepare, he insisted that he enjoyed watching the boats come and go and that he had all the time in the world. The delay gave me the opportunity to go into more details about my visit to La Amapola with Pepito, and about his death, and Hans's adventures aboard *La Sirena*, and about his death. Jupiter complimented me for learning so much about La Amapola, and confirmed again that Jamal was a drug dealer. He also thought that since Jamal was an Iraqi, and since Iraq was one of the countries receiving calutrons, it was likely that Jamal was involved in that business as well. And he further believed that since Carlos had an association with Jamal, Ali Amine, and Paco, it was probable they all worked together.

"Thus Carlos could lead us to Paco's boss, if Paco can't be pushed to do so," John suggested. "Do you know, it has even occurred to me that the big wheel behind all this might be someone who hangs out here; maybe even someone we all know."

I then suggested that he ask our COS in Madrid for further information on Chez Jacques and on El Ancon and La Amapola. "Pepito was killed in El Ancon," I explained. "Almost at the entrance. He and I stopped very near the place where he died just after I was at La Amapola with him."

"Yes, I know."

"You do?"

"Yes, in a way that's why I'm here," said Jupiter. He moved his chair to focus his full attention on me. "Tiger, you've been very helpful on this case. But I'd like you to leave Marbella and let these matters drop."

"Let them drop?" I asked.

"You see that butt you grabbed in Paco's office has a long history for such a small thing. The lab picked up traces of the same tobacco in one other cigarette butt I found. It was in your house."

"In my house? When?"

"You had already left for Paris. I didn't know that; so I dropped in on my way to the port. And I saw there an ashtray filled with butts and recognized the Turkish one. When I asked Luis who it belonged to, he laughed. At least fifty people were there for cocktails that afternoon, he told me, and they all smoked. So whoever it was obviously knows you both.

"Though we can't find a fingerprint on it, I'm not willing for you to take further chances. It's too hot for you now. It's time to leave. These encounters of yours with Carlos—which until now I thought were imaginary—have turned out to be authentic. Ever since his fingerprint was identified on that note he left in the safe, I've been worrying about you. This is not open warfare—your country is not under direct attack; and it's not fair to you to risk yourself. So I want you to forget the job and return to Madrid as soon as possible. Tomorrow would not be soon enough."

Chapter 35

I had never known Jupiter to be an alarmist. If anything he was a master of understatement. He was never less than calm and cool. There had been plenty of moments, most recently during our trip to Paco's office, for instance, when I had felt panic rising fast, and Jupiter had remained as placid as a summer sky. So when he told me so directly and forcefully that it was time for me to leave Marbella, I took him seriously. And yet I hated to leave with so much unresolved. The idea of skulking back to Madrid to get out of harm's way did not sit well with me.

In other words, despite his kind warning, I was not going to comply with his order. And there were other problems as well. Although it was almost the end of the season, leaving suddenly created the problem of changing plans. My departure was unfair to my husband, and to my eldest son, who was coming with his two small children for the weekend.

Consequently, I thanked Jupiter for his concern, and explained that I could not leave for three or four days at least. Then, since I did not want to appear ungrateful, I asked if he would have dinner with us in La Fonda, a popular restaurant in Marbella. To cheer up Fatima, I had asked her to dine that night, and Jupiter would make a perfect fourth. Despite his irritation with me for failing to follow his advice, he agreed to join us for dinner, and he was delighted to see Fatima again. When I stood up to leave, he ordered another coffee, claiming he had nothing to do except stay for a while to enjoy the cool breeze and the bustle of the port. I knew Jupiter too well to accept this white lie. Nevertheless I smiled back and let him get away with it.

Before I left my old spymaster, there was one other matter that I had to discuss with him. I gave him a quick summary of Fatima's account of her visit to La Amapola, then explained that I owed it to Fatima to help her save her sister.

When I finished, Jupiter just shook his head. "Don't, Tiger," he said. "Don't even dream of getting Salima out of La Amapola yourself. If we had some factual information about criminal activities there, I could probably get the Spanish authorities to investigate; but so far these are just rumors. Jamal's drug dealings are carefully concealed. The police know he's an international dealer, but that's not enough. They must have proof. And the others who use Chez Jacques and La Amapola," he explained, "are even more professional than Jamal. They know how to make themselves invisible to the law.

"Remember, as far as the Spaniards are concerned, Jamal and his friends are just wealthy Arabs who come to Marbella to enjoy vacations and to spend money. The Spaniards cannot make trouble for visitors who are indispensable for the economy of the coast."

Later, I had a similar discussion with Luis. He was just as sorry for Salima and Fatima as John was, but he was even more adamant that I should keep out of the mess Salima had put herself in. He did not want me getting mixed up in it. "If she wants," he said, "Fatima can denounce Jamal to the police. But you and I both know that will do no good. A Moroccan complaining to the Spanish authorities about an Arab husband treating his wife badly is not a serious charge.''

THAT EVENING, TO save time, Luis drove to the hotel to call for Fatima, while I went to the port to pick up Jupiter. After he joined me, I had difficulty finding a parking place near La Fonda; and once I found one, we had to walk through several narrow twisting streets and alleyways to reach the restaurant. This we didn't mind, since wandering through the picturesque old village of Marbella was part of the pleasure of dining there.

When we entered La Fonda, Luis and Fatima were already at the bar. But to my surprise they were talking to Bob Rhodentus and Alex von Ridder.

As Jupiter and I reached the bar, the head waiter came to tell Bob Rhodentus that a table would not be available for his party for at least another hour. The sight of their disappointed faces encouraged Luis to invite them to join us; and we all went into the patio together.

Fatima smiled when she saw the orange trees, the fountain and the bouganvillea, her first smile on this visit to Spain. "What an enchanting setting," she exclaimed. Soon after that, she began an animated conversation with Alex von Ridder. Encouraged by her charm, he told her she was his mother's favorite jewelry designer. And some years ago, he went on, he and his father had purchased a stunning birthday gift for their mother in Fatima's shop in Paris. Alex remembered this especially, because they had bought it from her beautiful sister, Salima.

Fatima's next words to Alex surprised me. For she told him that she had come to Marbella precisely to rescue her sister from a terrible Bluebeard of a husband. In fact, talking about Salima seemed to give Fatima relief from her anxieties. At the same time, although she did not go into all the details she'd given me, what she did say was enough to make those around the table listen attentively.

Then she and I both described La Amapola and its heavy security. And I mentioned my German friend, who had tried to get a look at the property by approaching it along the beach. He had walked along the shore, which between the high and low tide marks was supposed to be open to the public. But he was waved off by guards pointing automatic weapons. As I related Hans's tale, Bob and Alex became intrigued, and asked us all sorts of questions. They were obviously born adventurers.

"I bet my friend Bob here would enjoy rescuing someone from a place like that," Alex said half jokingly. "He used to be a Navy SEAL, the most highly trained, skilled American small attack force there is."

Bob grinned at Alex, then returned the compliment. "My big-mouth friend here was in a similar elite German program, and he'd be just as keen to help out a beautiful lady who is trapped in a high tower. Not to speak of my brother, Rick, who's showing up here tomorrow. He's a human fish in the water and his hobby is karate. He's also a master of shuto choke-holds, which he learned in the Orient."

There was a moment of silence around the table. Bob broke the spell by gazing at us with a roguish smile. "Why not let us try it? We need a little action while we're waiting to learn what the lawyers decide about *La Sirena.*" Someone chuckled (it sounded like John Derby); and without further encouragement, Bob went on. "For this operation, three would be a perfect team. One of us could guard the beach and our escape route, while the other two rescued the beautiful damsel from the jaws of the monster. Has anyone here been in the house? We need some sort of a floor plan, or at least an idea where this beautiful girl is being kept."

"I've been there once, briefly," Fatima volunteered. "But I was so distressed at my sister's frightful condition that I can't recall much. Let me think. . . . Ah yes, after the guards let me through the main gate, I was escorted to the back door and into the kitchen, then through the dining room, the main salon, and out onto a porch, which leads down a few steps across a lawn which descends to the beach." Fatima took a deep breath. "We took the same route when I left. But after I passed through the dining room, I noticed a hall. My sister told me that it goes to the wing where her room is located. Her room, she said, lies at its end. If you turn right down the hall, it takes you to the kitchen. Salima turned left. There were doors on either side, but I could not see which one was hers, because her husband grabbed me by the arm and practically pulled me out of the house and into a car. I'm afraid that's all I can recall."

"That's very helpful," said Bob, taking a small pad and pen from his pocket and sketching a few lines. "But it's too bad you don't have some idea of distances and cover, like bushes and trees, especially from the beach to the house."

I glanced at Jupiter, who gave a tiny affirmative nod.

"There's a store in town that delivers gourmet delicacies to La

Amapola," I said, assuming my most guileless look. "And I know the owner, Antonio; he also delivers to us. After I learned that Salima is a prisoner in La Amapola, I became curious about the place, and I asked him to describe it in detail. It was my old OSS instincts working, I guess. It seemed like a good idea."

"You were in the OSS?" Bob Rhodentus asked.

"Long, long ago," I answered, with a smile. "During what we liked to think was a real war."

"You're a surprising woman, Countess," Bob said.

All eyes turned my way. "According to Antonio," I continued, "the distance from the water to the lawn is some thirty meters. Where the lawn meets the sand, there is a small gazebo, just a round roof, open on all sides. And then the grass stretches some sixty meters to the front terrace, which extends the width of the house. The wall on that side of the house is made up of glass doors, which in the daytime are usually open. The house itself sort of rambles, because of the extra long wing on the left side as you come from the sea. This wing was probably added years after the main house was built. There is a cover of bushes and trees on the right side of the house, as you approach from the sea. On the same side, and parallel to the house for some fifty meters, is a lattice with vines. This extends to the back door. But there is no cover for the ten meters from this lattice shelter to the back steps."

When I finished, everyone's attention was still glued on me. My husband was shaking his head, and he was giving me an unhappy look. He now realized that I had done more than just hide inside Pepito's van when I visited La Amapola.

After a moment, Bob spoke. "That's certainly a helpful description. But is it accurate?"

I nodded, adding lamely, "Antonio is totally reliable."

Jupiter lowered his head to hide his smile, then said, "Fatima is right. The master bedroom is at the end of the wing, as she described. There's also a small porch, with glass doors, opening off that bedroom."

Now it was my turn to be astounded. How did he know that? Jupiter returned my glance serenely; nobody else seemed curious about where he had secured this information.

There was another silence around the table. A few moments before, I had presumed that Bob and Alex were kidding about rescuing the beautiful maiden—as perhaps was the case. But now somehow the nature of our conversation had changed.

What Jupiter said next made me realize that he had not only accepted the idea of the rescue, but was considering taking part in it himself. "How do you visualize we could accomplish this rescue?" he asked Bob and Alex.

"I would have to study the details with Alex and my brother, after he arrives," Bob replied, "but it's obvious that we would enter the property most easily by sea. Fortunately, we happen to have a lot of scuba gear with us, since we intend to have a look at the hull of *La Sirena*." As he spoke, it occurred to me that I, too, wanted very much to take part in the rescue. It also occurred to me that I would have no problem with the boy's scuba gear, since scuba diving had been for a long time one of my favorite hobbies.

Meanwhile Bob Rhodentus was giving Jupiter a long, careful look. He sensed that he was more than just a tourist enjoying the Marbella sun. After a time, he addressed John directly. "Three Glocks might be useful," he said. "The Model Seventeen or Nineteen would be fine. We could use three Trisicon night sights, too, but I doubt you can pick these things up at the local hardware store," he added wryly.

Jupiter gave him a wry smile in return. "No, I don't think you could; but it could be arranged elsewhere." The rescue had already advanced from a wild dream to the planning stage.

For a moment everyone was silent, until I asked, "What's a Glock?"

Bob turned to me, and in a low voice said, "They're the darnedest things. If the best thing to come out of Switzerland is the cuckoo clock, the best thing from Austria is the Glock. It's a fiberglass pistol that fires when wet, even underwater, a great weapon." He added, "The Austrians were smart enough to add metal strips inside the plastic of the Glock so they would be detectable by airport security systems." He paused and continued, "As for the Trisicon sight, Countess, remember the radium dials on old watches so they could be read in the dark? The hands and numerals gave off a greenish glow. The Trisicon night sight does the same thing, using radium isotopes. These let you sight the Glock accurately when it's pitch black."

Alex tapped me on the arm, and chuckled. "By the way, Countess, you could help us out if you would lend us a can of your aerosol hairspray."

"Why, for goodness' sake?"

Jupiter leaned forward and answered me. "An unusual benefit of hairspray, my dear Aline, is that it allows you to detect infra-red beams . . . though it's useless, I'm sorry to say, against a Sastec video motion detector."

The two young men looked at John Derby with still more interest. By now I was completely confused by all the technical terms, and I said so. Jupiter laughed and explained, "Don't look so surprised. I'm on the board of directors of several companies, some of which are heavily involved in producing high-tech security equipment. There's one in Minnesota, for instance, called Sastec.

"Sastec is a sophisticated alarm system of buried cables and video cameras. The cable is placed in sand two to three feet deep in a snakelike pattern. Within ten feet on either side of the cable, the weight of an intruder activates an alarm. And the video camera immediately swings to that specific area for visual observation." Jupiter took a sip of his drink before continuing. "You can set the weight you want to activate the alarm—above ninety pounds, say, so that dogs or other small animals will not trigger the system." He paused, then added, "But I doubt if they could use the Sastec on the beach. Bathers strolling by would constantly activate the alarm."

Alex and Bob both nodded in agreement. "However," Alex suggested, "I assume they have infra-red surveillance at night which covers the beach area." Turning to me, he continued, "That's why we need the hairspray—to detect the beams from that system."

Bob leaned forward and said, "We would need a local commercial fishing boat and a reliable crew and skipper." Looking pointedly at Jupiter, he added, "We would need someone on board who speaks Spanish and who would also keep an eye on our fannies while the rescue is underway."

Staring directly into Bob's eyes, Jupiter gave a hint of a smile. "The fishing boat could be waiting for you at five tomorrow morning at the dock opposite the El Duque bar, here in the harbor," he said. "The boat is called *La Lola*, the captain's name is Don Alberto," he continued evenly, almost blandly. "I have some friends in CESID, this country's intelligence service, who owe me a few favors. I can borrow the other equipment you need from them." Almost as an afterthought, he added, "Your timing could not be more perfect. Salima's husband has left the country. He will not be back for several days."

Again I looked at Jupiter in amazement. Obviously his afternoon in the port enjoying the cool breezes had not been a waste of time.

Bob's voice was more enthusiastic each time he spoke. "Alex and I should spend some time in the fishing boat offshore in front of the house. We need to study the beach, and survey the terrain. We could also learn how many guards patrol the place, how long their tours are, and so forth." He continued to speak directly to Jupiter. "Oh yes, some good binoculars would be useful." Bob spread his hands and looked around the table with an "it's as simple as that" expression. Alex nodded in agreement.

BOB, ALEX, AND John then spent an hour or so fine-tuning the details of the operation. And I listened to them, fascinated by the project, wondering how I could take part. I would find a way, I knew.

Once things seemed set, Jupiter turned to Fatima, all smiles, for he was clearly delighted with the way things were turning out. "From what I've heard tonight, Fatima, I think the boys' plan is workable. And well worth undertaking. In fact, I doubt that you could find a more competent team. And, quite honestly, I feel that this is the only way you will be able to rescue your sister."

"But this thing you are talking about could be so dangerous," objected Fatima. "I appreciate your generosity and courage. But the scheme is too perilous. Although I just met you two tonight," she gestured toward Bob and Alex, "I can't believe that you would risk your lives for my sister. Neither of you know her. I . . . I just don't know what to say."

Bob reached across the table and took her hand. "You don't have to say anything, Fatima. For Alex and myself, this would be a fascinating adventure—rescuing a beautiful damsel from a monster." He grinned. "And physical activity and excitement is just what we need right now."

"You will take advantage of these young fellows' offer, Fatima, won't you?" Jupiter encouraged. "The hands of the Spanish police are tied. Even though they may be aware of illegal activity at La Amapola, they won't interfere in a marital dispute between foreigners. And even if the Spanish police could stage a raid, in a shoot-out with those Arab guards, your sister could be killed."

Bob spoke directly to Jupiter again. "We'd be willing to go ahead with the rescue, but we'd have to do it as soon as possible, because we have other problems to take care of. Our reason for being here concerns *La Sirena*. In a few days we hope to take the boat over. Putting the ship in order afterwards will take up all our time."

"Are your lawyers really optimistic?" Jupiter had a new alertness in his tone.

"They are about to obtain the warrant to enable the local police to board the yacht. They will expel my stepmother—by force if necessary—and hand the boat over to me and my brother."

"Hold on," said Jupiter. "How many people know about this?"

Bob shrugged, "No idea. My lawyers hope to have this settled within the week."

John's lips pressed together. The gesture, I knew, meant that Bob's remarks had created some kind of a problem for him. The others did not notice, however; and Jupiter said no more.

Since we had finished dinner, he took advantage of the lull to say good night, pleading jet lag from his long trip the day before. I almost laughed out loud at that. Jupiter was impervious to such weaknesses. He was leaving, I had no doubt, to make arrangements for the Glocks, the fishing boat, and all the other gear. And he was probably up to something else as well. Jupiter was not only extremely anxious to penetrate the compound of La Amapola, but he was also interested in *La Sirena*.

The rest of us left La Fonda. Nearby was a small nightclub where sometimes there was good flamenco. Both Fatima and the boys eagerly agreed with Luis's suggestion that we "look in."

It was about one o'clock, an hour when tourists had left and locals poured in. Gypsies performed seriously then for those who could not be fooled by a mere racket of stamping feet and artless twists and turns. The place was cramped and dark, small candles glowed on most of the tables. As we entered, a lone spotlight was focused on a gypsy wailing his song of unrequited love to the chords of a guitar. Before we could find a seat, a small gypsy girl in bare feet ran into the spotlight; she might have been ten years old, at the most. As she began to move to the rhythmn of the music, each gesture of her skinny little body was filled with magic. The crowded room hushed. Every spectator became electrified by the matchless grace of the child's impassioned dance. When the tune ended, she disappeared into the shadows to enthusiastic applause. A moment later, a gypsy, presumably her father, appeared. He was holding a hat and pushing his way between the tables. Pesetas spilled into the hat; and the little girl reappeared from the shadows, trailing behind him and smiling shyly.

We finally found a table, and I sat down next to Alex von Ridder. Fatima, Luis, and Bob squeezed around as best they could on a bench. Somehow, despite the hubbub, I was able to whisper to Alex. "Do you know why Jack Wilmington canceled his marriage to Nancy?" I asked.

"Well, to tell you the truth, Countess, Bob and I had something to do with that," the young German whispered back. "We didn't want Jack Wilmington to be as unhappy as R.K. Rhodentus seems to be right now."

"What do you mean?"

"Well, Bob and Rick had a note from their father that said he was curing his marriage wounds in some far away place. Since he hasn't surfaced yet, they imagined he's pretty broken up. We are convinced that Nancy betrayed Mr. Rhodentus with some other man. He's not one to take failure easily. Meanwhile, Jack Wilmington was under the impression that the story was the other way around—that Bob's father left Nancy because he was having an affair with another woman. But we're quite sure that was not true.

"We told all these things to Jack Wilmington. And we also told him about Nancy's legal efforts to keep *La Sirena*—she is starting all kinds of half-baked legal actions—and he decided that the wisest thing would be to put the wedding off until all the uproar dies down. He's known Bob and Rick since they were born. He didn't want to put himself in the middle of a fight that involved old friends on both sides."

"When you were kind enough to receive us yesterday," Bob added, for he had managed to hear Alex's and my conversation, "we avoided giving the disagreeable details. We didn't want to say anything that was not necessary. But our legal problems with Nancy are really an ugly mess."

"We've been unfortunate with both our fathers," Alex interrupted. "Mine was murdered by terrorists; and Bob's has disappeared. Just when the project in the Caribbean seems close to bearing fruit. . . ."

"Did you ever learn who killed your father?" I asked.

Alex looked glum. "Only that a group called Action Directe took credit for it. A bomb was planted in the car and exploded by a remote device." He shook his head. "Imagine the kind of person who waits for a car to approach, then presses a switch and watches it blow up!"

A loud clapping to the beat of a *buleria* announced the arrival on the tiny stage of a new group of gypsies. Conversation became impossible. It was now about two-thirty; and since it was Saturday, the place was more crowded than before. From my darkened seat, I saw people streaming in and out under the naked bulb of the narrow doorway. It seemed impossible that more could fit into the crowded room. The dense smoke of hundreds of cigarettes was unbearable, and I suggested to Luis that we leave. Fatima agreed. But the boys remained behind as we stood up.

"We'll pay this bill," Bob offered. "You invited us to the dinner."

"Thank you," Luis replied.

Pushing our way through the crowd of sweaty flamenco fans, we finally reached the door. With relief I stepped out into the fresh air. Luis disliked my driving home alone; but with two cars there was no other solution. Anyhow Marbella was quiet at night. And safe: the town depended upon tourism for its livelihood.

The night was beautiful; and the scent of jasmine drifted to me from someone's garden. I walked slowly down the hill to where I had left my car. Since Luis had been able to park nearer the restaurant, he and Fatima were already in his Citroën, driving slowly behind me until I reached my car. As soon as Luis saw my hand on the door and knew that I was safe, he sped off.

When I put the key in the lock, I found the door was open. I must have been talking to Jupiter as I was parking and forgot to lock it, I thought. But as I climbed in, the interior light did not go on either. Nevertheless, unconcerned, I put the key in the ignition and started the engine. Just as I did, the smell of a familiar tobacco teased my nostrils—sweet, pungent Turkish tobacco! And before I could react, a gloved hand touched my shoulder.

I heard then a soft voice, which I recognized only too well. "Señora Condesa, please move your car down the street."

Terrified, I slipped the car into gear, while thoughts of how I could defend myself or escape raced through my mind. Two gloved hands were now resting on the back of the passenger seat. Why gloves on a hot night? my mind screamed.

"Please continue, Countess. No, not too near that streetlight."

Carlos spoke so quietly and was so close that fear was racing up my spine like an electric current, numbing my senses, making it difficult for me to follow his instructions. "Do not be nervous. We are old friends. Now turn right at the next corner, if you would be kind enough, Countess. Someone could appear on this street."

My hands wavered on the steering wheel. Immediately, a gloved hand slid in front of my face, indicating the desired direction. The right turn took us into a narrow, deserted one-way street with little light. Behind us, there were apartment buildings. But this was a commercial street, and everything around us was closed. I wanted to cry out, but stifled that impulse fiercely.

"Pull the car over to the curb," he ordered.

I did that, but left the engine idling and the lights on.

"Perhaps it would be best to turn off the engine and the lights."

When I did as he commanded, we were buried in darkness. But now Carlos said nothing. His silence and stillness was more terrifying than anything he had done or said. Driving had given me the illusion of some kind of control, and his directions had kept him occupied. But what was he planning now? My anxiety was growing wilder each second. Then, finally, his right gloved hand reached over my shoulder. I shrank down against the door, searching desperately for the handle. Perhaps I might be able to yank it open, fall out, scramble to my feet, run. Yet in the moment I considered these possibilities, I knew I would not get far before a bullet tore into my back. Carlos was always armed. And he was a crack shot.

The gloved hand continued to reach beyond me, removing the keys from the ignition. Gently the quiet voice said, "I'm joining you in the front seat. Don't move."

In a flash he slid over the back of the seat and was sitting beside me. The nearness, the feel, the smell of this man who had killed so many innocent people made me stiffen. He settled comfortably in his seat, as if preparing for a long drive in the country. In the dim light, I was aware that he wore light-colored slacks, a pale shirt open at the neck, and a dark jacket. I caught a brief flash of his sunglasses, reflected in the whirl and sparkle of a passing car. Aware of my glance, he self-consciously adjusted the rims on his nose.

He waited quietly for a time. Then, sensing my discomfort, he said gently: "Señora Condesa, I do not intend to hurt you."

The remark did little to ease my fear. I said nothing . . . had nothing to say. Again there was a long silence, until he said, "I wanted to talk to you."

For the first time I looked openly at him. My gaze must have somehow disturbed him, for he looked away. And again there was a long, unpleasant silence while he stared down at his gloved hands resting on his lap. When he finally spoke, his words were a kind of strange apologia for his life. "Once in London there was a man I had never met. This man trusted me enough to let me into his home. Everything he stood for I was brought up to hate. I killed him for that, and to prove my ability."

While he spoke, I wondered how long it would take Luis to realize my car was not behind his. Or would he just speed on with Fatima, take her to her hotel, stop there and chat for a while before going home? In which case it would take him too long to realize I was in trouble.

Carlos continued to explain. "That act was a turning point in my life." He paused, and I had time to wonder what he would say next. "You live in another world from me, Countess, the world of that man in London. I once lived in that world as well. But I want you to know about my world, and to understand why I have chosen it. The first time I saw you in your home in Madrid, you were gracious to me; and you continued to be kind whenever I saw you. I felt you liked me then; and even now that you know, I hope you still do." He paused. "I do not want you to have the wrong opinion of me."

Dreadful thoughts were racing through my head. By the time Luis knew something was the matter, I'd be dead. . . . How would Carlos do it? I asked myself.

But my neighbor kept talking. In my frantic agitation, I struggled to make sense of his words. The fact that he was speaking in such a calm, natural tone gave me the courage to look at him again. What was he talking about now? I wondered, trying to keep my trembling hands still. "It will be impossible now for me to see you again for quite some time, Countess," he was saying. "Yet I had the wish, the intense desire, to speak to you, not masked, but as myself, as the man you were always gracious to when I visited your home. Does this seem strange?"

I thought it was exceedingly strange, but I did not answer. My eyes skimmed over him, wondering where he kept his gun. Even when he worked at Luis's insurance company, he'd been armed, Alfonso Domínguez had said. Would he pull his gun and shoot me after he'd finished justifying himself?

"You are not pleased, Countess, I can see," he went on. "Well why would you be? Forgive my methods, but I had no choice. If I had approached you on a street corner, you would surely have cried for help."

This was true.

"What was it you wanted to tell me, Carlos?" My own voice startled me; it seemed incredible to be actually speaking to this man.

"I wanted you to know that although people in your world look upon me and others who fight by my side as criminals, in my own world I am a hero and fight for an honorable cause."

He searched through his coat pocket. My heart clenched, expecting him to pull out a revolver. But instead, he withdrew a small flat silver cigarette box, which he opened and offered me. "Would you like one, Countess?"

"No, thanks." I made efforts to keep my voice calm.

Slowly, he took a cigarette; then he found a lighter in his pocket and lit the cigarette. Now the familiar aroma of his tobacco filled the car; and the heavy scent began to oppress me. Settling back in his seat again, Carlos went on smoothly, softly. "It is important for people like you to learn that in my world, although I would prefer not to use violence, it is the only way to change the capitalist system to a better one. Of course, I could have been a lawyer, or a doctor, or a philosopher, but I wanted to be more important than that, more useful to humanity. I am a soldier and I'm involved in a war, a war for the world. And I intend to continue fighting to bring justice to everyone. It is better to kill a few for the sake of a better life for the majority, don't you think, Countess? I tell you this, because I want you to respect my work." He lowered his window and tossed the cigarette out. A tiny bright spiral skimmed through the darkness. His calm nonchalance left me astounded, but fear still gripped me. I sensed he had other reasons for meeting me.

And now, suddenly, the other shoe dropped; and his gentle tone turned harsh. "I saw you had dinner tonight with Señora Rhodentus's stepson and the von Ridder boy."

What interest could Carlos have in those boys? I wondered, as my fears took even wilder flight. Did he intend to kill them, too? Was he justifying himself in order to soften me? Nodding assent, I waited.

"And the attractive dark-haired woman is the sister of Jamal Abad's wife?"

Once again I nodded.

"The American named Derby, who arrived with you at the restaurant—is he a good friend of those young men?"

"No," I answered, neither wanting nor daring to say more. Was Carlos aware of Jupiter's true profession? Has Carlos been bugging my phone? Did he bug our table at the restaurant? What does he know? My mind was jumping erratically.

"I would like to know, Countess, if it is true that those men are taking over *La Sirena*. It is important. . . ." His voice faltered as the lights of a car suddenly illuminated the dark street.

Some twenty yards behind us, another car had pulled up, and it had left its lights on, shining full onto my car. My heart leapt. Luis! The bright lights made it impossible for me to see the car. But, please, make this be Luis, I pleaded silently. Then the lights dimmed, and in my rearview mirror I recognized Luis's Citroën. A wave of hope swept through me. But almost immediately I was again filled with terror. Carlos had a gun in his hand! If Luis approached the car, he would surely kill him. My husband was going to die unless I did something . . . fast.

In that moment, two other cars screeched around the corner and pulled to the curb behind Luis. Carlos and I both knew, that this was the police.

"Carlos," I screamed, "hand me my keys! Now!" Surprisingly, he did as I asked—I supposed he saw the situation the same way that I did. I took the keys and fumbled with the ignition. "Those fellows will kill you," I said. "I'm driving to the corner. There are dozens of narrow paths among the apartment houses around here; they are too narrow for any vehicle. My car will block the road until you have time to escape."

As I spoke, I started the engine, and in no time we were at the corner. I jammed on the brakes.

"Countess," he said quietly as he opened the door, "you will please notice that I am leaving you now. I am not taking you hostage—as I could easily do." Without another word from either of us, Carlos jumped like a shot into the night. As if by magic, he disappeared into the shadows. Behind me the three cars started forward. I leaned on the steering wheel, trembling.

Luis came running to me, and as he opened the door, relief swept over me. I collapsed into his arms. "It was Carlos, darling. Carlos."

The next moment, four policemen with weapons drawn surrounded us. "Where is he?" they cried.

Without speaking, I gestured weakly toward the dark apartment buildings. My husband, as always, was coolheaded in emergencies. Efficiently he pulled me out of my car and hurried me to his. Meanwhile the police were making a racket running into the narrow streets and emerging again empty-handed. I knew he was somewhere very close by with his gun cocked. They knew it, too, yet they soon gave up. Luis handed my car keys to one of them and asked him to drive behind us. Then we sped home.

Fatima had moved into the backseat; she was so terrified she hardly said a word on the way to her hotel. Luis and I were exhausted by the emotion of the last ten minutes and didn't feel like speaking, either. After we finally dropped Fatima off and pulled into our drive, Luis put his arms around me. I relaxed as he told me how he happened to return for me. He had driven slowly, expecting my car to appear. When he saw that my Seat did not show up he became uneasy. And as he thought about it, he realized that something might be the matter. On his way back to find me, he passed the police station and alerted them just in case, and then raced ahead himself.

When he found my car and pulled up behind me, his headlights revealed another person in the car with me, but since there appeared to be no immediate danger, he decided to wait for the police. When the police did arrive and he saw me suddenly speed off, he directed the police to follow. "The rest you know," he ended with a kiss on my cheek. "But why did you help Carlos escape?"

"Darling," I said, "he had a gun in his hand and would have shot you or anyone who approached the car. By helping him get away, I thought I was saving your life."

Later, it was difficult for me to sleep. My feelings were mixed, confused, but predominantly sad. Somehow I couldn't help but feel sorry for this confused young man who had been taught to be a terrorist from childhood. How would my own children have turned out if they had received a similar education? I asked myself. All night I twisted and turned. At one point, when I realized that Luis was not in bed, I glanced around the room. Then I realized he was as upset as I. He was sitting in a chair near the door, his pistol on the table next to him, and his shotgun across his lap.

Chapter 36

L uis spent the morning trying to contact John Derby to tell him about Carlos; I went to the hotel to have lunch with Fatima. She sat at a small table at the far end of the room. I spotted her immediately when I entered. Fatima always stood out wherever she was; but today she looked particularly striking. Her long black hair swept back into a loose chignon revealed the beauty of her oval face. She held a small blue flower in her long slender fingers, obviously plucked from the centerpiece. She twirled it around, examining every side. I could tell by her absorbed look that she had a jewelry design in the making.

"Oh, Aline, what a terrible experience for you last night. Imagine being taken prisoner in your own car."

But I didn't want to talk about last night's adventure—it was too fresh and too frightening. So I asked Fatima if the rescue was going ahead as planned. She reached across the table, clasped my hand and smiled. "Yes. And I just had to talk to you about that. I'm bursting with nervousness. I wish there was something I could do besides sit tight and wait!"

Bob and Alex had been to her suite that morning, she explained a moment later, to lay out their plans for her approval. "I can't get over those two," she said, "they're like movie heroes, and handsome, too," she added with a laugh. "Please don't mention that to my husband." I remembered that Raul Aziz was very jealous of Fatima; but then she may have given him reason to be.

I agreed that Bob and Alex were brave and handsome.

"But not foolish, I hope," she said with a dramatic sigh. "The younger brother, Rick, seems very bright. You didn't meet him. He's staying here at this hotel. He's short, thin, wears glasses, and looks like a college professor. Though he didn't have much to say, I could tell he's as excited about the rescue as his brother. And just as adventurous."

Fatima ordered a shrimp cocktail, grilled chicken, and all sorts of other things, but my experience of the night before was still too fresh to inspire any interest in food. I asked for a simple salad with freshly sliced tomatoes. While Fatima concentrated on the flower in her hand, I thought again of my fright when I found Carlos in my car. Now that the scare had passed, I was beginning to think that Carlos had been sincere with me, in his peculiar fashion. He approached me as a friend. . . . Yes, he wanted information I could give him. But he asked for it as a friend might, and not as an extortionist. And yes, he wanted me to understand his motives . . . and to approve of them. Why he did not find these as silly and clichéd as I did, I'll never know. And why he wanted my approval, I'll never know, either; but I felt certain that he did. Hearing his gentle voice reminded me of the charming young man I knew from so many months before. I remembered his kindness to my cook, the funeral, the children, his gracious manners, his sense of humor, his considerate attitude—all that made Carlos such an enigma. Yet I knew his visit doubtless had a purpose beyond the ones that were obvious to me. I decided that I should take our meeting as a signal to be on guard. My habitual optimism this time could prove fatal.

Fatima interrupted my thoughts: "The boys spent about four hours at sea early this morning in front of La Amapola. So far they don't see a problem. And I'm sure they are right. They give me enormous confidence. But it is Salima who worries me. She could easily panic. And she's not a strong swimmer, you know."

"At least the boys are giving her a chance for freedom," I answered, as gently as possible.

"But Salima does not know either of them. Do you realize that when they reach her, she might easily refuse to go with them. Everything is so confused and distorted for her now, Aline. To her everyone is a criminal. Everyone is dangerous. She may well think the boys are worse than her husband."

"You are probably right," I said, beginning to glimpse a strong reason why I should take part in the rescue.

"If I were with them, Salima would know we were there to help her; and she would come with us without complaint, but I don't know how to swim and I would be an obstacle." Fatima sighed. Then she switched to a slightly different topic. "Do you know, Aline," she continued, reaching across the table and taking my hand in hers, "I'm dumbfounded that everyone is willing to take the risk. Truthfully, last night, I thought the project was mere fantasy. But Aline, you'd be amazed! Overnight they've constructed a serious plan of action; and they are determined to make it happen." Fatima leaned across the table still farther and whispered, "Tomorrow—or actually tonight—several hours past midnight, they have assured me, Salima will be out and safe." She sat back in her chair, her eyes wide with excitement.

That is, I thought, if everything goes as planned. My mind flashed back to the courageous Jeds, our three-man teams dropped behind enemy lines during World War Two. A radio operator, a demolition expert, and a native of the country always worked together. At night we would gather in the radio room at OSS offices in Madrid, waiting for the Morse code message of a successful drop. I remembered the shouts of joy and the hugs when that terse report was received. But I also remembered other evenings that stretched into dawn, when no report came. We knew then that the drop had failed, and that our agent was dead, or worse, picked up by the enemy and probably tortured for information. Of course, I said nothing to discourage Fatima's excitement, or her hope.

"According to Bob," she was saying, "John Derby is a true wonder. He's been able to obtain technical equipment and everything else they needed at the snap of a finger. He's astonishing. How is he able to do so much so effortlessly?"

I smiled. My spymaster's work "effortless"? The years of discipline and struggle to build and maintain a perfect cover had not been easy for Jupiter. But thanks to that, his undercover work had remained undetected. Jupiter's foolproof, worldwide, import-export company had made him a respected and widely recognized businessman. Today it was therefore "effortless" for me to explain how he could provide so much help to the boys so easily.

WHEN I RETURNED home from the luncheon, I was surprised to see my small traveling bag neatly stacked with my makeup case and one large suitcase near the front door. As I climbed the stairs, I realized that Luis was on the phone. His voice came to me through the open door of his study. When I entered, he stood up to face me. By the way he was holding his shoulders, I could tell that his anxiety from last night had not diminished.

"What is it, darling?" I asked innocently.

Soberly, he looked at me. In his glance was a forceful expression that I had rarely seen. "Aline, you are leaving for Madrid on the ten-thirty flight from Málaga tonight. I'll be flying out ten minutes later for a meeting in Barcelona tomorrow, after which I'll join you. I've also spoken to the children; they won't be coming here this weekend. María-Luisa has packed your most important things; the rest will come by car with Andrés. Everything's decided. I won't discuss it further." He turned around and walked back to his desk, pretending to be searching for an important paper.

I was dumbfounded. This behavior was so unlike Luis that it seemed ludicrous. He was always considerate; he rarely dreamed of changing plans without consulting me.

"Luis, what is going on?" I asked, sounding as incredulous as I felt.

"Ask John Derby," said Luis quietly. "He'll be here at six o'clock."

So this was John Derby's idea! I supposed Luis had told him about my meeting with Carlos. Well, I reasoned, I'm not surprised that they're worried.

I looked at my husband's bent head as he studied his papers. His handsome face was slightly obscured by the long stems of the abundant flower arrangement on his desk. Looking at these, I remembered the carnations Carlos had sent me several weeks before. Obviously Luis was more upset about Carlos than I had believed. And yet, surprisingly, I was starting to feel less worried about him than before. Perhaps having actually spoken to him, and the fact that he had not harmed me, had removed the immediate pressure.

At any rate, I felt I could now relax a bit. Of course, Carlos remained dangerous. I never forgot that.

Meanwhile, the futility of arguing with my husband was obvious. So I rushed off to do the million things necessary before what would surely be our final departure for the summer.

When Jupiter arrived, he looked as though he hadn't slept in days. His clothes were rumpled, and he was still wearing the same dark cotton slacks and shirt he wore at dinner last night. His eyes were red with exhaustion, and a dark stubble beard peppered his face. Obviously, he'd been very busy. Yet an air of exhilaration and intensity hung about him like a fragrance I knew well.

He was restless. Eliminating the usual greetings, without pausing to sit down, he suggested that the three of us go for a walk on the beach, where we could count on not being overheard.

". . . or ambushed," I heard him mutter to himself as we passed across the terrace. Then he even glanced back as if to assure himself that only Luis and I were following. What had happened, I wondered, to warrant all this nervousness and precaution? Or were the preparations for Salima's rescue making him so tense?

We left our shoes on the stone wall separating our lawn from the beach and trekked barefoot along the sandy pebble-strewn coastline. On the barren stretches ahead of us, seagulls were grouping for the night. Far up the shore one lone man was casting a fishing line where small waves lapped over a reef. A chilly breeze slid over the retama bushes scattered across the large open expanse of the field on my right. I rubbed my bare arms, wishing I'd brought a sweater. Luis was walking on the other side of Jupiter. Watching my husband framed by the lovely stretch of ocean sparkling in the day's last light, I suddenly felt consumed by nostalgia for the summer that had ended. A sort of end of season gloom swept through me, amplified by the cawing of the birds flying in circles overhead.

"Well, what's the story, John?" Luis asked, but as he spoke, he was looking at me; and I saw the worry in his eyes.

"For reasons that will no doubt be obvious, we have kept Paco Cabanellas under surveillance ever since the death of Hans Schmidt." He paused and we waited. This was hardly startling news. "The surveillance has now paid off. We believe that the operation Ali Amine and Carlos have been planning is about to take place here on this coast. And that it could happen at any moment. From all we can tell, it's going to be something enormous, involving gigantic amounts of explosives."

He waited for a time to let that sink in; then turned to me. "The meeting with Carlos in your car last night, Aline, proves that he has been observing you. This means you must get out. It's quite clear, Aline, that you are now too close to something Carlos is interested in." He paused and then laid his hand on my shoulder. "In my opinion, you may already be a target for Carlos, Aline." Jupiter waited for my reaction.

"John," I said, "Carlos frightened me last night; yet he was polite, even friendly. In fact, he may be grateful that I helped him escape."

My words were greeted with a stunned silence. Luis shook his head in disbelief. Jupiter's face turned red. "You mustn't be taken in by him, Aline," he said. "No matter what you do for him, he will betray you. If he had any regard for you at all, he would not have broken into your car." He shook his head. "You can't actually be telling me that you never felt threatened by him last night?"

"Well . . ." I admitted softly.

"He's a criminal psychopath; he has no sense of right or wrong. All the more reason for you to leave immediately."

I stammered something about the flowers Carlos sent a few weeks earlier.

Jupiter wouldn't let me continue. "Oh, he has manners all right. He often sends flowers to those he plans to kill. I want you out of here, Aline. Now. This isn't a 'maybe' or 'in a few days' any longer. Carlos is dangerous and unpredictable, and never more than now."

His words made absolute sense, I had to admit. And yet at the same time, behind John's indignant attitude I divined something else. I was beginning to suspect that his main reason for wanting me far away was that he worried I might try to join in the rescue. And if I did do that, and if Carlos was still following me, he would find out about that. His next remark made me all the more certain that was the case.

Jupiter bent down and picked up a flat stone, which he skimmed over the water, watching as it made little ripples on the surface. Then he looked from me to Luis, as we continued to walk along the beach. "I would have preferred not to be so blunt, but Aline is stubborn. I want to be certain she'll be on that plane tonight. And if Carlos is still watching her, I want him to see that."

Luis spoke for the first time. "John, you told me that Carlos is currently providing a radical branch of the PFLP with weapons. Are they coming from somewhere around here?"

"Yes, Serge is now in Madrid with Jerry. He gave me that information. We have been aware for some time that Carlos has been setting up an arms depot somewhere on the coast. I wouldn't be surprised if the questions Carlos asked Aline had something to do with a problem he's having trying to ship weapons to or from here. And the fact that he mentioned *La Sirena* leads me to think that Carlos may want that boat for that purpose. In which case your friend Nancy would be in serious trouble."

The sand felt cool and damp under my feet; seagulls lifted before us, circling stupidly, then landing again a hundred feet further on. Jupiter raised his voice loud enough to carry above their cries. "And there's another thing: We have just received proof that Carlos and Ali Amine provided the materials for the explosion in Beirut yesterday. Did you read about it? Or see the television coverage? Over twenty people were killed, forty more seriously wounded. Four were Americans; eleven were children."

I looked at Jupiter. The three of us had stopped walking and were now facing the surf breaking on the beach. Luis's silence was ominous. Jupiter's expression was somber. "The Beirut explosion is not the big operation we have been expecting." He shook his head gravely. "You evidently think, Aline, that because Carlos was nice to you that he wouldn't harm you. But I can assure you that he would put a gun to your head as quickly as to his worst enemy."

Luis spoke. "There's no question about it, John. Aline will be leaving in a few hours."

"That will not be too soon."

I had not said a word. I was far from convinced that Carlos intended to kill me. And even if that was true, I still did not want to leave Marbella without trying to help with Salima's rescue.

We were now nearing Carmen Franco's beach house. A fisherman was loading his boat on the beach, while a companion was preparing the floats and boxes for the night's catch of squid. Jupiter glanced at his watch and suggested we turn back and pick up the pace. He had an urgent appointment in a half hour. "Carlos's depot will provide weapons to terrorists from all over Europe. Case in point: Two inspectors from Scotland Yard have just trailed an IRA terrorist to Marbella. The IRA agent was here to obtain weapons."

By now we were back in front of our house. As I walked over to the wall to pick up my shoes, it occurred to me that Jupiter may have found some clues about the location of Carlos's depot that he had not told me. Jupiter and Luis were now beside me, also putting on their shoes. Jupiter placed a hand on Luis's arm and one on mine. "I trust you are both convinced by now that it's not safe here."

"And what about you?" I asked my old spymaster. "Carlos also mentioned your name last night."

Jupiter frowned and shook his head, but said nothing. I knew well that this was precisely the kind of situation he enjoyed. Of course he was keyed up about the coming night. And he knew I was, too. He sensed that I wanted to be in on the rescue.

We walked across the long stretch of lawn up to the terrace. Evening was beginning to set in; and fishermen's boats now began to stand out against the graying horizon. I wanted Jupiter to talk about the rescue; but I could never do that in front of my husband. So all I said was, "Fatima told me Bob and Alex are going ahead with their plan."

But Jupiter avoided going into details about that. "Yes, I'm very optimistic. They're tremendously competent. And they've been busy. Now they have all the information they needed and are resting. Their plan is to set out in Don Alberto's boat *La Lola* at midnight." That said, Luis asked John if he wanted a drink before leaving, but John insisted he was in a hurry. Together we accompanied him to his car, which gave me no opportunity to tell him that I intended to join the boys tonight. Just as Jupiter was stepping into his car, he added, "Don't tell anyone you're leaving. Complete secrecy is indispensable right now." And then he was gone.

WITHOUT TAKING TIME to eat, Luis and I left for the airport. Even as we approached the terminal, I could feel my husband's tension easing, though I knew he wouldn't be completely relaxed until he saw me board my plane.

Meanwhile I had already made up my mind how I would avoid that and return to Marbella. I was more determined than ever to embark with the boys and Jupiter on the *La Lola*. I had the terrible premonition that if I was not with them, Salima would refuse to go; and she might even do something that would put them all in danger. At the same time, if Carlos was following me, he would also think I was flying to Madrid. So I felt no guilt that I would add to the boys' risks. Much as I hated to worry Luis, I doubted it would come to that. I knew I could be back in Madrid tomorrow, long before he returned.

Since we had over an hour before departure, Luis went into the bar for a toasted cheese sandwich. I told him I wanted to pick up the *Paris Herald Tribune* and that I'd meet him in a few minutes. Then I made a telephone call to my maid in Madrid. When the Señor

Conde calls from Barcelona, I told her, she should tell him I'm having dinner with friends and would return very late.

When I entered the cafeteria-bar, Luis was finishing his sandwich, engrossed in the racing results. But after I sat down, he lowered the paper, and we began to talk about *La Sirena*.

"That yacht problem is really a complicated mess," said Luis. "It's impossible to know who's right, the boys or Nancy." With a shrug of the shoulders, he went back to his paper. Watching him calmly turn over the pages as the minutes ticked by made me nervous. I couldn't concentrate on the *Tribune*. So when I saw that Luis had run out of cigarettes, I immediately offered to get some for him.

The tobacconist's stand was quite close to a line of telephone booths. Quickly I darted into one and called Jupiter. "I'm calling from the airport. No matter what you say, I'll be on *La Lola* within an hour, John," I said. "Don't leave without me, because without me, the whole operation may fall apart. According to Fatima, Salima is likely to be so terrified of the boys that she will refuse to go with them. But she will surely come with me. And don't worry about Carlos following me. Everyone—my husband included—will think I'm on the plane to Madrid tonight. And, oh yes, John," I added before hanging up, "be sure the boys bring scuba gear for me."

After my manifesto, Jupiter sounded resigned, almost relieved, it seemed to me. "Well," he sighed, "at least my conscience is clear. I warned you of the dangers. Luis can't accuse me of leading you down the path of irresponsibility." His voice grew brighter then. "But, now that you are coming, I can let you know that Serge will be here also. He is taking a plane from Madrid to Málaga right now. You may even see him in the airport. He will be very useful. The boys are experts in their line, but we may have some surprises. Welcome aboard, Tiger."

As I emerged from the booth, the Madrid flight was being called over the loudspeakers. I had to hurry, because domestic flights departed from the other end of the airport and Luis was waiting for me at the departure gate. When I got there, he told me that the Madrid departure had been delayed for a half hour, and that he would be leaving before me. Although I knew my original plan would fool him—I was going to walk out of the bus that took the passengers to the plane—this made "my escape" much simpler.

Luis's news was a relief, but I tried to appear properly disappointed as I walked with him toward the Barcelona gate for his flight.

Chapter 37

As *La Lola* left port and headed for our position off La Amapola, Jupiter handed me my underwater gear. I was relieved to recognize the same Regulator U.S. Diver type that I had used several years ago in the Caribbean. The wet suit was light, and came with a hood; and the tank, a steel seventy-two-cubic-inch model, was also familiar to me.

Bob Rhodentus checked my equipment and gauges carefully. "It's fortunate that you're familiar with this stuff," he said as we braced ourselves against the swells of the bumpy sea. "Now, let's get John, Rick, and Alex and go over our procedure once more."

The boat was rolling from side to side, but we were able to squeeze into a tight circle around him. "When we are in position," he began, "I will take a compass heading on some bright light onshore near La Amapola."

I suggested the illuminated dome of the mosque, which was high on the hill and could be easily seen.

"Good idea, but I'll have to check it again when we are in position. Now," he continued, "since it's such a dark night, with no moon and a little swell, I chose Regulators over Rebreathers. They're less cumbersome, and though they create bubbles, no one will spot them at night. We'll approach the beach in a tight triangular formation. I'll take the point. Aline will be directly on my right, with Alex outside of her. Rick will be on my left. Stay extremely close. If anyone gets lost, that could screw up the whole operation."

Handing me a compass and a waterproof watch to strap on my wrist, he went on. "When we get on station, I'll determine the compass heading. If things get fouled up, you can find your way back to the boat. Are there any questions?" Nobody responded. "Good," he said. Then turning to Jupiter, he added, "John, since you will be our contact on board, maybe you want to suggest something."

Jupiter gave a negative nod. A prickle of nervous anticipation ran through my body, as the adrenaline began to flow.

"Now, let's check our equipment. Aline, check your flippers. We have also given you a pair of 'Booties.' We'll have to do some walking."

We were now about a half mile off the beach of La Amapola. Since the coast shelved off gradually, we were able to anchor. After carefully surveying the terrain on shore with night-vision binoculars, Bob called us together again for a final briefing. "Aline was correct. The lighted dome of the mosque lines up with La Amapola and our boat at two hundred and seventy degrees. If we have problems, you'll find *La Lola* on the reciprocal bearing of ninety degrees. She will have one white light high on her mast. We'll leave our scuba gear just above the water line opposite the gazebo. That will be our reference point. The tide is ebbing; so our equipment will be further from the water later on." Looking at us one by one, very soberly he said, "Any questions?"

No one spoke. He went on, "We each know our procedure when we get ashore. Once in the water, we'll submerge to ten feet." He paused again. When nobody said anything, a big grin came over his face. "Okay, troops. Let's mount up and rescue the fair damsel. Aline, you come over last."

The three men splashed into the sea, and from the water Bob motioned me to follow. While I was sitting on the fantail about to put on my regulator, Jupiter gave me a tight hug, whispering, "Good luck, Tiger." Then holding onto my mouthpiece with my right hand and my controls with my left, I entered the water backward. When I surfaced, the darkness around me was complete. Above us, the stars winked, there was no moon.

We formed up in a triangle and submerged to ten feet; proceeding on our compass heading. I had little difficulty following Bob's trail of air bubbles. The plan was to surface after six minutes to verify our position; then again six minutes later. From then on, we would remain underwater until we reached the shore. Once there, I was not to get out of my gear until the guards were out of action.

As soon as Salima was out of the house and on the beach, Alex would signal *La Lola* by flashlight to move closer; and he would then take her out on a rubber raft.

Glancing at the luminous dial of my watch, I saw it was one-thirty. We were due back on the boat by two-thirty, at the latest. The water sweeping through the Strait of Gibraltar was cold, but my exhilarated state made me oblivious to it. Several times, I remembered Hans's ordeal that night off Tangiers. I marveled at his strength and perseverence in saving his life then—only to lose it a few days later.

The bubbles from the rest of the team's regulators were reassuring. As we neared the beach, I concentrated on the job before me. Surprise, timing, and speed would determine our success. Since I was the only one of our party who had set foot on La Amapola, once the boys had dealt with the guards, I would lead them through the cover of trees and bushes to the lattice corridor where I had observed Jamal and the others. Then we'd move on through the back door to the kitchen and the hall leading to Salima's bedroom. Serge was responsible for securing the front gate, the guards, and the alarm system. The boys had determined that the heart of the electronic communications system was there. Until that was eliminated, all the surveillance cameras would still be functioning. After completing that task, and if there was time, Serge would join us.

My prime responsibility was to convince Salima to come with us. But if it turned out she was drugged, or if she resisted, Alex would carry her out bodily. Meanwhile, Bob planned to skirt around the other side of the house to make certain all was safe when we moved out with Salima. Yes, it seemed quite easy.

Six minutes. Our first surfacing was flawless. The lights of La Amapola were right on line with the mosque. In the distance, the glow of cars on the Málaga-Cádiz highway looked like a long blurry caterpillar. To the left, the flicker of lights from Gibraltar. Just as I was beginning to enjoy the sights, Bob pointed to the menacing beam of a searchlight behind us, coming from a boat bearing directly on our position and moving fast. Quickly we submerged to twenty feet and listened as the roar of the engine and propellers passed overhead. As I treaded water waiting there, a sense of fear shot through me. Had our plan been uncovered? Would this unknown boat force *La Lola* to change position? If so, that would make our return difficult, if not impossible. Whoever it was, he was slowing us down. My underwater watch marked 1:48.

The boys' observation over the past few days had determined that there was a changing of the guard at two a.m. Their intention was to capture four guards at once.

Eliminating the second surfacing, Bob pushed the pace. And when we came up barely forty meters from the shore, we were almost on time. Before us, in the light of a small bonfire, four guards were laughing and passing bits of what were probably grilled sardines, a favorite delicacy on the coast when cooked over an open fire. We covered the last forty meters slowly and carefully. Then my companions beckoned me to stay where I was. Then with Bob leading, they moved smoothly up onto the beach and removed their scuba gear. Afterward, they slithered along the sandy beach in single file. The guards' boisterous voices showed they were drinking. As the boys had hoped, they were paying little attention to their duties.

Although I could not see what Bob was doing, I knew his first task was to use hairspray to locate the infra-red beams on the beach. He would search for an opening we could pass through without setting off the alarm system. For several interminable minutes, I was alone, waiting. When I heard Alex's low whistle, I jumped. Then recovering my composure, I crawled ashore, removed my scuba gear, and placed it alongside my companions'. Alex was next to me now. He whispered in my ear to follow directly behind him on my stomach, and to stop when he stopped. I went so closely behind him that his feet were almost in my mouth. I was terrified that any small deviation from the path he took might set off the alarm. Finally the tips of my fingers touched grass; and I knew we had reached the lawn that led up to the house.

Now safely beyond the infra-red beams, Alex rose to one knee and moved ahead to join Bob and Rick, who were crouched behind the gazebo. I copied his movements. From here, we could easily see the guards who were some thirty meters away. Fortunately, they were passing a bottle, and eating and laughing, confident of the capabilities of their security system. Bob motioned me to remain in place; then with quick hand signals, he gave commands to his two companions. As one body, they moved quietly toward the guards. Never has a happy party come to a more abrupt end. One guard collapsed after a few moment's under Alex's choke-hold. Another took one of Rick's shuto hand chops and fell to the sand unconscious. The third and the fourth guards sank to their knees and held up their hands. Both were staring down the barrel of a Glock. All four guards were speedily trussed up and gagged, facedown in the sand.

I was excited and impressed. The operation had taken less than thirty seconds. Rick then flipped open a walkie-talkie and tersely informed Jupiter at the other end: "Beach secure. What about the front gate? Advise." I was close enough to recognize Jupiter's clipped reply, "No report yet."

Everybody looked at Bob. After a pause, he motioned me to come forward to lead the team to the house. Since I had not encountered any electronic security for the entire length of the trellis during my previous visit to La Amapola, I counted on the same situation holding.

However, the other parts of the property were another matter. Dismissing the possibility of land mines and crouching low, I led the party to the right and toward the trellis. It was so dark that calculating our position was almost impossible. The only light behind us was the dim glow of the guards' fire. And if I looked very carefully out to sea, I could make out the single small white light on the mast of *La Lola*. Fortunately, the dome of the mosque shone brilliantly above us. Using the line from the boat to the dome for direction, I moved ahead. The going was tortuous and took more time than I had predicted. But finally, when I stumbled head on into the trellis, I gave a sigh of relief. With my left hand on the lattice frame, I made my way along it until I reached the end, where I stopped.

Bob came up beside me to survey our position. Suddenly, he pressed my arm and pointed. The glow of a cigarette was only fifteen feet away. Was that a guard at the back door? He pulled me back, and we retreated silently down the trellis and beyond, until we were behind bushes and out of hearing. Now Rick again flipped open his walkie-talkie and informed Jupiter of our problem. Then he inquired again about the front gate. And again I was close enough to the device to hear Jupiter's laconic answer: "Front gate secure. Wait for party." A flood of relief surged through me.

Precious seconds ticked by while we waited for Serge. I looked at my watch—almost five after two! We were at least ten minutes behind schedule; and we were not yet inside the house. Bob and I went back to the end of the trellis and watched the tiny ember of the guard's lighted cigarette. Again Bob nudged me to back up. When we were far enough away, he leaned close. "We'll have to divert him. Find cover some twenty yards away, and start making a noise. Be a cat or some kind of wounded animal. But make the sounds intermittent, so the guy doesn't know what the hell it is. This will make him curious and hopefully move him off the porch into the driveway. That's all I need."

I looked at him doubtfully. "Don't worry," he murmured. "Just give the performance of your life. Now go." He gave me a little shove. I had no choice. I slid along on my belly, then sat behind a bush of adelfas and started groaning like an injured animal. At my first sound, the guard responded: *"Quién va? Quién está allí?"*

I stopped. After perhaps ten seconds, I began again. I must have given a good performance because I heard the guard descend the steps to the driveway. As soon as he entered the shadows, Bob twisted a garrote around his throat, and he went over backward, sinking to the drive without a sound.

When I returned to the others, it was a thrill to see that Serge had now joined the rest of our group. His arrival had been absolutely silent. As I approached, Bob said something in his ear; and Serge's response was a quick gesture, drawing his right forefinger across his throat. That was doubtless what he had done to the security guards at the gate. Next Bob indicated to us with silent hand commands that he would circle the house and secure the porch leading from Salima's bedroom to the garden. In case we needed additional help with Salima, Bob would rendezvous with us once again at the back door in four minutes, when we were supposed to have Salima in tow. Without another motion, he slipped away.

As planned, Rick, Serge, and I entered the back door. Despite the hour, in the kitchen were two servants in *chilabas* hunched over a small table eating. Serge motioned for us to go ahead through the pantry, while he took care of them.

Time was precious. Rick and I moved on. Not a ray of light filtered under the doors along the corridor of the bedroom wing. But at the end was a glimmer from one small electric bulb, and as we reached a corner, we saw two guards in olive-green khakis. They seemed to be playing some sort of card game; their automatic weapons were propped carelessly against the wall. One man was in the act of lighting the other's cigarette. Rick handed me his Glock. Then, before either guard had time to react, he had slipped by me and put a choke-hold on one, while I covered the other with his fancy pistol. There was no struggle and no noise. And in seconds both guards were bound, gagged, and unconscious on the carpet.

As we stepped over their prostrate forms, Rick glanced at me and winked. But my thoughts were not as lighthearted. What would we discover when I entered Salima's room? Just before I put my hand on the door, Serge joined us.

As my fingers clenched the knob, I discovered to my dismay that the door was locked. Rick quickly frisked the guards for a key, but with no success. "I'll try," I whispered. The best safe-cracker in the USA had been my teacher at the spy school in Virginia; but that was a long time ago. My rusty skills would have to do. With a slight bow, Rick handed me a thin steel blade. Surprising myself and Rick, too, I released the lock in seconds, and eased the door open. My action was silent, and for a moment those inside were unaware we were there.

The enormous room was furnished like a sitting room, with a bed in a far corner. Two double French doors were covered by thick draperies, which hung to the floor. The remnants of a meal was on a table. Salima was sitting in an armchair, her head resting on the back of the chair with her eyes closed. Near her, a woman in a gray *chilaba* was pouring tea from a silver oriental teapot. Neither woman had yet looked up when, as softly as I could, I called Salima's name. The maid jumped. Her head spun in my direction, and for a brief second she stared at me. Then she scampered like a mouse across the room. Rick was faster; he tackled her as she grabbed a wall telephone. He placed his hand over her mouth while Serge wrenched the wires loose. The woman was clearly terrified; her eyes showed she was certain that we intended to kill her.

Despite the noise, Salima still had not opened her eyes. I called her again and went to her side. When I gently tapped her shoulder, her large blue eyes opened, and she looked at me with an empty gaze. For a moment I feared she was drugged. But when I smiled, she grabbed my hand and stood up. To my immense relief, she embraced me. She then glanced at the other side of the room, where Rick had grabbed a linen napkin from the table and was proceeding to gag the maid. During the entire procedure, the Arab woman had not let out a sound. Salima watched with obvious satisfaction as he tied the maid firmly to a chair. Her expression told me she despised the woman.

"Salima," I said, taking her hand in mine. "I want you to come with us. We're going to help you out of this place . . . out of this prison."

"No, I can't. It's impossible," she whispered. "The place is loaded with guards and alarms."

I tried to explain that my friends had neutralized the guards, as well as the security systems, and that we had everything under control.

"No, no, you are wrong. There's more security than normal. There's a big meeting tonight. I heard several cars arriving; but you probably didn't see them; the guards parked them near the gate where they would be out of the way. No, please go, I'll never get away. You must leave before they find you."

Despite my assurances that her sister was waiting to take her home to Morocco, Salima became more and more frantic. She kept shaking her head, and beads of sweat started to form on her brow. I glanced at Rick and Serge, who were both looking at me, clearly worried. I had to think of something that would put some heart in her. She began to mumble, "Oh, it's horrible, horrible." She glanced at the maid tied up near the bed, and she suddenly looked terrified. Moving slowly towards the chair, she sat down and grasped its arms as if she was afraid we'd tear her away.

"Salima, your husband is returning here in a few hours," I said firmly. That was the truth. My next words were necessary lies: "He is on a plane from Paris with two of his friends. Their destination is Málaga. They are coming here to use you like a slave, Salima. Unless you come with me and my friends." She looked up at me, her expression pained and pitiful. My words had affected her, but still she wavered. Her fingers nervously clutching at the fabric of the armchair.

This time I put my hand on her shoulder and spoke more softly. "Salima, you must trust me. We can't come again. Right now we are all risking our lives for you." She continued to waver. And I looked toward my friends, wondering what we would do.

But she slowly stood up and stretched out a hand to pick up a sweater from the table next to her. She put it on over her light silk dress, and started to walk silently toward the door. Rick jumped ahead and opened it, and Serge placed himself behind her. I put my arm in Salima's, and silently the four of us tiptoed out. The guards' bodies in the corridor gave Salima a start. But we quickly skirted them and reached the back door safely.

When we stepped outside, Bob was not there. Rick hesitated. I knew he was concerned, but we also knew we had to keep Salima moving; so we continued quietly through the dark trellis and down the lawn toward the diminishing glow of the guards' fire on the beach. In the distance a dog was barking, and I thanked the stars that we had to contend with human guards who were easier to control. Salima had begun to tremble.

The peaceful, caressing air of the summer night and the lapping of the waves on the beach were a strange contrast to the turmoil going on in my head. When we approached the shore, Alex rose from the shadows; and I introduced him to Salima. In the glimmer of the dying bonfire, we moved past the unconscious bodies of the four guards; and Salima shook as she looked down at them. Fear was again welling up in her.

Bob had still not appeared. Very strange. It was 2:15. We were falling further behind our schedule. Silently we waited . . . five long worrisome minutes. We had to be back at the boat by two-thirty. Moving Salima on the raft would make our return trip more difficult.

It was now nearly two-twenty. *La Lola's* beckoning light was rolling back and forth about three hundred meters out on the light swells. It was agony to have Salima so near safety and not to proceed. But orders were to wait on the beach and proceed out together.

Although Rick, Alex, and Serge had not said anything, I could see their growing desperation. Their glances moved from the lights of the boat to the dark house up on the hill. I looked at my watch— 2:21! The more time we waited, the greater the danger. The coastguard patrol could appear, or a guard we had missed could realize something was wrong. Obviously something had happened to Bob.

Salima's expression as she stared at me was full of apprehension. Intuition told her our plans were not working as intended. Alex looked from me to her. I knew he was worried about keeping her on shore any longer. We had to make a decision.

"We'll have to return to the house and find out what has happened to Bob," I said. "We can't leave him. And we can't keep Salima on the beach any longer. Alex, why don't you take Salima out to *La Lola*. If something has happened to Bob, the three of us will see what we can do."

"You're right," Serge said.

Then, with my arm in Salima's, she and I went together down to the water. Alex had inflated the raft, and I explained to her that he would take her to a boat where she would be safe. As I walked into the water with her. I pointed to *La Lola's* lights offshore. She followed my gaze out there, and then turned a frightened face to me. "It's so far. I don't swim. This water is awfully cold, Aline. I'll drown."

I grabbed her firmly by the shoulders: "Do you like living with Jamal?" I said harshly. "You won't drown. Trust me. Lie down on the raft; and Alex will pull you to the boat. Do what I say and stop complaining, Salima. You're putting all of us in danger."

My words got through to her; and without further complaint, Salima scrambled onto the raft. We watched Alex tow her out to sea until they disappeared in the darkness.

Rick then picked up one of the guards' weapons, gave it a quick inspection, and turned to me. "This is a 380 caliber Mini-Mac automatic, made in Atlanta, with a full magazine. In automatic mode, it shoots one hundred twenty rounds per minute, including the time for changing the clip. Each clip holds twenty rounds. Or you flip this switch," he pointed, "and it fires single rounds." He patted the gun. "A really great weapon. Just slip off this safety, and you're ready to go."

He handed it to me, and I was surprised at its light weight. With a gesture toward the house, he beckoned Serge and me to follow him. I glanced again at my watch—2:25! We should be climbing back into *La Lola* by now.

Without exchanging a word, the three of us grouped together and moved toward the house. Although we assumed that the surveillance systems were knocked out, since Bob was obviously in trouble, we were aware that danger could lurk anyplace. So we took as much care as the first time.

The long rambling building loomed large and forbidding before us. When we reached the terrace, crouching low, we broke off to the left, circling the portion of the house we had not visited before. We advanced cautiously, keeping within the protection of trees and bushes whenever possible, carefully measuring and testing each step, fearing a trap or a surprise. But my worst fear was that we might find Bob's dead body stretched out on the ground.

Rounding the far corner of the building, we could see a light bathing the bushes about a hundred feet further on. Still more carefully, we crept ahead, until we were next to the stream of light. It was cast from a French door a few feet away. At that moment, we all froze; a figure was rising from the shadows. . . . It was Bob Rhodentus, apparently unharmed, and he was waving to us to come closer. He turned around and squatted not far from the door. He was observing something inside. It was something very important, I realized. Otherwise he would never have wreaked such havoc with the schedule.

Voices were coming through the open door. Rick and I inched up behind Bob and cautiously raised our heads to peer into the room. The first glimpse almost paralyzed me. Sitting in a large overstuffed chair, puffing on a cigar, the booming voice, the loose, jowly face! I struggled to restrain a gasp of surprise. In front of me, no more than three meters away, was R. K. Rhodentus! Facing him, seated on a chair with an automatic weapon balanced on his knees, was Nicky Maniatis!

Now I understood Bob's absence. His astonishment at seeing his father must have been enormous. But scanning the room further brought still more shocks. Carlos was standing there. Exactly as I remembered him from the first time I met him. As I watched, he walked to a desk in the corner. My heart thumped.

Carlos pointed a finger at R.K. His voice was intense, measured, yet charged with fury. "I don't want your damned worthless checks. I want cash. I'm going to make the call myself, and you can tell him to pay me—in cash." I remembered the note he left in Paco's office: "one hundred thousand dollars short." This was obviously another chapter in that story.

"You're too hungry, Carlos," R.K. said, blithely waving his cigar. "Relax. You'll get what you're owed."

I was so startled to see Carlos, R.K., and Nicky together in the same room that I had not yet glanced at the others. Before Carlos made another reply to R.K., a woman rose from a seat in a far corner and was moving onto center stage. At first I couldn't believe who it was. Her manner, her looks, her face, were a far cry from the poised, confident woman I knew. But all these changes notwithstanding, the woman was Nancy Rhodentus. She wore wrinkled pale cotton slacks, her hair was disheveled, and there was no makeup. She lifted a hand and waved it at Carlos, then at the others. With her lovely face tense and bitter, and her voice cracking with anger, she cried. "God damn it, Carlos! R.K.! This argument is stupid. You're always fighting about money." She concentrated her gaze on Carlos. "I know. I know. My one-time loving husband is a pain in the ass who acts like a billionaire when he doesn't have a pot to piss in. I know he's all smoke and mirrors. But f—— him. The real money comes from shipping the stuff you have in the ship, and we won't have a ship for much longer—not after R.K.'s kids take over La Sirena. So why don't we make a treaty and stop fighting and ship the stuff." She moved toward the open door. Had she seen us? We quickly spread out flat on the grass, but then she turned around and paced in the opposite direction.

Nicky must have been there longer than the others. Cards laid out in a game of solitaire were on the table next to him. He stretched a hand to a glass and poured some red wine for himself as the others watched. Even from our position outside the door, we could feel the violent tension.

Then my eyes were drawn to a short thin obviously Arab man in the corner behind the bar. At first I thought he was a butler. With a glass in his hand, he walked out from behind the bar, then toward Nicky. Something about his manner and movements looked familiar. When he turned sidewards, I realized why. He was Ali Amine. He spoke softly to Nicky I gathered in Arabic. Because then Nicky turned to R.K. "My friend says he can't risk going to Switzerland again. He also wants his money delivered in cash . . . here, not there."

R.K. shook his head vehemently. "You tell that damn Arab he's going to have to wait a long time. What he wants is impossible. We already agreed to do it my way. So that's it. No changes.

"Now," R.K. continued, "about Ali's dispute with Carlos. It's about time Carlos learned that Ali had double-crossed him. Well, what the hell. If Ali thinks money ought to go to him, and not Carlos, fine, why not? It's no skin off my back. But if Carlos doesn't like that, they settle that between themselves. I don't intend to pay twice. You two work out who I owe it to. As for what I do owe you, Carlos my friend," he said, turning to Carlos, "you won't get any cash from me until I'm damn sure that it's safe and convenient to me. If you wait a year, you'll have to put up with it. I'm not taking any chances now." R.K.'s voice had the old self-assurance; but he looked less healthy and much older than he had the last time I saw him. Perhaps his slouch in the low armchair made him appear heavier; but he now had a paunch I didn't remember; and his face was fuller.

The hand with the cigar pointed at Nicky again. And his face was increasingly flushed with anger. Something was obviously eating at him. "Do you know something, Nicky? I don't intend to put up any longer with the crap those two guys have been handing me," R.K. said, tight-lipped. "The new passport that Carlos gave me—and which I paid Ali Amine for, very generously—is Yemenite." He looked at Carlos. "It's not worth a cent, as far as I'm concerned. I'm not going to Yemen or any of the countries that accept a f——ing crazy Yemenite passport. What do I want to go to Cuba for, for God's sake? Eight months in Czechoslovakia was enough. I'm going back to the West. And I'm going to rebuild the situation that you guys so royally loused up eight months ago."

With difficulty R.K. rose to his feet. He was not wearing Western clothes, I realized now, but a voluminous *chilaba* hung in deep folds around his body as he walked over to Nancy, who had slipped into a chair near the back of the room. When he reached her, he leaned over to say something.

R.K.'s whispered words seemed to calm Nancy. Evidently these two understood each other.

As I watched the two of them together, I tried to add up what was going on. For instance, what brought R.K. to La Amapola in the first place? Was Jamal's drug business one of the sources of his fortune. Or perhaps one-time fortune might be more accurate, I thought, the way the others were talking. Where had it all gone?

At the same time, R.K. was also very obviously involved in Carlos's arms deals.

So, I concluded, this internationally respected businessman was up to his eyeballs in the dirtiest business imaginable. What made him do that? I wondered.

My eyes shifted to Serge, who had moved close to me. He was spellbound.

Meanwhile, Nicky tapped the gun on his knees and faced R.K. His expression chilled me. In his excitement, he was talking faster than usual. "You arrogant American capitalists who brag about your millions. When it comes to paying, you chicken, you white-assed bastards. We risk our lives for you, and you find fine print in the contract. Sorry. Well, f—— you.

"Since you decided to pass out of circulation, you've exposed us all trying to cover up your trips, getting passports, helping you maintain another identity. Now you have absolutely screwed things up with your delays and your pointless trips. You've refused to pay Carlos, Ali, me, or anyone else. Just get it through that bloated head of yours that you're not in a paneled office surrounded by a flock of constipated overpaid lawyers." Again he caressed the automatic weapon on his lap. "This is our lawyer, judge, and jury, and I'm beginning to think you are about to be found guilty.

"Have you ever seen Ali work with his knife?" he went on. "His work is beautiful, delicate. He's an artist. I once saw him skin an Israeli agent. Something to behold. Even after an hour, the agent was still alive. You owe us money, Mr. R. K. Rhodentus. Screw your excuses. Cash! Now! It's your only hope." He flipped the safety off his weapon. Threatening silence filled the room.

My eyes were drawn to Nancy, who didn't seem at all impressed. She merely sat slouched in her chair with her lips tightly pursed, watching the proceedings through blazing eyes.

R.K. gave Nicky a long, cool look. For a moment I saw flashes of his old charisma. But then I realized that I was wrong. It wasn't charisma I was seeing but bluster. "I think Nancy was right, do you know that, Nicky? As long as there is a boat to use for transport, we should take advantage of it. Meanwhile, there's a helicopter coming to pick us up. We fly away in the helicopter. It carries us to a small strip in Morocco, and a Lear will take us to Algiers. The shipment follows in *La Sirena*. The shipment arrives in Libya. I am paid, and you are paid. Simple. Isn't that so, Carlos?" He turned. Carlos was not there. "Carlos? Damn you. Where are you?" R.K. looked around the room. "Where is that guy?" The others looked, too. Carlos had disappeared.

Nicky stood up, placing his weapon on the table next to his chair. "Forget Carlos," he announced. Glancing at his watch, he added. "The helicopter will be here in less than two hours, and it will take six of us. To hell with Carlos! If he's gone, let him take care of himself."

I glanced at my watch. To my dismay, it was now 2:48.

Bob raised a hand to catch our attention. "We have to take them," he whispered to us, very softly. "Now." Then he gestured to Serge and Rick, directing Serge to enter the room from the other side and Rick to stay put. A single finger raised told us they were going to burst into the room in one minute. He then motioned for me to stay flat on the ground.

I was still wondering where Carlos had disappeared to when Serge appeared at the open door on the other side of the room. At that moment, Bob and Rick rushed through the French doors.

The four inside must have put considerable faith in La Amapola's security system. For as my three companions vaulted into their midst, they simply stared at them with a dazed look. That split second of surprise was all our team needed.

Ali Amine was the first of the four to perceive what was happening; he was starting to draw one of his knives when Serge struck him with a spinning back kick to the solar plexus, followed by a lethal chop to the throat. As he sank toward the ground, Serge gave him another brutal chop to the head and a rib-smashing kick. There was no love lost between those two. Nicky sagged like a limp doll from a choke-hold of Rick's. Bob had a Glock pointed at his father. For a second, I thought he was going to kill him.

Meanwhile, I unlocked the safety of the Mini-Mac, and switched to single-round fire. Then I concealed myself just outside the French doors.

While Serge, Bob, and Rick were dealing with the men, Nancy opened a drawer of the table and pulled out a revolver. She then aimed it at Rick's back. Almost like a reflex, I pulled the trigger on my weapon. Nancy screamed as my shot caught her wrist and the revolver flew from her hand. She sank to the carpet, staring at the blood pouring from her forearm.

Serge now reached behind the collar of the unconscious Ali, and withdrew a short delicate stiletto. With a cry, he yanked back the Arab's hair, and with the knife in his right hand braced it against Ali's throat.

"No, Serge," I called out. "Don't!" Serge looked at me for a moment through raging eyes. Then he shook his head and dropped Ali's unconscious body.

R.K. had kept quiet from the beginning of the action. But then he spoke to Bob and Rick. "Thank God you came when you did," he said with almost palpable relief. "I don't know what . . ."

"Oh, shut up, Dad," Rick said.

"Richard!" R.K. pleaded.

"He said shut up," Bob said, waving his Glock menacingly at his father.

R.K., tears streaming down his jowls, raised both arms in supplication, but his two sons turned away.

Nancy was beginning to moan. I slipped through the door and moved to her side. I quickly examined her wounds; despite the blood, they seemed superficial.

With a towel from the bar, I did what I could to bandage her wrist. Bob was snapping out terse orders: At his direction, Rick ripped out phone wires and lamp cord, while Serge used these to bind the other four. "That will keep these people until the police get here. That'll be one hour maximum."

Turning to me, he said, "Run down to the beach and check on the guards; start putting on your gear. We're going to leave for the boat in one minute. Rick will advise *La Lola*. John can call the police from there." Looking at his watch, he shook his head.

As I stepped through the door, Rick flipped open his walkie-talkie.

I moved fast. Many problems still faced us.

Carrying the Mini-Mac in my right hand, I raced down the lawn toward the beach.

About halfway there, I heard a movement behind me. Before I could react, a strong hand clamped over my mouth with such force that I almost fell over backward. My weapon dropped to the ground, and at the same time, an arm steadied me. Then I heard a familiar voice, "Don't cry out. I'm here to help you." The pressure on my mouth relaxed. I turned; and Carlos was standing only inches away. "Get out fast. This place is going to blow in exactly three minutes." His dark, attractive features were tight with anxiety. There was no doubt in my mind that he was telling the truth. "Run for it, Countess." With that he disappeared into the shadows.

I ran as fast as I had ever run in my life, not away, but back to the house. When I reached the house, Serge was tending Nancy's wounds. Rick and Bob were preparing to leave.

"Bob!" I shouted. "Get everyone out right now! Carlos met me out there and told me this place is going to blow up. In three minutes, he said." I looked at my watch. "Now, it's less than two minutes!"

Bob looked at me, skeptically. "Carlos?" he asked. "Who's Carlos?"

"A crazy terrorist. And don't argue. He's telling the truth! He dashed away as soon as he warned me. You must all go!"

Serge's voice boomed. "Carlos knows what he's talking about. Let's get the hell out. Right away. This must be Carlos's arsenal and we're on top of it. And he's set it to blow."

Rick and Bob looked at him incredulously.

Serge, who was moving toward the open door, turned, "Look kids, we're talking explosives. This guy knows explosives. And I know him well. Now get moving."

"We need time to get these guys down to the beach," Rick said.

"No. There's no time. Leave. Get moving."

I looked at Nancy. She was terrified. Despite all I had heard tonight, my heart went out to her.

"Serge," I called out to my friend. "I've got to help Nancy." I then rushed to help her. But before I reached her, Serge grabbed me around the waist, carried me back to the door, and threw me out onto the grass like a rag doll. The next thing I knew, Nancy was sprawled next to me. Then somebody picked me up and shoved me toward the beach. I began to run, faster and faster. Two others were racing by my side. My breath was coming in gasps; I stumbled and fell. Again somebody picked me up. The two figures running next to me were now ahead. Someone else was coming up behind, the rapid thumping of his footsteps made me push harder.

I felt sand under my feet when the blast occurred. There was a flash like a hundred suns. And then a wave of heat. Then the roaring blast of wind hammered me to the ground. With my hands over my head I sensed hot debris scattering all around. Palms and bushes must have given me protection from the flying pieces that shot out from the enormous blast. One explosion followed another. Instinctively, I squirmed deeper into the sand. Without daring to move, I listened to the sounds of the blasts.

Finally I jumped up; and frightened, bruised, and cut I raced along the beach, looking for the spot where we had left our gear. The bound guards were frantic with fear; but we ignored them. My friends were already donning their scuba gear as I scrambled into mine. In no time, we were all in the water. Bob lifted his flashlight and signaled *La Lola*. "Go!" he shouted to Rick and to me. "Get to the boat as fast as possible. I'll take care of Serge." I'd forgotten that Serge had no underwater gear.

As soon as I was at a safe distance from shore, I surfaced to look back. La Amapola was swollen and bursting with flames, its now roofless frame, silhouetted against the sky, looked like a sea monster spitting its flaming breath two hundred feet high into the dark night.

JUPITER AND ALEX helped me on board. Together we gazed toward shore. Flames were still shooting high, and sporadic explosions still ripped the silence. Carlos had obviously assembled an enormous cache of arms and explosives under La Amapola. What hatred he must have felt for those inside, I mused, to have destroyed such a fortune.

"So tell me what happened, Tiger," John said after giving me some time to catch my breath and calm down. "I always suspected the arms and explosives depot was there, but I had no idea it was so gigantic."

Briefly I related the story of Salima's rescue and the discovery of Carlos, Ali Amine, Nicky Maniatis, and the Rhodentuses. When I finished, Jupiter asked me to repeat the story of the dispute that led to Carlos's spectacular revenge.

"Well, well, well," Jupiter said, with a toss of his head and a grim smile, after hearing the story a second time. "So Bob Rhodentus," he beamed at me, "stumbled into a convocation of terrorists. I'm sorry that one of them turned out to be his and Rick's father . . . that their father turned out to be the fat, bankrupt spider at the heart of the web. But in just about every other respect, your discovery was a happy outcome to our long investigation. And the explosion not only destroyed the weapons cache, it has also reduced some of the most dangerous terrorist networks' capacity for violent action—for a while at least. Our friends and colleagues around Europe and the Middle East can relax for the time being about the big attack against our countrymen that we feared. Without explosives or weapons, they won't be able to pull it off, whatever it was. In a way, Tiger, we have much to thank your friend Carlos for. He did much of our work for us . . . as well as saving your life." He touched my hand lightly. "For which I am very grateful.

"And there's one other interesting piece to this fascinating web—the money. Don't you think it's interesting, Tiger, that these people who profess their undying faith in truth, justice, freedom, equality, and so on, should turn out to be greedier than most capitalists?"

"Do you have any idea what was the point of their quarrel?" I asked.

He thought for a moment. "No," he answered, "not really. Not from what you heard. But it looks as though R.K. was broke. And the rest of them were scrambling to grab as much as they could of the scarce resources he still had. Evidently, from what you told me Ali tried to double-cross Carlos. And Carlos's fury and indignation led him to set off the explosion." He drew in a long, slow breath. Then said in an almost inaudible voice, "There's quite a lot of irony in all this, isn't there?"

"Yes, John," I answered. "Quite a lot."

And we both turned again to look at the great bonfire that had been La Amapola.

I wondered about Nancy then. And with sadness, I realized that she must be dead. Even though we pulled her out of immediate danger, she was hardly in any condition to dash away from the explosion. No one who was much closer to the house than we were could possibly survive that holocaust. I now knew Nancy had much to answer for, much that I had never suspected before we stumbled upon "the convocation of terrorists," as Jupiter called it. But I couldn't stop liking Nancy. I didn't want her dead.

Meanwhile, the sounds of fire engines and police cars racing along the highway came out to us. Their red flashing lights moved closer and closer to El Ancon. Suddenly there was a shout from the water. It was Bob. Jupiter assisted him and an exhausted Serge who just lay panting on deck. "We're okay," said Bob. "Let's move." Don Alberto started the engines, a crewman cut the anchor line, and we were off. Jupiter started kidding Rick. "The plan was to rescue the beautiful girl only, not to blow up the whole place," he laughed.

But Rick was in a dark mood. He and Bob stood on deck grimly watching the diminishing flames. I could see that what they had found out about their father was affecting them deeply.

"And how is the beautiful maiden?" I asked, to divert everybody's attention. And besides, in all the excitement, I had completely forgotten about Salima.

"She's sleeping in the cabin," Jupiter answered. "She'll be all right, I think, once she's had a good rest. And a good measure of love and affection," he added.

I went into the cabin and looked in on Salima. She was wrapped in an old wool blanket, sleeping, and Alex was sitting by her side, holding her hand. I gave him a smile, and then went back on deck.

No sooner was *La Lola* underway than a Coast Guard cutter came bearing down on us at full speed. We all scrambled into the small cabin just before a powerful searchlight focused on our craft and a bullhorn ordered Don Alberto to heave to. *"Qué pasa?"* they inquired, friendly enough, more interested in what was happening on shore than in us.

"Don't know," Don Alberto replied. "We were fishing, and there was this enormous explosion over there." He pointed in the general direction of La Amapola. "It scared the hell out of me and the fish, too. So we're leaving."

The lieutenant laughed. "Okay, Don Alberto. See you ashore." And the cutter sped off toward the roaring flames.

As the little boat chugged toward the port of Banus, Jupiter came to stand next to me. My wet hair was flapping in the wind; and although we were now far away from El Ancon, I could still see the glow from La Amapola.

"When we dock," Jupiter told me, "Alex will take Salima to Marbella, where Fatima is waiting with a doctor and two of her father's bodyguards. They will take her to the airport; and soon she'll be on a Lear on her way to Morocco." Then he said, "When you were all so late, and I saw that explosion!" he exclaimed. "My God, Tiger, I was worried!"

"So was I," I answered. "So was I."

Chapter 38

A lthough it was nearing the end of September, the weather in Madrid was as hot and dry as it had been in August. Meanwhile, Luis and I had been expecting a call from Jupiter ever since we came back; but six days had passed and no news. I had not yet dared tell my husband about my part in the rescue, although I had related to him everything else I knew about the assault on La Amapola and the events that resulted from that.

The newspapers covered the explosion, but they accepted the official reports, which avoided all mention of terrorists. The explanation was that the house blew up because a large propane tank had carelessly been installed in the cellar. There was a leak, and a spark, and a flash. . . . No bodies were recovered from within the house. So it would never be known who, or even how many, died there.

Meanwhile there was no news from Morocco about Salima and Fatima. I telephoned Fatima's home repeatedly. But the message was that she was out of the country.

Finally Jupiter called. He was in Madrid; and he asked us to dine with him at Jockey. Luis couldn't join us, however, since he had a card game.

When I arrived at Jockey several hours later, John Derby was sitting at the small bar in the front of the restaurant. He stood up to greet me. And I liked what I saw; he looked relaxed, rested, and fit. Tonight he had the sparkling eyes and ruddy complexion of a man who'd spent his life in the open country, rather than in the sterile commercial airliners where he spent all too much of his life. "Aline, I'm delighted you could join me on such short notice," he said, taking my hand. I laughed, knowing he was fully aware that I'd been expecting to hear from him ever since we left Marbella. Always a shy man, he let my hand go immediately. "I'm sorry to miss Luis," he continued, "though perhaps it's better we catch up alone. I don't suppose you told him you'd been in on Salima's rescue?"

I shook my head, and he smiled. "You're lucky you escaped that explosion. What would he have thought?" He smiled wickedly. "Oh, by the way, you'll be pleased to know that Serge may join us for coffee."

Gerardo, the maître d' of Jockey, appeared to escort us to our table. As soon as we were seated, I beseiged John with a barrage of questions, "What's happened to the boys? Any news about Salima?"

"So far no news from Morocco, although I know the plane arrived in Casablanca with the two girls safe and sound. The most interesting news I have, however, concerns your old friend R. K. Rhodentus."

"Don't tell me he escaped the fire?"

"No. I'm quite certain he did not. But our people at home have checked into his background. They've come up with a few details you may like to hear."

By now our first course had arrived. John picked up his fork and dove into his smoked salmon, leaving me hanging on his next words. "To begin with," he finally said between bites, "the fortune R.K. started out with came from his wife. Her father was the founder and chief stockholder of ATM, the big multinational, and she was his only child. From the beginning of the marriage, R.K. kept trying to prove he was the business wizard that his wife's father was. He would put together deals, takeovers, what have you. And none of these really worked. At the same time, he was always chasing women. Anyhow, he and his wife grew tired of each other; and he left her, or she left him, about the time Rick was born. But even after the divorce, R.K. managed to keep his hooks in his wife's family business and its connections (I strongly suspect he had something on her father that he used as leverage). But her father did manage to 'encourage' him to leave the United States. Thus R.K. became an expatriate, with homes in France and England. He never saw his kids, and friends of the family say they hated him."

"It's more complicated than that," I broke in. "He did give them *La Sirena*. And they weren't exactly doing jigs after he died."

"It's always more complicated than that," John said, with a wave of his hand. He was now warmed to his tale, and he wanted to get on with it. "R.K. managed to obtain much status in European capitals thanks to his connection to ATM. But eventually his ex-father-in-law put a stop to that; and R.K. was forced to find other means of supporting his expensive tastes. That's when he began his association with terrorists and drug dealers."

"And what about his friend Karl von Ridder?"

John put down his fork and spoon, then touched his lips with the napkin. "R.K. had him killed. Von Ridder was a respected banker in Germany, the kind of associate and friend R.K. needed to maintain credibility. When Ridder caught on to R.K.'s illegal dealings, R.K. knew he had to eliminate him or go to jail. Ridder was a very fine and honorable man. As soon as he began to suspect R.K., he approached the West German authorities. And as a result of that, the West Germans set up a 'sting,' which would not only have netted R.K. himself, but most of his contacts in the terrorist and drug worlds. Sadly, R.K. found out about that (he had an informant in Bonn). He then gave the word to eliminate von Ridder, and disappeared. You have a pretty good idea of his odyssey after that."

"And Luis and I actually liked that man. He had such force; he radiated such energy."

"That's one of the qualifications for the profession of con man, Aline."

"And what's the news of the other Rhodentuses, John? Have they taken over *La Sirena?*"

John smiled. "Yes. The legal situation clarified quickly, which of course was helped along by the disappearance of Nancy Rhodentus. I also said a few words to a friend at the State Department; and some of their lawyers pulled a few strings. So now the boys have the yacht." His smile broadened. "And when they stepped on board, the boat was totally deserted. The entire crew had vanished. I recall that Hans Schmidt had some doubts about them. He turned out to have to have been right. Would it surprise you to learn that the Spanish police have discovered that the boat was used to transport weapons and drugs?" I shook my head no. "Nor was I. The police found the remains of a drug shipment in the hold. That explains in part why you saw Carlos in Germany with Jamal.

"Fortunately, the boys are familiar with yachts; they're already setting about hiring another crew."

"Do you know if Nancy got out of the explosion alive?"

"Sorry. No news of that lady. But it's my opinion that she's dead. However, my contact in the police said it was impossible to identify anyone they found in the ruins. They don't even know how many died there. So there will always be a question about Nancy."

"What about her connection to R.K.? What did the Agency have to say about that?"

"Serge has that report; I'm sure you'll be hearing all about it from him." John looked toward the entrance. "Don't know what's keeping him. He should have been here by now."

For a while I did not speak. Poor Nancy. I couldn't get the old line out of my head: "What's a nice girl like you doing in a place like this?"

For desert, Jupiter ordered baked Alaska; he had a terrible sweet tooth. The more rich and outlandish the concoction the better. As he was digging a fork into the mound of ice cream and cake, he turned to me with twinkling eyes. "Well, Tiger, it seems we found out more than we realized that night at Cabanellas's office.

"Those French code names were the first layer of an elaborate system for the transport of weapons and other illegal materials to the Middle East. Since I last spoke to you, a team of experts has been working to construct a model of this system. It looks to be sophisticated beyond anything we've previously encountered. The whole substructure is mathematical, and incredibly complex. Yet even with limited information, we've been able to intercept several shipments; and we've effectively shut down operations between a shipping agent in Libya and one in Kuwait. And we're just beginning."

Slowly he took another spoonful of the rich dessert. I watched as he consumed it. Finally he spoke again. "We've had an interesting development with Cabanellas. The Spanish authorities picked him up and confronted him with the evidence that we found in his office. With some urging, he divulged a a great deal of valuable information. . . . They offered him some sort of plea bargain; and he took it. Our Paco is such a weasel, but at times, weasels are useful. As a result, we've identified two companies in Germany and one in France that were violating COCOM regulations. And we have further information that should lead us to at least five others.

"Paco was released only yesterday in Málaga; but not surprisingly, he requested police protection. He feared his old colleagues might make another attempt on his life. I guess he's not convinced that all of them are dead. And he's right. Carlos, for one."

"What about Hans Schmidt?" I asked.

"Poor Hans Schmidt. He was perhaps the most unfortunate of all. Some time ago, Nicky Maniatis, representing R. K. Rhodentus, tried to buy calutrons from him. And he refused. Meanwhile, completely independent of that, Hans's daughter fell for Paco Cabanellas. And Paco had a falling out with his 'friends,' who placed a bomb in his Cigarette . . . and Hans became an avenging angel. A good man, Hans Schmidt. And brave. But a loner. He had to do it all himself." He shook his head. "That wasn't wise."

I was glad to hear John's news about Hans. For it confirmed my own feelings about him. I had always sensed he was a decent person, whose tragic flaw was that he was rash and unpredictable. We were still discussing Hans Schmidt when, a few minutes later, Serge strolled in. Gerardo brought him to the table.

Serge's shaved head made his Slavic cheekbones more prominent, and made him more alluring than ever. As he settled down next to me, the waiter brought another cup of coffee. Serge appeared to be in a particularly optimistic mood, and when he spoke I understood why. He'd just received word that Ali's network had fallen apart after it was learned that Ali was dead. "Carlos is probably the one who spread the tidings," he said, and then looking at me, he added, "So now you no longer have any worries about that guy either. He's undoubtedly in the Middle East. In Baghdad, I'd say."

At that moment, Silvia and Ignacio Coca were on their way out of the restaurant and stopped by to invite us to join their table at El Corral de la Moreria, a popular flamenco nightclub. And we agreed to meet them there a bit later. After they left, Serge patted the pocket of his dark-blue suit. "I have something here that John wanted me to show you," he said.

John suggested that he save it until we were at the nightclub, and then asked for the bill. A half hour later, when we entered the club, we found the place charged with excitement. Antonio, a famous gypsy dancer, would perform. He alone was enough to draw a packed house. But it had been announced that he would be dancing with a new and extremely talented partner. And so the hot stage-lights played upon the expectant faces of people waiting impatiently for their appearance. Elegantly dressed men and women were squeezed into every inch of space. Beaded gowns and wispy tulle skirts crushed against silky tuxedo legs.

Since it was almost impossible to move around the room, everyone who knew each other—and many of us did—laughed and waved helplessly to one another.

With an expertise born of years in the business, the owner, another Antonio, lead us through the crowd toward the Coca's table. Silvia's cheeks were flushed with excitement; and I could see from her animated gestures that she was fascinated by the man she was talking to. As I followed Antonio to the table, I saw through a break in the crowd that he was in fact Paco Cabanellas—much to my surprise. He was nodding calmly as a buddha at something Silvia was telling him. Well, I thought, I guess it's not a big leap from jail to a nightclub.

"Aline, my dear, so glad you came," Ignacio said when I finally reached them. Fortunately, he seated me between Jupiter and Serge. I was not eager to be near the odious Señor Cabanellas. Meanwhile, Jupiter immediately leaned over and began talking with him.

The crowded room made it necessary to squeeze chairs and tables closer than usual, and our table ended up almost on the stage. Now and then, Paco turned briefly to greet people; but he and Jupiter continued talking. Some time later, with the arrival of Dominguín, there was another round of greetings, and more of a squeeze to make room for the celebrated bullfighter.

Taking advantage of the noise and commotion, Serge whispered in my ear. "I want you to read the report Langley sent on your friend, Nancy Rhodentus. The last time I talked with them was only an hour ago. The report's been coming in bit by bit all day. That's why I stayed in Madrid, and why I arrived late tonight. It's quite a tale!"

He took a folded piece of white paper out of his inside pocket and handed it to me. "Read it for yourself. It's brief. And when you finish, I'll tell you the rest." As I took the printed sheet, he added, "Prepare yourself for a shock."

The print was small. But since we were near the stage, I could lean close to the footlights. The restlessness of the flamenco fans and the noise was also a help; I was able to read without anyone paying attention to me.

The report began:

NANCY RHODENTUS WAS BORN IN VENEZUELA IN 1945, NEE NANCY ROSARIO MARTINEZ AGUILAR. SHE STUDIED IN THE UNITED STATES FROM 1963–1967, AND MARRIED AN AMERICAN STUDENT IN 1965, WHICH EVENTUALLY GAVE HER US CITIZENSHIP. HER BROTHER, ROGELIO MARTINEZ, WENT TO SCHOOL IN PANAMA, AND BECAME INVOLVED WITH DOMINICAN TERRORISTS AT AN EARLY AGE. WHILE IN THE US, NANCY MARTINEZ BECAME INVOLVED WITH A LEFTIST GROUP AT BERKELEY. HER CLOSEST FRIEND IN THOSE YEARS WAS SUSIE TURPIN, WHO IS A KNOWN MEMBER OF THE WEATHERMAN'S GROUP. IN 1967 NANCY MARTINEZ OBTAINED A DIVORCE AND WENT TO PARIS. THERE SHE JOINED HER BROTHER'S LEFTIST ASSOCIATES, INCLUDING ILLITCH RAMIREZ, CODE NAME "CARLOS THE JACKAL," WITH WHOM SHE HAD A SHORT LOVE AFFAIR.

ROGELIO MARTINEZ AND ILLITCH RAMIREZ HAD BEEN STUDENTS TOGETHER AND HAD BELONGED TO THE SAME COMMUNIST GROUP IN CARACAS.

IN 1974 IN PARIS, WHEN CARLOS KILLED TWO SECRET SERVICE POLICEMEN, MANY OF CARLOS'S VENEZUELAN AND CUBAN COMPANIONS, AMONG THEM NANCY MARTINEZ, WERE COMPROMISED. HER BROTHER ROGELIO WAS NOW A KNOWN INTERNATIONAL TERRORIST. AND SHE WAS IN NEED OF A SAFE COVER. AT THIS TIME SHE MET R. K. RHODENTUS, A WEALTHY AMERICAN INDUSTRIALIST, AND MARRIED HIM IN 1975. IT IS NOT KNOWN WHETHER HE HAD PREVIOUS KNOWLEDGE OF HER CONNECTION WITH TERRORISTS.

NANCY MARTINEZ MET NICOLAS MANIATIS, CODE NAME "AGUILA," EITHER THROUGH HER BROTHER OR THROUGH "CARLOS THE JACKAL," WHO MET "AGUILA" IN A CUBAN TERRORIST CAMP SOME TIME EARLIER. THERE ROGELIO MARTINEZ BECAME A SPECIALIST IN COMMUNICATIONS, AND CARLOS BECAME AN EXPERT ASSASSIN. BOTH ROGELIO AND CARLOS LEARNED MILITARY AND OTHER UNDERCOVER SKILLS AT THE CAMP. MANIATIS WAS ONE OF THEIR INSTRUCTORS. AT THAT TIME, "AGUILA" WAS ALREADY A MEMBER OF THE PFLP. AROUND THE TIME OF HER MARRIAGE TO RHODENTUS, NANCY WAS INVOLVED IN AN AFFAIR WITH MANIATIS IN PARIS. SHE SPEAKS SEVERAL LANGUAGES INCLUDING FRENCH, SPANISH, ENGLISH, AND SOME GERMAN.

When I handed the paper back to Serge, I felt weak and confused. Fortunately, there was no need to talk. John was in conversation with Dominguín, and everyone else at our table was absorbed in the general excitement.

Serge understood my silence. Leaning closer, in an especially soft voice, he said, "Since that report came in, I've received more news. We think Nancy also trained in Cuba for a short time after graduating from Berkeley. We know for certain her friend Susie did."

As he spoke, I was trying to sort through my feelings about Nancy. It was hard for me to believe she was a trained terrorist, and I said so.

"Sorry to give you such unsettling news, but," he shrugged, "she was a clever, well-educated, beautiful woman. When she offered her services to the PFLP, they leapt at the chance to use her. It didn't take much to recognize her potential. With her great style and elegance, she could attract important men—Jack Wilmington, for instance. He's a respectable, honest American. And he was damned lucky to escape her."

"Do you think Carlos was in touch with Nancy during the shoot at Paco's ranch last November?" I asked.

"Yes. I'd say Nancy is pretty good proof that the man you saw in the country was Carlos. For one reason or another, they had to be in contact. Remember, she had just come in from Germany and they had probably been out of touch. There were doubtless pressing matters the two were handling which could not be discussed by phone or trusted to a letter. They were no longer lovers at that time; but they continued to work closely together; and did meet periodically."

We were interrupted by the waiter, who had managed to push through the crowd with our drinks. Since no one paid the slightest attention to us, Serge continued, "R. K. Rhodentus was the perfect cover. Nancy was always with him, she sat in on confidential meetings, hired his secretaries, his bodyguards, made important decisions."

As he spoke, I wondered how I could have been so blind. Yet, I mused, no one else who knew Nancy would have suspected her. Serge went on, "Nancy used R.K.'s houses and apartments as safe houses for a variety of terrorists when they had to go underground." He stopped for a moment, and a slow grin crawled over his face. "Well, the only safe house her friend Susie's going to be in for some time is the maximum security prison in Leavenworth. Recently she was picked up with a group of Weathermen. They were robbing a bank and two policemen were killed." I continued to shake my head in amazement.

"But, Serge," I asked, "are you certain Carlos is no longer in Marbella? I'm afraid you and Jupiter told me that to make me feel secure."

"You can feel *absolutely* secure, Aline. He's far away; and the others we saw that night in La Amapola, as far as we know, are dead."

Just then the burning lights became a single narrow spot. The crowd quieted down to excited whispers and the clicking of ice in glasses. Backstage the steady repetitive clapping of several pairs of strong hands set the rhythm. The clapping went on, now ringing out across the room, where it seemed everyone had stopped breathing. Suddenly, like a magician from a cloud of smoke, the star appeared within the circle of light and stood for a moment, still and imperious. Antonio was not a large man; but he had the magnetism of a mythological figure.

A small blue light now focused on a girl in a long ruffled gypsy skirt sitting languidly in a chair facing him. Antonio's chest was held proud and high. And as he looked at her, his brow was furrowed. He was playing the role of the jealous lover. The clapping continued, steady and strong. As if hypnotized, the gypsy girl rose from her chair and approached the man slowly, gradually raising her arms above her head in sinuous patterns.

"Another surprise for you, Tiger." Now it was Jupiter who whispered in my ear.

But I wasn't listening. When the girl lifted her face, I saw that it was Sofia Cabanellas.

Oh my God! I thought. Carlos's girlfriend! The last person I expected to see tonight! Involuntarily, my eyes swept the room, searching for her lover. Despite Serge's reassuring words, I couldn't help feeling that he was nearby. During the past months, Carlos seemed to appear wherever Sofia did.

If he was in the club that night, however, I failed to see him. And as the seconds passed, I found my attention drawn ever more powerfully into the spell of Sofia's dancing. She was magnificent.

Her long graceful fingers began to snap, marking the beat. Her beautiful supple body moved slowly, sinuously. And these subtle gestures transfixed the audience, as if she had touched them with a magical current. All eyes were concentrated on her alone. Each enchanted movement sent a wave of pleasure throughout the room.

The dancing came so close to the edge of the stage that Sofia's measured footsteps sent little puffs of dust onto our table. At that moment, Jupiter leaned over close to me. He had more to tell me. And he was quite comfortable with the noise, the music, and the dancing, knowing no one could overhear our conversation because of it.

"That girl there," he said, indicating Sofia. "She is one of the more interesting people to show up in this tale.

"Carlos was in love with the girl. He actually had a lawyer contact the authorities on her account. He asked for protection for her. Claimed that she was not involved in any of his terrorist activities. And in fact, there's no evidence that she was." His eyes lifted up to the stage. Mine never left her; they had remained fixed on her. "But it's fascinating, isn't it?" he went on. "Carlos the Jackal falls for that lovely thing! And yet, if you look back, Sofia was usually in the places where you saw Carlos."

"I noticed that," I said.

"At least, you can now be sure his appearances were not products of your imagination. The girl will be watched, of course, but I imagine her affair with the Jackal is finished. After what happened last week, it's my bet that Carlos will probably remain in the Middle East—or somewhere behind the Iron Curtain—for a long time."

"There's one other character in this tale who needs some explaining." I asked Jupiter, "What do you know about Nicky Maniatis?"

"Nicky was quite a guy!" John said. "And completely phony. He had nothing at all to do with boat building, for instance. That business actually belonged to a cousin with the same name; and Nicky seems to have acted as some sort of commissioned sales representative for him. But that was only a cover. His luxurious lifestyle was financed by his terrorist activities."

Jupiter was seated just behind me now, talking into my ear. Both our chairs were turned toward the stage. As I listened to him, I continued to watch Sofia's skilled and elegant movements. She was brilliant. This one blazing performance would make her the most dazzling new dancer in the flamenco world. Her delicate beauty added an ethereal quality to her dancing that further entranced everyone in the room. Everyone except John Derby. But Serge was mesmerized by her performance.

John glanced at the stage now and then, but for the most part, he was watching those around us. "Nicky and Nancy were lovers, of course. And he was the one, I believe, who persuaded her to marry R.K. As Luis witnessed at Paco's shoot, Nancy's marriage proved no obstacle to her relationship with Nicky. They were probably lovers right up to the end."

On stage, Sofia moved toward Antonio and began to circle him seductively. He pretended not to notice her, but continued to clap out the rhythm of her movements. Then he suddenly stamped a foot, as if to break the trance, and the two of them faced off warily, each taking the other's measure. Their feet then began stamping in an intricate pattern; and the couple started taking turns dancing toward the other. One advancing, the other retreating, the rhythm and volume escalating with each turn.

Jupiter lifted his watch in front of my eyes, to get my attention, and then tapped it forcefully. I realized that he was going to leave. This might be my last chance to talk to him for some time.

The dancers now held each other in a tight embrace, with Sofia's head crushed against Antonio's chest. But suddenly he flung her away. And she spun off in a series of unbalanced turns, then crumpled to the floor, while Antonio launched into an elaborate dance, his legs moving sharp and angular, snapping out from his almost rigid hips like knives.

John was about to get up. "I must sneak out, he said. "I have a plane early tomorrow morning."

"Where are you going now, John?" I asked.

"I'm starting a business in China. I think that country has a great future."

"China?" I asked, incredulous. "Good heavens, that's far away."

"I don't intend to lose myself in China; I'll be back and forth, but my interests for the near future will be the Far East, not the Middle

East." He looked at me steadily and I knew he would be leaving for Baghdad that night, not China.

The dancer's stamping reached a crescendo that was nearly deafening. And it abruptly ceased. Then Antonio stealthily approached Sofia, now lying prostrate on the floor. He reached down and encircled her upper arm with his hand and gracefully lifted her to her feet. Then they advanced in a slow pattern toward the front of the stage, and toward each other; their steps complex, their arms moving in counterpoint. They danced faster and faster as they approached each other, until they were in a frantic embrace just inches from the edge of the stage. In one powerful motion, he bent her back, and she arched out away from him as supple as a bamboo stalk. Her head and shoulders hung suspended beyond the edge of the stage as above a bottomless abyss. The lights blacked out; and the roar of applause swept through the small room like an aural stampede. Sofia had become a star; there was no doubt of that.

As the houselights went up and the dancers were taking their bows, Jupiter stood up and said goodbye to the Cocas, with apologies for having to leave so soon.

On stage, Sofia was smiling broadly, almost innocently. "You don't need Carlos," I said soundlessly. "You have inside you more than he could possibly ever offer you. Forget him, Sofia."

Jupiter turned to me to say goodbye. But he stopped before he did that, bent down, and in an uncharacteristic impulse, whispered in my ear, "Oh, I forgot to tell you, Aline. Jamal was found murdered in a suite in a hotel in Algiers!" He took a deep breath. "Terribly mutilated. Not a pretty sight. Nobody has a clue who killed him. That man had many enemies! I leave you to guess who did it."

He kissed me shyly on the cheek, not giving me time to say a word. And then he was navigating through the crowd. I watched him until he disappeared.

Six gypsy dancers bounded out on the stage, and the musicians lifted their guitars and started to play "Sevillanas." The women raised their arms in graceful circles, twirling and spinning, their muticolored skirts billowing. But I scarcely noticed them. For I sat in my seat stunned. Not even the loud staccato clapping penetrated my consciousness. My mind was occupied with a tremendous certainty: I knew who had masterminded Jamal's death. And this time it hadn't been Carlos.

· · ·

BEFORE ENDING THIS story, I need to mention one more thing. Two days later, my breakfast tray appeared with an unusual addition: an elegant package wrapped in silver-and-gold paper embossed with the name of Luis Gil, Madrid's leading jeweler. Attached was a small note in Luis's handwriting:

> Darling,
> Even though you think you got away with murder once again, not to mention worrying me to death on top of that, your role in saving Salima deserves this gift.

Hurriedly I stripped off the paper. Before me was a large suede case, which I quickly opened. Glowing up at me was a one-strand necklace of exquisite black South sea pearls.